KROX RISES

MAGITECH CHRONICLES BOOK 5

CHRIS FOX

CHRIS FOX WRITES LLC

Copyright © 2018 Chris Fox
All rights reserved.
ISBN-13: 978-1-7916-0098-3

For you, the reader. Thanks for sticking with me.

CAST OF CHARACTERS

The Magitech Chronicles are vast, and we now have a dizzying array of gods, demigods, drifters, Shayans, planets, and other stuff. Below you'll find a mostly complete list to remind you who's what.

If you find anything missing, please shoot me an email at chris@chrisfoxwrites.com and I'll get it added!

Gods, Wyrms, & Demigods

Arkelion- Son of Drakkon. Currently works for the Krox and was recently involved in the assault on New Texas.

Drakkon- The Guardian of Marid. Dwells on the world of the same name.

The Earthmother- A Wyrm of tremendous power. Sibling to Virkonna and Inura. Killed by Krox during the godswar. Her body is now used to lure primal drakes, which Krox has been enslaving for millennia.

Inura- The undisputed master of *air* in the sector. Inura was the chief architect of the *Spellship*. Sibling to Virkonna and the Earthmother.

Krox- One of the most ancient gods in the sector. Krox was dismembered during the last godswar, but his children have been conspiring to raise him. Nebiat finally succeeded in doing so, and is in control of Krox.

Marid- Marid is an elder god slain by Shivan in the early days of the godswar. Her body lies on the world of the same name, and is protected by her Guardian and son, Drakkon.

Nefarius- Nefarius is a Void Wyrm of immense power who ascended to godhood in the earliest days of the godswar. She is sometimes referred to as a he, though the reason for the change in gender is unclear. Nefarius was slain at the end of the last godswar, but her Guardian, Talifax, is conspiring to bring her back.

Neith- The first arachnidrake, and the eldest of the draconic siblings. Sister to Virkonna, Inura, and the Earthmother, but much, much older.

Shaya- A mortal raised to godhood by Inura in order to defend her people. Died, doing exactly that. Now entombed under the great tree on the planet Shaya.

Talifax- Guardian of Nefarius. Talifax's age and race are unknown, but he is rumored to be nearly as old as Xal.

Virkonna- The Wyrm of *air*, sister of Inura, Neith, and the Earthmother. Virkonna is known as the mother of the last dragonflight, and slumbers in torpor on the planet Virkonna, watched over by her children. Virkonna helped Inura build the first *Spellship*.

Xal- One of the eldest gods in the sector, and also one of the largest repositories of *void* magic. Xal allowed himself to be killed by a pantheon including most of the other gods on the list, because he knew eventually that would allow for his return. Best known now as the Skull of Xal.

Inurans

Jolene- A powerful Inuran matriarch. Mother to Kazon and Voria.

Kazon- Brother to Voria, son of Jolene. Kazon was mind-wiped alongside Aran, but has since returned to take his place in the Inuran hierarchy. Kazon owns a huge chunk of Consortium stock, but has turned over his voting rights to his mother.

Skare- A powerful Inuran patriarch. Skare is a rarity among Inurans. He's ugly. Skare is also corrupted by Nefarius, and is working with Talifax to raise their dark goddess.

The Krox

Frit- Frit is an escaped Shayan slave, one of the Ifrit, who were molded by Shayan slavers into beautiful women made completely of flame.

Kahotep- Son of Nebiat, grandson of Teodros. Kahotep, or

Kaho for short, is Nebiat's last surviving son. He is a powerful true mage and master scholar.

Nebiat- Daughter of Teodros, granddaughter of Krox, mother of Kahotep. Nebiat is a centuries old Wyrm, and one of the most powerful true mages in the sector. Her hatred of Voria borders on irrational.

Teodros- Son of Krox, father of Nebiat. Teodros was a hatchling during the last godswar, and played no notable role. However, he's spent the intervening millennia gathering strength, and building his people into a military powerhouse. Teodros orchestrated the rise of Krox, but did not live to see his work completed.

Shayans & Drifters

Bord- Bord is a lower-class Shayan born in the dims at the feet of the great tree. He was conscripted into the Confederate Marines just before the Battle of Starn, and has been cracking bad jokes ever since. Kezia's boyfriend.

Ducius- Thalas's father. Ducius has been a Caretaker of Shaya for many years, one of the most powerful political positions, second only to the Tender. After Eros's death, Ducius took up the role of Tender, and is currently the leader of the Shayan people. Ducius hates Voria. Kind of a lot.

Eros- Eros was the head of the Temple of Enlightenment on Shaya, and Voria's original master. Eros became Tender of Shaya when Aurelia died. Eros died shortly thereafter fighting Teodros in the Chamber of the First.

Kezia- Kezia is a blonde, curly-haired tech mage drifter born in the dims, not far from where Bord was raised. She was conscripted in the same wave, and went through basic training beside him. Bord's girlfriend.

Thalas- Son of Ducius. Thalas was Voria's second in command for several years. He was executed by Voria for insubordination during the Battle of Marid.

Voria- Daughter of Jolene and Dirk. Sister of Kazon. Voria served as a major in the confederate military, and commanded the *Wyrm Hunter* until she acquired the mythical *Spellship*. She now commands the Shayan defense against Krox's inevitable invasion.

Ternus

Governor Austin- Austin is a young, ambitious politician in the wrong place at the wrong time. He is woefully unprepared to lead his people during a time of war, and is desperate for allies that can help his people survive. Seriously distrusts magic.

Fleet Admiral Kerr- Commander of the Ternus fleet during the Battle for Marid, and subsequently promoted to Fleet Admiral and placed in charge of all Ternus fleets.

Nara- Former space pirate, now powerful true mage. Nara was mindwiped by Voria, and conscripted into the Confederate Marines. She's fought alongside Aran, Crewes, Bord, Kez, and Voria ever since.

Pickus- Pickus is a freckle-faced grease monkey turned tech

mage who has somehow found himself as Voria's right-hand man.

Virkonans

Aran- Born on Virkon. Manipulated by Neith into being mindwiped in preparation to forge him into a tool to kill Krox and Nefarius. Aran is currently the Captain of Aran's Outriders, a mercenary unit based out of the *Talon*.

Kheross- Father of Rhea. An ancient Wyrm from an alternate timeline where Virkonna was overcome by a sea of blood. Kheross was corrupted by Nefarius, and despite being cleansed on Shaya, still bears the mark. He's currently allied with Aran's Outriders, but Aran doesn't trust him, and Kheross knows it.

Rhea- Daughter of Kheross. Rhea is an unknown quantity. She believes herself to be a human Outrider, but is in fact a *void* Wyrm. She is a powerful war mage, with limited true magic. She is currently being held on Yanthara, in the custody of the Temple of Shi.

Yantharans

Marcelus Crewes- Brother of Sergeant Crewes. Marcelus is a prosecutor living on Shaya. He prosecuted Voria during her trial.

Sergeant Crewes- Brother of Marcelus Crewes. Sergeant Crewes was born on Yanthara. He voluntarily joined the Confederate Marines, and was quickly assigned to the

Wyrm Hunter. He is one of the strongest tech mages in the sector, and his mastery of *fire* is unrivaled.

Sarala- Priestess of Shi, and former girlfriend of Sergeant Crewes. Sarala is the head of the Temple of Shi, and is responsible for guiding new members to the Catalyst. She dated Crewes briefly in secondary school, but that ended when Crewes enlisted in the Confederate Marines.

PREVIOUSLY ON

You guys all know the drill by now. The previously on is where I get to snarkily relate the previous book, and is always my favorite part to write. That said, having recaps for every book is getting longer and longer, and we're reaching a point where it is no longer feasible.

You can check out all the recaps at magitechchronicles.com/previously-on, but from here on out I'm only putting the most recent one in each book. And there will be at least several more. The godswar has really started to heat up, and I cannot wait to show you guys where it goes.

One last thing before I let you get to the recap. **We've begun play testing the Magitech Chronicles pen and paper RPG**, so if that's something you're interested in, sign up to the mailing list at magitechchronicles.com and I'll get you some details.

The first ever game was run at the 20BooksTo50k convention. I played with five science fiction authors, several of whom I'm betting you'd recognize. By this spring I'm hoping you'll be playing too.

Okay, enough about me. Let's get to the recap.

Last time, on The Magitech Chronicles...

War Mage kicked off with Voria bringing the *Spellship* back to Shaya, to have the gunk cleaned off the walls. Said gunk is the Blood of Nefarius, which corrupts any living thing it touches. This began as a minor subplot in book three, back when we thought the Krox were the only thing to fear.

We flash to Aran, who has just parked the *Talon* inside the *Spellship*. He's come to rendezvous with the person Shaya has sent to clean the ship, and it turns out to be Ree. She accuses Nara of being a traitor, and Nara reacts badly because she's a little preoccupied.

Their spat is interrupted as Ree and her mages are attacked by Kheross. Wait, who now? There was a throwaway line near the end of book three where Aran teleports onto the *Spellship*, and meets the Outrider, Rhea. She helps him find the door, and realize his destiny and all that junk.

While they are talking, they hear a roar in the distance from a large creature, say something the size of, oh, I don't know, maybe a colossal Wyrm. Rhea mentions that's Kheross, and that he used to be a friend before he was corrupted by the blood.

Aran and the company kick Kheross's draconic ass, but not before he carves up a lot of Ree's mages. She's left angry, both at Aran, and at Nara. The latter is mostly because Ree blames herself for Frit's escape, and thinks that Nara was in on it.

Nara doesn't help matters, because at the end of *Spellship* she woke up to find someone named Talifax sitting in her room. Talifax is the Guardian of Nefarius, and is super mysterious. Nefarius is a rival of Krox's, who was apparently killed during the godswar. Talifax wants to bring her back so that there will be more books after Krox is killed.

Anyway, Talifax sent Nara a dream where she killed Voria, and claims that it's going to come true. Then, he did something impossible. He gave Nara her memories back.

Those memories are coming back one at a time, and Nara is quite justifiably freaking out. She knows she wasn't a good person before, and fears going back to her old self.

Meanwhile, Eros is cracking out with the Mirror of Shaya. He knows something bad is coming for Shaya, but can't provide any details about what it is, so he sounds like a rambling lunatic. He and Voria do a lot of posturing. Her priorities are getting the *Spellship* cleaned, and also cleansing Rhea and Kheross, the refugees Aran brought back from the timeline where the *Spellship* was discovered.

Eros and his council perform their cleansing ritual, and it works on Rhea. The Outrider is squirreled away by Eros to Yanthara, because he's preparing the plot for Krox Rises and knows Aran will need to pass by there. Kheross, whose cleansing doesn't work, is given into Aran's custody and put in the brig of the *Talon*, since there is no pound for *void*-corrupted Wyrms and Aran can't find him a good home anywhere else.

Right around the time you were yawning for the first time wondering when the politics would stop, the Krox lay the smack down at New Texas, and I delivered more *pew, pew* than a church. They kick Ternus's second largest colony squarely in the nards (those are testicles in case it wasn't clear) with a large-scale invasion.

Ternus puts up a bat signal for Voria. This is a dramatic re-enactment:

Ternus: You signed a treaty, so, like, help us and stuff.
Eros: No. Suck it.
Voria: Don't be a douche, Eros.
Eros's douchiness intensifies.

Ternus: But, we're like dying and stuff.

Eros: Nope, not gonna help. I have a vague premonition that something might attack Shaya, so we need literally every ship and every mage to protect our world. Just in case.

Voria: Just in case you get attacked, you know, like New Texas?

Eros: Exactly. We need to be able to protect ourselves.

I should write movie scripts. Anyway, Voria gives Eros the middle finger. She takes the *Spellship*, and heads for the capitol of Ternus, because she's also had a vague premonition. She thinks Nebiat is going to attack something else besides New Texas, and worries that if she goes there, she won't be where she needs to be.

Early spoilers: this is happening because they're both being manipulated by Nebiat's dad, Teodros. He's been quietly pruning possibilities to show them things he wants them to see, while obscuring things he doesn't want them to know.

Flash back to Nara. She experiences a memory from her distant past, before she was enslaved by Yorrak. It turns out she was in the Zephyr program, which was a Ternus experiment to create Tech Mages.

The Zephyr version of her character is the template for the Spellsniper class in the pen and paper game, which is exactly what it sounds like.

Anyway, when Nara comes back from this memory she finds that Talifax has been controlling her body. While she was incapacitated he used her body to steal the *Talon*, and has almost reached Shaya's umbral shadow. She's about to turn around when Ree and her spellfighters come after her.

Nara doesn't want to risk going back, because if Talifax can control her then maybe he really can make her assassinate Voria. So she bugs out with the *Talon*, and leaves Shaya, disabling Ree's fighter as she zooms by.

Aran is more than a little annoyed that his ride has been jacked, and the rest of the company is pretty pissed at Nara too. They have to decide a course forward, and Crewes suggests that Aran resign from the Confederacy and form a mercenary company.

So he does.

They use the money from Virkon to buy out their contracts, and to purchase brand new spellarmor from Kazon. If they still had a ship they'd be set. Since they don't, Aran proposes a plan to the on-world Ternus representative...Admiral Nimitz (one of the guys who prosecuted Voria back in *Void Wyrm*). Nimitz agrees to look the other way, and Aran and Davidson steal the *Wyrm Hunter* from the Confederacy.

Aran also contacts Ree, and shames her into coming with them to help Ternus, because she feels responsible for both Frit and Nara's escape. She's brought a dozen spellfighters, further augmenting the relief force Aran leads to New Texas.

Speaking of Frit, she's brought her sisters to the Heart of Krox, where they were originally born. When she gets there, it's nothing at all like she'd hoped. Her people are mindless slaves, incapable of language. Her sisters and she are alone, and have nowhere to go.

Cue Nebiat's arrival. She shows up with her son Kaho, the dude who lost a hand to Aran back in *Spellship*. Frit realizes they've been manipulated. They have nowhere to go except with Nebiat, and so they all agree to serve her. Frit goes along with it despite her reservations, and quickly finds that she has an ally in Kaho, who also hates Nebiat.

Nebiat's goal is to locate something called magibombs,

which is a super original name, I know. I'm quite proud of it. Anyway, she wants to use these magibombs to destroy Colony 3, thus robbing the entire sector of its food supply for decades.

Meanwhile, Voria puts out a call to Shaya, and to her shock, many, many people answer. Drifters and Shayans alike leave their world to help New Texas, and she ends up with a city full of people living inside the *Spellship*. Many are *life* mages, and quickly finish cleaning the ship. They also never lack for beer, since Drifters.

Nara arrives at the abandoned facility where Ternus trained the Zephyrs. It's been abandoned, but she's hoping to learn more about her past, and has no idea where else to go. Only a few of her memories have returned, but more are coming back.

Not long after she arrives, she finds her old combat suit, rifle, and pistol. Talifax appears and she asks him why he wanted her to come here. She gets her answer when Frit and Nebiat arrive. Talifax placed her in Nebiat's path intentionally, though Nara has no idea why.

This next part was hard to write, because Nebiat is devilishly smart.

If she captured Nara she'd kill her, instantly. Because letting her live is *muhahaha* villain stupid. However, she gets a missive from dad, and Teodros tells her not only is she not going to kill Nara, but she's going to give Frit the *Talon*, and the magibombs, and have them destroy Colony 3.

Nebiat protests that you don't give super important tasks to underlings, but Teodros insists. He tells Nebiat to bring the rest of the Ifrit back to the Erkadi Rift, effectively removing her from the war for the time being. She's pissed, but reluctantly obeys. She knows her dad is planning something big, and just hopes whatever it is doesn't screw her.

Aran arrives at New Texas, and we get some of the most fun combat I've ever written. Aran and his company combat drop into the Ternus equivalent of the Pentagon, called Fort Crockett. They punch through the Krox assault, and everyone gets to show off. Looooots of *pew, pew, BOOM, RAWR*. Good stuff, I'm telling you.

Ternus dispatches a reporter called Erika Tharn to record the drop, and Tharn follows the company in as they punch through all enemy opposition. They get inside, and the footage is broadcast all over the sector, finally giving Ternus hope that they can fight back against the Krox.

Unfortunately, while Aran makes it in, the best he can do is hold the Krox at bay. Sooner or later they'll overwhelm the facility. He deals with waves of incorporeal wights and some powerful demons, but if they don't get backup they'll only be able to keep them at bay for so long.

Frit arrives at Colony 3 fully intending to destroy it. Nara realizes that the reason Talifax placed her in Frit's path was so that she could persuade Frit not to do it. Nara succeeds, and Frit realizes that killing hundreds of millions of people, and causing billions more to starve is going too far, no matter what Shaya did to her and her sisters.

Frit's sister, Fritara, a total teacher's pet sent by Nebiat, tries to kill Frit. Nara is forced to execute her, and saves Frit's life. Just when things are looking up, Ree and her squadron of spellfighters arrive. They're here to hunt Frit, and Frit doesn't know what to do.

Nara suggests contacting Ternus and offering to turn over the bombs, so they do. They surrender. Ree attacks anyway. They pilot the *Talon* into the Ternus battle stations, and Ree ends up getting shot down by Ternus. She dies. It's very sad. Not like, were Crewes to die level of sad, but more like...she could have come around and been a cool ally.

Meanwhile Voria goes to New Texas, even though she knows that this is giving her opponents time to spring some sort of trap. She gets there just as Aran has finished up like nine chapters in a row of straight combat with endless demons. He's holding on, but barely.

Voria casts a spell from the *Spellship* which engulfs the entire world, and effectively counter spells the binding holding all the undead and demons in check. The corpses collapse, and the demons turn on their masters.

Aran and company finish saving the Ternus command structure, and everything is happy, yay! We've beaten the Krox.

Here comes the trap.

Teodros's whole plan was to hit Shaya. Eros was right. Teodros is the Guardian of Krox, and is basically a demigod. He shows up at Shaya with an army of undead dragons. Basically he animated every dragon that died over the last three decades, and uses them to assault the tree.

There's a big battle with the Shayan forces losing (if only they had the *Wyrm Hunter*, and Ree's fighters, and the *Talon*, and the *Spellship*). Eros falls back to the Chamber of the First where the reservoir of immense magic designed to raise Shaya is housed.

Teodros beats Eros down, kills Erika (the Warmaster, not the reporter), and drinks the pool. Eros gets the last word though. He mutters a death curse, which puts a minor compulsion on Teodros. That becomes really important later.

Nebiat arrives in the Erkadi Rift and finds out all about dad's plan. It turns out he's going to resurrect Krox, but with some stipulations. Krox will be a slave, and Teodros will be in the driver's seat. It's an audacious plan, and it requires a massive amount of *life* magic...which Teodros just stole from Shaya.

There's just one tiny problem. Eros's death curse causes Teodros to build a critical flaw into his spell. When he tries casting it, his wards fail, and Krox eats him. *BURRRRRP.* No more Teodros. Nebiat sees the mostly finished spell, and remembers how Nara stepped in and finished casting hers back on Marid in book one.

Why not do the same thing?

She finishes her father's spell, and seizes control of Krox. Nebiat rises as a goddess, backed by the power of one of the oldest gods in the universe.

Not bad for a cliff hanger, eh?

PROLOGUE

The first problem Nebiat encountered in becoming a god was dealing with the lack of sleep. She'd been a Wyrm for centuries, and could choose not to sleep when it suited her, but like most of her kin she found it a welcome respite from her many troubles. As a god, sleep was denied her.

There was no escaping the endless sea of possibilities. No respite. That was proving more challenging than controlling the Mind of Krox, and disquiet fears that she might not be able to manage either appeared in many possibilities. She could, quite literally, see herself being subsumed into the god her father had attempted to control.

What will you do now? Krox's immense voice rumbled in her mind. In some ways they were the same entity, a mobile star that could sail through the heavens of its own accord. But in others Krox was completely alien, and as unknowable as the stars themselves.

I don't know. Admitting that terrified her. *I must find a way to make them fear me, and soon, or Voria and her blasted allies will seize the offensive. It is in your best interests to work with me. They are coming for us both.*

The Mind of Krox pulsed thoughtfully, and she watched as Krox spun out countless possibilities. It happened so quickly, billions upon billions weaving out in every conceivable direction. She couldn't follow them all, not yet, but she kept up with much of it. She saw her death, and her rise, and Krox's return, and many other variations.

This possibility is the most intriguing. Krox offered. A possibility pulsed, growing more distinct than the rest. *Destroy their capital, and their spirits will break.*

Nebiat saw, and she was pleased. A world lay before her, a shining jewel surrounded by a sea of glittering droplets, the thousands of orbital stations protecting the capitol of Ternus. In that possibility Nebiat arrived in the sky over their world, and laid waste to the planet.

She didn't recognize the magic she used, some sort of tremendously powerful *earth* spell. Yet it hardly mattered, as she didn't possess nearly enough *earth* to cast a spell like that. Krox had immense reserves of *spirit*, nearly infinite. Thanks to her father's theft from Shaya, Nebiat possessed a large quantity of *life* as well. But she possessed little else, and that limited her actions.

How would this possibility come to pass? She made it a demand, though the god did not seem impressed.

Permit me to travel to the Earthmother's grave, and we will draw the power from her body. Krox showed her a possibility where she orbited a familiar world. The world where most of their hatchlings were birthed. The world where the goddess known as the Earthmother had been slain.

Nowhere in the sector is there a stronger earth catalyst, not even the Fist of Trakalon, which I myself severed from the mighty titan.

Nebiat drew *void* from her immense reserves, more than any mortal had ever had access to, though a trivial amount compared to the *spirit* or even *life* she possessed. She briefly paused as she wondered how to cast a spell without hands, but quickly realized that she understood the magic in a way she never had before.

It didn't require crude gestures. It required will. She reached out and opened a vast Fissure, wide enough to accommodate the bulk of a star. It shimmered for a moment, and then the magic became unstable. The edges cracked, then dissolved, exactly the way any Fissure would when exposed to the light of a star.

Nebiat fought to rein in her temper, and narrowly succeeded. There were so many frustrating details her father had no doubt prepared for, but that she was completely unaware of. *If I cannot open a Fissure because of our own light, then how are we to travel?*

The barrier on Fissures exists for our protection. Krox's voice contained no emotion, save perhaps patience. The god seemed otherwise indifferent. *If we, or any potent magical being strong enough to be considered a god, were to enter the depths, then we'd be set upon by our own progenitors and torn apart. The Fissures keep them from coming to our plane, and visiting the same fate upon every living thing in the cosmos.*

Nebiat felt something gather within the Mind of Krox, a surge of all eight aspects of magic combined into one harmonious song. When that song faded she was simply... elsewhere. The void around her was tinged with a deep purple, the familiar heart of the Erkadi Rift.

Below her lay an ashen world, grey with the deaths of billions who'd fought to defend their draconic mother from Krox's final, brutal assault. She could see those memories, and witnessed Krox in all his glory. She understood, as she watched the memory of him dismembering a planet-sized dragon, that the Mind of Krox was a very small part of a greater whole.

Yes, we are much diminished. But that can be remedied, and coming here is the first step. You have seen how we traveled, a method we call translocation. We simply mold reality so that we are somewhere else. There is no spell. There is no magic that can be countered.

Nebiat had so many questions. Who were these progenitors? There was an eternity to learn, but only if she survived the war with Voria and her blasted Confederacy. *If this magic cannot be countered, then how do we defend against it?*

Krox pulsed the first emotion she'd experienced, a complex mix of amusement and exasperation. *By foreseeing the possibility that such an event might occur. A rival god's approach sends ripples through Neith's web, and clever gods can detect such ripples. Fortunately, I possess such abilities, and any god that might challenge us will know this. Unless they are strong, they will not risk a direct confrontation. The wisest course when presented with a god of near equal strength is to flee and wage your war through proxies. Vessels, like this Voria you detest so much. Or Shaya, her forebear.*

It had never occurred to Nebiat that Krox could peruse her memories the same way she could his. Of course he'd seen everything. There was far less to observe, as she'd lived only a tiny fraction of his vast timespan. She'd not yet ascertained his true age, but billions of years seemed likely. Millions at the very least.

Mollified, Nebiat observed the world they'd arrived at. She saw with fresh eyes—well, with whatever Krox used to observe. There were so many spectrums, so much that had been hidden from her before she'd merged with a god.

She could see the life forms dotting the planet. She

could see the places of power, most created from blood or body parts raining down to the world in the aftermath of the battle between Krox and the Earthmother.

Krox had devoured a full third of goddess's massive body, including everything above the shoulders. Presumably, her mind had been absorbed, and the same fate awaited Nebiat if she was not careful.

The headless body of the Earthmother lay on the world below, a full continent in her own right. The millennia had covered her with an endless forest, each tree a miniature version of the very same redwoods that grew on the hated moon of Shaya.

Within that forest lay countless drakes, each a primal that had been drawn to the world by the magical song of the Earthmother. Unfortunately, drakes were merely animals, because their minds had not yet developed. Given enough decades they would fully awaken, but only a handful below were that old. Most were little more than beasts. Though useful beasts.

Their minds are yours. Something surged within Krox, and a wave of *spirit* washed over the world. As one, every drake looked skyward, and any old enough to have grown wings leapt into the sky. They soared toward her, basking in the light of their god as Krox bound them. *But that is not why we have come. We have come for her.*

A tendril of *spirit*, kilometers thick, extended from the Mind of Krox and wove through the planet's atmosphere until it reached the Earthmother's corpse. The tendril latched onto a rent in her scaly hide, directly over the heart, and wonderful brown pulses of *earth* began flowing up the tendril and into their star. Nebiat could feel the power immediately, each pulse unimaginably powerful.

After a half-dozen pulses, they stopped, and Nebiat felt a

sudden emptiness. She watched as the tendril retracted back into the main body. *Why did you stop?*

If we drain her fully, then the primals will no longer come. I have taken sparingly from her, so that she remains a powerful long-term asset. I have raised countless armies over the millennia, and will no doubt raise countless more after you and I have merged.

Nebiat saw the sense in that, and didn't press the issue. She had enough *earth* to cast the spell she'd seen in the possibility. It was time to pay a visit directly to Ternus, and show them the might of a god.

1

SURPRISE, BITCHES

Aran stepped through the *Hunter*'s airlock, entering Alamo Station. The mushroom-shaped station sat atop an enormous umbilical cord that stretched to the world below. A space elevator, Pickus had called it.

The rest of the company followed him, all wearing full battle dress, despite being aboard the most secure Ternus facility in the sector. The governor had requested it, probably to fulfill some sort of PR goal of showing the 'brave heroes' from New Texas.

Aran forced himself forward, into the middle of the strangest spectacle he'd ever imagined. The corridor ended on a stage, with a sea of bright lights glaring down on him from above. Beyond that lay a shadowed audience in stadium seating, and he'd guess there were at least a hundred. Perhaps significantly more, as the upper rows disappeared into shadow.

Aran turned back to the tunnel he'd exited from, and found Tharn standing right behind him. The older reporter wore a simple, black flight suit that somehow managed elegant, and her bright white hair had been pulled into a tight bun. She reminded him, both in bearing and appearance, a little bit of Voria.

He pitched his voice low so only she would hear. "They're really broadcasting this to their whole world?"

The rest of the company piled out of the tunnel, with Crewes in the lead, and Kheross lurking in the rear. Each carried their weapon openly, and their armor gleamed under the lights. Even Aran had to admit they looked damned impressive.

Kezia's hammer gleamed under the lights as she stepped onto the stage, passing Tharn. "Would you lookit them all. They're joost here to gawk at us?"

"Can't really blame 'em," Bord began as he sidled up in his scout armor, "I mean, have you seen my lady? I'd have stood in line to see you in person."

Kezia came to a dead stop, and turned and faced him. "Bord, I do believe you just paid me a classy compliment."

His faceplate slid upward, exposing an exuberant grin. His dark curls peaked out like shrubs badly in need of cutting. "I've been practicing all week for that one."

Tharn gave a small wave to draw Aran's attention, then she nodded out to the audience with a wry smile. "To answer your question, yes, this is being broadcast to the entire sector. I gather social media isn't a thing on Shaya. Every person within 30 light years will be discussing this interview for weeks—I can promise you that."

She gave Aran a grandmotherly smile, which was partly a performance for the cameras, though he also felt some real affection there. "This way."

The reporter escorted Aran over to a large U-shaped table where a pair of men already sat. Each held a glass of water, but they were only holding them, not drinking. It all felt very staged. Even their faces had been painted with a faint layer of cosmetics, hiding the blemishes that self-conscious Shayans would simply have removed with *life* magic.

Aran moved to the opposite side of the table, and the rest of the company followed.

Crewes was the first to reach the table. "Sir, if I sit in this thing it'll get smoked. Like, even outside my armor it wouldn't be good for this chair."

Aran agreed. "Noted. I'll take care of it."

Aran reached for the well of *air* in his chest, and drew enough to create a tendril for each member of the company, Tharn included. He scooped them up and set them in chairs molded to fit them. Weaving so many would have been taxing, once. Since meeting Virkonna it was trivial.

"You're in the wrong line of work, sir." Crewes cradled his hands behind his head as he settled into the translucent chair. "I could get used to this."

"You and me both, sir." Kezia leaned back. "It's almost like we're gonna get five minutes of R&R before the world starts blowing up again."

Nervous laugher echoed up from the audience, and Kezia froze self-consciously, as if suddenly remembering they were all staring at her.

Bord hopped to his feet, and thrust an armored gauntlet at the audience. "You think you can laugh at my lady? She's a proper hero, and you'd best show her the respect she deserves. You keep it up and I'll turn the lot of you into frogs. See if I don't. I'm a powerful mage." He dropped his voice to a conspiratorial whisper. "They don't got no idea what you can do with spells, I figure. I bet they'll buy it."

"Captain Aran." A handsome dark-haired man in his early twenties set down his glass and rose from the other side of the table. The man wore a black suit with a white shirt and black tie, of the sort their businessmen seemed to love. His hair was artfully sculpted with some sort of hair product, and had probably taken hours to perfect. The man offered a hand, and offered a plastic smile. "I'm Governor Austin, and on behalf of my people I would like to thank you for your heroic actions on New Texas. Countless people owe you their lives." The smile didn't quite reach his eyes. Staged, like everything else. If anything, Aran sensed animosity in the man. Why, though?

Aran refrained from pointing out that it was actually Voria who'd saved the planet, and accepted the handshake with a plastic smile of his own. The custom was growing on him, mostly as a result of his time spent with Davidson. There'd been a lot of that on the trip from New Texas, and that was going to be sorely missed. Davidson was still the only officer he'd met, in any military, that he could relax around.

"Thank you, Governor." Aran released his hand and returned to his improvised chair. "Everyone involved in this war, at every level, had a hand in pushing back the Krox. If not for the combined efforts of all involved, I don't think I'd be standing here today. Ternus should be proud."

The other man cleared his throat, then gave Aran a respectful nod. "Captain. I don't know if you remember me, but I'm Fleet Admiral Kerr. We met briefly at Marid, though in your defense you were otherwise occupied."

"Yes, freeing Drakkon, but I still remember you, Admiral." Aran offered a tight confederate salute. Kerr returned it.

The governor returned to his seat and looked as if he were about to say something when an aide with a device clipped to his ear ran over and bent to whisper something urgent.

The governor paled, and then turned to Tharn. His face went splotchy, and his amicable expression turned ugly. "Turn those things off. Now. NOW!" He rose to his feet and rounded on the film crews, who seemed unsure how to respond, at first.

Tharn cocked her head quizzically, but after a moment the silver-haired reporter waved a hand and the lights on the drones died. They rose into the air, and the stage lights dimmed enough that Aran could see the confused faces in the audience.

"Why did I just terminate a sector-wide feed, Governor?" Tharn demanded. Elegantly, of course. She raised a hand to straighten her bun, the silver curls immaculate under the lights.

"Because I told you to, Tharn," the governor snarled. "I've just received word that a second sun has appeared in our system." The governor rose shakily to his feet, and his hands were shaking as he spun toward the aide. "Get me a viewscreen. What the blazes is happening out there? I need answers, people."

The aide seemed used to the abuse, and didn't react as he touched the device on his ear, triggering a large holographic sphere in the center of the table's U. A representation of the Ternus system burst into sudden clarity, complete with every station and every ship tagged in real time. The bulk of those defenses were, quite naturally, arrayed around the planet's umbral shadow, where most foes would appear.

That left the Ternus defenders totally unprepared for the blazing star that had appeared near the planet's nadir. That star dwarfed the planet, but Aran sensed that the size wasn't the true threat. It wasn't comprised of radioactive material, or whatever stars were made of. No, this thing was comprised of pure magic, most of it *spirit*. More than existed anywhere in the sector, so far as he knew.

"That's no star," he muttered, then rose to his feet. "That's a god, an elder one. If I had to guess? We're looking at Krox. Governor, your planet is about to be assaulted. You need to evacuate everyone you can. Now."

It was far too late.

Tremendous magic built up somewhere in the distance, endless oceans of incredible power. Not *spirit*, as he expected, but *earth*. He had no idea what the spell did, but sensing that much power made Aran suddenly understand why Neith had hidden herself away, and why Virkonna had chosen what amounted to a voluntary coma.

Krox's power dwarfed them all.

2
GRAVITY

Nebiat appeared in the sky over Ternus, the planet and its moons rotating beneath her. They were far smaller than she, their proportions about what one would expect when considered next to a star. Her arrival immediately altered the attitude of every satellite, every ship, and even the planet itself.

Those closest to her were drawn in by her gravity, disappearing into the roiling, white mass that comprised her body. Their memories, and thoughts, and even atoms were added to hers, strengthening her the tiniest bit.

The ships fortunate enough to be closer to the planet were not immediately pulled in, and many were already beginning to react to her arrival. She realized that with her senses she could perceive the face of every individual citizen on the world below. She saw the first few, a minority certainly, look up into the sky and notice a second sun suddenly appear.

Many were too self-absorbed to realize there'd been a change. The distracted fools were lost in one form of entertainment or another, and couldn't be troubled to look out a window. They would go to their deaths oblivious.

Wait. Do not destroy this world. Krox cautioned.

That took Nebiat aback, so much so that she abandoned the spell she'd been about to cast. *We came here specifically to destroy the capital of my enemies, to show them the kind of power they are dealing with. That was YOUR suggestion, remember?*

I did not advise you to destroy this world. Krox countered. *I advised you to make them fear you. Destroying this world will do that, but it will also limit their viable responses. They will know that you intend their obliteration, and they will have no choice but to band together and resist. That will breed the possibility of our defeat. Instead, you must show them a fate worse than death, and then show them that their own survival is possible if they abandon their allies.*

Nebiat begrudgingly admitted, internally at least, that it made sense. She refused to give the god the satisfaction, though she wasn't certain he was even capable of experiencing that sort of emotion.

Very well. I will deny my enemy this world, but allow some of their citizens to flee, and to spread word of what happened here.

Nebiat drew deeply from the well of *earth* she'd stolen from the Earthmother. She concentrated on the world below, and felt every atom making up its structure. Like most worlds, the core was comprised of molten rock covered by a thick outer crust, also of rock.

She focused on that rock, and willed it to become much more dense. Nebiat began with the iron, already dense, and made it more so. She continued outward with each mineral she encountered, replicating the process until she reached the planet's crust.

Silver, gold, granite, marble, and a hundred other substances grew increasingly dense, the entire planet thickening and hardening over the course of a few moments. The spell's effects were very nearly instantaneous, at least from the perception of the poor fools living on the rock below.

Her work had two immediate effects. First, it dramatically increased gravity. Second, and much more insidious, the planet's core began to cool as the thermal energy was spread through a much greater quantity of matter. In a handful of months that process would strip the planet of its protective magnetic field, though the suddenly unstable orbit would likely prove its undoing long before the magnetic field's absence could kill them.

Nebiat was completely unprepared for the sudden vacuum as the immensity of *earth* magic left her. Completing the spell—if something this powerful could even be called a spell any longer—drained nearly all of the *earth* magic she'd siphoned, plus a good bit of her own reserves.

Divine acts come with a corresponding cost. Krox explained. *If you wish to war upon this sector you will need more magic, and you will not find it here. You must devour a Catalyst, one of significant strength.*

Nebiat savored a final glance at the doomed enemy capital. Her work was done here, and she could safely tend to other matters while news of the attack spread.

She considered Krox's words, and realized the deity was right. They needed more magic. It was time to tend to that. She focused on the potent magical song Krox had used to translocate them, then duplicated it.

They left the skies over Ternus, leaving a doomed world in their wake.

3

RUN

Aran hesitated only a moment, overwhelmed by the immensity of the magic pouring out of the god and into Ternus. He didn't need to understand the spell to know what it meant. Ternus was doomed, and so was everyone who tried to fight that thing.

He quickly scanned the room, and saw two other exits. There was no going back the way they'd came, since the *Hunter* had already left the dock, and probably the system. They had to find another way off the station, and they needed to do it now.

"Governor." Aran drifted into the air, his spellarmor gleaming under the lights. "Do you have a ship standing by? My company can escort you to safety."

Austin nodded, then wiped sweat from his forehead. His hands were still shaking, likely from adrenaline, or the increased gravity. "My vessel is docked next to the *Talon*. Get me there alive, and I'll give you your ship back." The governor's complexion was ashen, and he slowly swayed back and forth. "Kerr, what do we do about that thing? Give me options."

Kerr rose slowly, his teeth gritted in obvious pain, and fought the increased gravity as he moved to the holo, the blue glow bathing his weathered face. "We do what the captain suggested, and we send a priority one evacuation order, system wide. Anyone able to flee, should. That includes the *Hunter*."

The governor directed a withering look at his aide, who seemed to be dealing with the sudden gravity better than either of the others. "Make it happen, Jared. Order every vessel to lift off. Quickly."

"Right away, sir." The aide closed his eyes and tapped the device on his ear.

Aran's stomach lurched as whatever spell Krox had cast reached completion. The magic faded, but the effects of the spell did not.

A final wave of immense gravity pressed down on him, and the *air* tendril strained to hold up his armor. He could feel his weight increasing, and that of the others. The scream of metal came from all around them as the walls began to twist and buckle.

"This place isn't designed for this kind of gravity," Kerr forced out through gritted teeth. "We need to get off this station before it comes apart."

Panicked screams rang from the audience as they were pressed into their chairs by the suddenly increased gravity. Anyone without significant physical conditioning was in no position to even stand, much less run.

Another deep groan passed through the station, and the hologram showing the system flickered. When it returned it showed a sea of glittering dots falling toward the planet. Horror bloomed as Aran realized that their orbits were rapidly decaying because of the increased gravity.

"Bord," Aran roared, forcing his armor into the air with a

surge of *void*. "Grab the governor. Kezia, you're carrying Kerr." He spun to face Tharn. "Can you lead us to the *Talon*?"

"B-bay 34," she managed. She clutched at her chest, and her face began to turn red. She took a single step forward, then started to collapse.

Aran willed his armor across the distance, and caught her just before she hit the deck. "Come on, people. Let's go."

Bord wrapped an armored arm around the governor, while Kezia scooped up the fleet admiral.

"That way." Tharn raised a trembling hand. She was in fantastic shape for a woman her age, but the human body was only designed to withstand so much. "Not far." Then she relaxed against Aran's armor, unable to move.

Aran gave the audience one agonized glance, then whirled and zipped up the corridor. He hated triage, and in that moment he finally gained a little more sympathy for Voria. Making decisions that got other people killed sucked, but if someone didn't make them, then more people ended up dead.

He zipped up the corridor as fast as he thought safe, winging around the few people strong enough to manage a walk. Most were still back in their seats, and Aran knew what that meant. They were dead. All of them. And there wasn't a damned thing he could do about it.

He glanced down at Tharn, who'd lost consciousness. He had no way to check her vitals, so he kept moving as quickly as he could. She did not look good. Her skin was pale, and she'd stopped sweating. If she was breathing it was too shallow to make out.

The rest of the company had formed a single line behind him. As they charged up the corridor Tharn had indicated, he began to see berth numbers. Two, four, six. They had a ways to go.

They'd made it another few hundred meters, when the corridor ahead of them buckled. The ceiling caved in, twisting under the weight of the bulkhead above.

Aran extended a hand, and gritted his teeth as he reached for the *void* in his chest. He pulled up as much of the magic as he dared, and forced it into the wall of metal now blocking their path. It groaned and began to rise, millimeter by millimeter. "Crewes, a little help."

"On it, sir." Crewes trotted forward, then ducked nimbly under the gap Aran had created. He planted both hands against the collapsed ceiling, then heaved upward with a yell. After a moment, the metal began to rise. "All right, that's the way we do it. Get through. Now, people. We got places to be."

Aran waited for the rest of the company to scramble past Crewes. He wrapped Tharn in a net of air, then flung her gently up the corridor to safety next to Bord and Kezia.

"Hold on, Sergeant." Aran squared his shoulder, and got ready to charge.

"Oh, I am not gonna like this, am I?" The sergeant winced, and the metal above him groaned ominously.

"No time to argue." Aran channeled *fire* to increase his strength, and *void* to increase his mass. He sprinted forward, and caught Crewes in a flying tackle.

They rolled over and over again down the corridor, sparks flying as their armor scraped the walls. Behind them came a tremendous boom as the corridor collapsed, obscuring their view of the way they'd come.

"Well that sucked." Crewes climbed to his feet. He was the closest to Tharn, and scooped up the unconscious reporter. "Best get moving."

"Twenty-four through thirty-six is that way," Aran read aloud, then started up the corridor. The rest of the squad followed, their pants of exertion loud on the open missive linking their spellarmor.

He zipped past 26, then 30. "Looks like we're nearly there."

Aran pulled up short next to the airlock, and felt something ease in him, a tension he'd been carrying since Nara had stolen the *Talon*. There she was, miraculously untouched, sitting in a berth that hadn't yet come apart. Above her he could see fires burning through the metal, and knew it was going to get worse, quickly.

He cycled the airlock, which groaned in protest as the thick, metal door slid up into the roof. Aran accepted Tharn as Crewes forged past him and moved to stand near the inner airlock controls. They filed inside, then Crewes stabbed the big, red button. The door slid shut behind them, sealing briefly, then the opposite door slid up to reveal the *Talon*'s familiar blue membrane.

"C-captain," Tharn gasped. Aran glanced down at the reporter's face. Her eyes bulged, and a blood vessel burst in her right eye, filling it with blood. She clutched at her chest. "C-can't breathe."

The older woman spasmed suddenly, and Aran gently set her on the floor of the airlock. "Hang on, Tharn. We're almost there. Bord, get over here."

Bord set Kerr gently against the wall, then moved to Tharn's side. His face bore uncharacteristic concern. "You just lie back now." He rested a hand on Tharn's forehead, and golden energy blazed from his palm. It pulsed into Tharn for several seconds, then ceased.

Tharn's complexion hadn't improved, and her eyes fluttered closed again. Bord looked up at Aran, and shook his head. "There's nothing I can do, Captain. I can fix a cut, or a bruise. Her heart's giving out, and the rest of her won't be far behind."

"Will getting her into the *Talon* help?" Aran gently picked the reporter up. She was so light.

Bord shook his head, and wiped at some moisture in the corner of his eye. "I don't think so, sir. The damage is done."

Aran carried Tharn through the membrane and back aboard his ship for the first time in nearly a month. The *Talon*'s golden corridors were a welcome sight even in their current circumstances.

The extra gravity was absent inside the *Talon*, a fact that was less evident in his spellarmor since it insulated him from the stresses. He set Tharn against the far wall, and took a step back so Bord could take a look at her.

Bord knelt and pressed two fingers to Tharn's throat. Tears streamed down his face, and he gave a tiny shake of his head as he looked up at Aran.

Aran stared hard at Tharn, and realized that her chest was no longer rising and falling. Tharn was dead. He compartmentalized the pain. He hadn't known the reporter well, but he'd liked her, and seeing her die so suddenly was…he didn't have words for it. It showed that any of them could go, at any time, even when they thought they were safe. "Bord, Kez, get Tharn's body down to medical and see that she's cared for. Then help Kerr and the governor to the bridge."

Aran tried not to think about it as he zipped up to the bridge, and found Crewes already entering one of the three matrices. Aran slid wordlessly into the central one, and quickly stabbed all three *void* sigils as the rings rotated around him. "Tharn didn't make it."

The sergeant's face fell. "Ain't right, for her or any of

the others. I hope all them zeroes ain't been skipping leg day, 'cause they're gonna need everything they got." The words might have been harsh, but the tone was as sympathetic as Aran had ever heard. Crewes's eyes shone as he stared at the scry-screen. The sergeant punched a *fire* sigil, and the scry-screen sprang to magical life. It showed the world below, with much more clarity than the Ternus device.

Several moments later Bord and Kezia hurried onto the bridge. Each deposited their charge atop a bench on the far wall. Both Kerr and Governor Austin seemed to be recovering, physically at least. Austin's gaze was unfocused, and he was muttering to himself under his breath.

"Hold on to something," Aran instructed as he linked to the *Talon* and observed the situation outside through its senses.

The situation was pretty damned grim.

The station was doomed, and looked as if it would take the continent with it. The whole structure had already begun to list, and while stabilizing thrusters were continuously firing, they weren't doing anything to deter the process.

"This thing is about to trigger an extinction-level event," he said, "We can't be here when it does."

Metal paneling along the space elevator's umbilical cord began to buckle, and the whole station was jerked violently downward. If not for the *Talon*'s inertial dampeners, they'd have been hurled to the deck.

"Sir." Crewes tapped another *fire* sigil, then a *dream*. "Looks like the station clamp is inoperable, and we ain't going anywhere until it's removed."

Aran cocked his head and saw through the *Talon* once more. A large arm with a magnetic clamp had been affixed to the upper hull. "Kerr, is there a quick way to get this dealt with?"

The fleet admiral's forehead shone with sweat, and all he could manage was a quick shake of his head. The governor was in even worse shape, though surprisingly, Kheross had moved to his side. He bent to check the man's pulse, then turned to Aran. "He lives. For now."

"I'm going to try to keep it that way." Aran tapped an *air* sigil on the silver ring, then another on the gold. He poured a healthy mix of blue-white magic into the matrix, and willed the spell into existence.

Lightning streaked from the spellcannon, arcing up into the clamp. It played across the chrome surface, grounding into the dense metal. A moment later there was an echoing thunk, and then the clamp released them.

"What did you do?" Bord blinked at him from the third matrix.

"Their clamps use magnets, and they require power. I shorted them out," Aran explained as he cautiously guided the *Talon* around the clamp and toward the hangar door. Aran tapped *void* on the bronze, then the silver, then the gold ring.

The cannon fired again, this time a simple level three void bolt. The spell slammed into the hangar door, and a *Talon*-sized hunk disintegrated, exposing them to the vacuum of space. Explosive decompression ripped loose cargo, debris, and anything else that hadn't been strapped down.

Aran waited for the turbulence to subside, then smoothly guided the *Talon* through the hole and into orbit over the world. Below him the space elevator's momentum had increased, and the gigantic cable slowly toppled toward the planet below.

They shot away from the doomed planet, but Aran kept the scry-screen focused on the station. It was impossible to look away as it slowly slammed into the continent beneath it. They were insulated from the horror at this distance, but Aran knew that anything on that continent that hadn't died in the initial impact was unlikely to survive the nuclear winter it would bring.

All around them stations burned like embers as their orbits decayed and they too fell toward the world below. A few large ships blasted off from the surface, but none of the small seemed able to escape the planet's newly increased gravity. They were trapped in a nightmare.

Aran flipped the *Talon* around, and scanned for Krox. A brilliant white star still hovered in the sky, but only for an instant. He didn't blink, or look away, but Krox simply vanished.

He turned wearily to Crewes. "Get a missive to Davidson, and tell him to turn around. The governor's ship went down with that station. We're going to need the *Hunter*."

4
HOPE

Voria knew she was dreaming, but also knew that what she witnessed was no ordinary dream. It had plagued her every night for weeks, in one variation or another. Each time, she appeared in the sky over Shaya in the midst of the largest orbital battle she'd ever participated in.

Shayan ships, backed by a Ternus fleet, which included the *Wyrm Hunter*, had formed a protective screen over the shield protecting the great tree and the cities clustered at her feet. There were many vessels in their ranks that Voria didn't recognize, including dark, menacing ships that she knew must have been created by the Inurans.

Voria never spent much time examining the ships, because a far more dangerous threat filled the skies over Shaya. A god had come, and while she'd never seen the four-armed deity, she knew it must be Krox.

The god smashed the shield protecting Shaya, and wrenched the great tree from the world, its roots tearing out the farms and settlements as the home she'd known her entire life ripped free of the planet. Krox tore that tree apart, and withdrew an ancient black spear, many kilometers long, from the corpse.

At the same time a lady of light, Shaya herself, appeared in the sky to oppose Krox. Krox swung his mighty spear, and the lady of light answered with a double-bladed staff comprised of pure light. She parried desperately, but it was clear that she was not nearly as strong as the god who'd come to devour their world.

Voria's eyes opened, and she stared at the ceiling to her quarters, aboard the *Spellship*. Her heart thundered in her chest, and she forced several calming breaths. Dread permeated every part of her body and her mind. She never saw how the battle ended, but it wasn't much of a stretch to assume the lady of light would be overwhelmed by Krox.

She rose from her luxurious bed, and began pulling on her uniform. She needed to be in the Chamber of the First shortly, to help conduct the restoration ritual that would stabilize the planet in the wake of the most egregious theft of magic she'd ever heard of.

Teodros had drained the pool, leaving them without the magical strength to keep the shield in place. If there was one silver lining in her recurring nightmare, it was that the shield existed when Krox arrived, so it must mean that the ritual she'd be conducting today would be successful.

Small comfort.

Voria tied her hair into a tight bun, and then began sketching her teleportation spell.

She appeared in the Chamber of the First, vertigo washing over her as she adjusted to her new surroundings. The wooden ceiling vaulted high above them, the natural whorls of the grain making beautiful patterns. Except where it had been marred with battle damage, from Eros's last stand.

She smoothed her uniform, freshly washed with a little *water* magic before she'd gone to bed. She didn't clean up very well, but if today's ritual was a success, that would hardly matter to these people.

Seven men and women, the finest surviving mages, were already gathered around the Pool of Shaya, or what remained of it. Each wore their ceremonial white robes, but while the clothing was the same, the people who wore it were most certainly not. Ducius's face, normally twisted into a permanent smirk, was somber, his eyes haunted. The others all wore variations of the same expression, and why not? Their entire way of life had just been violated.

"Caretakers," she called in a clear voice. They turned as one to face her, and she fixed her attention on Ducius, then gave him a respectful nod. "Tender."

"Tender over what?" Ducius barked a bitter laugh.

She half expected Ikadra to comment on that, but the staff said nothing, though the sapphire pulsed thoughtfully.

"Of this." Voria extended a hand and a swirling ball of liquid light appeared in the air above her, golden and potent. It was the stuff of *life* itself, hundreds of liters undulating in the air, bound by the magic she'd wrapped around it. "Eros's legacy isn't much. A remnant of the vast pool that once lay here, but it is a beginning. It is enough to conduct the ritual we've come together to enact, and it buys you time to refill the pool enough for a similar ritual in a year's time. Eros served us well, in the end, and salvaged our future."

"*Our* future?" Ducius asked suspiciously. He snorted, and for just a moment he resembled his old self. "Does that mean you count yourselves among us? That would be a first."

Ikadra clicked rhythmically on the floor as she approached the pool. "It does. It means that I am staying on

Shaya, and that I will be overseeing her defense." She stopped a meter away from Ducius, and from the pool. "Make no mistake, Caretakers. Krox has risen, and he is coming. He will be upon us soon, and in nearly every possibility our world is destroyed. But in a few, we survive. What we do in the next few weeks will determine which possibility comes to pass."

She hadn't seen their survival, but telling these people there was no hope would only hasten their destruction. They needed hope more than they needed the truth.

Voria raised Ikadra and gestured at the roiling ball of liquid light, slowly pulsing over the center of the room. She maneuvered it over the pool, and gently lowered it to the very bottom. A soft, muted gold shone as she allowed the liquid to flow into the pool. A glimmer of what it had once contained, but vastly better than the cold darkness that had existed until a moment ago.

"What comes now?" Ducius whispered, his gaze fixed on the pool.

"Now I show you the power of the *Spellship*, gentlemen." Voria raised a hand and began to sketch. She sketched as she'd never sketched before, sigil after sigil. "Among other things, my vessel is a magical amplifier."

The latticework of glowing sigils grew, mostly *life*, but many *water* as well. Voria deftly wove them into a framework that would allow the other mages in the room to add their own magic.

"What is it we're doing, exactly?" Ducius asked. None of the others seemed brave enough to speak to her, and their shell-shocked expressions worried her.

"We're going to refill the pool, as much as it can be." Voria placed Ikadra at the center of the spell, and released him. He hovered there, bathed in the magical energies.

"Ikadra will channel the magic of every *life* mage aboard the *Spellship*, and thankfully we possess many. In short, they are returning a portion of their own strength. Each will be slightly lessened, but it will buy the time we so badly need."

She turned to the lot of them. "I expect the same contribution from each of you, and will offer it myself."

"Of course." Ducius turned to the spell and began sketching *life* sigils. A warm, golden glow snaked up his arm, then left him in a burst of light. It flew into Ikadra's sapphire, and was almost immediately joined by one from another Caretaker, and another.

Voria extended an arm as well, and her arm began to glow. She felt a portion of her power—a small, but not inconsiderable portion of her *life* magic—returned to the spell. It wouldn't prevent her from casting her magic, but it would mean she could cast fewer spells before needing to rest.

She lowered her trembling arm, and nodded to Ikadra. "The rest is up to you."

"It's a good thing I am the sector's most amazing staff," Ikadra glowed. "You guys want to see something really cool? Watch this."

Ikadra's tip began to glow intensely, and the glow worked its way slowly down the staff until it reached the base. A beam of pure, white brilliance shot out of Ikadra into the pool. Wave after wave of golden energy flowed from the staff, all the power they'd lent amplified repeatedly by what might be the strongest eldimagus in the sector's history.

The pulses only went on for a dozen heartbeats, then they stopped and the glow slowly faded. The sigils comprising the spell fused, then disappeared. Ikadra hovered over the pool, which glowed far more brightly than it had after she'd deposited the reservoir Eros had saved.

She leaned over the lip of the pool and looked down. The golden energy barely covered the bottom, but it covered it completely. Voria's face slid into a wide smile. "We've done it."

Ducius sketched a *fire* sigil, then a *dream*. He cocked his head, as if listening, then gave a satisfied nod. "The barrier has been stabilized. We've been losing a meter or two each day, and the rate seems to be accelerating. If this holds, we shouldn't lose any more habitable surface. You've really done it."

Voria nodded. "It will hold, for long enough anyway. If we cannot find a way to stop Krox, then it will hardly matter."

She could feel the elder god's approach, crowding out every other possibility. Krox would arrive within a few weeks time, and by then if she didn't have a way to stop a god they were all as good as dead.

5

TORPOR

Nebiat arrived in a familiar system, one she'd last seen when she'd rendezvoused with Frit and her sisters. The Blazing Heart of Krox, possibly the most powerful *fire* Catalyst in the sector, smoldered angrily in an empty solar system, untroubled by planets or other orbiting objects.

The only other circumstance of note was invisible to the naked eye, though not to hers. Countless primal Ifrit flitted across the star's surface, frolicking and basking in the glow of their god. They would be nearly as useful as the Heart itself, if she could find a way to bend them to her will, as she had the drakes.

I am the finest binder that has ever lived, Krox rumbled. *Enslaving them is trivial. The simple act of absorbing the Heart will see to that. These creatures know you are their god. They worship us, thus increasing our power.*

The implications of that single statement, so casually delivered, were staggering. *Explain. How does worship increase our power?*

Krox pulsed with amusement. *All life, all consciousness,*

exerts will on the universe around it. This will can be harnessed, and used to achieve desired possibilities. In short, the greater your influence, the greater your ability to shape reality to your will.

Nebiat considered that. *So if the entire sector worshiped us, what would it allow us to do, in practical terms?*

Very nearly anything, Krox rumbled. *We would have the freedom to devour every Catalyst, and could use the power, and that of the surviving mortals, to reshape the galaxy as we see fit.*

That presented some very tantalizing possibilities. Nebiat could undo the damage to her race that her father had wronged over the previous several decades. She could find a way to restore her people. *I assume that simply believing in us doesn't constitute worship. How do I secure these worshippers?*

Krox's mind showed her images of a vast swirling sea of stars bordering a super-massive black hole. She recognized it as the center of the galaxy that the humans had so amusingly termed the Milky Way. *Primals will be drawn from the galactic core automatically as we grow stronger. They come from the Great Cycle, created originally by Reevanthara, perhaps the greatest elder god to have ever lived. Simply existing will increase your power, but for the rest you must convince them to consciously accept you as their deity. In most cases this involves founding a religion that requires them to perform daily rites. These rites force concentration, the touchstone of all worship.*

Nebiat was fairly certain she understood the basics, and was eager to test it. Thankfully, she didn't lack for subjects. She eyed the Blazing Heart, glowing with near limitless *fire*. *How do I consume the Heart?*

Simply approach and allow me to merge with it, Krox instructed.

Nebiat flew closer, basking in the magical power. The

Heart pulsed a greeting, evidently recognizing the Mind of Krox.

Indeed, Krox rumbled. *The Heart remembers our unity, and longs to be restored.*

She seized direct control of Krox, a feat she'd not yet attempted. The feeling of power was heady, and she *was* the Mind. She reached out with a sea of grasping, white tendrils, each plunging into the body of the smoldering, red star.

Deep pulses of scarlet *fire* magic flowed up each appendage, and every pulse dramatically increased her strength. The entire process took long minutes, but when it was complete the Heart had faded to a dull, crimson husk. It floated there, a dead star, bereft of power.

Power that now belonged to Nebiat. It surged through her in a vast tide. Yet there was more than just power. There was consciousness. Memory. The Heart had been a god in its own right, at some point in the distant past. That god, she now saw, had been bested eons ago, and was one of the oldest parts of Krox's power.

Oceans of flame rolled through Nebiat, granting enough magic to burn the universe, if she wanted. She'd never felt so alive, not even when she'd merged with Krox originally. The process was invigorating, and continued to accelerate as she adjusted to the new power.

Invigorating slowly became overwhelming. There was *too much* power. Too much knowledge. Too much Krox. And not enough Nebiat.

Yes. Krox was again amused. *You begin to understand. Your own identity is precious to you, but you are less than an insect in a vast jungle. In merging with the Heart you have returned much of my strength. In time, as we absorb other Catalysts, you will grow smaller and smaller. Eventually you will be little more than a shading on my personality, a small part of my mind. We will be one, united in purpose.*

Nebiat shrieked in her own head, beating at the confines of the spell she herself had cast. Had her father understood the dark bargain he'd created? She wanted to live forever, but as herself, not as a footnote in Krox's story.

You have little choice. Your enemies gather, goddess. If you do not crush them, they will crush you. You must act, and each time you do we will be more me, and less you.

Maybe. Nebiat wasn't sure she believed Krox. This being had evidently found a way to keep its consciousness intact, and she would do the same. But it was right. She did need to deal with her enemies.

First, she would marshal an army, then she would destroy Shaya. Once Voria was dealt with there would be no one strong enough to pose a threat, and she could worry about finding a way out of the grisly fate Krox had in mind for her.

Tremendous weariness overtook her, and the sea of possibilities winked out around her. She struggled to contain her panic. *What is happening to us?*

Be at ease, Krox reassured her. *What you feel is known as torpor. You must rest while you assimilate the tremendous power you have absorbed. Then, you will be ready to flay our enemies.*

6

DAMAGE CONTROL

Aran strode into the *Talon*'s mess, now a temporary command center for Ternus personnel. He'd made the offer to have them relocated to the *Hunter*, but to his surprise the governor had refused, and insisted he didn't want to entrust his safety to any other vessel.

That made it hard to argue, and Aran had no choice but to let the man stay aboard. It made things even more tense than they otherwise would be, and tempers were already starting to fray. The Umbral Depths would make that worse.

Governor Austin sat at the table in the far side of the room, surrounded by a cluster of advisors, Fleet Admiral Kerr among them. Most had already been aboard when they'd arrived, along with a dozen technicians and engineers who'd apparently been studying the ship before turning it back over.

Austin's scowl deepened and he leaned across the table. "—We don't have a choice. I'm not risking any more ships." He stabbed an accusing finger at a harried, bald man in a business suit, complete with one of their odd neckties. "Every ship we've sent down there to retrieve anyone hasn't been able to make orbit. We're only feeding the problem."

"So you're abandoning them?" The man's thick eyebrows knit together, a stark contrast to his hairless scalp. "I admit we've run into problems, but—"

"Senator, do you think me an idiot?" Austin rose to his feet and planted both hands on the *Talon*'s golden table. He leaned over the poor man, looming like a Wyrm about to feast.

The senator shifted uncomfortably in his seat, but refused to drop eye contact. Aran guessed this to be part of a longer standing feud.

He lurked at the edge of the conversation, and considered departing, but before he could, Kerr caught sight of him. The fleet admiral disengaged from the table, and hurried over. He looked a good deal better than he had when they'd been evacuating. The heavy gravity had not been kind.

Kerr gave a tired smile as he reached Aran. "You're a welcome relief from that cock fight. The governor is all diplomacy, until he's stressed. Then he's a monster, and the surviving senate isn't taking it well." Kerr delivered a sigh, and smoothed his rumpled uniform. "I know it's petty, but lack of fresh uniforms is already getting to me. Every time I think about changing I realize this might be the last uniform I ever wear."

"Davidson might have a surplus from New Texas," Aran offered. He knew this was about a lot more than uniforms, though. "Listen. I know you've got a ton of problems to deal with, but we need to talk. Now that the immediate crisis is contained, I need to decide where this ship can do the most good. I can't stay here. You have my sympathy, but the *Talon* isn't a relief ship."

Kerr nodded wearily. "I understand, son, and you're right. This is a warship, and we need to get you back into the fight. You have no idea how hard I had to fight the governor not to try to commandeer it back. Once he agreed, I managed to get him to agree to transfer to another ship. Davidson will be arriving any minute. When he gets here we'll transfer command over, but the governor is going to try to convince you to escort us to Yanthara."

"Yanthara?" Aran asked, blinking.

"Before we were interrupted by the untimely demise of our world, we'd begun negotiations with the Inurans." Kerr shook his head, then spat against the wall. "Mercenary bastards are probably selling to the Krox too, but the governor's gotten it into his head that we need their ships. Before I could argue sense, but now? Now my position has reversed. Doesn't matter what I think of the Inurans, or their tech. I'd make a deal with the devil himself if it would give me a fleet to spit in the eye of a god."

Aran didn't know who this devil was, but he got the gist of it. Nor could he fault Kerr's logic. Ternus was screwed, and Shaya was too. That put both in a position to lean on the Inurans more than ever, and he had no doubt they'd use that to extort whatever they could. He made a mental note to contact Kazon when he could find a moment.

"I can't blame the governor for that, but make sure you have all the facts about these new ships." He frowned, remembering his inability to activate his spellarmor after Virkonna had bound it. "There's something wrong with the new metal they're using, enough to make a goddess sit up and take notice."

"Kerr!" The governor's voice rang out over the hum of conversation filling the mess. "Get over here. Logistics, man. They can't wait. People are dying."

Kerr gave Aran a helpless shrug. "I need to head back, but before I do there's something you need to know. The governor had intended to give you back the *Talon*, but there was a condition. He wanted to send you to Shaya for a prisoner transfer, and those prisoners are aboard. Your former friend and her companions are in the brig, awaiting delivery to Voria."

Aran planted a hand against the wall, and suddenly felt like he was back in the increased gravity. "Nara's aboard?"

"That's what I'm saying, son."

Boots clomped across the deck behind him, and after a moment Crewes walked up the ramp. He still wore his spellarmor, but the cannon must have been returned to the lockup.

"Sergeant, good timing. I've got some news." He waited for the sergeant to walk over before continuing. "Apparently we've got prisoners aboard. Nara and company. Will you head down to the brig and assess the situation? I'll be down in a minute."

Crewes nodded, a scowl sliding into place at the mention of Nara. "I'll see to it, sir."

Aran trusted the sergeant not to do anything rash, but he almost pitied Nara the tongue lashing she was likely to receive.

He took a long, slow breath, then turned back to Kerr, who'd already taken a step back toward the mess. "One last question, Admiral. I want to explain the situation clearly to Voria. What are we looking at for Ternus? From a technical perspective? How long do your people have?"

Aran had a rough understanding that the clock was

ticking on their world, but he needed to know exactly what was on the line if they were to have any prayer of dealing with it. Plus, tackling this problem meant he could delay dealing with others he didn't want to think about.

"I'm no physicist, but as I understand it we got a few problems," Kerr explained. His eyes went vacant. Haunted. "The gravity is a short-term nuisance, but a long-term killer. Most of our fauna, and a lot of our flora, aren't equipped to deal with their new environment. Initial estimates say that we'll lose seventy percent of our biodiversity in the first four weeks. Things get worse after that, but after seven weeks it won't matter. Our orbit will decay to the point where the surface is unlivable. A week after that it will be molten. Put simply, we've lost. We can't stop a god. What are we supposed to do to combat this?"

"I don't know." Aran forced himself back to his feet. He stowed the feelings, and focused on outcomes. He needed to be in control right now, of something, even if it was only his own body. "What I do know is that there *is* a way. Krox isn't the only god. We'll find others to help us. Voria has the *Spellship*, and you saw what she did on New Texas. She'll find us an answer."

He was saved from further conversation when a loud chime came from the portable holounit the Ternus command had set up near the table. An image sprang up, and showed the *Wyrm Hunter* entering the system through a Fissure. The weathered battleship brought a swell of pride. She was still flying, even after all the punishment she'd been through.

"We'll be taking our leave soon, looks like." Kerr sat in the chair Aran had just vacated. "I hope you're right, and that Voria pulls something out of her bag of tricks. I've got to be honest, though. I just can't see much hope."

Aran couldn't either, but hearing that wasn't going to make anyone fight harder. They needed more than the truth. They needed hope. "We've been through some crazy shit, Admiral. I've killed dragons. This time I'm just going to have to aim a little higher."

7

WHY?

Aran left the mess and threaded a route down to the ship's lowest level, which contained their cargo hold, and adjacent to it was the brig. Crewes had stopped right outside the arched doorway leading into the brig.

Kheross stood next to him, arms crossed and his narrow face drawn down into a scowl. That scowl deepened when he saw Aran, and *void* flared in his eyes. "It's past time we talked, Outrider. Can you promise me my daughter survived the attack on Shaya? Where is she? I've lived up to my end of the deal."

Aran rubbed his temples and longed for the days when he'd been the one taking orders instead of giving them. "That's my very next problem, Kheross, I promise. You've done right by us, and I will see that we do right by you. But right now I don't know where your daughter is. When I do, you'll be the first to know."

Kheross gave a wordless growl, and stalked back up the ramp without another word.

"Yeah, keep walking, Scaly," Crewes called, but there was

no heat to it. He turned back to Aran once Kheross was out of earshot. "I figured it might be smart to be on the same page before we go in there, sir. How you gonna play this?"

"Honestly?" Aran scrubbed his fingers through his beard and wished for the time to trim it. "I don't know. Nara saved our asses. Many times. But the knife is still sticking out of my back, and I remember who she was before the mind-wipe." He shivered. "That Nara would knife her mother for a bent scale. Don't let me do anything stupid."

"Oh, I won't." Crewes's scowl would have sent Bord scurrying had he been there to see it. He and Kez were still overseeing the temporary clinic they'd set up in the medbay to help treat the near infinite flow of wounded. "She jacked our ride, then defected to the enemy. Remember that, sir. Keep it front and center. I know you hit that, and I know you care about her, but don't go soft, man."

"Thanks, Sergeant. I mean that." Aran appreciated the advice. He took a deep breath, and plunged through the doorway into the brig.

One of the *Talon*'s many latent enchantments was a magical silence that blocked the brig from the rest of the ship. The instant he stepped through, the noise from the Ternus personnel vanished, and he stood in a well-lit hallway with six cells, which seemed impossible as they occupied a space greater than what the room should have taken up on the ship. You had to love extra-dimensional spaces.

All three cells on the far side were occupied. The first held Frit, her ebony skin smoldering. A river of bright flame cascaded down her shoulders, and she stared impassively at him with those twin pools of flame. She didn't look away or drop her gaze, as she once would have.

Aran returned her stare kilo for kilo, and only dropped it

when he shifted his attention to the next cell. It held a Krox hatchling that, Aran quickly realized, he recognized. He was nearly three meters tall, forcing him to hunch against the ceiling. His wings barely fit in the cell, and there was no way it could be comfortable.

The last cell held Nara, but Aran stiffened and forced himself to focus on the hatchling.

"Hello, Kaho. How's the hand?" Aran nodded down at the hatchling's clearly intact limb.

"Splendid." Kaho gave him a reptilian smile, which revealed hundreds of razored fangs. He raised the hand and flexed clawed fingers. "The scales are a little discolored, but it serves as a reminder never to grow overconfident when tangling with a war mage, even a human one." Kaho's face fell. "My brother wasn't so lucky, as you know better than anyone. I forgive you for his death, for whatever that's worth."

"Really, Scaly?" Crewes barked a harsh laugh, and moved to stand in front of Kaho's cell. "You 'forgive' the Captain for cooking your miserable excuse for a brother, after he attacked us, again? Well, that's real white of ya. I hope you forgive me for putting my foot up your—"

"Sergeant." Aran's voice was soft, but there was steel there, and Crewes recognized it.

The sergeant's jaw clamped shut, but he continued to glare at the Krox. Aran took a step closer to the bars, and met Kaho's draconic gaze unflinchingly. "I'd advise you not to speak again, unless spoken to. Crewes has more right than most to hate you. Your people burned our worlds. You've killed our friends. You're hell-bent on eradicating our species. The only reason you're alive is so that Voria can rip every last secret out of that scaly head of yours."

Aran was mildly surprised to realize his hand had tightened around Narlifex's hilt. The weapon thrummed in his grip, pulsing with anticipation of a kill. A kill Aran couldn't deliver, at least not yet.

"Forgive me, Captain." Kaho slid awkwardly to his knees, and prostrated himself on the floor of his cell. "I should never have spoken so familiarly to you. I do not wish to challenge you, but I beg you to hear what I have to say."

Frit eyed the Krox with pity, but then her eyes snapped accusingly up to Aran. He ignored her.

"Lies, whatever it is." Crewes barked a short laugh. "You know how I know? 'Cause your mouth is moving. Gods-damned binder."

"Lies or not, let's hear what he's got to say." Aran folded his arms and glared down at the Krox. He was very aware of Nara watching him from the neighboring cell, but she'd said nothing yet. Nor had Frit, though she continued to glare.

"You have every right to hate me and my species." Kaho rose to his knees, but didn't make eye contact. "You have every right to kill me. But before you do, I beseech you. Consider that my species is just as varied as your own. We have free will, whatever you might think. I have no love for my mother. I have even less for my grandfather. Their plans for the galaxy would benefit me even less than they would you. She will kill me, human, when she learns that I have gone over to your side."

"Gone over?" Crewes gave a loud snort. "'Course you'd say that when you're in a cell. How stupid do you think we are?"

"Pretty stupid, actually," Frit snapped, finally entering the conversation. She'd transferred her glare to Crewes. "Didn't Nara steal this ship right out from under you? Why don't you open this cell, and I'll show you just how stupid, human?"

Crewes scowled down at the Ifrit as he leaned closer to the bars. Deep, hot flames appeared in his eyes, and Aran could feel it even from where he was standing. "As soon as the captain gives the word, trust me, I'll be opening that cell, and you'll get to show me just how dumb I am. You go ahead and use all the fire you want, kid. Won't stop me from pounding the traitor out of that smug face. Can't believe I ever trusted you."

"Trusted?" Frit snarled. She slammed the glowing bars with both fists, and was hurled into the wall of her cell in an explosion of blue light. She rose quickly, rolling her shoulder as she turned to face Crewes again. "Your people *made me in a pattern inducer*, and then put a collar on me. You forced me to fight, to kill my own people. You pretend to be so morally superior, but your whole way of life is built on enslaving others. Enslaving my kind. You'd better believe I escaped as soon as I could." Her eyes flared to match his. "Do whatever you want to me. You can kill me, but you can't take my freedom. Never again. I'll die before I fight for you, collar or no."

A wave of weariness crashed over Aran, and he closed his eyes. He took a deep breath, and then opened them. "Frit, we're not going to make you do anything, whatever you may have done. I'm not any more fond of slavery than you are, and I agree that how your people were treated was tragic."

He shook his head sadly, then turned to Crewes. "Sergeant, go get Kez. Tell her I want her to stand guard over the brig. I need a moment alone with the prisoners."

The sergeant paused and leaned in close. "Sir, you ain't going soft, are you?" Crewes looked as concerned as Aran had ever seen him. The sergeant never questioned him so directly, unless they were in private.

"Not a chance." Aran's voice was frosty steel and, thankfully, so was his resolve. He met the sergeant's gaze and dropped his voice low enough that only Crewes could hear. "But you're letting them get to you, and riling them up in the process. I need intel, and we aren't going to get that if Frit is hurling herself at the bars."

Crewes blinked a couple times, then nodded. "Understood, sir." He shot a glare at Frit. "This ain't over, kid. You'll get your chance to take a swing at me. I promise you that."

She didn't reply, but she did glare at him as he left.

Aran waited until Crewes had departed the silence field to face Nara. He took a step closer to her cell, and sized her up. She wore a form-fitting dark-grey suit of unfamiliar mesh-layered material. Some sort of stealth tech, Aran guessed. Her dark hair had been bound into a simple ponytail, and her face had gone pale enough to highlight the sea of freckles. She looked scared.

Aran considered his anger. He remembered the sleepless nights, and the questions. It all boiled down to just one word. A word he carefully stripped of emotion. "Why?"

A single tear slid down Nara's cheek. He felt nothing. No satisfaction, no sarcastic 'oh, here it comes'. He felt nothing. It had all gone to ashes.

"His name is Talifax," Nara began. She glanced at Frit, then back to Aran. "I haven't ever said his name aloud, until now. He first appeared to me the night we left Virkon, right after we…"

"I remember," Aran prompted. "Who is this Talifax?" The name was maddeningly familiar, but his mind slid off the word, around it somehow, unable to hold onto it for long.

"Forgive me for speaking out of turn, but Talifax is the Guardian of Nefarius," Kaho supplied. All eyes shifted to the Krox, who gave Aran a respectful bow. His tone conveyed respect, but also fear. "Talifax is known in our histories. He is called the great manipulator, the herald for the darkest god to ever war upon this sector. My great-grandfather, Krox himself, was terrified of Nefarius, and wary of Talifax. A greater god knew fear at the mere mention of the name."

"And this guy showed up while I was sleeping next to you?" Aran demanded of Nara. "Why didn't you wake me?"

Another tear slid loose, and Nara looked away. If she was faking she was even better at this than he expected. Her voice dropped to a whisper. "He gave me my memories back."

A chill worked its way through him, and Aran lowered his arms to his sides. He took a reflexive step back from the cell, his subconscious throwing up emotional walls as he recognized the Nara of old. "That explains a lot. I'll have more questions when time permits, but right now I've got a crisis to tend to. You're going to have to sit tight until we sort it out."

"What's going on?" Nara whispered. She wouldn't meet his gaze, and instead moved to sit on the cell's bench.

"You must have felt it." Aran took a step toward the silence field, but paused to face Nara before leaving. Did she really not know? Her expression showed genuine confusion. If she were really working with the Krox, her confusion didn't make sense.

"I felt something," Frit whispered. The rage had burned out of her, transforming her into the timid Ifrit he'd first met, even if just for a moment. "Something terrible."

"You're gods-damned right it was terrible. That god you love so much? Those people of yours that you're angry we killed? Well guess what? Krox leveled Ternus." Aran could feel the heat rising in him, and faint *fire* magic suffused his entire body. The rage was a living thing. "Your god showed up and dick-punched a whole planet. Millions dead. Hundreds of millions more are going to die. Maybe billions if the Ternus scientists can't find a way to save them."

Frit's eyes widened in horror, and even Kaho seemed taken aback.

"Krox is here?" Nara pulled her knees to her chest, and huddled against the wall.

"Not anymore." Aran shook his head. "He, or it, used magic on a scale we've never seen, something involving a massive amount of *earth*. Then he left, and we have no idea where he went. There was no Fissure. He isn't using the Umbral Depths to travel."

Kaho blinked rapidly. "Not using the Depths? How is he traveling then?"

"You tell me." Aran moved to stand in front of the Krox's cell. The anger was still there, smoldering, but so was the realization that his prisoners probably didn't know anything more than he did. About this, at least.

"I don't know." Kaho dropped his gaze to the floor of his cell. "I've never heard of such a magic."

"Great," Aran sighed, and turned his attention back to Nara. He forced his voice into an emotionless tone. "I'll come back when I can spare the time and we can have a nice, long chat. You've got that long to get your stories straight. I'd encourage you to remember that if you lie to me, it won't matter. Voria will get at the truth. I promise you that."

Nara's eyes shone, but she gave him a crisp nod. Aran turned and departed.

8
UNEXPECTED GUESTS

Voria had been on her feet for nineteen hours by the time she wandered back to her quarters. She'd tended to the worst of the emergencies, and gotten another crop of refugees settled. Too many people no longer found Shaya safe, ritual of restoration or no. She couldn't blame them.

Thankfully, Pickus had risen to the occasion, and masterfully handled a bewildering array of logistical concerns. That meant she could finally sleep, and she sighed contentedly as she slid across the carpet, her eyes fixed on the floating bed on the far side of the room.

"Umm, Voria?" came a male voice from the shadowed corner of the room.

For a tiny moment she thought it was Ikadra, as he was the only one in her quarters capable of speaking, but the staff hovered next to her. And besides, the voice had an accent. An Inuran accent.

Voria's hand shot up, and she sketched a level three binding, then flung it at the shadowed corner. The spell flew unerringly toward its target, but simply ceased to exist, dissolving into thousands of tiny mana fragments.

The figure stepped from the shadows, and she sucked in a breath when she recognized Kazon's bearded face.

Behind her brother stood a...haze. Her eyes slid off its features, and she could sense, well nothing from it. The absence of magic scared her more than anything she could have detected.

Kazon wasn't capable of counterspelling, and that meant that whatever this thing was had casually batted a powerful spell aside. She only hoped they came in peace.

"What are you doing here, little brother?" Voria's attention was fixed on the hazy figure. She picked up Ikadra, and held him defensively before her.

"I'm terribly sorry, but Inura insisted..."

"Inura?" Voria blinked. "You've brought a god into my quarters?"

"Holy shit," Ikadra said, sapphire pulsing. "I thought I recognized the obfuscation spell."

"I brought myself," a cultured Inuran voice replied from the shadows. Those shadows finally fell away, and illuminated a largely human face, with a few disquieting differences. His eyes were slitted, like the Wyrms on Virkon, and his fingers were a little too long for a human. "I apologize for startling you, but you no doubt understand my need for caution."

Voria froze. How did one banter with a god? Where Neith felt like a being of immense power, this god was much more like any other mage, or Wyrm, she might meet. But she couldn't afford to forget that Inura would be so much more than he appeared.

"No doubt." Voria gave an understanding nod. "You're here now, so presumably something has changed. Have you come to teach us to use the *Spellship*? Goddess, I hope so, because otherwise we've no way of dealing with a god of Krox's strength."

She struggled to contain the hope, but some of it clearly leaked into her tone, and she hated the sympathetic light in Inura's draconic eyes. "Limited help, yes. I have many other tasks to attend to, but I can help you prepare for Krox's arrival. I have seen the possibility of your victory. It is remote, but distinct. I will lend you what aid I can, but I will not risk exposing myself in battle. Not against Krox. Not while I know there is a greater threat out there."

Voria bit back her anger, knowing the words would accomplish little. It wasn't easy. "So what is it you are prepared to offer then? How can you help us defend ourselves?"

"If you are to fight a god," Inura's wings flared behind him, "then you will need a god to oppose him. I cannot stop Krox, but you can."

"What are you saying?" Voria knew she was tired, but she simply wasn't tracking.

"I'm saying that we must elevate you." Inura gestured at Ikadra. "Ikadra is my finest creation and—"

"Did you hear that?" Ikadra broke in. "You all heard it right? Finest creation."

Inura gave the faintest of sighs, and continued as if he hadn't been interrupted. "—is the catalyst, and with the proper rituals and infusion of magic, you can ascend to godhood. Voria, I'm asking you to fill the same role I once asked Shaya to fill."

Voria went numb. She pictured another, very similar woman, in similar circumstances. Had that been the way of it? Had Shaya really been a mortal tasked with defending her people? Voria had assumed the lady of light from her dreams must be Shaya, but if Inura was to be believed...then it was her.

Inura nodded, as if he'd heard her thoughts. "That was the way of it. She was a warrior, and a healer, and a leader. She led the Vagrant Fleet for three decades before I called upon her. Her people needed her, and so we constructed the *Spellship* to serve as both her vessel and her Catalyst."

"I'm standing right here, dad." Ikadra's sapphire pulsed. "Not even a hello, or an acknowledgement? I should totally write a book."

"You've grown, Ikadra, and not necessarily for the better." Inura frowned at the staff, and Voria was left with the distinct impression that he regretted his creation. "I intended you to be a tool, not comic relief. I am tempted to reset your personality to before you met Shaya."

"That would be a mistake," Voria found herself saying. She cleared her throat, and continued. "Ikadra can be juvenile, it's true. But he has proven immensely resourceful, and his rather, ah, unique world view has allowed me to view possibilities that would otherwise have remained hidden."

Inura cocked his head, and eyed the staff critically. "Very well, I will leave the personality matrix intact, against my better judgement." He turned back to Voria. "Kazon and I have business elsewhere, but I will leave you with everything you need."

Before Voria could protest or Kazon could offer a goodbye, the god raised a hand, and a wave of light assaulted Voria's senses. Memories and power, almost indistinguishable, rushed into her mind in a torrent of inexplicable strength. The light overwhelmed her senses, and when it finally cleared there was no sign of her brother, or the wayward god.

She felt no different, except more exhausted.

"Well that was an odd end to a long day." She stumbled to the bed, and sat heavily, then tugged off her boots. A flash shot through her mind like a bolt of lightning, and she saw the *Spellship* in orbit over Shaya, magic streaming up to it from the world below. It lasted only an instant, and then was gone.

What good was godsight if she couldn't control or understand it?

Patience. Inura's voice echoed in her mind. *In time you will understand.*

Weariness crashed over Voria, and she collapsed into bed, asleep before her cheek touched the soft satin.

9
GODSPEED

Aran waved his hand as he stepped through the golden doorway into his quarters. A shimmering pane of opaque blue energy cascaded down to fill the doorway, and afforded him privacy. It was the first he'd had since before the 'interview' they'd had scheduled on Ternus.

He knew he'd accumulated a lot of emotional debt, not just the crisis on Ternus, but also the revelation that Nara was less than a dozen meters away. With her Krox allies.

Emotions were such bullshit.

Aran moved to the scry-screen, and tapped a *fire* sigil, then a *dream*. He waited for the missive to connect, praying desperately that she would answer.

Voria's weary face filled the screen, stress lines creasing each eye and a single lock of errant hair having escaped from her bun. She stifled a yawn, then stretched luxuriously. "Good morning, Captain. Your timing is excellent. I've just encountered something vanishingly rare in the sector, a good night's sleep."

Aran sat down on his bed, which sagged lower in the air,

then righted itself. "I plan to get one of those myself as soon as we're done talking. We've got a lot to catch up on."

"Indeed. I felt...something a few days ago, and suspect you can tell me more of the cause. In either case I have news. Why don't you start." Voria rose, and moved to her nightstand, where she faced the mirror and stuffed the errant lock back into her bun.

"The highlights?" Aran rubbed his temples, and considered the most important parts. "Krox assaulted the Ternus home world. Their planet is doomed, and it's likely to be a slow death. Krox saw to that. They are in dire need of a divine miracle, or at least some magic well beyond anything I've seen or heard of."

"The strength of the magic was...unparalleled, at least in my experience." Voria paled, but her resolve didn't waver. "Even all the way out here I felt the strength of it. Whatever Krox did rippled through every possibility. But what can be done can be undone."

Aran nodded, and rose. "It was a power play, the sort of thing Nebiat would approve of, I think. They want us scared and on the run, and they're doing a damned good job of it so far."

"A fair point. They have ensured I can do nothing to aid Ternus, for the time being at least." Voria heaved a sigh and finally turned back to the scry-screen, now looking as pristine as ever. "Krox is coming for Shaya, and this time he will not stop at the pool. This world, and everyone on it, are doomed unless we can stop them."

Aran hoped he didn't sound as desperate as he felt just then. "So...how do we do that?"

"We have allies, of a sort." Voria looked over her shoulder, then back. "I can't say more, but there is a plan in place. One I will tell you more about in person."

"That meeting might be a little ways off." Aran folded his arms. "Governor Austin requested an escort to Yanthara. For a meeting with the Inurans to purchase a new fleet. He's quite insistent."

Voria's eyes narrowed. "Blast it. They're purchasing corrupted ships, and there isn't a damned thing we can do about it. We can't ask you to sabotage negotiations; they need the ships too badly. But if you go, at least you could monitor the situation."

"That seems like a really flimsy reason to fly to Yanthara," Aran ventured. "We could do a lot more good tracking down some sort of super weapon, or even visiting our...friend in the Umbral Depths."

"Good uses of time, but there's another reason to go to Yanthara." Voria frowned, her eye twitching in what Aran took for irritation. "Eros did something 'clever' near the end. He secreted Rhea to Yanthara, at the Temple of Shi, where she couldn't be found by Krox or his agents. He seemed quite concerned that they might come for her, and that she has some grand role to play before the end. As far I know, the girl is still being kept in a magical coma, because they have no idea what to expect when she wakes."

Something eased in Aran's shoulders. He sat on the bed and tugged off one of his boots. "That's a bit of good news. At least it will keep Kheross off my back. He's desperate to get to his daughter, and make some sort of amends."

"Or to convince her to become a weapon against us." Voria became 'the major' again. "Never lower your guard, Aran. I'd have thought Nara taught you that."

"Speaking of." He heaved a sigh of his own. "She's aboard, in the brig. Along with Frit, and Nebiat's son...the true mage."

"Kahotep?" Voria blinked. "That's an unexpected windfall. Have you interrogated them yet?"

He shook his head, and reached carefully for his next words. He relaxed, and told Voria the unvarnished truth. "I'm not ready. I need to be in a good place when I deal with Nara. She's got her memories back, and believe me when I tell you that the woman those memories belong to terrifies me. You back that woman up with all the power we've accumulated? Part of me thinks we should end her, before she somehow escapes. She'll be unstoppable, especially working with Frit and Kaho."

"That part of you is pragmatic. What about the rest of you? What do you think you should do?" Her tone gave no hint as to what the right answer might be. "You don't answer to any government any more, so no one can really stop you from meting out whatever justice you'd like."

Aran exhaled a long, slow breath, and he truly thought about it. "I think we should hear them out, separately. We should learn everything we can, and compare their stories. Since those stories are rehearsed, we should assume most of what they tell us can't be trusted. That said, I've already learned one thing I was hoping you might be able to shed some light on."

"Oh?" Voria's eyebrow rose.

"Kaho seemed to recognize a name Nara used. She claimed she was manipulated by someone called Talifax."

The blood drained from Voria's face. "I see."

"I take it you recognize this guy?"

"I recognize legends, yes. The Guardian of Nefarius, who is only said to appear at times of great change. Before wars that annihilate entire sectors, and kill gods."

"This guy sounds great." Aran sat on the bed again. "I guess it's at least a little reassuring that you recognize him. I have no idea if Nara is on the up and up, but at least she wasn't outright lying."

"Take care with her, Aran. Your feelings are a luxury you cannot afford."

Aran barked a short laugh. "I've got Crewes to make sure I don't do anything stupid. Do you have anything you want me to pass to the crew?"

She hesitated, and her mouth worked as if she was going to say something. Nothing came out, and Aran instantly recognized the kind of magical manipulation Neith had forced on them. Voria was trying to speak about something she wasn't allowed to. She smiled suddenly. "Only my good wishes. We'll save the rest for when we meet in person. Just know that we are not without allies."

"So tell me about this temple." He tugged off his other boot, and set it next to the first.

"It's called the Temple of the Shi, one of two religions found on Yanthara," Voria explained. "It was a clever defense, really. The Temple is a *dream* Catalyst, and its magic warps reality around it. That makes scrying very difficult, if not outright impossible. Be forewarned that the priestesses are notoriously touchy."

"Sounds like fun. I'll contact you when I reach Yanthara."

"Godspeed, Aran." Voria gave him an approving smile, nodded, and then terminated the missive.

Aran lay down feeling marginally better about the situation. The rest of his problems could wait until morning.

10

OFFER YOU CAN'T REFUSE

Aran stifled a yawn as he entered the mess, where Governor Austin was holding court, hopefully for the last time before the transfer. Aran moved to the manifester, the technical term for the magical device they usually called the 'food thingie', and thought of coffee and a glazed pastry. Both appeared.

"Man," Crewes rumbled, entering the mess a moment after Aran, "I'd forgotten how much I love this ship. You know that, right, ship?" Crewes patted the wall affectionately, then moved over to the manifester. A moment later a plate of steak and eggs appeared, making Aran rethink his choice.

"Captain," Austin called from behind him, "would you please join us for breakfast?"

Aran's shoulders slumped a bit. He was hoping to get some caffeine in him before dealing with more of the governor's endless demands, but it looked as if he wasn't going to have that option. He picked up his pastry and his coffee, and headed over to join Austin.

There were several empty chairs, and Aran took the one

next to Kerr. His was the only friendly face at the table. The rest had made it clear that they thought it folly to give Aran the *Talon*. He knew, because they'd loudly argued it within earshot. More than once. Thankfully, Kerr had repeatedly pointed out that it would be a monumentally bad idea to try to seize a ship from a well-armed company of tech mages. They still didn't seem to get it.

"Morning, gentlemen." Aran nodded at Kerr as he sat down, then at the governor. He mostly ignored the aides and senators crowding the nearby tables. Aran sipped his coffee, then looked up to find the governor staring at him. "What did you want to see me about, sir?"

Austin eyed Kerr reprovingly, and sipped his own coffee. "The fleet admiral tells me that he's already alerted you to the fact that we'll need an escort to Yanthara. It's my hope that returning the *Talon* is sufficient payment, since you know that my world's financial status is dubious at best, and catastrophic at worst."

"Of course, Governor." Aran gave him a grateful nod, and mirrored the man's posture. Voria had mentioned that helped when dealing with people. "We're at your disposal. We can get you to Yanthara, and there's no need for additional payment. Our contract for New Texas was quite generous, and I appreciate the return of *my* ship." He put the faintest emphasis on the word 'my', and could see from the way Austin's eyes narrowed that he didn't miss it.

"Excellent." The governor shifted uncomfortably, as if deciding how to approach a topic he wanted to discuss.

Aran took an experimental bite of his pastry. It was good, but he resisted wolfing the whole thing down. He sipped his coffee, and waited.

Austin leaned back in his seat, and eyed Aran for several long moments. "We're far enough along in negotiations that

I suppose it's time you were brought into the loop. Kerr mentioned we were purchasing a new fleet?"

"He did." Aran sat back as well.

"These ships are quite unlike anything currently used in the sector." Austin seemed remarkably proud, as if he'd personally invented said ships. "They can harness, and absorb, magic. I am assured that they can challenge even a god, if there are enough of them attacking at once."

"They sound impressive." Aran took another sip, and waited for the other shoe to drop.

The governor beamed the first genuine smile Aran had seen. This one actually reached his eyes, which shone with a feverish intensity. "Before we can battle a god of Krox's strength, we'll need to 'power up' these ships, so to speak, and that's where you come in. We want you to oversee the process."

Aran set his coffee cup down and gave the governor his full attention. "And where will you get this power?"

"There are a number of potent Catalysts in the sector," the governor explained. "We'll simply choose the ones that provide the magic we need."

"So let me see if I understand this." Aran popped the rest of his pastry in his mouth, and took a few moments to chew before finally leaning forward and looking Austin directly in the eye. "You want to raid Catalysts to steal magic to power up your ships so that you can go toe to toe with a god?"

"Precisely." The governor's smile hadn't slipped.

Kerr, on the other hand, recognized Aran's tone, apparently. He had the good grace to look embarrassed.

"Governor, I see two problems with this plan." Aran held up a single finger. "First, the rest of the sector will immediately see you as a threat. Every magical power from Virkon to Drakkon will fear these ships, which brings me to my second point." Aran added a second finger. "These ships are created from a metal that a literal goddess warned us was corrupted. These ships are bad news, Admiral, and while they might seem like an attractive option right now, I assure you that option will come back to bite you, probably sooner than you expect."

Austin's face went ugly, and his hands balled into fists. "I understand you've already got a dog in this fight, Captain, but let me be perfectly clear. New Texas lies in ruins. The capital is on the brink of annihilation. We very nearly lost Colony 3 as well, our last truly habitable world. There is a real chance we have already lost this war. Unless you can propose an alternate solution, or offer another means of producing the armada we need, then there's really no need for further discussion on this point. We're buying these ships. Unless you have another answer?"

Aran did not. He took a slow breath, and reined in his temper before speaking. "That's fair. I understand the predicament you're in, but I can't in good conscience help you create these weapons knowing what a risk they pose."

"I told you he'd say that," one of the senators crowed. The light shone off his bald head, making him strongly resemble a sinister egg. "Use Kerr's solution."

Aran looked wearily to Kerr, and the admiral nervously cleared his throat. "Just tell him, Austin. It's the only way you're going to get him to agree."

"All right." The governor leaned across the table. "If you help us, then we'll contribute our entire armada to defend Shaya against Krox. I've heard he's coming for your world, and I know you can't stop him alone. Help us get these ships ready, and we'll help you win this war. I can send Davidson's fleet right now, and as soon as our ships are ready, we'll return to help as well. What do you say?"

Aran was silent for a long moment. He weighed the pros and cons, and in the end simply couldn't come up with something that felt like a right answer. "I'll tell you what, Governor. Let's get you to Yanthara. You meet with the Inurans and get your ships. Once you have them, then we'll talk."

He rose from the table and offered the governor his hand. Austin shook it, and he had a surprisingly firm grip. "Very well, Captain. It's a start. I'll let you get back to your...magic."

Aran didn't bother correcting him as he headed for the bridge. He couldn't wait to get these people off his ship.

11

YANTHARA

They spent four endless days crossing the Umbral Depths. On the positive side, the governor and his retinue had relocated to the *Wyrm Hunter*, and since they couldn't risk missives in the depths he'd been blessedly free of Ternus politics.

On the negative, that provided Aran plenty of time to think about their prisoners, and to agonize on what to do with them. He still didn't have a concrete plan, though he'd at least come up with the beginnings of one.

Aran headed up the ramp to the bridge where Crewes was piloting. Not that they needed a pilot, as they were flying blind and in a straight line. He spotted Kez and Bord sitting on one of the benches along the sloped wall where Bord was giving Kez a shoulder rub. Aran hid his smile with a hand, and moved to speak with the sergeant.

"Morning." He gave Crewes a nod, which his friend returned.

"Mornin', sir. We'll be arriving in a few minutes, if your numbers are right."

"They're not my numbers. I just read the chart. But that's not why I'm here."

Crewes spun the matrix's hovering chair around to face him and gave Aran a grin. "You're finally gonna deal with Nara, aren't you?"

Aran cocked his head. "Guess I'm more predictable than I thought."

"Sometimes." Crewes shrugged. "It ain't a bad thing, 'cept in combat. You want some company, I'll head down to the brig with you."

Aran tensed. "You aren't going to like my play, but I need you to back it." Crewes's hatred for Nara, and for the Krox, was one of his few blind spots.

The sergeant studied him for a moment, then nodded. He unbuckled his harness and hopped from the matrix, his massive legs bunching as he landed. Even without the power armor he was damned intimidating.

"I've always got your back, sir." Crewes lowered his voice as he started for the ramp to the brig. "Just tell me you aren't going soft. You can't let her go."

"I'm not going to let her go." Aran followed Crewes down the ramp, then paused and turned back to Bord and Kez. "You two, with me. I want you here for this."

Bord stopped his massage, and Kezia's eyes fluttered open. She brushed a lock of golden curls from her face, and blinked in his direction. "Down to the brig? Are you going to interrogate Nara, finally?"

"Something like that." Apparently they'd all been waiting, which he should have expected. Nara's betrayal didn't impact only him. "Come on." He turned and started after Crewes, taking his time as he made his way down the gently sloping corridor.

When he passed through the veil of silence into the brig,

Crewes was already standing in front of Frit's cell. He looked over his shoulder at Aran. "Get a load of this crap. Frit's found herself a boyfriend."

Kaho and Frit each sat on their respective benches so that they were as close to each other as they could get. It was impossible to miss their body language, and it killed something inside of Aran. There was definitely affection there, and a good degree of trust. Frit had gone over fully to the Krox, and if she had, it made it more likely Nara had as well.

"Sergeant, go get the collar from lockup," Aran ordered. He needed to give Crewes something to do, so the sergeant didn't have time to needle the prisoners. That would only make this harder.

He moved to stand in front of Nara's cell, and found her staring up at him from her bench, her dark hair framing brown eyes and that sea of freckles. "I'm guessing we're almost to Shaya? If you're handing me over to Voria I'll go quietly, but...do we have time to talk to first?"

"We're not going to Shaya." Aran folded his arms. A glance at Frit and Kaho confirmed that neither seemed interested in their conversation, though he assumed both were listening. "We have a minute before Bord and Kezia get here, and the sergeant gets back. Say what you need to say. I'll hear you out."

She exhaled a long, slow breath, and rose, then approached the bars. He steeled himself against whatever alibi she was preparing. "I mentioned that Talifax returned my memories."

"From when you served Yorrak?" Aran asked, interested in spite of himself. She'd been a master manipulator, and if she had her memories back, she was once more. He couldn't forget that.

"Some of them." She nodded, then plucked absently at

her sleeve, as if giving herself something to do. "Others are from before Yorrak, even. I was part of a Ternus program called the Zephyrs. Their version of tech mages, basically. Yorrak broke into the facility and kidnapped me. When these memories came back, it was an overpowering experience, especially at first. I had no idea where I was, or what I was doing. By the time I recovered from the first memory, Talifax had already used my body to steal the *Talon*, and I found myself in orbit near the umbral shadow."

"So it wasn't your fault." Something eased in Aran. "You were just a pawn." He so badly wanted this not to be her fault, though the detached part of him knew he wasn't being objective.

"No!" Nara's eyes flashed. The ferocity took him back a step. "The returning memories aren't an excuse. I could have turned around right then, but I didn't. I ran, because I was afraid, and because I wanted answers. I should have come back. Should have told you what happened."

"Why didn't you?" Aran asked quietly.

Nara shuddered again. "I first saw Talifax right after I woke up from a nightmare. A nightmare that he sent, and told me was a vision of the future." She looked up at Aran searchingly. "Aran, in the dream I assassinated Voria. I saw it. It was like...a memory that hasn't happened. Not just some illusion, or a binding. I gunned her down in cold blood, and I knew for certain it would really happen if I stayed. I had to get away. I couldn't be the reason we lose this war."

Aran didn't answer immediately. It all sounded just plausible enough to accept. Nara had just the right amount of guilt. Just the right amount of justifications. Just the right amount of sympathy. Not too much, but enough that he wanted to wrap his arms around her.

She might be telling the truth. Or she could be playing him. He'd act like it was the former, and prepare for it to be the latter.

He was saved from having to answer by Kezia walking into the brig, closely followed by Bord. Bord had his hands in his pockets, and lounged sullenly against the wall near the door. He didn't even look at Nara, or Frit.

Kezia, on the other hand, walked directly to Nara's cell, and stared fiercely up at her. "Tell me you had a good reason."

"Not good enough." Nara's shoulders slumped, and she returned to her bench.

Some of the fire went out of Kez, and she retreated to stand near Bord. She turned away from the cells, very pointedly, instead slipping into Bord's arms and resting her blonde curls against his chest.

"What about him?" Aran nodded at Kaho. "How did you end up working with a Krox?"

Kaho's scaly head turned in their direction, and Frit looked up a moment later. Both were staring at them.

"Talifax arranged it." Nara pulled her knees up to her chest on the bench. "He sent me to the facility where Ternus housed the Zephyrs, at the same time Nebiat and Frit arrived. I was deliberately placed in their path so I could stop Nebiat from destroying Colony 3." A ghost of a smile flitted across her face, then was gone. "We succeeded. We stopped her there."

That was good at least, though it bothered Aran that Talifax wanted the Krox to fail at Colony 3. Why? It could be as simple as weakening all his enemies, but it could also be part of a larger plan.

"What happened to Ree?" Aran kept his tone neutral. He didn't want her telling him what she thought he wanted to hear, especially since he'd already seen the footage.

Nara paled, but then she rose and began to pace. "She didn't leave us any choice, Aran. Frit was only trying to escape captivity. That isn't her fault."

"Firing on Confederate fighters is," Aran pointed out. "She killed Ree, or as good as."

"That self-righteous bitch didn't give me a choice," Frit snarled. She wrapped her hands very pointedly around the crackling blue bars, and did not remove them, even when smoke billowed out from where her fingers brushed the energy. Hot, fiery tears fell down her dark cheeks. "Ree hunted me like an animal. She followed me across half the sector, because she'd rather see me dead than protect her own world. What other choice did I have? We asked her to stand down, but she just kept coming..."

Unexpected grief welled up in Aran. Not just the loss of Ree, who, even though he'd never much liked her, had been one of their staunchest allies. He'd also lost Frit, and Nara. He took a deep breath, and composed himself before answering.

"Ree was a fanatic, but the fact is that you killed several mages escaping Shaya." Aran approached Frit's cell. "I don't blame you for trying to run, but I've read the report. You were going to carpet bomb the sector's breadbasket with the most lethal weaponry manufactured in this decade. You don't get to claim the moral high ground after that."

Frit's mouth worked but she had no answer. Her shoulders slumped, and she gave a single nod, then returned to her bench.

Metal steps thumped down the ramp, and the sergeant appeared a moment later, now wearing his bulky armor. The silver metal glittered menacingly under the lights, but it paled compared to the scowl he leveled in Nara's direction. "I grabbed the collar and the control rod. I assumed you'd want to deploy soon, so I suited up. You want the lovebirds to get ready too?"

"No," Aran replied, deciding out loud. "I want Kezia to stay here and look after the prisoners. I do not want to come back to any surprises."

"Ah, man, we're always getting left behind." Bord kicked dejectedly at the wall.

"You aren't getting left behind. Go get suited up, Bord." Aran turned back to Nara. "You're coming with us too. He sketched a *void* sigil in front of the magical panel, and the bars to her cell winked out. Sergeant, give her the collar."

"Sir, this is a bad idea. She'll put a knife in our back." Crewes moved to block Nara's cell, so she couldn't exit.

"No, she won't," Aran countered. He faced Nara. "She'll work with us for two reasons. First, I think she wants the same thing we do. Second, and more importantly, you're going to be holding the control rod, Sergeant. If she steps out of line, then do what you need to do."

Crewes reluctantly handed the collar to Nara, and she snapped the thin, golden necklace around her neck. The sigils flared, then it faded against her skin, almost invisible.

"I realize none of you will believe this," Nara said quietly. Her gaze flitted between them, as if seeking a friendly face she didn't find. "I never meant to hurt you, and I will do whatever I can to protect you."

"Sir," Crewes asked, his voice nearly cracking as he eyed Aran searchingly, "why, man?"

Aran tightened his hand around Narlifex's hilt. "We're walking into the unknown, Sergeant. I have no idea what to expect at the Temple of Shi, but Eros left Rhea here for a reason and I want the magical backup in case we run into any surprises." He turned to face Nara, and looked her directly in the eye. "Honestly, though? The main reason is that if I leave her here, even in that cell, I feel like we're going to come back and find out that our ride has been jacked. Again."

"You know what? You're right, sir. I don't trust leaving her here either." Crewes gave a nod of acceptance. "Come on, ex-friend. We've got a package to pick up."

Aran headed for the ramp. He prayed that the Temple would be straightforward. They needed a win, and he needed to get to Shaya so he could help Voria get ready for Krox's assault.

12

THE TEMPLE OF SHI

Kheross was already waiting impatiently in the cargo hold when Aran arrived with the rest of the squad. Bord moved to don his scout armor, while Nara lurked as far from everyone else as she could get. Crewes loomed behind her, his cannon 'accidentally' wandering in her direction.

"This had better work out as you've promised," Kheross growled, his eyes flaring with *void* magic. His muscles bunched under his archaic, crimson armor, a subtle reminder of the threat he posed.

After all the turbulence, Aran found the straightforward animosity refreshing. "It will, as long as you keep your temper in check while we retrieve her. These priests are supposed to be touchy. Voria was very specific about that. If I thought you'd stay behind I wouldn't even bring you. You want your daughter back? Keep it in your pants for a bit, and we'll get her."

The Wyrm gave a non-committal grunt and moved to stand before the blue membrane protecting the bay from the vacuum outside. Yanthara lay below them, a lush, green world, orbiting a large, orange sun.

He walked to his Mark XI, and sketched a *void* sigil before the chest, then slipped inside the familiar armor. His HUD flowed to life, and a thin trickle of *void* magic flowed from his chest. The suit rose into the air, and he guided it over to hover next to Kheross, next to the membrane.

"It troubles me," Kheross rumbled, "that I have never heard of this Temple of Shi. Who is this god, and why should I fear his priests?"

Aran realized that he wasn't entirely equipped to answer the question. He turned to Nara. "Have you heard of it? Voria told me it was a *dream* Catalyst, and that the priests are very unpredictable."

Nara pursed her lips for a moment, then brushed a lock of hair from her face. "I'm not familiar with it, no. But I think I understand why Eros would have hidden her here. Divination can be blocked, and the easiest way to obscure it is with *dream*. If he wanted to prevent her from being found, this would be a great hiding place."

Aran nodded gratefully, then turned back to Kheross. "I guess it doesn't much matter who they are, as long as they don't give us any grief about retrieving Rhea."

"Sir," Crewes said quietly. He raised the faceplate on his armor, exposing a troubled expression. "I know the Temple. My ma used to take us when we were kids. She still worships Shi, even on Shaya. The major's right. They don't brook no nonsense, and I'd step lightly around their priestesses."

"If you know of any customs we're screwing up, make sure you tell us." Aran glanced through the membrane, and saw the world rapidly rushing up at them. His connection to the *Talon* alleviated the need to fly the ship directly, which would be damned helpful when preparing for combat drops. If he'd known about this back when they'd assaulted the second burl they'd never have needed Pickus to save the ship.

They descended into a seemingly endless expanse of trees. There were redwoods, like on Shaya, but also dozens of other species Aran didn't recognize. A haze of undulating magical energy permeated the trees, elusive but powerful just the same. The magic pooled in violet eddies, permeating the entire forest in all directions, and the forest seemed to cover the entire continent.

The notable exception was a vast tree stump, easily a kilometer across. A modern city sprawled across it, with Ternus-style skyscrapers competing with the trees to reach the sky. Smaller buildings clustered around the skyscrapers, like mushrooms, and countless streams of vehicles flowed between them, lines of marching ants.

The *Talon* glided lower of its own accord, and angled toward a steep-sloped pyramid constructed from long planks of redwood. Unlike many of the other buildings this one was surrounded by small groves of trees, and seemed much less crowded than the rest of the city.

Only a few figures walked the mulched pathways threading between the many gardens, and a few more stood at balconies on the Temple's upper floors. Each wore robes of scarlet and purple, which obscured their entire body, save the eyes and a bit of dark skin around them.

Bord nodded down at one of the robed figures. "They must have some lovely ladies if they need to dress 'em up like that."

No one responded, and after a moment Bord sighed. "I miss Kez. I feel like I should punch myself for that joke."

Aran caught Nara's wistful smile, though it seemed no

one else did. It vanished nearly as quickly as it had appeared, replaced by something approaching guilt. That surprised him. Not that she might feel that kind of emotion, but that she would express it. The Nara he'd met before the mindwipe was calculating, and always in control.

This new Nara, if she was on the level, didn't much resemble the woman he'd encountered just after his mindwipe. Nor did she seem like the Nara he'd fought alongside. This new version was much more reserved, a blending of both women.

"Do you feel the immensity?" Kheross asked, those dark eyes focused on the forest around them. "Something is out there, and it does not like us."

"Speak for yourself, scaly." Crewes slugged Kheross lightly in the arm, then nodded at the trees. "This is home. Even the gods-damned trees think you're a slimy stain. They're just fine with the rest of us, though."

Aran guided his armor into a fast walk and headed for the compound's main structure. They received a number of looks from robed figures as they approached, but no one made a move to stop them. There was no fence ringing the grounds, and they were able to thread their way up the mulch-lined walk, all the way to the Temple's wide double doors.

The doors swung open of their own accord, exposing a wide hallway lined with marble. Pedestals lined the entryway, each containing the bust of a fierce warrior. Aran could feel the *dream* radiating from each, and caught *fire* as well.

A robed figure appeared suddenly, just inside the Temple's doorway. One moment the space was empty, and the next a purple-garbed figure blocked their entrance. Judging from the curves, they were looking at a woman, but beyond that the only other detail was her eyes. They were swirling pools of purple-pink that shifted and changed as he watched.

"Welcome, Aranthar, once of the Last Dragonflight, now agent of the Coalition of Light." The woman's clear voice rang out, the words accented so that consonants often blended together, and emphasis was placed in strange places. "Do you seek access to the house of Shi?"

"I do." Aran drifted toward the doors, but the woman didn't budge.

The priestess turned toward Crewes, and took a step closer to the sergeant. She stretched out a robed arm, and rested her gloved hand on the barrel of his cannon. "And what of you, Linus Crewes? Do you seek access as well?"

"Linus?" Bord asked, blinking. "Your first name is Linus?"

Crewes's faceplate snapped up, and he leaned down toward Bord's smaller armor. "Something funny about that name, Bord? You maybe wanna make a joke? Make it rhyme with something?" The malevolence made Bord wilt like a flower.

"No, no jokes. Sorry, sir."

"Linus?" The priestess said, drawing the sergeant's attention. There was emotion buried, but Aran valued Crewes's privacy enough not to dig. "You do not recognize me, do you?"

Crewes shifted his attention to the priestess, and he gave a quick nod, then dropped his eyes to the deck. "Yeah, I remember, Sarala. A guy don't just forget a woman like you."

The fabric over her mouth whispered, and Aran suspected she was smiling. She patted his armor over the bicep. "You *do* remember. You look good, though your burdens are many. Be welcome, Linus Crewes of Yanthara. You have come home."

"Uh." Crewes looked more uncomfortable than Aran had ever seen him.

"He's freezing up," Bord whispered audibly. "Oh my god...he's crashing and burning."

Crewes eyes began to smolder. Orange and red flame licked out where the white used to be, and when he turned to Bord the orange went white-hot. "You're getting on my last nerve, and we just got here, Bord. If you open your mouth again, without instructions, I will make basic your *second* least favorite memory. Are we clear?"

Bord's face went pale, and a moment later the faceplate to his armor snapped down. His voice was a bare whisper. "Crystal, sir."

Aran used the opportunity to get Sarala's attention. "You seem to know who we are, and I'm hoping you're expecting us. Eros, the Tender of Shaya before his death, left a... package for us."

Sarala's swirling pink eyes narrowed, and while Aran couldn't see the frown he had no trouble imagining it. "And what makes you think we'd turn the Outrider over to you? Eros told us that the one who came for Rhea would be a woman. Voria, I believe her name is."

"That's the major," Crewes supplied. "We work for her. Well, we used to."

"Voria's a little busy at the moment." Aran kicked himself for not realizing there would be some sort of security around this. Of course, it would have been helpful if Voria had mentioned it. She probably hadn't known. "She's on Shaya, rallying her people for an assault by Krox. And she wasn't the one who discovered Rhea in the first place. I did. And I have a responsibility here, and a promise to fulfill. Listen, Sarala, I know that we're not Voria, but there has to be something we can do to show you that we're the right people to turn her over to."

Aran prayed, for his sake, that she'd be reasonable. Kheross throwing a temper tantrum could level several surrounding blocks if the Wyrm cut loose. That was the last thing they needed right now.

"Hmm," Sarala murmured. She folded her arms and moved to stand before Aran. Something pulsed from her, a mixture of *fire* and *dream*. She didn't sketch any sigils, which made the magic more similar to what a war mage would use. She leaned closer, and studied him with those bright, swirling eyes. "I believe there is no deceit in you, on this matter at least. And I trust Linus. If you have his loyalty, then you cannot be altogether bad. But I still do not trust you, and I will certainly not allow you into the inner confines of the temple."

Aran took a deep breath. "Okay, that's fair." He thought furiously. "What about Crewes? You said you trust him. Will you let him inside?"

Sarala was silent for several moments. She didn't break eye contact the entire time, and Aran found it difficult to maintain. He kept her gaze until she transferred it to Crewes. "This would be acceptable. Come with me, Linus. If you wish to undergo the trials, then I will allow you to take custody of the Outrider."

"Trials?" Crewes eyes were very wide, and his voice was very small. "Not like, puzzles and stuff, right? You know I hate that shit."

"Sergeant?" Aran asked.

Crewes shoulders slumped. "Fine, I'll come inside and do your tests."

13

THE REDEMPTION

Skare strode onto the bridge of the *Redemption* and turned in a slow circle. The pristine vessel was quite unlike any other ship they'd produced, and he appreciated the minimalism. There were few consoles, and no matrices. The only features were a trio of comfortable chairs, all facing a massive scry-screen.

He moved to stand opposite the chairs, and clasped his hands behind his back as he stood to wait. It didn't take long. Within moments he heard Jolene's cultured voice as she explained the ship's features to their prospective clients.

"Don't let the simplicity fool you," Jolene was saying as she entered the bridge. Her hair had been cut even shorter, a page-boy cut that was coming back into fashion. She was followed by a young man that Skare recognized, but had never met. Governor Austin, the leader of Ternus.

He was reputed to be astute, but passionate to the point where his temper occasionally ruled. That kind of weakness could be exploited, particularly during times of intense stress, as when a god doomed your capital world.

"I thought these magic ships required, what did you call

them, matrixes?" the governor asked, his displeasure manifesting into a frown. "How will my people fly the ship?"

"Welcome, Governor." Skare called, approaching the Ternus delegation with open arms. A cloud of soldiers had followed Austin, including a grizzled man with dozens of medals pinned to his uniform. That one eyed him critically, and the ship around him skeptically. That would be Admiral Kerr. Skare smiled warmly. "Jolene, would you mind if I field his questions?"

"Of course not." She gave him a predatory smile, then extended a hand. "Please, I know how much you enjoy talking about your creation. Governor, Skare designed the *Redemption*."

Skare gave an embarrassed smile, and it was only partly an act. He'd labored for years to create this vessel, and not for the purposes that everyone assumed.

"To answer your questions, Governor," Skare began, "the matrices do exist, but not in a conventional form. We can visit them if you'd like, but I can show you a representation here. Caelendra, display the ship layout and increase the magnification on the arcanotubes by two hundred percent."

"Of course, Lord Skare," a cultured feminine voice came from all around them.

A moment later an illusion of the ship's internals appeared, and then zoomed in on the lowest section, near the heart of the ship. It showed twelve identical black tubes, each connected with a silvery array of coils that fed directly into the ship's spelldrive.

"Those are spell matrixes?" the governor asked. He cleared his throat, and looked at his retinue, as if for guidance. None was provided, other than a few helpless shrugs. He turned back to Skare, who waited expectantly. "Where are the rings? Do the mages get inside the tubes?"

"They do." Skare nodded, magnanimously, of course. "A mage's physical needs are tended to. Their vitals can be tracked from the bridge, and they can remain in stasis for up to four months."

"How do they eat?" Kerr asked, his frown still firmly in place. He removed his cap and tucked it under his arm, then leaned in closer to study the hologram.

"They're fed intravenously," Skare explained. He gestured at the hologram. "Caelendra, show us tube six, please."

The illusion zoomed in and showed the outside of the tube. It centered over a small window, and beyond that window was the sleeping face of a young woman, no more than eighteen or nineteen.

"Her name is Zoraya," Skare explained magnanimously. "She comes from Yanthara, where her entire family lived in poverty. She signed a seven-year contract with us, and she'll spend the vast majority of it in that tube. She fuels this vessel directly, alongside seven other mages. She provides the vessel with *fire*. Others provide different aspects, giving the ship a mixture of abilities based on its complement of mages."

Skare paused dramatically, and allowed his face to fall into carefully crafted sorrow. "There is a cost for all this enormous power, unfortunately. The ship serves as a sort of magical battery. It is designed to drain magic, and at the end of her term Zoraya will have sacrificed the entirety of her magical ability. It will belong, in its entirety, to this vessel."

"So this thing burns out mages?" Kerr asked. He folded his arms, and delivered a no-nonsense look. "Mages are rare enough as it is. Why would Ternus sacrifice the few dozen we have to fly ships around?"

"You misunderstand me, mister—". Skare knew how

Ternus officers valued their rank, and enjoyed needling the man with his feigned ignorance.

"Fleet Admiral Kerr," the man snapped.

"Admiral Kerr," Skare continued apologetically. "The magic, once absorbed, is a part of the ship. The ship is, in essence, a giant eldimagus, and when Zoraya is drained of her power the ship will possess it, and be able to call upon it in the same way. The ship's commander controls the vessel through an implant we will provide, of course. This puts the power in the hands of your government, and not any random officer who wishes to disobey your commands whenever it's convenient."

The reference to Voria wasn't lost on them—Skare was certain of it. The governor was nodding along, but Kerr was still skeptical.

"I still don't like losing mages," Kerr argued. He shook his head. "Do what you want, Governor, but I don't like these things one bit."

Austin raised a hand to silence Kerr, then turned to Skare. "What can these ships can do that makes such a sacrifice worth it? You know what we face."

Skare sighed and gave a slight shake of his head. "I wish I'd been able to arrange a proper demonstration, but an explanation will have to suffice. I'm told you're having trouble with a god, yes?"

"You know we are." The governor's eyes narrowed. "And my patience is not infinite. No more games, Skare."

"Fair enough. These ships drain magic. Gods are comprised of pure magic," Skare explained. He dropped the volume of his voice slightly, to express the gravity. "Gentlemen, with enough of these ships you can not only kill a god, but empower your own fleet in the process. Every time these ships win a battle they grow more powerful, even as your crews grow more experienced. If you need to battle a god, then I can think of no finer weapon. For the first time you'll be the masters of your own fate, and no longer playthings at the whim of gods and mages."

The governor adopted a thoughtful expression, and began rubbing at the sleeve of his jacket, where a watch would be. Skare knew most officials wore a comlink there, and that a comlink was often associated with their wealth, as that was how they checked their balances in their mighty computers.

"The vessel includes a full artificial intelligence built using your own tech." Skare knew he needed to press, and he pressed hard. "All they lack are mages, and they'll be ready to save your world."

"What are they going to cost us?" Austin asked. "You know our money is tied up in relief efforts, and we're not likely to be able to acquire credit with our world...as it is."

"And this is the part," Skare smiled mischievously, "where I get to prove you wrong about us, Governor. From a fiscal perspective giving you money is a bad investment, I agree. But having Krox devour the sector is hardly good for business either. We will give you an armada, on 100% credit. I will charge no interest for the first three years, and after that we'll adjust no more than two basis points a year."

Austin blinked, then turned to his advisors. They had a whispered conference, and the only part Skare caught was when Kerr said something about that 'pasty-faced clown.' Skare smiled into his hand.

Finally, Austin turned back to them. "You've got yourself a deal, Skare. You get us a fleet of these ships, and if we survive this war we'll pay back every penny. You've got my word on that."

"Splendid." Skare walked toward Jolene, and paused

near the bridge's wide doorway. "Welcome to your new flagship, Governor. The *Redemption* is yours. I'll get out of your hair. Caelendra, transfer command authority to governor Austin of Ternus."

"Acknowledged, Lord Skare." Caelendra's cheerful voice echoed across the bridge.

Skare strode away with Jolene in his wake. She hurried to catch him, then eyed him sidelong. "That was masterfully done."

"All I needed to do was convince them that we share the same interests." Skare shrugged. It hadn't been that hard. "Now we sit back and let them create the weapons we need."

14

THE MIRROR OF SHAYA

"Where are we going?" Ikadra asked, his innocent voice echoing down the empty corridor. This portion of the *Spellship* was deserted, and likely had been for countless centuries. Voria was left with the impression that something was watching her from the lingering shadows that the period magical lights failed to banish.

"To the Chamber of the Mirror," she explained as she advanced up the corridor. "I had it moved here from Eros's vessel, and haven't had occasion to use it. Now, I need answers."

"Oh." Ikadra pulsed thoughtfully. "Hopefully we see something cool."

She did need answers badly, but she knew that this move underscored her desperation. Divination was hardly her specialty, and she'd watched Eros hurl himself at the Mirror over and over, with little success. Trying to master it had taken too much of his attention at a critical time, and she couldn't afford to make the same mistake.

Unfortunately, her need for answers was genuine. She

had to try at least. Would it even interact with the godsight she'd been given?

Voria took a deep, steadying breath as she stepped into the Chamber of the Mirror for the first time since discovering it. That was its true name, though it had been merely an empty room when she'd first come aboard the *Spellship*. It contained a simple pedestal, with no clear indication of what the room had been intended for.

The only significant detail had been the room's magical resonance. It hummed in a way she'd rarely heard, a deep thrumming melody that contained all eight aspects of magic. They were heaviest in *fire* and *dream* though, confirming that the Mirror had something to do with divination.

Those energies reverberated off mirrored walls, each showing endless reflections of Voria and Ikadra, and of the single object occupying the room. That object, the Mirror of Shaya, possessed an identical magical resonance.

Voria moved to stand before the ancient eldimagus, a slash in the air with a perfectly reflective surface that bobbed up and down slowly over the pedestal. The Mirror appeared two dimensional, disappearing from view when it rotated so that she was looking at it sideways.

The Mirror vibrated as she approached, almost as if greeting her. The spinning stopped, and it shifted to face her. It didn't seem to have an intelligence in the same way that Ikadra did, but at the same time it seemed aware of both its surroundings and the needs of its viewer. If she was fortunate, it might help her unravel the maddeningly unspecific task that Inura had left her with.

"Can you show me things as they were?" she wondered aloud, not really expecting an answer. "Show me Shaya, while she still lived."

It was a vague request, and yet the Mirror's surface began to ripple and change. The surface clouded in mist, and when it cleared, the Mirror provided a portal onto the bridge of the *Spellship*, though Voria somehow sensed that it was a wholly other time, in the distant past.

A tall, raven-haired woman stood with hands clasped behind her back. She wore her hair loose, and her blue uniform was slovenly. It could have passed for a confederate uniform, with the same gold trim, though the patch on the shoulder was of unfamiliar design.

The woman rested one hand on the hilt of a spellblade, suggesting she was a war mage. She certainly had the physique for it, and despite her unkempt appearance there must be some discipline in there somewhere.

Her attention was fixed on a scry-screen, and that screen showed a moon that was both familiar and alien. The surface was barren and lifeless, comprised of grey-green rock with no atmosphere. The moon orbited the same gas giant she'd stared out her window at as a little girl.

She was looking at the moon of Shaya, before her goddess had brought it life.

The woman standing at the scry-screen turned to face Voria, and Voria gave a start until she realized the hawk-eyed woman was staring past her, not at her.

"Blast that Wyrm," the woman snarled. "He should be here." She took a deep, even breath, then seemed to collect herself. "Has everything been prepared as I've instructed?"

"Yes, Battle Leader." A man in golden armor that was shockingly similar to current Shayan fashion hurried into view and knelt next to the woman, Shaya, she realized—it could be no one else. He offered Shaya a golden staff, tipped with an immensely powerful sapphire. "Ikadra has been prepared as you've instructed."

"Huh huh," the staff said, sapphire pulsing. "We're going to play hide the staff."

"None of your antics today, old friend." Shaya's tone softened a hair, though her features didn't relax in the slightest. "Explain to me how this will work. No jokes. We're pressed for time."

"Right." Ikadra's sapphire dimmed. "Are you sure you want to do this? You don't have to. We can get out of here right now. It isn't too late."

The raven-haired beauty took the staff in her hand, then turned back to the screen. She stared at the barren moon below her, and smiled. "I'm certain. This is the proper course. My death is inevitable. It doesn't have to occur here, but it will occur regardless of what route I choose. If that is the case, then why not ensure my end matters? My death will mean a future for the Vagrant Fleet."

Ikadra's sapphire pulsed forlornly, but he said nothing. That silence spoke volumes, and told Voria of the long and storied history they must have had together. It mystified her how the staff had managed to maintain its optimism after all the horrors he'd no doubt witnessed.

Shaya turned to her lieutenant. "Take Ikadra and the *Spellship* to Virkon. Present them to Inura, and ensure that blasted Wyrm finds a way to hide them as discussed."

"Of course, Battle Leader." Her lieutenant sank to one knee, then pressed his hand to his heart. "We will never forget your sacrifice. And we will honor your wishes. If all comes to pass as you have foreseen, our people will ensure that this world flourishes, and we will watch over the sector until you rise again."

Shaya rolled her eyes, though the man on the ground didn't seem to notice. "I've no doubt, old friend. Just don't go overboard with the whole I'm a goddess thing. You still remember when I used to scramble through air ducts, and come home covered in rust. Don't go all worshiper on me in the final hour."

Her lieutenant rose, and removed his helmet. The sandy-haired man clutched it under one arm, and gave Shaya a boyish grin that reminded Voria a bit of Aran. "To be fair, you *are* a goddess now, little sister. You were always the best of us." He snapped his fist over heart once more.

"Goodbye, brother." Shaya smiled, and then began to glow with immense white light. The strength of the glow was staggering, and was made no less so when Shaya suddenly teleported out of the *Spellship*.

Voria's perspective shifted to match and she now hovered in orbit over the moon that would somehow become the home where she was born. Shaya maneuvered around the world, finally stopping near the Telethal mountains, which were unmistakable even without the tree to give them perspective.

Shaya's body was comprised entirety of light, and while Voria couldn't guess at her actual size, she'd been near enough Wyrms to make a safe guess. Shaya was nearly the size of Drakkon, which made her considerably smaller than Neith, and a speck compared to Krox.

Space folded in on itself, warping and changing at the edge of the system, far from the light of the sun. The strange magic resolved into an unfamiliar god. It could be nothing else. The being towered over Shaya, despite her increased size.

The giant appeared humanoid, from the waist up anyway. Below that his form blended into the void, and made him appear a disembodied torso. His body was comprised of the stars themselves, cosmic dust linking limbs defined by constellations. Shivan, she realized, recognizing his description from her time in the library on Marid.

"I do not understand," Shivan thought, the force of his voice knocking Shaya a step closer to her world. "Why did you allow this possibility to occur? It should have taken nearly four centuries for this confrontation to commence. You could have run."

Shaya gave a wicked, almost flirtatious smile. It would have horrified any Caretaker, or any devout priest of the temple. It did not at all match the chaste giver of life they painted Shaya to be. The goddess raised her hand, and began sketching a spell.

Life and *air* and *water* swirled around Shaya in a growing cloud of unfamiliar power. Voria couldn't begin to guess what the goddess was doing, and from the very mortal expression on Shivan's cosmic face he wasn't having any more luck.

The god raised a spear of immense power, one that strummed a memory. She'd seen the weapon before, and now that she thought upon it she'd seen the god, too. She remembered the chaos on Marid and touching the goddess for whom the world had been named.

"Worldender has slain countless gods." Shivan slowly raised the weapon, but Shaya made no move to dodge or hide. "It slew Marid herself, in a single blow. What will your tiny magic do that your betters could not?"

Shaya laughed, a high, musical laugh, that echoed somehow through space. She shook her head sadly. "Do you know why Inura and Virkonna chose to elevate me, Shivan?"

The magic around her swirled faster, and further out around her, until it formed a nimbus of power with Shaya's blazing form in the center.

"I admit the decision puzzles me." Shivan lowered the spear a hair, and seemed to consider the question. "Investing so much power in one as young as you...your perspective barely covers a century. How can you understand the complexities of this war? Why put so much power in the hands of an infant?"

"Perspective," Shaya supplied. The spell around her grew to a crescendo. "I can see things that elder gods cannot, with my limited, mortal perspective. I remember being born, and I've lived with the certainty of my own death. I understand the cycle of life far better than you ever will. What I do today will ensure your rebirth, Shivan. I will set you on the path to undo all the harm you have wrought. Come, let's end this."

The spell burst outwards even as Worldender left Shivan's hand. Shaya made no defense. Quite the opposite. She extended her arms and thrust her chest forward, as if embracing the spear. The weapon burst through her heart, slamming her into the moon below.

Light, and sound, and magic, and memory burst up from the world below as Voria witnessed the death of a goddess. Shaya's body cratered an area west of the mountains, precisely where the tree would one day stand. She lay on her back, limbs splayed brokenly around her. Worldender, the vicious black spear of the gods, had pinned her to the earth, and sank deep into the moon.

Only then did Shaya's magic begin to take hold. The energy swirled up and around the haft of the spear, covering it in a layer of *life*, and then *water*, and then all eight aspects at once. The magic rolled out of her in inconceivably vast waves, each swirl sinking into Worldender.

The weapon began to transform. Bark sprouted along its surface. Roots snaked along the ground, finding purchase on the barren rock. Long, slender limbs jutted from the main body. The tree grew quickly, an impossibly tall redwood replacing Worldender's dark form. Onward and upward the tree grew, its roots finally obscuring Shaya's body.

A wave of magic rippled outwards from the very tip of the tree, and the familiar bubble she'd lived with her entire life slowly descended from the tip, protecting a wide swathe of the moon. Within moments, ferns and bay trees and redwoods sprouted from the barren ground everywhere the bubble protected. A virgin forest grew swiftly, the wild growth covering nearly a quarter of the moon.

High above, Shivan stared down at the world, his cosmic gaze still confused. "I do not understand. Her sacrifice deprived me of a weapon, nothing more. I fail to see my rebirth, in any possibility." He shook his head sadly. "Such a waste."

The god turned, then disappeared as suddenly as he'd come.

Voria blinked as the second reality disappeared and she was back in the Chamber of the Mirror. She still didn't understand how Shaya had ascended, but she knew how she'd died. More importantly she knew why Krox was coming.

He wanted Worldender, and no doubt to consume Shaya's body. Either would ensure the sector never recovered. Voria had to find a way to stop him, but to do that she needed more information.

"She's under the tree," Voria whispered. "Under the pool. That must have been Eros's secret, and what Inura meant. Why the Mirror chose this memory to show me."

It was time to visit the goddess in person.

15

BULLSHIT SIDE QUEST

Crewes stepped through the temple's ivory doors, uncertain of what to expect in the dark room he entered. It was utterly silent, and after the doors swung shut behind him, it was blacker than the depths.

A sound like whispers rolled out of the darkness, all around him. And then a wet, earthy smell bubbled up, the kind he associated with the deep jungle. Had he been teleported somewhere?

"Man, I hate this creepy religious crap." He flicked his external light on low, which illuminated Sarala's robed form a couple meters away. "Where are we?"

Something roared in the jungle, a tiger from the sound of it. Tigers were no joke.

Crewes fed a bit of *fire* to the armor, and a soft glow arose from its surface, better illuminating the area around him. As he'd feared, they were surrounded by dense jungle. He hated the gods-damned jungle. It had been the reason he'd been so eager to get off this blasted world in the first place.

As if on cue, the jungle burst into life. Insects began

their shrill song. Monkeys shouted in the distance, answered by another troop even further away. It pressed down on him, and Crewes spun to face the spot where the doors had been only to find unbroken jungle.

"You know where we are, Linus," Sarala finally said. She gave a soft laugh, and slowly lowered her cowl, exposing a more mature version of the face that had tilted his whole world, once upon a time. The motion exposed braids of dark hair tied into long, ropy fibers. She eyed him playfully, and a brief smile played across full lips. "We are in Shi's domain. I know how...uncomfortable it makes you. I know you hate the trees, and Shi knows it too. That's why this is the trial. Your weapons and tools will be stripped from you, and you will need to persevere. Not even your mark of Van will help. *Fire* has no power over *dream*. Not in her domain."

Crewes snapped his faceplate back up, and scowled at a girl he'd once hoped to marry. "Are you saying I gotta walk through the jungle, with no gear? Why? And where am I even going?"

Sarala's entire body dissolved into purple smoke, then flowed back into her human self a few meters away. She gave him a wink, and then a low, throaty laugh. "Find Shi, Linus. Her light will guide you. Do not rely on your tools, for they will betray you."

"What are you going to be doing?" Crewes took a reluctant step after her, and a fallen branch cracked under his armor's weight. He didn't love the idea of being without his gear, and he liked the idea of being alone even less.

"This is your trial, and yours alone. I can observe, but you will not see me again unless you succeed." Her form dissolved, then flowed along the jungle floor until it disappeared behind the wide trunk of an iroko tree.

"Well that's just gods-damned great." Crewes snapped

his faceplate down again. "I know gods got their rules, but Shi's just gonna have to make an exception. There's no way I'm ditching my armor in the middle of a jungle."

He willed a healthy flow of *fire* into his spellarmor, then channeled it into the booster. A fat plume of flame burst from his back, and the armor jetted up into the air. It took him almost twenty seconds to snake his way clear of the canopy, and he'd guess the tallest trees topped two hundred meters. They spread out at the top, jealously preventing the trees below from getting their share of the sun.

Once he broke the canopy, the night sky glittered above him, a sea of stars that were as welcome a sight as anything he'd ever seen. They represented freedom, and he wished he could just fly away, and bail on this whole planet, just like he'd done when he'd enlisted. But he couldn't. He had a job to do, and the captain was counting on him.

The kid didn't have too many people in his corner, and Crewes was damned if he was gonna be one of the ones who let him down.

Crewes scanned the jungle, and turned in a slow circle. It extended in all directions, as if he were thousands of kilometers from where they'd landed with the *Talon*. There was no sign of civilization, or of any sentient creature. This was the deep jungle. Here and there a cloud of massive bats flitted over the trees, diving to scoop up insects, then disappearing into the canopy when they'd had their fill.

He might not be able to see anything, but he realized that he could feel something. Something big and magical lurked just beyond the edge of hearing, somewhere to the south. Crewes began flying toward it, and fed another chunk of *fire* into the booster. He ate up the kilometers, grateful that he'd decided to keep his armor. Walking the same distance would have taken hours, if he was lucky.

A faint, violet light filtered through the cracks in the canopy ahead, closer to pink than to purple.

He gained some altitude, and studied the glow. That had to be the destination, and he'd guess he could reach it in a matter of minutes.

Faint, feminine laughter bubbled up from the jungle, though it was impossible to determine the source. It came from everywhere, even above him.

A wave of unfamiliar magic rippled around him, and his spellarmor...dissolved. And so did his clothes. Crewes was naked, and suddenly weightless.

"Oh shit." He began to plummet toward the canopy below.

16

GHOST LEOPARD

Crewes tumbled end over end, at first. It wasn't his first time falling, and he knew getting control was critical. He extended both hands, and felt the wind drag at them, but he was spinning too fast to get control.

The canopy rushed up at him, each revolution bringing it closer. If Crewes didn't slow his momentum, then he was going to die. He'd survived the breath of a demigod, but he was going to die from falling damage.

"Nah, it ain't going down like that." Crewes closed his eyes, and concentrated on the *fire* smoldering in his chest. It had been a part of him for years, and the strength had grown when he met Neith.

The captain had told him that there wasn't much difference between a war mage and a tech mage. But Crewes had never tried to use his magic without his armor, or his gun. Why would he? They worked fine. But now he had no choice, and he was gonna find out if he had what it took to be a war mage.

Crewes flung all his limbs out, increasing his drag. Then

he drew from the *fire*, just as he would have to power his booster. The magic built within him, and he sent it down his arm, toward the palm of his hand, like he was casting a fire bolt.

A weak jet of flame burst outwards from his palm, and he spun in that direction. "Well, all right then!"

Crewes did it again, this time with more success. His tumble became a lazy spin. He did it again. And again. After several more bursts his feet were angled downward, and at least he was falling in a straight line.

That gave him a really good look at the rapidly approaching jungle.

"How do I get into this shit?" He shrieked, a distant part of his mind grateful no one heard how high pitched his voice had gone. Bord would never let him hear the end of it.

He took fast, shallow breaths as the trees rushed up at him. Crewes fired a burst of flame at nine o'clock, then another at three o'clock. It pushed him out and away from a thick branch, but he slammed into another beneath it. Something cracked in his chest, and he roared as his elbow slammed into another branch.

The sent him back into a spin, one he had no hope of controlling. So he didn't try. Crewes pulled his knees up to his chest, and wrapped his uninjured arm around them. "This shit worked once before, and it's all I got."

He tugged at the *water* magic in his chest, and pulled as much as he could, as fast as he could. Crewes willed the *water* into a thick sheen of ice, which sprouted all over his skin, and then quickly grew outward. He kept the process up as he fell, and the next time he slammed into a branch it hurt a lot less.

More ice formed, until he was completely encased in a ball. Crewes held his breath, and continued to create more ice. His snowball bounced off the trunk of one tree, then went into free fall. It was agony not knowing how far down the ground was, but now that he was below the trees he couldn't see shit.

The ball spun and his stomach lurched, over and over and over. He was just thinking about losing his lunch when all momentum suddenly ceased. Ice exploded around him, a wave of shards that stung and shredded his unprotected skin.

His head slammed into something, and he lost his breath when he crashed into the jungle floor. Every part of his body screamed, especially his left arm, and his ribs. Crewes gave a low groan, and kind of wished he were dead.

After his breath returned, he gritted his teeth, and rolled over into a sitting position. "I ain't been this bad off since Nebiat took a liking to me."

He scooted back a bit into a convenient root, and rested against it as he looked around the jungle and tried to figure out what came next. "I mean, I guess Sarala did warn me." Crewes rose shakily to his feet, and realized that if he was going to walk he'd need some sort of crutch. "I guess walking would have been smarter, but then I ain't never been accused of being a fast learner."

A long, straight tree branch lay directly under where he'd impacted. It was the perfect size and shape, just fat enough to fit in his hand, and rose about a half meter taller than his head. It ended in a jagged tip that Crewes thought he could make pretty lethal if he poked something with enough enthusiasm.

He used the branch as a crutch, and started into an uncomfortable shuffle up the ridgeline, in the direction of the glow he'd seen. This far beneath the canopy there was no natural light, which made the amethyst glow all the more noticeable.

The hairs on the back of his neck suddenly rose of their own accord, and Crewes was positive something was watching him, out there in the trees. He pretended not to notice, and limped his way across the jungle floor. It was slow going, but it wasn't like he had anything better to do.

His makeshift crutch made walking possible, and he was surprised how strong and supple the wood was. He had no idea what kind of tree it had come from, but the branch was almost unnaturally straight, like a spear. If he still had a belt knife he could probably carve the tip into exactly that.

Something flashed across the edge of his vision. He caught sight of rippling ferns, and a brief flash of fur. It was a tawny color, and had the kind of distinctive spots every child was warned about before entering the forest.

Not a tiger then.

"Ghost Leopard," he growled. Great cats roamed the deep jungle, and leopards, while not the largest, were the most dangerous. They could take down a full-sized human, especially one with bare feet and his dong hanging out.

Crewes would have confronted the cat, if he'd had the ability, but he knew it didn't work that way. The cat would follow him, and wait for him to exhibit weakness, or to go to sleep. Then it would tear out his throat, and probably bring him back to its cubs. When he'd been a kid he'd heard stories that ghost leopards could carry a full-grown man up into the canopy, and when it happened blood would rain down for seven days and nights.

He couldn't afford to wait for it.

"Here, kitty, kitty," Crewes called, nice and friendly, like. "I'm bleeding all over the place and I taste real good. Why don't you come get a nibble?"

Another flash of fur passed on his left, but then it was gone, leaving nothing but swaying ferns in its wake. Even if Crewes weren't wounded he still wouldn't have risked chasing it, as ghost leopards were known for being crafty. Some said they were holy creatures, killing those who offended Shi. He'd never put much stock in rumors like that, but now he wasn't so sure.

The jungle went silent. No monkeys. No insects. Only the distant cry of a bat broke the shroud that smothered the trees around him.

Crewes put his back to a tree, and readied himself. He wasn't disappointed.

A furred form flashed down from above, and if not for thousands of hours of training he'd have died right then. Instead, he went on offense. Crewes sucked in a deep breath, and exhaled a cloud of super-heated magical flame. His own personal napalm.

The cat twisted, and somehow flung its body out of the path of the flame. Crewes judged its landing point, and aimed his walking staff like a rifle. Somehow, by some miracle, it responded. A sheen of ice shot from the tip and coated the ground where the cat landed.

It slipped, and gave a frustrated growl as it rolled into the shadows.

"That's right, kitty. You want more of the same you come right on back," Crewes boomed. He felt a lot less confident, though. He was still bleeding, and without Bord to patch him up, sooner or later the blood loss was going to make him woozy. That's what the cat was waiting for.

A frustrated roar came from a dozen meters above him, and he glanced up to see the cat glaring down. It didn't make any attempt to attack, but it also didn't leave. Crewes leaned back against the sturdy wooden spear, and tried to decide what to do.

"Of course it ain't a demon, or a Wyrm, or something I can punch, or even understand," he managed through gritted teeth. "It's gotta be some crazy ghost cat who won't stand and fight. Man, I tell you, this quest shit—"

The cat leapt from the tree, and he tensed, but only for a moment. He wasn't the target. The leopard landed a few meters away, and began to groom itself. Crewes sighed, and hung his shoulders. "Part of the bullshit quest, I bet. Gotta confuse me before you eat me, huh? All right, then. I'm just gonna keep walking. You attack me whenever you want."

The cat stopped licking itself and delivered a baleful look, as if it understood what he'd said, and was absolutely certain he was some fresh-faced wipe. Crewes's mom had delivered similar looks, often, while he'd been growing up.

He ignored the cat and started threading through the trees again. The cat followed, but prowled around the edges of his vision. Each time it passed he tensed, but it no longer seemed interested in attacking him, and he started to wonder if that's what it had been doing in the first place.

But what else could a great cat want with him? Maybe it was a spirit animal. That was a thing, he'd heard. Followers of Van mostly just burned things, but followers of Shi all got to pick out their own cuddly animal to get tattooed, and have monogrammed on their frigging robes.

Crewes leaned heavily on the spear, and inched his way up a sloped ridge. The amethyst glow was stronger there, and he suspected he'd have a decent view if he could reach the top. He hobbled up, though it took a couple eternities to reach. "Never thought I'd miss the Umbral Depths, or that crazy spider."

A few more painful steps brought him to the top of the

ridge, and he could finally see down into the valley below. A deep purple-pink glow rose from the center of what could only be an impact crater before the jungle had covered it. The bowl-shaped valley was too symmetrical to be anything else.

At least he could see his destination. He started walking again, gritting his teeth with every step. Man he hated the jungle. "Come on, cat."

17

PRAYER

Voria blinked a few times as she entered the *Spellship*'s massive amphitheater for the first time. It wasn't merely that the room was cavernous, or even that the slowly ascending rings of seats held nearly five thousand people, all of them magically active in some way.

What surprised her the most was Pickus.

The mousey tech-turned-tech-mage had clearly become a leader. He adjusted his glasses, his freckled face splitting into a grin as he patted a drifter on the shoulder, then turned to listen to a young woman, just out of her teens. Their adoring gazes spoke volumes. They trusted the fiery-haired young man.

The young woman tapped his shoulder and gestured in Voria's direction. Pickus turned and spotted her, then hurried over with a smile. "There you are, ma'am. I haven't seen you in two days. Hope things are going well with the Mirror. Have you puzzled out what Inura expects us to do?"

It warmed her that he'd said us and not you. She smiled back, her burdens slightly lessened. She could see why they trusted him. "I'm working on that now." She slid her hand up Ikadra's golden haft, and rested her weight against the warm metal. "I need to confer directly with Shaya, or her shade, or...well, whatever remains. The answers are there—I'm certain of it."

"She's down there." Ikadra's sapphire pulsed a somber beat. "I can feel her. This was the last place I saw her before she died." After a moment the sapphire brightened. "She's the reason I like poo jokes. She's a good person. Shaya will help you, Voria. I know it."

"Thank you, Ikadra." She wished she could properly convey that gratitude. His continued confidence helped more than the staff would ever know.

Pickus kept darting glances out at the audience, and Voria followed his gaze.

"Are they expecting an address?" Voria nodded at the crowd. Nearly every face was fixed on them, though many were having their own conversations.

"No." Pickus's grin was replaced by a tight, fierce frown. "I told them you don't have any time for their nonsense. And a lot of it *is* nonsense. It's my job to insulate you from this stuff." He paused for a moment, and tugged at his collar uncomfortably. "Uh, it's also my job to ask you the questions no one else is gonna ask."

"Indeed." Voria forced a smile, knowing he needed to see that she was receptive to this. And she was, as every leader needed checks on her authority. "I need you to feel you can question me, Pickus. I don't claim to understand our ultimate role. If our plan succeeds, I suppose I'll be a goddess and terms like 'major' or 'admiral' or whatever else I might adopt are meaningless. But Shaya has already shown me that such power will not make me any less fallible. I'll need you more than ever."

"Well this question ain't too bad, as questions go." His

smile crept back onto his face. "It's just that...I need a title. I need something to show these people that I'm your number one guy. I mean, not like, romantically, but in a professional sense. They all know I work closely with you, and people seem to listen, but there are lots of factions forming. People want a leader, and right now they're looking to the old systems of power. They're listening to the Caretakers, and the new Tender. That's not a bad thing on its own, but we need to make sure you've got your own power base to counter theirs."

He was right.

Voria released Ikadra, who hovered beside her. She folded her arms and stared out at the crowd, really seeing them now. The rifts were there already. The seating wasn't as haphazard as she'd first suspected. Each group had gathered around their leader, and she saw a dozen men and women who'd each possessed power before their world had been attacked, all leading their own small factions.

There were others she didn't recognize, and each stared suspiciously at their neighbors. That wouldn't do, not if they were to have any prayer of success.

"What kind of title did you have in mind? I'll happily grant it." She smiled at Pickus again, affectionately this time. "You earned that back in the Umbral Depths, and have many times since."

"Oh." Pickus blinked. "I kinda thought you'd have an idea. I mean, respectfully, ma'am, I'm just a tech with a junior college certification, and a couple Catalyzations."

"Not anymore." Voria swept him into a hug. He tensed, but then returned it. She held him for a long moment, then released him, and slowly faced the crowd. She sketched an *air* sigil, amplifying her voice. The *Spellship*'s magic responded, carrying it equally to every corner of the room.

"Good morning, citizens of Shaya. I have not officially welcomed you to the *Spellship*, so please, be welcome. I have spent several hours communing with our goddess."

Whispers rippled through the room at the sudden shift in topic, some scandalized, others amazed. A few, mostly drifters, were slurred. She let the chaos build for several moments before continuing.

"This ship," she called, "once belonged to Shaya. Our goddess was known as a battle leader, a fact that surprised me, though in retrospect it shouldn't. Our lady was a warrior, and a healer. She was also a brilliant strategist, and she planned for the future. Our future."

Voria paused and paced the length of the stage. She had them now. They all stared at her with rapt attention, a sea of faces praying for answers. Answers she hoped she could deliver. "Shaya left behind the tools we need to fight Krox. I'm going to commune with her again, and use the clues she left behind to assemble the tools we need to survive against a god. While I am doing that I want to officially introduce you to Administrator Pickus. Most of you already know him. Pickus is captain of this vessel in all but name. If he gives you an order I expect it to be carried out as if I had issued it. If he makes a suggestion, then I ask that you consider it. And, most importantly, I ask that you lend your expertise. The administrator will need a great deal of help that you are uniquely suited to provide."

"Now they're all gonna start jockeying for my ear," Pickus hissed, shooting her a reproving glance.

She gave him a knowing smile, then turned back to the audience. "Be strong, citizens of Shaya. We will prevail." She waved, and they gave a desultory cheer. It was better than nothing, she supposed.

"Well, I did ask for a faction." Pickus gave a nervous

laugh. "I'll see if I can't bring some order to this mess, and start building some sort of bureaucracy. I'm pretty good at logistics, but people are a lot harder to manage than engine parts."

"I've no doubt you'll excel, as you do everything else. I'll return as swiftly as I'm able." Voria turned from the stage and walked back to Ikadra. "Take me to the Chamber of the First, old friend."

An explosion of applause sounded behind her, and she looked over her shoulder to see Pickus moving to the center of the stage to take control of things. The ship was in good hands, which gave her the freedom to tend to this.

"It's time." Light flared from Ikadra, and then they were elsewhere.

She'd grown used to teleportation, and quickly oriented herself in the Chamber of the First. It wasn't so depressing as it had been in the wake of Eros's last stand, but neither was it as brightly lit as it had been at the height of its glory. She avoided looking at the burn marks on the walls, untouched since the battle.

The pool emitted a strong, golden light that warmed her both physically and internally somehow. The magic called out to the portion embedded in her chest, like calling to like. This was definitely the right place.

"I suppose now we need to find a way to commune with her." She glanced at Ikadra. "I realize I'm opening myself up for all manner of juvenile responses, but do you have a suggestion?"

"Wellll, you could try praying." Ikadra's tone was uncertain. "I don't really know how this is supposed to work. I mean, I want to say something witty, but I can't...'cause Shaya's dead, and I feel all bleh. I mean, the magic keeps her around somehow. But not like she was. We need to get her attention somehow."

Voria nodded slowly. She didn't quite understand the link between Shaya and her people, but it seemed some vestige of the goddess' mind survived, and that she might be able to reach it. If ever there was a place that could be accomplished from, then this was it.

She approached the pool, staring down into the quarter-full earthen bowl nestled between artfully carved floorboards, the center of their recent ritual. Voria took a deep breath, then sank slowly to her knees. She didn't know much about worship, but many of the ritual prayers required supplicants to kneel. It was difficult reconciling that with the woman she'd seen in the Mirror, but it was really all she had.

"Shaya, mother of us all, please help your children in their hour of need," she intoned, the words coming unbidden despite not having been used since she was a child. She closed her eyes, and bowed her head. "I do not know how to do this. I don't understand what is required of me, and Inura's instructions were maddeningly unspecific. I can see why his side lost the war. This cryptic signs-and-portents nonsense is getting my people killed."

A faint musical laugh sounded in the distance somewhere, just beyond the edge of hearing. A moment later a breeze passed through the room, bringing with it the scent of spring. Bay leaves, and earthy ferns, and the unmistakable scent of redwoods.

Drink. A voice whispered through her mind, much like Neith, though far weaker, and more elusive.

She blinked, and looked around. Other than the pool there was nothing the voice could mean. "You want me to drink the *life* magic? But we just performed a ritual to sustain the tree. There isn't enough. If I take from that reserve..."

Light exploded from the pool, yet the golden brilliance did not blind her. The waters at the bottom of began to rise, slowly filling the pool. The level continued to rise until the magic passed the one third mark, which was over double what they'd had when they'd completed the ritual.

Voria could only gawk like a first-year student. "How?"

Drink.

Voria nodded numbly, and bent to reach into the pool. She scooped up a single handful of *life* magic, the warmth spreading through her hand, and then the rest of her body. She raised it to her lips, and gulped it down greedily.

Wonderful light burned through her, suffusing her limbs, and even her mind. She felt the strength of the gods, their unmistakable power, pure and terrible, and miraculous.

More. Drink and see.

Voria didn't need to be prompted this time. She drew another scoop from the pool, and drank it just as greedily as the first. More power suffused her, heady, and urgent.

See.

The floor below her began to dissolve, and she scrambled backwards in a primal attempt at flight. Below her lay a vast cavern, and in that cavern lay the sleeping body of a goddess, still brimming with power.

The woman's eyes began to open. Then Voria was falling. She tried to sketch a spell, but couldn't force her disjointed mind to do anything. She fell faster, directly toward Shaya's enormous eye. Voria closed her eyes at the last moment, just before impact.

18

THE VAGRANT FLEET

The light faded, though the warmth remained. Voria expected to find herself floating in the cosmos, or perhaps dropped into the remembrance of some long-ago battle of the gods. The very last thing she'd expected was to find herself back in her own quarters, aboard the *Spellship*.

It was depressingly normal.

"What am I missing?" She tapped her lip as she turned in a slow circle, and quickly spotted details that didn't fit. The coverlet on the bed was scarlet instead of blue. There was an empty wine bottle on the mantle, and two more on the carpet next to it. Clothing had been dropped haphazardly across the room, likely over the course of several days judging by the piles.

Most importantly, perhaps, the bed was occupied.

Voria crept closer and slowly raised a hand to cast, or to counterspell if needed. The woman in the bed stirred, and blinked sleepily up in Voria's direction as she rose into a sitting position and the scarlet coverlet fell away. She had thick, dark hair, and almond eyes, and Voria would place her somewhere in her mid-thirties. A mid-thirties human, anyway. This woman could be any age, if she were some other race.

"Who are you, and what are you doing in my chambers?" Voria demanded. She suspected that this was an illusion, or a dream, or whatever Shaya had pulled her into. But she needed to play along, and see where it led.

No answer. Unsurprisingly, the woman seemed unable to see Voria.

The woman dragged herself reluctantly from bed, and cradled her head in her hands. She gave a groan, and reached for the bottle on the nightstand. After a futile shake she dropped the empty bottle to the carpet with a sigh.

"Magic it is," the woman slurred as she wove a path to the nightstand. Her accent was most definitely Shayan, though it was more clipped than Voria's.

The woman took a deep breath when she reached the nightstand, and still seemed utterly oblivious to Voria's presence, suggesting that Voria was witnessing a memory. The woman sat in the chair before the mirror, and slowly raised her hands to her temples. She sketched no sigil, but potent, golden energy flowed down her fingers and into her head.

"Ahhhh." The woman's eyes fluttered open as the glow died. "Much better. That third bottle was definitely a mistake." She scratched the back of her neck, and slowly rose. "I'm pretty sure I've got something important going on today."

The air next to Voria shimmered, and a spectral shade appeared, translucent and pale. It strongly resembled the woman in front of the mirror, but Voria sensed that this version was older, and had seen a great deal more loss. It could only be one person.

"Shaya?" Voria ventured.

The ethereal woman nodded. "Or as close as you're going to get. I'm a shade. A creation I picked up from that blasted Wyrm. They're quite useful as contingency plans, as this meeting has demonstrated."

Voria took that in, and tried to decide how to proceed. "So you have all of Shaya's memories?"

"Effectively." The shade shrugged. "I was made about two months prior to her death, so everything she felt at the end...well, I can only imagine." The ghostly woman shuddered, and looked at the younger version of herself with an obvious swell of pity.

"And her." Voria nodded to the woman at the nightstand. She struggled to keep judgement from her tone, and evidently she failed. "She's the younger version of you?"

"Yes, well, in my defense I'd been at war for decades." Shaya winked at Voria. She *winked*. "I've heard the thoughts and prayers of your people, Voria. I know about the religion they established. A real shame, that. I'm sorry it morphed into something that hurt you personally, and your family."

Voria licked her lips. She was still phrasing a reply when the Memory-Shaya rose from the desk and exited the quarters. Voria hurried after her.

Shaya sauntered up the hallway whistling a catchy tune, one Voria didn't recognize. She headed for the bridge, and Voria followed. So did the shade.

"You must have picked this memory for a reason." Voria quickened her step, and narrowed the gap to Shaya. "Why? What is she about to do?"

"Krox is coming again, isn't he?" the shade asked.

Voria nodded soberly as she watched Shaya enter the very same amphitheater she'd been in not more than an hour ago—well, an hour, assuming time passed linearly here.

"Yes. Krox is coming," Voria admitted. The pain and anxiety came flooding back, the understanding of just how doomed her world really was, with only her as a fragile shield. "And I need to be there to stop him. I lack the means, and it terrifies me."

"As it terrified me." The shade delivered the same look of pity to Voria that she'd given to the memory they were following. "As you are no doubt aware...gods come in varying degrees of strength. Krox is an elder god, the sort of thing that helped forge the universe countless eons ago. Even a fraction of his power will be nearly impossible to overcome, and for you to stand a chance you must undergo an investiture of divine power. You must consume what I have left, and draw from the faith of your followers. The resulting power will elevate you to the lowest rung of godhood. It may not be enough, but unless things are a good deal easier than when I went through this, I suspect you'll have to make do with whatever you can come up with. Gods like Inura are, in my experience, incredibly unreliable. You'll have to work with what you've got, just like I did."

The shade nodded toward Shaya, who had stridden out onto the stage. Inura's unmistakable form was already waiting there, his leathery wings arching above him. Long, white hair cascaded down slender shoulders covered in tiny scales, almost human, but so far removed. The Wyrm-god beckoned impatiently at Shaya with one hand. The other held Ikadra's unmistakable golden length, his sapphire blazing with magic.

Shaya took her time crossing the stage, and didn't increase her pace an iota.

Voria smiled. "It's somehow comforting to know that I'm

not the only one who's put up with arrogant gods. And it's nice seeing her—you, I guess—thumb your nose at Inura."

"I detest that Lizard," the shade whispered conspiratorially. "He's even more smug than the rest of them, but he's on our side, at least. Virkonna used to serve as a stabilizing influence, but ever since her mother...well she's withdrawn from the war entirely."

Voria fell silent and focused on the proceedings. Inura had used the same term, investiture, to describe what she'd need to do. She was about to see the process, which is exactly what she'd hoped to discover.

Shaya finally reached Inura, though she looked more than a little queasy.

Inura wore his fury plainly, his features twisting into inhuman rage. "Do you have any idea how important today is? Nefarius comes, mortal. If we are not prepared we will be scoured away."

Shaya's eyebrows knit together like thunderclouds heralding a storm. Her eyes went frosty and she glared at the Wyrm-god.

"If you don't like the candidate," Shaya began quietly, "then you don't offer her the job. You want me to walk? Fine." She turned and began retracing her steps.

"You're refusing an investiture?" Inura's jaw fell open, and he eyed Shaya with clear disbelief.

Shaya kept walking, the pants of her uniform swishing together as she approached the doorway leading back to the corridor.

"Wait!" Inura thundered, his voice echoing across the entire amphitheater, out across the crowd. Silence fell, total and complete.

Shaya paused, then slowly turned to face Inura. Her features were calm, but it was the deceptive calm of a riptide—placid on the surface, yet turbulent below. Voria could feel the woman's rage. "Say what you're going to say, Wyrm."

Inura's lips pulled back in a snarl. "Do not speak to me like—"

"Like you're an up-jumped lizard playing at godhood?" Shaya thundered, seizing the conversation. Her hand shot up and she sketched an amplification spell. Her voice rolled out over the audience, and from the spell she'd cast Voria suspected that Inura's voice would likewise be amplified. She wanted the audience to hear their dispute. "I will speak to you any damned way I please, Inura. I've earned that right over three decades of war. Where were you when our world burned? Where was the last dragonflight at Osmium? I kept the Vagrant Fleet together. I led our people. We have been hunted, and if you really are a god, you're a poor one. You've done nothing to shield us from Nefarius. Nothing but slow our destruction."

The woman's fury spoke volumes. What must she have been through?

Voria had so many questions. How much time elapsed between this moment and Shaya's death? Was this before Krox had become their enemy? Apparently they overcame Nefarius at some point, but how? She stifled her questions, and focused on the conversation. One thing at a time. First she needed to understand this investiture, and then perhaps she could seek other answers.

Inura's jaw worked, but before he could respond, Shaya spoke again. "If you want to give me a slice of your power, then I will take it. I will use it to shield these people, to keep them alive and fighting, just as I always have. But don't pretend that you're doing me some sort of favor. Don't act as if making me a minor god is anything other than painting an even larger target on my back. Talifax already wants me dead, and now Nefarius will too."

"You're right." Inura's wings drooped, and something like sympathy entered his slitted gaze. As expected, Shaya's spell carried his words to the audience. "We are taught that investiture is a holy gift. My own was delivered to me by my mother, a gift she only gave eight times in the whole of her enormous lifespan. Every Wyrm aspires to it, as it is the pinnacle of our existence. The idea that it is an unwelcome burden is...unthinkable."

"It isn't that we aren't grateful," Shaya said. She folded her arms, and stared at the god like an equal, all quiet dignity. It was the first glimpse Voria had seen of the woman Shaya would eventually become. "But I'd remind you that my people were never part of any dragonflight. We've had to, for good or ill, determine our own destiny. And whether you give me power or not, I will do everything I can to ensure that my people always retain that self-reliance. Gods can't save us. We need to save ourselves."

Inura gave a disquieting frown, full of razored fangs. "Let us be about this. The ritual is short, but it will require the aid of your people. Not just those in this room, but every last mortal in the fleet around us. They must believe in you, Shaya, or this will not work."

The first crack in Shaya's confidence appeared, and Voria couldn't blame her. No one could control how an entire people felt about them, and if Shaya's people were anything like Voria's then there would be a lot of contention.

Shaya took a deep breath, and her gaze rose to meet Inura's. "They'll support me. How does this work?"

"It's a fairly simple process." Inura reached back absently and plucked Ikadra from where the golden staff had been hovering in the air. The staff was smaller than she was used to, about a half meter shorter, though otherwise identical. Inura offered it to Shaya. "This is Ikadra, my latest creation. He's young, and impressionable. Please refrain from ruining him, if possible. He has a vital role to fill, many millennia from now."

"Hi there," Ikadra pulsed. His voice young and friendly. "Nice to meet you, Mrs. Shaya. I'll be guiding you through the investiture today. All you have to do is hold me, and stand over in that ring on the center of the stage."

Voria noticed a circle of runes that had been drawn on the floor. They were a standard Circle of Eight, but within each sigil lay hundreds of tinier sigils. The circle, despite its small size, might be the most complex she'd ever seen. It had a permanent feel to it, and she suspected she'd find the same in her version of the *Spellship*.

Shaya moved to stand in the circle, and patted the staff. "So I guess I get to keep you afterwards. You like jokes, Ikadra?"

Ikadra's sapphire pulsed slowly. "Uh, I don't know. I've never heard one."

"Focus," Inura snapped. Whatever momentary sympathy he'd expressed had evaporated. "Let us be about this."

Shaya took a deep breath, and then nodded. "Okay, I'm ready. What do I have to do?"

"Survive." Inura raised a hand and began to sketch. Voria studied each motion carefully, knowing she'd likely have to duplicate this spell later. Most were *life* or *air*, though *water* and *spirit* were involved as well.

The spell was perhaps sixth level, and the idea that she'd be required to cast it was terrifying. The sigils quickly fused, and a wave of brilliant golden light burst out over the audience. That wave suddenly reversed, and a tide of magical energy flowed from the audience, into the circle containing Shaya.

Oceans of power flowed into Ikadra's sapphire, far more than the audience alone could provide. Voria cocked her head, wondering where the extra was coming from. She glanced at Inura, and while a potent quantity of life streamed from him to Shaya, there was no way it could account for the sheer volume.

"Come," the shade said, speaking for the first time since the ritual had begun.

The amphitheater fell away, and her perspective spun as she left the *Spellship* and flitted into the void above it. She didn't feel the cold, any more than she needed to breathe in a memory.

Her new perspective stopped and she inspected the *Spellship* and the surrounding fleet. Thousands upon thousands of vessels in all shapes and sizes dotted an unfamiliar system. Most resembled sleek Inuran ships, though they were different enough that they belonged in another era. There were so many of them.

A wave of pure, brilliant, white light burst from one, and then another, and then dozens, and then hundreds. Every ship sent a ray of light toward the *Spellship*, the united voices of an entire culture pouring their hopes, and dreams, and their faith into the drunken woman Voria had observed.

The light concentrated on the *Spellship*, building in a corona until Voria had to shield her eyes against the brilliance. It exploded outward, a pulse of magic that rippled through the entire fleet. When it faded a towering woman stood near the center of the fleet, a colossal version of Shaya, comprised completely of light.

The shade materialized next to her. "I'll never forget that

day. It changed nothing, in the end, but it gave my people hope."

Voria faced the woman, the ghost of the mother of her entire culture. "Thank you, Shaya. I know what I have to do now."

19

SYMBOLIC REPRESENTATION

By the time Crewes limped down into the crater his feet had been sliced to ribbons. He kept walking mechanically forward, his teeth gritted, and short, fast breaths coming through his nostrils with every agonizing step. Each one brought him closer to the immense amethyst glow. If not for the spear, he'd long since have fallen, and he increasingly trusted its steady length as he forced himself forward.

At some point, he realized, the branch had changed, and was now more of a staff. The surface was the same, but now lined with intricately carved pictograms, the kind he'd seen both in the Temple of Van and the Temple of Shi. Together those pictograms seemed to tell a story, but Crewes was too tired and in too much pain to try to puzzle that crap out. The changes to the tip of the staff were easier to process. The jagged end was now a flat, black stone. Obsidian, if he had to guess. It was a real spear now.

The ghost leopard continued to shadow him, and when his feet finally stopped obeying, and he stood swaying in place, it began to pace impatiently across a clearing ahead of him. Crewes licked parched lips, and glared at the cat. "That light ain't going anywhere, and I need a minute."

The cat gave a low whine.

"Gods. You're almost as bad as the major." Crewes forced himself back into motion, and started following the cat. He had no idea when he'd stopped assuming it would attack him, or when it had transformed into him following the thing.

But the cat seemed to know where it was going, and he could see its shadow up ahead, silhouetted by the strange amethyst glow.

Crewes held up a hand and studied it. The way the light played on his hand wasn't odd or anything, but wherever it touched his skin tingled. The magic was quieter than *fire*, but also more insidious. He could feel it seeping into him, more and more the closer he came to the Catalyst. Was it him, or was the magic getting stronger with every pulse?

His head began to spin, and suddenly the world canted drunkenly. He fell onto his back in a patch of damp jungle debris, and found himself staring up through a break in the trees. The night sky filled his vision, countless stars backlit by the swirling pink energy that bubbled up around him.

It seeped into his body, and his consciousness began to expand. A riot of colors permeated everything, tree trunks suddenly glistening with multicolored tapestries. *Dream* magic had washed over them continuously for so long that it had seeped into the wood, and into the soil.

And into Crewes.

As he watched, a scene began to play out in the sky. It was a battle on a scale that dwarfed any of the scrapes he'd been in, and he'd seen a lot. On one side of the sky lay a pulsing, red star, its malevolence both terrifying and somehow enticing. Before that star stood a protective god, his body as large as a planet. The god was a disembodied torso, basically, with a well-muscled body.

That body was translucent, and somehow comprised of cosmic dust, and magic. Crewes felt the familiar call of *fire*, and the more insidious song of *dream*. He realized he was staring at the being who'd spawned the twins, Shi and Van. At one time they'd apparently been united.

Arrayed against these two gods were dozens of smaller gods, supported by hundreds of Wyrms. The cosmic being, Shivan, towered over the smaller gods, but it did not save him. Wyrms streaked at him from all directions, and to his shock Crewes realized he recognized the largest. "If that don't make a man feel small, I don't know what does."

It was Drakkon, the water Wyrm's massive bulk made tiny next to an elder god. Drakkon dodged a fist as the god lashed out, but the blow crushed several slower Wyrms. The cloud of remaining dragons rose up around the god, stinging, biting, and casting, like insects against an armored warrior.

Crewes didn't pretend to understand the magic he was seeing. He wasn't a true mage or a war mage, or none of that. He was just a tech mage. But he knew the battle playing out was one that had shaped the sector for centuries. Maybe longer.

In time the battle turned against the cosmic god, and while many of the assaulting Wyrms had been slain, enough remained to finish him. They pierced his skin, disappearing inside, where they evidently wreaked havoc.

His body thrashed wildly back and forth, twisting and arching as he struggled to reach the smaller gods tearing him apart from the inside. A hot, angry tear appeared in his midsection, and began to spread across his entire body.

Shivan began to tumble from orbit, twisting slowly

toward the jungle where Crewes still lay. As the body descended it split, one half pure *fire*, a flame that Crewes knew better than his own face. Van, his very first Catalyzation.

The other half fell to the northern hemisphere, the amethyst shard kicking up a spray of intense magic as it created the very crater that he'd been walking in. Where, in theory, he was lying on his back, but somehow also seeing it play out.

It was maddening. "Man, I hate this shit. What did spider-bro-chick call it? My 'reductive' world view. I kinda like not having to care about this crap."

A low, feline growl came from less than a meter away where the cat sat on its haunches. The amethyst energy swirled around it, seeping in just as it had with Crewes. The glow built, and a distant song swam out of the jungle. The energy grew brighter, and brighter, then abruptly faded.

When it dissipated the cat was gone. In its place stood a set of Mark XI armor. The surface now had an iridescent sheen it had lacked before. He climbed to his feet with a groan, and reached down to pick up his spear. Only there was no spear. There was a gods-damned spellcannon in its place, right where the spear had been sitting.

His spellcannon, with the same iridescent sheen the armor had. "I hate this symbolic representation crap. What in the actual fu—"

"You have received her blessing." Sarala's musical voice came from the jungle. A moment later it came from an entirely different section. "You bear her mark now, Linus."

"Man, I hate this woo woo shit. Can you just stand still for a minute?" Crewes moved to his armor and sketched a *void* sigil in front of the chest. He stepped inside, and winced as his lacerated skin came into contact with the interior. He took several rapid breaths, and his eyes teared up from the pain. "Does this mean we can get out of here? I don't have to like...talk to the goddess or anything? That's what I've had to do in the past."

She finally materialized before him, her cowl down, exposing her face. "You've spoken to a goddess?" Sarala blinked her large eyes at him, and Crewes had a very uncomfortable thought that seemed totally inappropriate to the situation. Her long, flowing robe obscured, but it did nothing to hide the curves.

"Yeah, well, I wouldn't recommend it." He reached down with a grunt and hefted his spellcannon. "So weird that it became a spear. Of course, it was weird that I had to truck around the jungle buck-ass naked."

Sarala gave a laugh at that. "I told you, you needed to approach Shi with nothing but your own tools. You have done so, and learned the secret no one who has not initiated with both twins knows."

"That they used to be one god?" As Crewes watched, the ivory double doors appeared behind her. They appeared in the space between blinks, as if they'd always been there.

"Shivan, he was called." She pursed her lips, and her eyes took on a far away look. "I have communed often, and learned a bit of his history. But it is still Shi that I serve. And Shi does not dwell in the past. She seeks the future."

"Uh, okay." Crewes didn't really understand all the god machinations. Makinations? Hells if he knew. "Since I passed her test, does that mean she's gonna let me take the Outrider chick? Captain's got a deal with this Wyrm that's been following us around like a stray dog, and I'm real eager to send it packing, if you know what I mean. He'll leave as soon as we get her back."

He took a painful step toward the ivory doors. Hopefully

Bord was still on the other side, because damned if he didn't miss that smart-ass kid's *life* magic.

"You now possess the magic to retrieve her," Sarala explained. She shifted into a cloud of mist, and swirled around his armor. "I will take you into her dream. She must be woken, and it is a delicate process."

"Of course it is." He shook his head, then spat onto the jungle floor. "Can't ever be easy, can it?"

20

MEMORY LOOP

Rhea glanced over her shoulder at the towering vessel, unique among all ships in the cosmos. Their charge was safe. The *Spellship* stood gleaming, ready for battle, just as she had for millennia.

"Down, Rhea!" Her father's voice cracked. Rhea instinctively obeyed, and dove for the ground.

A moment later a void bolt slammed into the wall above her, disintegrating a large chunk of pristine metal. She was tough, but that spell would have killed even her.

"Thanks," she called to her father as she rolled behind another pillar. She drew her spellrifle from her void pocket, and fed it *air* to increase its already enhanced accuracy. "Time to push back?"

Kheross, her father, crouched behind a neighboring pillar, his dark hair whipping about him in the breeze. He hefted a pair of wicked axes, his signature weapons. "Past time. I'll go in hard on the right. As soon as they commit to me, end them."

He didn't wait for her response, nor should he have. They'd honed their teamwork over decades, and she was ready as he sprinted around his pillar and into the open. A hail of void bolts streaked out of the enemy ranks, the black-armored hatchlings eagerly focusing on Kheross. Every last one wanted him dead, with good reason. His reputation had been built kill by kill, for centuries.

Rhea leaned around the pillar and lined up her first shot. These hatchlings were tough, so she thumbed the selector to level four. That would drain her quick, but she was fairly certain none of these bastards was cool enough to walk away from a level four spell.

She selected the Aranthar's Piercing Spike spell, which drew equally from *fire, earth, void,* and *air*. The spell was costly, but their founder had used it to end countless Wyrms, and his descendants had kept using it for a reason.

Rhea stroked the trigger, and the bolt shot into the closest hatchling. She fired a second, and then a third, all at different targets. All three hatchlings were still focused on Kheross, and as she'd hoped, all three lacked the magical defenses to survive. Each slumped to the deck, pools of dark blood flowing from the hideous wounds her spells blasted into their bodies.

Her father danced through the surviving hatchlings, and their dark blood sprayed across his crimson armor as he made short work of his opponents. A few moments later eight draconic corpses lay steaming on the metal decks.

"Do we press the offensive?" She called as she scanned the corridor for any more hatchlings. Nothing yet.

"No." Kheross turned to the behemoth behind them, and she looked again too. The *Spellship* was awe-inspiring, pristine and pure, even after all this time. "Our mission isn't to kill the spawn of Nefarius, much as we enjoy it. We're to protect the ship, at all costs. Nothing gets inside. This ship is far, far more important than either of us. We don't leave this room."

The control room overlooking the hangar flashed suddenly as spells were exchanged inside. The glass shattered, and a blue- and white-garbed Outrider came crashing through. Urslaa, her elder sister, landed in a crouch, then rolled to the side as a void bolt slammed into the area she'd just vacated.

Rhea's rifle snapped to her shoulder almost of its own accord, and she sighted over the hole where her sister had emerged. A scaly face appeared, and she adjusted her aim to center the crosshair over its heart. She stroked the trigger, and her last fourth level spell took the creature full in the chest. The force blasted it backwards, and out of sight.

"I was gonna wait until you were done to interrupt," came a sudden voice to her right, "but it looks like this might go on for a while."

Rhea whirled to see the strangest sight she'd ever seen. A man stood before her in unfamiliar spellarmor, his skin dark, like mahogany. He cradled a spellcannon, and while it seemed primitive, that didn't mean it couldn't kill.

"Are you an ally?" she asked, cautiously of course. There was something familiar about him. She'd met him before, if briefly. He'd stood over her bed. Now why would he have been doing that?

"Yeah." He propped his cannon on an armored shoulder. "And I'm gonna need you to come with me."

"Do you have a name?" Rhea plastered her back to another pillar, and scanned for targets. The hatchlings were all down...until another wave came. "You might want to get into cover. The spawn of Nefarius will kill everyone here, and they won't care that you're not a part of the last Dragonflight."

"Uh, I'm pretty sure they can't see me. This ain't real. You're in a dream, or some shit." The dark-skinned man raised his free hand and pointed the armored gauntlet at something she'd only just noticed. A set of ivory doors carved with unfamiliar glyphs.

The doors touched something in her memory. "I've... seen those before. Been through them. A long time ago, I think."

"Not that long." The dark-skinned warrior snorted. "I guess they put you under to help with the healing, or to program you, or some other crazy shit. Don't much matter. I'm here to collect you and bring you back to your scaly dad. Name's Crewes, by the way."

"My father is right there." She nodded in Kheross's direction. "And I don't understand what you mean by 'scaly'."

"Listen, lady," the man began, clearly exasperated. "I ain't got answers. The captain has those. You want to know what's up, you talk to Aran. I'm just supposed to bring you back. I don't much like your dad, but he's awfully keen to see you." He pointed at her father, where he crouched behind the next pillar, seemingly unaware of this Crewes. "That's just a memory. A fragment, kind of. He ain't real. Now come on. This place gives me swamp ass."

Rhea froze. No more spawn had come around the corner, and neither her sister or her father had moved...at all since Crewes had appeared. They were frozen in place. Could he be right, and if so, where in the depths was she? Could this really be a dream? What an awful form of torture.

"Very well, I will trust you. For now." Rhea opened her void pocket and dropped the spellrifle inside. She gestured at the ivory doors. "You first, so I know it's safe."

"Sure." Crewes shrugged. He pushed at one of the doors with an armored hand and it opened easily, allowing his bulky armor to slip through. On the other side lay an...entry hall of some sort. The walls were cut from planks of sturdy wood that had an ancient look to it. Strange spears and shields lined the walls, archaic and useless on the modern battlefield.

Several people clustered near the middle of the temple, if that's what it was. Rhea's attention was drawn to a familiar one, who so very closely resembled her father. He had the same hair. The same scarlet armor. Likely even the same axes. But there was one violent change. His eyes burned with the hellish purple of the spawn. Somehow, her father had been turned by Nefarius.

"I'm not going with you...not to that...thing." She sneered at the fallen wretch that might have once been her father, but no longer. He hadn't seen her yet. She could still refuse to step through.

"Lady, I can already tell we're going to get along." Crewes's face broke into a wide smile. "I don't have much love for your pops either. But Captain said to bring you, so we need to get moving."

"Captain?" She asked, unsure who he might mean. She gave the others a cursory glance, and her jaw went as slack as a raw recruit when she recognized another man. "Goddess below...that's the first Outrider. Aranthar himself."

Crewes leaned in, and sized her up. He gave a conspiratorial whisper. "I'll tell you what. Do me a favor, kid. Keep the hero worship to yourself. The captain hates it, and he got enough of it back on Virkon. Best if you act like you have no idea who he is."

It was so much to take in, the revelation that her father had fallen, and that somehow she'd ended up in a timeline with the living version of the man who'd risen to godhood, then died defending the order she'd been born into. Numbness washed through her, and she wished she could curl up and hide.

But she couldn't. Like it or not, this had to be faced.

Rhea rose and gave the other version of her father, the memory version she realized, a final, longing look. She knew in her heart he wasn't real, and wallowing in an illusion was irresponsible. Outriders never quit.

She prayed that some fragment of the man he'd been had survived the corruption, even as she knew in her heart that he hadn't. He'd been the one to teach her that loved ones, once infected, must be put down, or driven off.

"All right, Crewes." Rhea took a deep breath, and nodded at the dark-skinned man. "Lead the way. I will feign ignorance, if you think it best."

21

CONDUIT

The Temple of Shi made Aran uncomfortable. There were too many entrances and exits, and a whole load of unfamiliar cries from the trees surrounding the structure. He blamed that for throwing him off his game.

Only after the doors closed behind the sergeant did Aran realize he'd neglected to ask how long this trial would take, and what they should do in the meantime. He surveyed the company. Bord stood well away from Nara, his arms crossed while he leaned nonchalantly against the marble wall. Nara stood a few feet away, and was obviously pretending not to be hurt by it.

She brushed a lock of dark hair behind her ear, exposing her freckled cheek. Damn if she didn't look innocent, which only put his back up more.

"If these priests," Kheross rumbled suddenly, "do not deliver my daughter soon, then I promise you I will level this entire wretched temple."

"I'm sure you will," Aran replied absently. He didn't have the mental energy to deal with Kheross's posturing. He needed to focus on what came next. Very soon he'd get a call from the governor asking him to join their new fleet. Was helping that fleet pillage a Catalyst worth gaining their support against Krox? How did he make a choice like that? "Nara, do you know off the top of your head how long it will take to get from here to the Skull?"

Nara drummed her fingers along the ebony haft of her staff, the fire rubies slowly rotating above her. She looked up suddenly, the soft light from above making her eyes shine. "A little over three days from Yanthara, in the *Talon* at least."

"And from there to Shaya? About seven more?" Aran had a vague understanding of relative distances in the depths, but Nara's gift from Neith meant she could probably tell him to the minute when they'd arrive.

"Six and a half," Nara corrected. "If you allow for a day to take care of whatever you need at the Skull, we're looking at twelve to thirteen days to arrive at Shaya." She cleared her throat, and tried to hold his gaze, but then broke eye contact instead. "You're trying to figure out if we'll arrive before Krox, aren't you? I know he's coming. And I know we have to be there, whether we like it or not. Frit might be able to tell you how long until he arrives."

"I thought she wasn't in contact with anyone among the Krox." Aran rested his hand on Narlifex's hilt, and the blade thrummed.

"She isn't." Nara rolled her eyes, the gesture clearly meant for herself. "I'm an idiot sometimes. She's a flame reader. She can use divination."

"Maybe." Aran shook his head and gave a half laugh. "You understand why I can't trust any intel I get from her. Besides, I'll take Voria's estimate over Frit's any day. Voria's got the *Spellship*, and the gifts our...friend in the depths gave us." He couldn't say Neith's name of course.

The ivory doors swung open with a loud creak, smothering the conversation. Bord snapped to attention, and Kheross uncrossed his arms. The Wyrm began flexing his hands, and Aran half feared he'd summon his axes.

An armored figure appeared in the doorway, and at first Aran wasn't certain it was Crewes. The sergeant's armor was similar, but the differences were notable. It had grown slightly, and many of the harder edges had softened into metallic curves. But the largest change was the color. The armor had taken on an obviously magical glow that make it appear ethereal and ghostly...ghostly pink.

Bord's raucous laughter echoed through the temple, and he stabbed a finger at the sergeant. "You musta pissed someone off good. Your armor...is the prettiest thing—" The wheezing laughter deepened. "—the prettiest thing I've ever seen. Wait 'til Kez sees this."

Crewes stalked over to Bord, and his faceplate snapped open. He leaned down over Bord, whose self-preservation finally began to kick in. The laughter wilted to a nervous chuckle, and Crewes didn't say a word. All he did was scowl.

"It's not that bad," Aran offered. But it was that bad, and as soon as the sergeant found a mirror, he'd know it. "What happened in there?"

"One moment, sir." Crewes leaned in even closer to Bord. "My armor is a nice, manly magenta."

"But, it's—" Bord unwisely began.

"What color is my armor, specialist?" Crewes growled.

"Uh, magenta, sir." Bord amended.

"That's what I thought." Crewes gave Bord one last glare, then turned to Aran. "Mission accomplished, sir. Took some doing. Sorry you had to wait so long."

"So long?" Aran raised an eyebrow, and nodded at the ivory doors. "It's been ten minutes, tops."

Sarala emerged a moment later in her multicolored robes. The fabric swished as she moved to stand next to Crewes, then placed a gloved hand on his armor. "We ask that you keep the nature of your vision of Shi to yourself, though there is no official prohibition about speaking of the journey."

A third figure emerged from the doorway. Aran had only really seen Rhea once before, when she'd been asleep in his quarters on the *Talon*. Like Nara she had dark hair, but the similarities ended there. This woman was taller, and physically stronger. Her arms bore the corded muscle earned over long hours of swordplay, and he bet if he inspected her palms he'd find callouses.

She walked like a warrior, despite the fact that she bore no armor or weaponry. Her expression betrayed no emotion, not even curiosity. She scanned the room like a professional, assessing them all in a few heartbeats.

"You." She nodded to Aran. "The others seem to defer to you, if their stance is any indication. I take it you're in charge?"

"Rhea..." Kheross said, his tone agonized. He took a single step closer, but made no move to embrace her. "You're alive, and...unburdened."

Rhea spared a single disgusted glance for her father, and the disdain there stopped him in his tracks. Aran wouldn't have thought it possible to pity Kheross, but in that moment he did.

Rhea's eyes flashed with *air* magic, mini-storms playing across the irises. "I can smell Nefarius's stink on you, father. No, not father. Kheross. You are no longer any kin of mine." She turned back to Aran, and squared her shoulders as if fortifying herself for a last stand. "I realize you've just met me, but if you have any sense you will kill him. You can no longer trust Kheross. He's a conduit to Nefarius. He should be put down. Now."

Kheross made a choking sound and gawked at his daughter. That seemed like a fair response to your own daughter calling for your immediate execution. His tainted eyes closed, and he exhaled a long, slow sigh. He wiped the back of his hand across his mouth, and then turned away from his daughter, for what Aran imagined would be the last time. "Thank you, Captain. You have lived up to your end of our bargain. Our accord is at an end. Where we go from here is up to you. I would just as soon take my leave, and never cross paths again."

He didn't have the leverage to afford pity, not in the face of everything.

"What do you mean by conduit?" Aran demanded, meeting Rhea's gaze, and finding a challenge there. He settled his hand instinctively around Narlifex's grip.

"A conduit is an extension of Nefarius, infected with his taint." She moved to stand next to Crewes, and he realized she was almost as tall as the sergeant. "The blood has seeped into the thing that used to be my father. Everything he sees, everything he observes, everything he thinks...all of it belongs to Nefarius. The goddess, or god, or whatever the depths it is...it's listening to us right now. And the longer you keep him around, the more it knows. We saw this corruption often, and there were only two responses. The weak exiled their corrupted, and most quickly came to regret it. The strong did the merciful thing, and killed them. This taint will consume him, eventually. But long after that happens Kheross will continue to act like my father, and like your friend, if that's what he is to you. Nefarius used our emotions against us, so we learned to live without them."

That knocked him back a step. No damaging secrets

leapt out at him that Kheross could have relayed, but the idea that everything was available to an enemy like that was horrifying.

"So he's only dangerous if he's around us," Aran pointed out. "If we let him go, and he leaves, then he can't watch us any more and we don't need to worry about him being a conduit. I don't like turning on an ally. What do you think, Sergeant?"

Crewes blinked a couple times. "Me?" He studied Kheross silently for a long moment, then scuffed the temple floor with his boot. The armor left a divot in the stone, and while Aran couldn't see Sarala's face, the eyes told him everything he needed to know. She was pissed. Crewes cleared his throat. "I know I'm always starting shit with that smug bastard, but a deal's a deal, sir. Scaly here lived up to his end. He saved our asses on New Texas, and he ain't stabbed us in the back yet. We ain't got no beef with him."

Aran folded his arms and eyed Kheross. Crewes wasn't wrong, but leaving an enemy at their backs was risky. If Rhea was right, and he had no reason to suspect she wasn't, then Kheross was a ticking bomb. Which was more important, honor or pragmatism? Could he afford a mix of both?

"Kheross is a threat," Aran began, deciding right then that his principles were still worth something, "and if we let him live we might come to regret it. Or, we might not. He's done right by us. He's helped us. If not for him none of us would be standing here. I'm not willing to compromise my principles for a maybe. Kheross, you already said it. Our deal is at an end. You're a Wyrm, so you can find your own way off world. Don't make trouble, and don't bring yourself to our attention, and we don't have to be enemies. In fact, do everyone here a favor and leave the sector. Find a home somewhere else, far away from all of this. You've been cleansed by the best *life* mages on Shaya. I have to imagine that's bought you some time. Enjoy what freedom you can."

"Thank you, Captain." Kheross nodded gratefully, his dark hair ruffled by the wind passing through the temple's spacious windows. "I don't wish to provoke your ire, but...I have a final request before I take my leave."

"Oh?" Aran raised an eyebrow.

Crewes folded his arms, and scowled hard at Kheross.

Kheross glared right back, but directed his words to Aran. "Take care of Rhea. Accept her as your first Outrider. She can aid you, and you can give her what she needs most...a family."

"Done," Aran agreed. They were recruiting, after all, and from the looks of it she had a lot of experience. Experience they needed. She might even be able to teach him some things, and he'd take all the help he could get.

Kheross gave his daughter one last agonized look, then raised a long, delicate finger. He sketched a series of interlocking *void* sigils, and a Fissure tore the space next to him. He gave Rhea a final smile. "I'm proud of you."

"You're dead to me." Rhea started for the temple door, and didn't look back as Kheross stepped through and the Fissure snapped shut behind him.

22

NEEKO-KAN

Aran didn't release Narlifex's hilt until the Fissure had snapped shut behind Kheross. The blade pulsed disappointment. *Worthy foe.*

He hoped he never found out, not because he wasn't confident he could take the Wyrm, but rather because he didn't want to have to put down a one-time ally. He'd already had a belly full of betrayal.

"You'll come to regret that decision." Rhea shook her head, sadly. "My father is strong, one of the strongest Outriders in our time."

Bord maneuvered his scout armor a step closer, and eyes her curiously. "Outrider? You ain't got the slightest idea what you even are, do ya, love? Sir, are you gonna tell her?"

That innocent question left him no choice, really. Aran took a breath, and told the unvarnished truth. She seemed the sort that could handle it, and the last thing they needed was another lingering secret. "Your father was a Wyrm, Rhea. Not an Outrider. When the final battle for your world began he used a binding to alter your memory. You and your siblings were made to believe you were simple Outriders. It was a last-ditch effort to prevent Nefarius from taking you, from how Kheross told it."

Rhea took three calming breaths, and then looked down at herself. She closed her eyes, and her hands began to tremble. It must be an immense amount to process, and having been on the other end of a mindwipe he knew how it knocked your world into an unstable orbit.

By the time she opened her eyes the trembling had stopped. Her gaze now contained a resolve that had been lacking before. "Maybe what you're saying is true. Maybe it isn't. For now, I'll focus on my immediate problems. I have no unit, no armor, and no weaponry. If you give me a spellrifle, and tell me you're willing to oppose Nefarius, then I'm more than happy to follow you into battle."

"We've got several spare sets of armor on the ship. The rifle will be a little unfamiliar, but I'm sure you'll adjust quickly." Aran nodded at Crewes, and the sergeant took point. He moved his now-pink armor toward the exit, and Sarala followed him, talking in low tones. Aran glanced at Rhea as she fell into step next to him. "I don't have another spellblade to offer you, but I'm sure we can find you one when we make port at Shaya. And as far as hunting Nefarius, yeah, that's on the list. He's...compromised a friend of mine. First we've got to survive Krox, though. You help us do this, and Nefarius is next."

Aran didn't look at Nara, though he felt her tense at the mention of Nefarius. She hadn't really spoken, or made eye contact, since leaving the ship. Nara seemed content to fade into the background, and he didn't mind letting her. The more he thought about things, the less angry he felt. Not because what she'd done wasn't wrong, but because she seemed more worried that she might hurt Voria than about her own fate. It was possible it was an act, but his gut said otherwise.

The company paused at the temple doors, and Sarala took Crewes's gauntleted hand. Aran tried to avoid looking at them, and noticed that even Bord was trying to give them a bit of privacy. None of them could escape hearing what probably should have been a private moment.

"Linus, you have been given a great blessing." Sarala took the sergeant's gauntleted hand in her tiny one, but it was enough to get Crewes to pause and face her. He somehow managed dignified calm, despite the pink armor. Aran was proud of him, for more than one reason. The priestess gazed up at Crewes, and her tone was pleading. "Stay. Learn. You could be the strongest fire dreamer in a generation, and we're going to need a leader for what's to come. I have watched the flames, and I have dreamed of the future. Terrible darkness approaches. A Great War that will swallow the galaxy in flame and death."

Crewes smiled grimly at her, and rested his spellcannon on the shoulder of his armor. "And I'm the terrible thing that's waiting to deal with the baddies when they show up. I'd love to stay, Sarala. But I got a god to embarrass. I'm sure you could teach me to dream, or whatever, but unless you can help me fight better..."

"Dream is stronger than you give it credit for." Sarala gave a musical laugh, and raised a hand. Aran felt...something. An elusive magic that he himself did not posses. *Dream*, no doubt. A tendril reached out to Crewes, and touched his armor.

A swirl of purple-pink energy enveloped Crewes, and when it faded his armor was just...gone. He stood there naked, his dark skin crisscrossed with cuts and abrasions. The swirl of magic pooled on the floor, and gradually resolved into a large feline. The leopard's dark fur was spotted, and it provided perfect camouflage for the local jungles.

The great cat promptly sat down and started cleaning itself, as utterly apathetic as any house cat.

Crewes stood there, naked as the day he was born, cradling his spellcannon. He stared at the cat in horror. "Nah, nah, nah. That is some *serious* bullshit. You can make my armor turn into a frigging cat? I thought that was just part of the dream, or whatever. It can't do that on its own, can it?"

The cat stopped licking itself and fixed Crewes with a baleful stare.

Sarala adopted a nearly identical one. "Of course she can, though she will not do so unless you ask her to. I...cheated. I have a bond with Shi, you see. Most mages cannot do what I have done here. As I said...if you wish to prevent it." She approached him and ran a single gloved finger down his massive forearm. "All you need do is stay and learn."

Crewes glanced down at his crotch, and his cheeks heated. "Yes, ma'am, but like I said, I got a war to fight first. But uh, I'll come back. Now, uh, how do I get the cat to be armor again?"

"The cat," Sarala said, rolling her eyes, "needs a name. And once you give her one then she will do as you ask, whenever you ask. Though I would not abuse the privilege. Ghost leopards are...fickle, much like Yantharan women."

"Oh man," Crewes muttered. He lowered his spellcannon to cover his midsection. "Not a great time to be put on the spot. Captain, you got any suggestions for a name?"

"No, but Nara might." He turned to her. She seemed surprised by the sudden attention, and crossed her arms uncomfortably. "Nara, what's ancient Virkonan for cat?"

"Neeko," she provided. "Neeko-kan if it's a kitten."

"That look like a kitten to you?" Crewes jerked a thumb at the leopard. It was the first time, Aran realized, that he'd spoken to Nara since she'd defected. "Anyway, it's good enough. All right, Neeko. Turn into armor again, and cover my junk."

The cat rose and gave a lazy stretch, licked itself a few times, then dissolved into a swirling whirlwind of pinkish magical energy. It coalesced around Crewes almost instantly, reforming into Mark XI spellarmor. Certainly far faster than Aran could don his own armor, or even the tainted Inuran stuff.

"Neeko is a strong name." Sarala's voice took on an affectionate warmth. "She will serve you well, and remember, she can go places you cannot. She will protect you, and bring you home safely so that you have no more excuses to avoid being alone with me."

Bord nearly turned purple with the effort of not laughing, and seemed immune to Aran's warning glare. He should have brought Kez.

Crewes ignored them all, and bent to scoop Sarala up. "I know tradition's important, and I gotta show you I'm interested." She squawked as he hefted her into the air, and delivered a soft kiss over the fabric covering her mouth. Then Crewes set her down, and took a step backward. "I will come back, once we're done dealing with Krox. You know there's always another baddie around the corner, and I wanna learn what you have to teach. All of it."

"I'll hold you to that." Sarala raised a hand to touch the fabric where Crewes had kissed her. "In the meantime I will give you a parting gift. Neeko serves you. If the color of your armor displeases you, ask her to change it."

"Yeah? Just like that?" Crewes looked down at the armor.

"Okay, Neeko, give me something menacing. None of that pink crap."

The surface of the armor rippled, and darkened into a deep crimson, almost black.

"Much better." Crewes gave a satisfied grin.

Aran's armor chimed and the HUD flashed to indicate an incoming missive. He accepted it, and an unfamiliar face filled the bottom of the screen. A cultured Inuran sat behind an enormous desk. His suit was immaculate, and probably cost as much as Aran's armor.

The white, frizzled hair, narrow face, and bulbous nose couldn't be more at odds with the office and the suit. He looked like all the discarded parts that had been tossed back in the genetic box.

"Hello, Captain." The man steepled his fingers, and gave a practiced smile. "I'm glad I was able to reach you. I understand that you may be otherwise engaged, but I convinced the governor to have you present at the signing."

"Signing?" Aran asked. He had a sinking feeling from the man's Inuran accent that he knew exactly who this was. "And you are? You haven't given me a name."

"Forgive me, Captain. I assumed you knew who I was." The man seemed genuinely surprised. "My name is Skare, and I represent the Inuran Consortium in this system. I'm here to oversee a sizable arms deal. We're presenting the Inurans with their fleet, and Austin would like you there to inspect it."

Aran hesitated. There was a trap, of that he was certain. He wanted a look at the ships, but there was no way the Inurans would offer that unless they stood to gain something. He kept his tone neutral. "Why are you contacting me instead of the governor's office?"

Skare cocked his head and smiled. "The governor is in a,

ah, private meeting with Matron Jolene. She's one of our most powerful shareholders. I believe you've met, and that you're familiar with her daughter?"

"Jolene is Voria's mother, right?" Aran confirmed. The governor was having a relationship with a woman four or five times his age? To each their own. "When and where is this inspection?"

"In orbit, Commander. I will have the coordinates sent to the *Talon*. As for time...as soon as is convenient." Skare gave a polite nod, and cancelled the missive.

Aran suppressed a sigh. He wasn't nearly as adept as Voria at political maneuvering, but he was going to need to learn quickly.

23

ONE MORE JOB

Kheross loathed the creature he had allowed himself to become. He swam through the void in a desolate system, reveling in his native form after so long cooped up as a human. He enjoyed the cold caress of the vacuum, which tingled against his scales, but today it provided no solace from the guilt and fear that gnawed at him.

Not because of anything he'd done, but rather because of what he feared Talifax would ask him to do. Of all the beings in the galaxy, only Talifax had ever inspired true fear. He was more real than Nefarius, more tangible than a dark goddess that Kheross had never even glimpsed, not even in his own timeline.

"You fear me," came a voice from the darkness, its origin somehow unidentifiable, echoing all around him, "because you know it was I who orchestrated the death of your world, your people, and your dear mother. Because you know that even in this timeline I will triumph, and that your only hope for survival lies in collusion."

Kheross spun in the darkness, his eyes narrowing. A star

glowed in the distance, the only celestial body in the system Talifax had asked him to meet in. There was nothing else, not even a meteor or comet. He appeared to be utterly alone.

"The fact that you can cloak your presence isn't all that impressive," Kheross bellowed. "Just another one of your parlor tricks. Nor will I ever grovel at your feet, defiler. You've summoned me here, and I've come, but I am not your plaything. What do you wish of me?"

He flared his wings high above him, reminding himself that he was no mere Wyrm. He was ancient and powerful. And while Talifax might be able to slay him, he could never break Kheross's will. He refused to be broken.

"I seek no conflict. Stem your ire, Wyrm." Talifax's bulky, black armor appeared in the darkness, perhaps a kilometer from Kheross. He appeared so small, not much bigger than most humans. As old as Kheross was he still had no idea what species Talifax had originated from. Something he'd never encountered, perhaps extinct now. "I have a task for you, one that requires no great betrayal."

"And what makes you think that I will do your bidding?" Kheross asked. He gave a dark smile, hoping that he could somehow bait Talifax into attacking. If he were to die, at least he would die clawing at the throat of the thing he hated most in the galaxy. "You have no leverage, Guardian of Nefarius. Now that Rhea is cleansed you have nothing I want."

"Really?" Talifax mused. He blinked closer, now no more than 200 meters distant. "You seek nothing for yourself? Not redemption, or salvation? Would you not like to be cleaned of my mother's dark touch?"

Kheross barked out a bitter laugh. "There's no way you

would free me. How desperate do you think I am, that I'd trust your word in any accord we make?"

Talifax's metallic laughter echoed through the void somehow, perhaps only a figment in Kheross's mind. He reached up and slowly removed his helmet, exposing a face that, Kheross would be willing to bet, no one had laid eyes on in centuries.

It wasn't immediately clear what species Kheross was looking at. Talifax's skin was a thick, leathery grey. Twin tusks of dull ivory jutted from his jaw, and a short, prehensile trunk wriggled where a nose would be. His eyes were large and dark, and they fixed on Kheross.

"The galaxy possesses little memory of my species," Talifax explained. "Some remnants remain, but my people were broken long before the last godswar. I watched them die, world by world swallowed by the darkness, as our endless empire finally fell." He paused, and fixed Kheross with those strangely unreadable eyes. "What I do in service of my mother must be done, but I remember my people. I have a shred of what you might call honor left, perhaps even more than you, fallen Wyrm. If you aid me in a single task, then I will withdraw mother's dark gift. I will rip the blood of Nefarius from you, and claim it for myself. You are cleansed, and I am further empowered. A fair bargain, yes?"

Kheross considered that. It sounded too good to be true, which meant it was. He flexed his wings, but suppressed his agitation. "And what task would I be required to perform in order for this...magnanimous cleansing?"

"I require you to open a door," Talifax gave back instantly. He replaced his helm, obscuring those odd features. "It must be opened at a precisely determined instant, and you must ensure that its occupant be freed to perform another task. Simply open that door, and return to me, and I will free you."

"Why can't you do it yourself?" Kheross's eyes narrowed. This sounded far too easy. Was he being expended?

"Quite the contrary." Talifax seemed amused. "You are not being expended. You've dealt fairly with me, and you are being rewarded. You wonder why I would do this. Why I would let you live. Because you are no threat, Kheross. Your friends and family will never believe that you are no longer my creature, and even if they did that would not erase your betrayals. You have no allies. No place in this war. So, you see, you are no threat. Take the deal, Kheross. Become an air Wyrm once more, and seek out your mother in this timeline. She still lives, you know, on Virkon. You can even attempt to prevent Nefarius from killing her. You'll have a purpose again."

Kheross agonized over his next words. He knew he couldn't trust Talifax, but there was little to lose. If he performed this errand, and Talifax was lying, then he'd be right back where he was, and no worse off. If he was telling the truth, then Kheross might be able to assume another Wyrm's identity, and start over on Virkon. He could have the one thing he believed impossible. A future.

If Talifax was honorable. That was a very large if.

24

INEVITABLE

Nara said nothing as Crewes led her back down to the *Talon*'s brig. She followed him meekly to the cell, and stepped inside without having to be asked.

"You wanna get that collar off?" Crewes asked. His spell-cannon rested on his shoulder, but the barrel was close enough that he could bring it to bear before she could start casting.

Nara reached up and touched the collar, and a jolt of pain prickled up her hand. She forced herself to keep touching it, and reminded herself that this was what Frit had lived like for her entire life. "I'd feel better if you left it on, to be honest."

Crewes's face showed a rare emotion, confusion, which quickly boiled into anger. He slapped the blue button on the wall next to the cell, and the bars crackled into existence. "Man, I just do not get you." He turned on his heel and stalked from the brig without another word or a backward glance.

Nara retreated to her bench, the cell's only furnishing

other than a toilet.

"What happened?" Frit's small voice came from the neighboring cell, and Nara looked up to find her friend at the bars.

"We went to the Temple of Shi," Nara explained quietly. She felt inexplicably exhausted, just drained, emotionally. "Crewes went into the Catalyst where Rhea was being held, which is, I guess, why they came to this world in the first place. They didn't tell me much beyond that. As you can imagine, none of them trust me anymore, and I can't really blame them."

Nara's emotions went brittle, and she sat perfectly still to avoid cracking. She badly wanted to let it all out, but the very last thing that would help her in this situation was a good cry. She needed to keep it together.

"Now what?" Frit asked, glancing at the doorway to the brig. "Are they taking us back to Shaya to be turned over to the new Tender?"

"If they do," Kaho interjected, rising from his own bench in the far cell and approaching the bars, "what is this Tender likely to do with us?"

"I don't know." Nara shrugged, then pulled her knees to her chest. "Aran didn't tell me where we're going, or what's happening. I didn't see much. I'm sorry."

"It's okay," Frit offered. "I'm sorry we're badgering you with questions. I keep forgetting that you're a prisoner, the same as us. They see you as the enemy too. I never thought I'd see that."

"Me either." Nara knew she'd given her friends cause, though. She looked up at Frit, then Kaho. "I promise I'll share anything that I learn."

Oddly, neither one was moving. At first Nara thought they were both just standing there, but as the seconds stretched she realized that they were unnaturally still. Frozen somehow.

"I have altered time in a bubble around us," Talifax's voice rumbled from the shadowed corner outside her cell. Had it been shadowed a moment ago?

Dark, bulky armor stepped from the shadows, and she shuddered as Talifax stepped into the light, as much as he ever could. She didn't know if it was an enchantment, or a property of the metal, but she never seemed to be able to stare at it for long.

"What do you want?" Nara asked wearily. "Did you come to gloat some more? We did what you wanted, and saved Colony 3, but it stops there. I'm not going to kill Voria."

"No?" Talifax asked mildly. He stepped closer to the bars. "You seem certain of that."

She hazarded a look at Frit, but her friend was still frozen, mouth open to form words.

"I find it curious that you still hold loyalty to the woman after your memories have been restored." Talifax's armor radiated an intense cold, enough that Nara's arms went to gooseflesh. "But either way, what you believe is irrelevant. I have examined every possibility, and prepared for every contingency. When the time comes, you *will* kill Voria, and then you will rise in her place."

Nara gave a short, bitter laugh. "I look forward to disappointing you. I'm wearing a collar, and I'm in the brig of one of the most secure ships in the sector. What makes you think I'll even have the opportunity?"

"I wonder," Talifax continued as if she hadn't spoken, "will your defiance continue when circumstances conspire to place you precisely where I wish you to be? Will you be able to deny your fate when it has grown so large you cannot escape it? I find the answer...tantalizing. I must know, and waiting to learn is...delicious. It has been a very long time since an event I could not predict with perfect precision occurred."

In that moment Nara found hope. Talifax had made a slip. A slight one, but one that proved something she'd desperately needed to know. He wasn't omnipotent. He couldn't see everything, and he couldn't predict exactly what she would do.

If he somehow arranged for her to be in a position to harm Voria, then she'd simply find a way not to do it. Unless she was bound and didn't know it.

"Perhaps you are," Talifax said with mock innocence. "Or perhaps I realize that you will soon understand the benefits of becoming a god. Voria cannot successfully oppose Krox. But you? You are more intelligent, and utterly ruthless. You will do what is necessary to best Krox, and drive him from Shaya. To prevent him from claiming Worldender. Isn't that what you want? To win the war? Surely it cannot be better to stand idly by while your newly minted goddess is slain, and her world drained of all magic?"

Nara didn't know how to answer that. There were so many variables she couldn't predict. Variables Talifax seemed to have already accounted for.

She folded her arms, and turned away from Talifax. He said nothing, but a moment later she felt the darkness recede.

Frit began to move again, as if nothing had happened. She blinked down at Nara. "Wait how did you get from..."

"Talifax was here." She closed her eyes. "I don't want to talk about it. I just want to sleep."

That was the one refuge remaining her. She closed her eyes and hoped it came swiftly. She was so tired.

25

MAKE A SCENE

Aran adjusted the collar of his uniform, a simple Confederate jacket and pants with the insignia removed, and in its place the red and black Outrider's patch that Bord had put together.

He'd come alone, his logic being that if Skare tried something at this meeting, the rest of the squad would be free and could come rescue him.

Aran stood in a centered stance just outside one of a half dozen arms jutting off the main body of Lagos station, over Yanthara. Each could berth several capital ships, though the one he stood outside was completely empty at the moment, probably a stipulation by the Inurans. They did like their space.

That was reflected in Lagos station's design, as she was an Inuran-built facility, but belonged to the Yantharan government. The station's existence lent a lot of credence to the rumors he'd heard that Yanthara embraced tech much more readily than Shaya. That worried him. The open-mindedness was great, but it was also something the Inurans would be more eager to exploit than ever.

Movement drew his eye, and Aran glanced up through the station's transparent dome, which vaulted over the teeming city at the heart of the station.

After the incident back on Marid he mistrusted it immediately, especially since he didn't have his armor this time. The governor's 'invitation' had been very specific on that point, and Aran had reluctantly agreed. If it came down to his spellarmor he was already dead anyway. Had they also forbade weapons he'd have refused entirely though.

He rested his hand on Narlifex. "Keep an eye on things in there, bud. We don't want to start trouble, but this could be a trap."

Too many watchers. Narlifex mused in Aran's head. *I do not believe they will attack. Taunt, maybe. Try to trick, probably. Trap is too obvious.*

An enormous battleship made its way slowly over the dome, and Aran couldn't help but feel like the unnecessarily slow approach was for his benefit. That, and the camera drones he realized were swarming around the dock, both inside and out. He looked for, but didn't find, the reporter they belonged to. No sign of a reporter, just the drones.

The ship itself was a narrow, black wedge, not unlike the vessel Kazon had showed up in back on Shaya, just less brick-shaped than Kazon's had been. It had the same oily sheen, which drank in the lights from the promenade around him. Hundreds of shoppers went about their business, blissfully unaware that the tool of a dark god was flying directly over their heads.

The ship maneuvered into the berth closest to his position, and as it settled into place Aran understood that it was even larger than he'd suspected. This thing was half again the size of the *Wyrm Hunter*, and outclassed everything he'd flown short of the *Spellship*.

Every time he'd encountered a vessel that size with a spelldrive he'd felt its strength from kilometers away. He felt nothing from this ship. Absolutely nothing, as if no light, or magical signature could escape.

A hatch on the side opened, and a long metal ramp extended, made from the same oily metal. It attached to the dock with a loud clunk, and a moment later three figures emerged from the hatch. Skare was in the lead, and a little behind him came Governor Austin, and Voria's mother, Jolene. She didn't much resemble the major, with a severe sort of beauty and an extremely short haircut.

Austin and Jolene were deep in whispered conversation, and the matriarch gave a soft laugh as they approached.

"Captain!" Skare called from the catwalk leading from the dock to the ship. He gave Aran a friendly smile and waved his slender arm. Aran had the odd impression that the man was genuinely pleased to see him. "Thank you so much for joining us. I know you have pressing duties, but I'm quite proud of our newest technology, and want the opinion of the sector's greatest warrior."

Aran froze as the first part of Skare's plan became clear.

Trap? Narlifex asked.

No. Aran thought back, realizing that he didn't really need to speak to the blade. Right now doing so would be awkward. *Or not a lethal one anyway. I think he wants to show the Ternus colonies that we endorse this acquisition. That probably isn't the extent of it, but it's definitely a benefit.*

He eyed the drones out of the corner of his eye, and noted that nearly a dozen were focused either on Skare, or on him. Damn it. He was still getting used to the idea of cameras, and wished he had more experience with tech. If he had been, or had someone like Pickus been here, the trap would have been clear.

"Skare." Aran kept his tone neutral, and inclined his head slightly as he stepped onto the bridge. "I'm not sure what your proper title is."

"Patriarch, but Skare is fine." He waved dismissively. "Please, we are friends, Captain. Together, you and I are going to help turn the tide against Krox. This vessel is the first step. Please, come inside."

Aran reluctantly followed Skare up the catwalk, and gave Jolene and the governor a polite smile as he passed them. Neither seemed overly interested in his presence, the governor especially. His attention was all on Jolene, but it didn't seem to be romantic in nature. He stood like a dog waiting orders from its master. Yet the raw adoration that came along with binding was absent. He didn't seem to be bound, exactly. So what hold did Jolene have over him?

He'd need to inspect the man's aura to be sure, something he wasn't particularly adept at. Nara would be a much better choice, and he briefly regretted not bringing her with him.

Skare led him through a tall, narrow corridor. The walls glowed with their own soft inner light, which grew brighter in patches of sigils that illuminated as they passed. They'd only made it a few meters inside when a wave of nausea boiled up. Aran tried to shake it off and focus on his surroundings.

Everything he saw here could be of use eventually, if they ever had to fight these ships. It was worth a little discomfort.

"Are you feeling all right, Captain?" Skare had reached his apparent destination, a small room that on a much smaller vessel might have been a bridge. There were only three chairs, each linked to its own console. Data in sector common scrolled across each screen, but as the queasiness intensified Aran found it difficult to study them.

He shook his head to clear it. "I'm fine. What purpose does this room serve?"

"This is the nerve center of the ship." Skare extended his arms and gestured expansively. He shot a smile over his shoulder at Aran. "From here a single person can manage the entire vessel. Almost all functions are automated, and the ship contains a full complement of self-repairing drones to tend to the vessel's day-to-day needs. Even catastrophic battle damage won't disable her, and there is no crew to kill, really, save the vessel's captain. We're safely ensconced at the heart of the ship, protected by immense magic."

Sweat beaded across Aran's forehead, and Narlifex gave an agitated thrum against his hip. The vessel was doing something to him. Probably not quickly, but he definitely wanted to limit the amount of time he spent here. Skare had to know he'd feel it. The move seemed uncharacteristically blunt, even not knowing Skare personally. Inurans were notorious for their clever tactics. It was a message, though Aran still needed to decipher it.

"I don't see a matrix. Where does the mage pilot from?" Aran walked slowly around the bridge, his uniform growing damp from sweat as the nausea worsened.

He couldn't see any difference between the consoles, and they seemed interchangeable for controlling the ship.

"Caelendra," Skare said, speaking to the air around him. "Please display a holographic representation of the ship's spell matrices."

An illusion appeared above the center of the room, so that it was visible from all six stations. It bothered Aran that he felt no magical signature, but of course tech didn't produce any. The hologram showed a row of black tubes, each roughly person-sized.

This time Aran's sinking feeling had little to do with the nausea.

"When we designed these vessels," Skare explained cheerfully, "We wanted them to be as independent as possible, for as long as possible. Our stasis tubes allow mages to effectively work while they sleep. Their direct participation isn't needed to utilize the spellcannon, or even to open a Fissure. The vessel's pilot controls all magical functions, and the mages merely supply the energy."

A ringing began in Aran's ears, and heat rose from Narlifex, like a cat bristling its hackles. He needed to get out of here. "Governor, I apologize, but I think I caught a bug on the surface and I'm really not feeling well. Perhaps we can pick this up another time?"

About two weeks past never, maybe. He was never setting foot in one of these ships again. Unless as a part of a boarding party come to destroy it.

"Of course." Skare frowned sympathetically, and turned to the governor. "Governor Austin, the captain has given his blessing, as you requested. Shall we depart at 6 am sector standard? That is, as long as everything meets with your approval, Captain?"

Several drones zoomed closer, their lenses whirring as they fought for the best angle to capture his response.

Aran knew he was trapped. He couldn't protest. Or rather, he could protest and look like an idiot when he couldn't provide any proof that this ship was anything other than it appeared...a miraculous last chance for Ternus to win the war.

And there it was. Skare was making him sick, and putting him off balance, because he wanted Aran to make a scene. Probably so he could start undermining whatever goodwill Aran had already earned with the Ternus people.

"The ship is impressive, Skare. Let's hope it lives up your promises." Aran gave a polite nod, and turned on his heel.

His entire uniform was damp by the time he reached the catwalk, but the instant he left the ship the queasiness abated.

The whole thing felt like a taunt, like Skare was thumbing his nose at Aran, because he knew there was absolutely nothing Aran could do about it. And, of course, Skare had been the picture of politeness for the cameras.

All he'd done was ensure Aran was more wary than ever of those ships. If they were given a full complement of mages, and gods forbid were able to drain a Catalyst, then these abominations might give even a god a run for its money. That was beyond terrifying.

And that put him in an unenviable position, a position he knew would come back to haunt him. He needed those ships to stop Krox, but in the process was handing his enemies a weapon they'd later turn against him.

"Captain," Skare called after Aran as he reached the docking bay and stepped off the catwalk. He turned and saw the Inuran patriarch poke his head out the battleship's doorway, "We'll see you tomorrow, then?"

"Count on it." Aran turned and started for the *Talon*'s berth. He was in deep now, but had a feeling the only way out was through it.

26

A NEW BODY

Nebiat's consciousness slowly returned to focus. Krox had explained what torpor was, but she hadn't really understood it until now. The languid period wasn't quite sleep, but they lacked any other basis of comparison. It was more like non-awareness of the possibilities streaming out in all directions. A period of relative blindness, during which Nebiat had explored Krox's memories.

In particular she'd sought battles against other gods. She wanted to understand how such battles were to be conducted, to give her some idea of how to formulate a plan to destroy Shaya. Krox had participated in hundreds of such battles, each separated by centuries, or even millennia. In most he'd grown stronger, though he'd also lost a significant number.

Every battle he'd lost had a commonality.

Yes, Krox agreed. *Hubris. In every case I assumed my victory was assured, and placed myself in a vulnerable position. I took risks, and my enemies exploited them. I am curious to see if you repeat my mistakes, or allow prudence to govern your actions.*

She realized something terrifying in that moment. Krox didn't fear any potential fate. He didn't fear being killed, because a god couldn't really be killed. He could be dominated. He could even be absorbed. But such an act would only change him, and she knew from his memories that immense boredom was a constant problem. Any change was good.

We have finished absorbing the Heart. What will you do now?

Nebiat didn't answer. Instead, she concentrated on her physical form, on the roiling magical energy that comprised her body. That was part of the problem. It was so alien, and if she was a god, why did she need to be confined by such things?

She visualized a new form, one that would be uniquely her. At first, she considered making that form a Wyrm to honor her past. "No, no, that's far too predictable." If she'd still possessed a mouth she would have smiled.

So far as her enemies knew, Nebiat was dead or in hiding, and Krox was their true enemy. They knew nothing about her survival, and thus Voria wouldn't know to expect her. She needed to preserve that situation, and that meant creating a form that was different from anything she'd used in the past.

She thought back to one of the gods she'd seen in Krox's memory, the great Shivan. Shivan appeared as a towering human comprised entirely of stars and nebulae. Such a god would terrify mortals, far more than an amorphous blob of magic ever could.

More and more I value your addition to my mind, Krox rumbled. *You understand mortals, and how they perceive their universe. It is unclear to me why the form you are crafting will inspire more fear. Their end comes regardless of our physical form, and all know this—why should this form terrify them more than a star?*

Nebiat avoided addressing Krox directly as much as possible, but in this case enjoyed the answer. "You're right. You don't understand mortals. You just finished explaining to me that the basis of our power comes from worship. If we want followers, then we must inspire fear, true. But not too much fear. If we are too alien, then mortals will feel nothing but gibbering terror when they behold us. For us to capture their wills, we must be familiar. We must look, at least partially, as they do."

A pair of arms extended from the main body of the star, and then a pair of legs. After a moment's thought, a second pair of massive arms extended from the star, and then a neck and head emerged from the top. She reshaped her body, changing her form to resemble the stars, as Shivan had.

Nebiat was happy with what she'd created, but reminded herself that she was after a certain degree of fear. She elongated the eyes on her cosmic face, and removed the mouth. Finally, she grew a half dozen tentacles from the head, mimicking those who'd dragged her father into Krox's swirling mass.

And you believe this form will be effective in garnering worship? Krox seemed genuinely curious.

"I am positive." Nebiat was pleased. Finally, she felt as if she had a body again. "When we arrive at Shaya they will know their end has come, and when I magnanimously spare a fragment of their people, they will eagerly bend knee."

And when will you begin your assault?

Nebiat focused on the swirling clouds of Ifrit clinging to

various areas of her new body. They swam across her like schools of fish, basking in her magic and power. They were a potent weapon, but they were not enough. For her to conquer Shaya she still required more troops.

She knew just where to acquire them.

27

CON JOB

Voria's teleport deposited her near the center of the Chamber of the First, atop the small dais Eros had used for his grand speeches. Nearly three dozen men and women clustered around it, most of them more interested in glaring at their neighbors than in staring up at her.

Normally that would have been just fine, as she wasn't overly fond of the attention. But now she needed their cooperation, or their entire world would be little more than a memory. She needed to be a leader.

That was made doubly difficult by last night's nightmare, the same she'd been having for days. She saw the death of her world nightly, and, thus far, didn't have the foggiest idea how she was going to prevent it.

"I've come here today," Voria called, her voice cutting through the bits of chatter still going on. "To perpetrate the greatest con in the history of our people."

That got their attention. Every gaze swept up at her with rapt attention. Some showed anger. Others shock. A few amusement. But they were all focused now.

"Krox is coming to end our world. He has reclaimed his heart, making him stronger than ever." She paused for a moment and allowed the implications to sink in. Almost all seemed to realize what that meant. "Now, he will come for us. He is a greater god, and he will crush this world unless we can pull off a miracle." She licked her lips, and let her eyes roam the audience. "To resist we must have a goddess to oppose their god, and that is exactly what we're going to do. I am going to perform an investiture of power, taught to me by Shaya herself. Gentlemen, we're going to elevate me to godhood, so that I can shield our world against Krox."

Ducius cleared his throat, and attention shifted his way. He stepped forward and lowered a hood to expose thick, white hair framing a troubled face. "Voria, apologies for interrupting. Our previous...animosity is diminished, but you murdered my son. I will not blindly follow you, and I will not participate in pointless deceit. Are you suggesting we create a false god? If so, how will that stop a real one?"

Voria took a deep breath, and exhaled slowly as she composed her answer. "We are, in point of fact, creating a goddess. The investiture is real, and if you doubt that look behind you at the pool."

She'd been ready for the questions, and was armed with the best evidence she could have hoped for. Shaya had delivered that to her, and it should make convincing them possible.

"Goddess preserve, the pool." Ducius's eyes had gone wide, and he dropped to his knees next to it. "There's so much more magic. Is this...part of the ritual somehow? What have you done, Voria?"

She knelt next to him, and took his hand in hers. Voria held his gaze, and told the truth. "I've spoken with her, Ducius. I saw her become a goddess, and I saw her die. She refilled the pool, using her own strength. She offered it to help us defend ourselves. Performing this ritual will require us to drain the rest of her power. That puts this world in terrible danger, I realize. But no more than it already is."

"And the con?" Ducius released her hand and rose shakily to his feet.

Voria joined him, smoothing her confederate uniform as she rose. She still wasn't sure why she wore it. "Part of the ritual requires worship. The way Shaya described it was like spiritual currency. My ascension requires convincing our people that I will be powerful enough to stop Krox. If they believe it, then they can provide me with enough strength to defend our world. Krox is powerful, but he has no followers. Theoretically, I will."

"And if they do not believe?" Ducius's tone was a bare whisper. The rest of the chamber was silent.

She met his stare, and its gravity. "Then our death is assured. Either we convince our people that we can and will win, or we are definitely doomed to fail. If we succeed, then we have a chance of saving our world, and to be completely forthright, it isn't a very good chance. You're aware of what happened to Ternus, Ducius. Krox didn't just kill their world. He set up a cruel trap that will kill them slowly, over a period of months. It's like pulling the wings off a fly. And that being is coming for our world."

Ducius hunched over, and his shoulders trembled. Tears streamed down his face, and his throat worked as he sought words. "You want me to go to a people who know all of your crimes, and you want me to convince them that you're a goddess strong enough to stop Krox? And if I cannot, all those people will die? It seems we have little choice, then. We succeed, or we lose it all." He shook his head. "I cannot believe my boy is dead, and I'm helping his murderer become a goddess."

Several gasps went up throughout the room at that, but Voria raised a hand to quiet them. "No, he's not wrong. Every word of what he said is true. I am not worthy of being a goddess, but I am what we have, like it or not. You do not have to like me, but if you cannot ensure that our people do, then all of us are doomed."

Ducius mastered himself, and cleared his throat before speaking. "Very well. We have no choice. You are going to become a goddess, and armed with the righteous strength of the Shayan people you *will* oppose, and defeat, Krox. We will make him pay for his atrocities, and our united people will gladly help you claim vengeance. And I will go to my grave knowing my son's soul will never rest because of my actions."

"It's a dark bargain, isn't it? A bargain none of us wants." She turned slowly in a circle, her eyes touching every last person in turn. "Most of you love power. You'd jump at the chance to become a god. Me? I cannot think of a worse fate. I saw what it got Shaya, and I know that even if we succeed, my godhood will likely be a short one. Our likelihood of survival is slim, and we all know it, but is any one of you willing to give up?"

Voria licked her lips. Many faces were unreadable. She wished she knew what they were thinking. "I've called you here because each of you represents a faction. You are influencers and leaders. You are respected, and people will listen to you. If we are to stop Krox, then you must convince our people that they play a role in doing so, and that the lowest among them matters as much as our fiercest warriors. And, as quickly as able, we need to carry word beyond this ship, to Shaya itself. Every last citizen needs to be ready for what is to come. Can I count on you to do that?"

Reluctant nods dotted the room. They didn't like it, and she didn't blame them, but at least they'd try.

28

THE SKULL OF XAL

Aran tapped the final *void* sigil on the *Talon*'s matrix, and the Fissure cracked its way open across the black. The hideous purple glow along the edges illuminated the armada behind him, their wedge shapes indistinct, and menacing.

"Crewes, send a missive to the governor's flagship," Aran ordered as he guided the *Talon* back into normal space. He shivered in spite of himself. Not from the imagined chill, but from the memory of the last time he'd been to the Skull of Xal, at the very beginning of this whole mess.

"Yes, sir." Crewes tapped a *fire* sigil, then a second on the silver ring. The scry-screen lit a moment later and showed a Ternus technician. Her eyes had been replaced with cybernetic implants, and a cable snaked out of her temple.

"Fleet actual," she said in a monotone as she cocked her head.

"Please inform Governor Austin that we've arrived," Aran explained. He slid out of the command matrix, and approached the scry-screen. "Let him know that I'll be coordinating the raid directly with Admiral Kerr, but that he's welcome to listen in to comms if he'd like."

There was movement behind the tech, and then the governor's face filled the corner of the screen. "Captain, I'd like you to take the ships to an altitude where they can fire directly at the Catalyst. Draining it from range seems like the safest course of action."

"Respectfully, Governor, you put me in charge for a reason. I plan to send in a ground team to recon—"

"Why?" Austin asked coldly. The governor folded his arms in a way that perfectly expressed his impatience.

Aran forced a calming breath, and reminded himself that the governor had no idea what they were dealing with. None of them did.

"We're coming around the planet's horizon line now. See for yourself, Governor." Aran kept his tone neutral. The corner of the scry-screen shifted to show their approach, and as they rounded the grey-green world Aran shivered again.

The Skull of Xal floated in the void, massive ram-like horns curling from its brow and up under the jaw. Two ridges ran along the top of the Skull—thick, dark bone. None of that was the worst, though. The hellish purple light of *void* magic came from the mouth and eyes, the same power Aran could feel coldly smoldering in his chest.

"Take a look, Governor." Aran paused to allow the man a moment to see the Skull, then plunged ahead. "For us to access the Catalyst we need to enter one of the ocular cavities. There is a reason why slavers deposit groups on foot. Attacking from out here is futile, as you can't penetrate the bone protecting the Catalyst. We could fly the fleet inside, but that puts us at the mercy of the tech demons living there. We don't know anything about their defenses. They could have fortifications, gun emplacements, or who knows what kind of demonic monstrosities ready to attack. The last time I was here I didn't see the Guardian, but that doesn't mean one doesn't exist. That Guardian will be a demigod in their own right, and will be surrounded by a cadre of powerful mages. If you pilot these ships in there you're declaring war, and I expect the locals to react badly. Are you really prepared for that kind of fight?"

Austin's handsome face soured. "Very well. You've convinced me. What do you have in mind, exactly?"

Aran stared at the rapidly growing Skull as he remembered the frigid air and the bleached bone hills. "We'll move to the edge of the ocular cavity and deploy our forces. We'll keep several of your ships close at hand so they can fire at any hostiles that assault our landing zone. Once we deal with their initial sortie we can push toward the Catalyst. We'll assess, and decide how to proceed. There's every possibility we may not be able to get the ships to the Catalyst. If that's the case I expect you to abide by my decision, or you can run this op yourself."

"I will *not* leave empty handed." The governor smoothed his suit, and collected himself. "If you can't get the ships to the Catalyst, I expect you to expose every one of our mage candidates to the magic."

Aran licked his lips, the screams of the dying echoed out of remembered nightmares. "It's your people, Governor, but expect heavy casualties. The demons will defend their territory, and your conventional weapons aren't going to do much to slow them down. Anything short of grenades or explosive rounds won't even scratch them. And remember, if things go south I'm pulling the plug."

The governor eyed him as if he wanted to say something, but finally gave a short nod. "Very well. Good luck, Captain."

The missive ended, and the screen shifted to show their approach. They'd nearly reached the same eye where Kazon and Aran had been dumped what felt like a lifetime ago.

"Whole lot a zeroes are about to die," Crewes said as he exited his matrix. He wore a fresh uniform, with the Outrider's patch monogrammed on the chest. The sergeant ducked past the spinning rings, and headed for the ramp to the cargo bay. "I'll get the kids ready."

Neeko's lithe form rose from the corner and trotted after the Sergeant. The cat was utterly silent, and mostly seemed to keep to itself. Crewes didn't acknowledge it, or hadn't in Aran's presence. The cat didn't seem at all discouraged about being ignored, and Crewes had done nothing to keep it out of his quarters.

"This plan is madness," Rhea said from the third matrix. "You seem aware of the risks, even if those fools aren't. Why are you going along with this?" She asked it simply, with no accusation, just a request for info.

"Krox is coming for Shaya." Aran guided the *Talon* into the ocular cavity, and brought them to rest roughly where Yorrak had set down not so long ago, at the edge of a vast field of bone.

There was no movement in the bleached hills rising into the distance, and nothing silhouetted against the terrible violet magic hidden somewhere beyond them. Nothing yet, anyway. "The odds of us stopping a god of that magnitude are...slim. We're going to need allies, and Ternus offered to help us if I'd lead their fleet here. I may not like the weapons, but if they're killing Krox then we need them on our side. I'm aware there will be a price to pay later, but I want to make sure we're around to pay it."

"Good enough for me." Rhea nodded as she exited her matrix. She quickly bound her hair into a ponytail, then tucked it inside the collar of her flight suit. "Thank you again for the spellarmor. I'm going to go get suited up."

"I'll be down in a minute." Aran continued to concentrate on flying until after they'd landed. He briefly considered leaving Bord with the ship to ward it, but odds were good the *Talon* would be a lot safer than the people they were sending in. Bord's magic would be needed there.

Aran ducked out of the matrix and hurried down the ramp. By the time he reached the cargo hold Bord, Kezia, Rhea, and Crewes were already suited up. Much to his surprise, Nara was there as well, next to the sergeant.

Aran raised an eyebrow at Crewes.

Crewes eyed him sidelong as he checked the internals on his cannon. "I thought she'd be useful, and besides, let's be honest, you were gonna bring her anyway." Crewes gave Aran a grim smile. "I ain't stupid though. She's wearing the collar, and I got the control rod clenched nice and tight."

"Good call, Sergeant." He nodded to Nara, who returned it before snapping her helmet into place.

Aran moved to stand before his Mark XI. It still didn't truly belong to him the way his old armor had, but he was grateful to have state-of-the-art tech that wasn't corrupted.

He'd had time to think about what happened back on Skare's ship, and the more he considered things the more he wondered if the ship was draining his magic directly. Perhaps the tubes were just for show, and any mage on the ship was at risk. It was a horrifying thought.

Aran sketched a *void* sigil in front of the breastplate, and then backed into his armor. The familiar foam interior settled comfortably around his skin, and the HUD lit almost instantly as the armor drew a trickle of magic from his chest.

He triggered a missive to the squad, each of whom appeared along the bottom of his HUD. "We're going to fan out ahead of the Ternus Marines. Odds are good the alpha strike will be leveled in our direction, so Bord, you're going to need to be on it with the wards."

"Ain't nothing touching my lady." Bord's scout armor paused, and to Aran's surprise he snapped a deft salute. "I'll keep the rest of you nice and shiny too, sir, but I ain't gonna be able to do much for the Marines. Too many people."

"I can aid you," Rhea's quiet voice sounded over the missive. "I possess *life* magic, and am skilled in creating wards. My resources are likely more limited than yours, but I'll do what I can. It isn't my specialty."

"What *is* your specialty?" Aran asked. He probably should have figured that out on the flight here, but he'd been too busy planning his role in the war to spend much time working with Rhea. She'd seemed fine with the arrangement, and hadn't really left her quarters much except to eat.

As her commander, though, he needed to be the one taking the initiative, and he made a note to do that, if they lived.

"Destruction." Rhea's armored form drifted over to the blue membrane, and she paused to face him. "The same as every Outrider that came after you. You mandated that we all learn true magic as well, which is why I know basic wards."

"Sounds like future me is much better at this," he muttered under his breath. Aran fed a bit of *void* to the suit, then drifted through the membrane, and up into the air over the *Talon* and the transports dispatched by the Ternus fleet.

Icy crystals covered the bone, a reminder of the cold that he, thankfully, couldn't feel because of his spellarmor. The first time he'd been here he hadn't been so lucky. Back then he'd been fodder.

Dozens of Marines in the same effective position he'd been in were rushing out and assuming defensive positions wherever they could find cover. Behind them came a line of hovertanks, and Aran felt a brief surge of hope until he realized none of them were Davidson's. The *Hunter* had probably already reached Shaya by now, along with the rest of Ternus's remaining conventional vessels, which was where Davidson should be.

A few moments later clusters of grey-clad techs sprinted out of the ships. The shuttles lifted off, and the bewildered techs looked around as if seeking escape. Aran knew exactly how they were feeling. Crewes hadn't been wrong about a whole bunch of zeroes dying.

He fed *air* into his suit to amplify his voice, then rose over the ranks. "I want the hovertanks to flank our advance. Marines, find any cover you can and keep the enemy at range. If a tech demon advances, scatter. Force them to chase you into the tanks, or my mages, and we'll peel them off you. Also, keep moving. The cold can be lethal if we're out in it too long."

The Marines started moving, and Aran noted that each had been fitted with cybernetic implants, just as the tech he'd spoken to earlier. That chilled him more than the temperature ever could. Who knew what those implants even did? Nothing good, he was sure.

"Movement, Captain," Rhea's confident voice came over the speakers in his suit. "I count at least twenty hostiles. Estimate eighty seconds to contact."

"Get to cover!" Aran bellowed. "Armor, aim for clusters. Disrupt and slow. Don't go for kills. We need to stagger their advance."

Crewes cut into the channel. "Sir, got another bunch over the ridge at three o'clock."

The pounding of booted feet on pallid stone grew louder, and echoed at them from multiple directions. There had to be hundreds of them out there. Countless silhouettes appeared against the glow in the distance.

The demons' objective was clear. They were arrayed to prevent Aran's forces from reaching the Catalyst. This was going to be a bloodbath.

29

SO MUCH FOR DIPLOMACY

Aran realized immediately there was no way his limited forces were going to survive a push through the approaching demonic horde. Yorrak's quick in and out raids suddenly made a lot of sense, because they happened before the locals had a chance to mobilize. A larger force was cumbersome and easily spotted, and that gave the demons all the time they needed to get into position to intercept.

"Sergeant," Aran panted into his suit. "We're going to double time it up to that ridge, and take the summit. I want to hold it just long enough to piss them off, and then we fall back to the LZ."

"Copy that, sir. You heard the man, people." Crewes's thruster fired, and his armor soared up the ridge.

Rhea's Mark XI rose smoothly in the sergeant's wake, and Aran could feel the *void* magic she used, twin to his own. She stayed above and behind the sergeant, shadowing him in the way only a veteran would know to do. Again she seemed more skilled than anyone else in the company, himself included. And that was without tapping into any of the abilities being a Wyrm would give her.

Bord and Kezia sprinted up the ridgeline behind Crewes and Rhea, but they wouldn't reach the ridge more than a few moments after them. Aran glanced at the Marines below, then toggled his external speakers. "In a few moments we're going to kick a hornets' nest. Those hornets are going to come swarming down those ridges, and when they do they're going to be pissed off. Do everything you can to slow them, and to channel them into a kill zone that the capital ships can concentrate their fire on."

Aran flipped off his speakers, and poured *void* into his armor. He zipped along the ridge, quickly eating up the gap between him and Crewes. *Fire* worked for flight, but *air* or *void* both did it better. He willed open his void pocket, and withdrew his spellrifle.

They'd need to kite these demons, as letting them get into melee range meant a swift death. It would be too easy for the demons to physically overpower them through weight of numbers, and while their magic might delay that, eventually it would run out.

Once he'd reached the sergeant's position, Aran jetted up high enough that he nearly brushed the top of the ocular cavity. It afforded a better view of the bleached fields stretching into the distance, and beyond them he caught sight of the familiar icy glow of the Catalyst itself, the purple light filling the cavity where a human's brain would be.

Columns of demons trotted across the bleached plain, all making for the ridge where his company was assembling. Most demons carried either a spellblade or spellrifle, but there were plenty of spellcannons dotting their ranks. Odds were good they'd use *void* exclusively, and that did make them somewhat predictable. Unfortunately, being able to predict a hail of void bolts didn't mean they'd survive it.

"Crewes, Rhea, start dishing big spells to the group closest to us," Aran ordered. He zipped back down toward the squad, and wasn't surprised when a chorus of void bolts rose from the demons.

The dark spells hissed past him, and he twisted and rolled to avoid the barrage. He continued his evasive maneuvers until he was low enough to drop into cover behind a bony outcrop. A final void bolt hissed into the rock above him, echoed by angry cries from the demonic ranks.

"Bord." Aran risked a quick glance around the right side of the boulder, then ducked back as a void bolt slammed into the rock. "Get ready with the strongest ward you can manage. Kezia, the first demon to make it around those boulders gets a hammer to the face. Keep them off the ranged, and don't get lured out of cover."

Crewes and Rhea were already moving. The sergeant darted around the right side of the boulder, and aimed his cannon at a trio of demons who'd broken ahead of the main body and were sprinting in their direction.

"Aran," Nara gave a frantic call from where she'd crouched near the base of a boulder. "What about me?"

Aran smiled grimly as he peeked over a boulder at the onrushing demons. The front rank was a little over a hundred meters out. "I want you to create an illusion of a second group of tech mages cresting the ridge forty meters to our right, and then immediately after I want one on the left. We're trying to get them to waste magic. Even demons have limits and every bolt that hits an illusion isn't hitting a Marine."

Crewes's cannon bucked, and a ball of superheated

flame arced into the air. It detonated over the trio of demons, and coated them in superheated napalm.

"Most demons are all but impervious to flame," Rhea called as she sprinted into cover about ten meters from Crewes. She popped out of cover and cored a demon through the heart with a level three void bolt. The creature continued running for a few steps, then tumbled to the ground and didn't rise.

"I ain't trying to burn 'em." Crewes was already firing a second time, but this time the ball that burst from his spell-cannon was a pure blob of icy blue. The *water* magic followed the same course the *fire* had, and when it slammed into the trio of demons, the cold washed over their superheated bodies.

Cracks formed in their carapaces, and it exposed purplish magic underneath. The lead demon took a step, and its leg shattered. The others collapsed as well, their bodies unable to resist the extreme shift in temperature.

Roars sounded from the ridge to the right, and then a moment later to the left. Dozens of illusionary tech mages came flooding over the ridge, all copies of someone in the company, and the demonic host responded in kind. They peppered the illusions with void bolts, but Nara had apparently accounted for that when she'd cast her illusion.

Each tech mage dove out of the way, or cast a shimmering ward, or did some plausible thing to explain why the spell hadn't affected them. If anything, it convinced the demons that the groups were both alive and more of a threat than the real company. Another barrage of void bolts swept out of the demon ranks, with no more effect than the first.

A few were aimed in Aran's direction, and he ducked behind cover again. He'd gotten their attention. Just one more jab, and he'd pull them right where he wanted them.

He kicked off the ground and shot up into the air. A pair of void bolts passed perilously close to his leg, but he twisted around them, and gained altitude. Aran snapped his rifle to his shoulder, and sighted down the scope at the rear of the demon ranks. As expected, a tall demon stood behind the others, and was bellowing something in an unfamiliar language as it pointed furiously at Crewes and Rhea.

"Let's just remove that organization, shall we." Aran settled the crosshairs over the demon's neck, just under the chin. The armor it wore ended there, and there was a thin, relatively unprotected patch between the helmet and the breastplate. Just enough of an opening for the spell he had in mind.

Back on New Texas, Aran had been particularly impressed by the explosive rounds used by the Ternus defenders. They packed a lot of destruction into a single shot, and he was fairly certain he could accomplish the same thing magically.

Aran summoned a core of brittle *earth*, several dense fragments. He added a core of liquid *fire*, volatile and eager to expand and destroy. Over the top he wrapped a layer of *void*, in case the armor got in the way.

The rifle bucked and the spell streaked into its target. The demon didn't even attempt to dodge, and its eyes widened comically as it spotted the spell at the last moment. The spell sliced through its neck, and disappeared inside its massive body.

Fire exploded out its ears, mouth, nose, and eyes. The commander sagged to its knees, then toppled face first to the bleached bone. The demons closest to it seemed unsure how to respond, though those closer to the front were still charging. Perfect.

"Fall back!" Aran roared. His voice echoed through the

canyons and even with the spellcannon fire he had no doubt the demons heard it.

He flew back over the ridge's lip, and out of the demons' sight. The rest of the company wasn't far behind, and bounded down the bleached rock as quickly as the reduced gravity allowed.

Aran fed a bit of *fire* to his suit, and triggered a missive to Kerr's vessel, the flagship. As promised, it and two other black ships were entering through the membrane separating the ocular cavity from the vacuum outside. The foreboding wedges hovered low above the bleached plains, fifty or sixty meters from where the *Talon* was parked. Hopefully that meant the demons wouldn't see them until they made the ridge.

"Steady!" Aran roared over the external speakers as he whirled and sought a target on the ridge.

A moment later a tide of black forms swarmed over the lip. As soon as the first rank appeared they began to realize they'd been tricked by Nara's illusion.

By that point it was far too late.

Eighteen hovertanks kicked almost as one as they launched an explosive volley that cratered nearly a quarter of the ridge. That seemed to undam the flow of death, and the Marines added their automatic weapons fire, peppered with the occasional grenade. All of that just softened up the demons though.

The real threat came from the trio of capital ships, and Aran could feel something sinking in the pit of his stomach as their spellcannons powered up. He zipped behind cover, and spun to observe the ships. It was the first time he'd seen them fire, and as they might one day be firing at him he wanted to know as much as he could about their capabilities.

Each vessel extended a tendril of negative energy quite unlike a standard void bolt. This more resembled the liquid fire the sergeant used in that it flowed toward its target like an eel. That energy swept over a pack of demons, and cold sweat beaded Aran's brow when he realized what he was seeing.

The demons dissolved as if disintegrated, but that wasn't what was happening. Not at all. The beam of energy vacuumed up their essence, the magic, and possibly the soul, and delivered them back up the stream as a pulse of shining, black energy that disappeared inside the ships.

Dozens of demons died in seconds, some from the unholy barrage, and others from the Marines and their tanks. A few managed to cast, but only one found a target. The Marine had leaned a bit too far from cover, and a void bolt separated his arm and shoulder from his torso. He tumbled back with a cry, while Bord sprinted to his side, his armored hands already blazing a brilliant white as he brought his *life* magic to bear.

Elation lived for a fraction of a moment, but then Aran felt it. Tremendous, incredible, divine power. The kind he'd felt on Marid when he'd met Drakkon. The kind that any sane mage ran from.

"Aran," Nara's voice came over the comm. "What the depths is that?"

"Shit, even I feel it," Crewes interjected. "And I do *not* want to meet whatever that is."

Aran guided his armor out of cover, and zipped as high as he could, twisting to avoid more void bolts as he tried to catch sight of this new threat. It took several moments to gain enough elevation to see over the ridge, and several more to sort the chaos of battle. Beyond lay rank upon rank of demons that were clearly waiting to enter that combat. Not hundreds. Thousands.

Only one area of the plain was clear. An area just wide enough for a single person to walk. The sea of demons parted, allowing a comparatively short woman to pass. When she emerged from the demonic ranks Aran tightened his grip on his rifle. She was beautiful, and terrible.

Long, white horns curved up over her head, like a second set of ears. Leathery wings extended over her shoulders, and a long tail flicked lazily back and forth behind her. Her eyes were what drew his attention though. They were the same dark fires that Kheross had borne, but where Kheross had felt alien...this magic felt familiar. There was an undeniable kinship between them.

"Hello, Aran. Hello, Nara." The demonic queen, if that's what she was, folded her arms. "The pair of you may approach. The rest I will allow to scurry back to your vessels, but only if they do so quickly."

"We don't want a war," Aran quickly explained, and drifted a bit closer. He raised his faceplate so she could look him in the eye. "I think we share a common enemy. We—"

The awful feeling in the pit of his stomach came again, and he glanced over his shoulder. "Goddess, no." All three wedge-shaped ships were moving to attack. The first fired its unholy tendril, and the beam writhed toward the demonic queen like a living thing.

So much for diplomacy.

30

DARK BARGAIN

Aran winced as the terrible black beam snaked from the Inuran ship toward the demon's leader. Having seen what happened to the smaller demons, he wouldn't wish that fate on anyone, demon or no.

The dark monarch merely smiled.

She stepped forward with a flourish, and whipped a slender spellblade from a void pocket so quickly Aran wasn't positive he'd even seen it. The pocket flashed open, then closed, and then she was flowing into an offensive form. A form he knew well.

The tip of her blade touched the tendril. Magic surged—cold, but somehow urgent and overwhelming. *Void* pulsed from her blade, and the weapon plunged deep into the tendril. The magic struggled to free itself, wriggling like a living thing, but the demon leapt into the air and flared bat-like wings behind her. She kept pace with the tendril, and adopted a look of concentration.

Enormous power washed out of her again, this time sinking directly into the tendril. A pulse of bright black moved up, as it had whenever the tendril had absorbed a demon. When the pulse hit the ship the vessel gave an almost living groan.

The pulse reversed course, and was quickly joined by several more.

"My gods," Aran whispered into the comm. "I think she's draining the ship, the same thing they were trying to do to her."

"Sir, it ain't too late to bug out." The sergeant sprinted over to stand near Kezia, who'd covered Bord while he tended to the wounded. "Ain't no way we're going to survive against something like that. Looks like she's just getting warmed up."

The groan became a metallic shriek, and the vessel abruptly entered free fall. A final, weak pulse of light flowed out of it, and the inert ship tumbled end over end...toward the Marines below. "Nara, I need all the gravity you've got. Now. Let's move that thing."

Aran poured *void* into his armor to increase his mass and streaked up and under the doomed vessel. He slammed into the side of it, and poured more *void* into his armor, until he was heavy enough to make a difference. The ship reluctantly began to budge, then jerked hard as Nara added her own magic. It crashed to the ground in a spray of bone fragments, which the Marines were thankfully armored against, then toppled toward the demonic ranks, crushing dozens in a spray of rock and debris.

"That could have been a lot worse, and she's got two more targets to hit us with," Nara said. "I know I don't get a vote, but if I did I'd be with the sergeant. We need to get out of here. I'm betting that at her age that demon knows true magic too. Those ships aren't going to do anything but slow her down for a few seconds. We need to go."

Aran couldn't always pick up Nara's emotion from her

voice, but this time the quaver was unmistakable. She was terrified. They all were.

The remaining pair of black ships turned and slowly departed through the membrane. The Guardian of Xal—she could be no one else, Aran realized—had her chance to destroy them, but she landed gracefully amidst her own ranks, and merely watched them go.

It didn't take the Marines long to realize their rides were leaving, and their ranks broke almost as one. They started sprinting for the *Talon* en masse. It was the only remaining ship, and thus the only thing worth defending.

"Bord, Kez," Aran said, thinking aloud, "get down there and organize the retreat. Pack everyone in that you can. Crewes, Rhea, get the *Talon* warmed up and in the air the second we're done loading. Let's move."

"Uh, sir, you ain't doin' nothing stupid, are you?" Crewes demanded over the comm. His armor was already in motion, and he feathered his thruster as he made for the safety of the *Talon*. The rest of the company quickly followed suit.

"I am, actually. Nara and I are going to go have a little chat with our new friend." Aran rose over the *Talon* and studied the membrane. "Be ready to flee, as quickly as possible. If this goes south, you've got command, Crewes."

"I don't like it, sir, but I trust you." The sergeant had already landed near the *Talon*, and was directing Marines inside.

"Well, here goes." Aran piloted his armor toward the demons, gliding slowly over their ranks. He stopped a good three hundred meters away, and used *air* to activate the external speakers. "Hey, there. Sorry we got interrupted, and thank you for letting the survivors leave. As I was saying, we've got a common enemy."

"You speak of Krox." The woman's eyes flared a deep, terrible purple, and the song inside Aran's chest answered. "You and Nara may approach. No others. I will grant you an audience, and I will hear why you have violated this place, in your own words. Then, I will decide your fate."

It wasn't really a decision at all. Aran sent a missive to the company. "Follow the rest of the plan. Get the Marines in, and retreat to a safe distance. Sounds like Nara and I are going to a demonic tea party. You good with that, Nara?"

"Wouldn't miss it."

Aran sent a missive directly to Crewes, and the sergeant's face popped up on his HUD. He frowned at Aran. "You don't think you're coming back, do you?"

"Why all the doom and gloom? Of course I'm coming back," Aran countered. "If she wanted us dead she could accomplish that right now, so I'm hoping it doesn't come to that. If it does you've got some choices. That puts you in charge of this outfit, and I know how much you hate being in charge. Voria will need you if I don't make it."

"And she'll have me." Crewes frowned at Aran. "But not today. You gotta crawl for this bitch, then you crawl. Come back alive. I can't do this shit like you can. We need you."

"I'll do my best. Take care of them, Sergeant." Aran killed the missive, and drifted a little higher. He looked past the membrane at the two black ships that had retreated. One contained the governor, and Aran thought he probably should check in before going with this demon. Then he reminded himself that the Ternus forces had just abandoned them.

He faced the demon, who'd walked closer. She now stood no more than a dozen paces away, and that afforded him his first good look at her. She was beautiful, oddly. If you took away the barbed tail hovering over her shoulder, and the leathery wings, and the horns curling from her temples, then what you had was a lithe, athletic woman with violet-hued skin. She topped two meters, making her slightly taller than him.

"Lower your magical defenses, and I will take you to see my father," the demon intoned in a melodious voice. She raised a delicate hand, and sketched a *void* sigil. Then another.

Aran relaxed when he recognized the teleport, and a moment later he and Nara appeared atop a wide ledge not far from their host. A broad throne cut from bleached bone sat behind him, and stairs wound down from their perch, all the way to the valley where they'd just been fighting.

The vantage provided a great tactical view of the Skull's interior, and he realized they were somewhere above the ocular cavities. Probably right behind the demon's forehead.

Below pulsed a blazing, violet sun, a mini-star that Aran knew from experience contained a vast, vast sea of *void* magic. That magic still contained part of the mind of Xal, and Aran shivered as he remembered his brush with the dead god. Somehow, after all he'd seen, the death of Xal was still the most tragic event he'd witnessed.

"Yes," the demon whispered. "It was a tragedy."

Aran shifted away from Xal's lingering magnificence, and faced her. Nara had quietly moved to stand behind the demon, but if having an enemy at her back concerned her, Aran couldn't tell.

"Do you have a name?" Aran asked. He was very careful not to make it a demand.

The demon nodded, but didn't speak until she'd ambled to the throne. She took her time sitting, like a cat finding a place on the mantle, and only then did she lick her delicate lips and offer a reply. "The name I was born with is Malila, though there are few still living who'd remember it, or my species. My title might better help you understand who I am. I was known as the Hound of Xal. My father loosed me to harry his enemies, and to slay them."

Aran glanced down at the blazing violet Catalyst, then back at Malila. He didn't like that she could apparently hear his thoughts. "I've only experienced a fraction of Xal's memories, but he showed me his death. He knew Krox was a threat, and he was right. He predicted Krox's rise, and I'm betting you know it."

She frowned at the mention of Krox. "I am aware. To address your...irritation, yes, I can detect everything both of you think. I am in your minds, listening, and I have been since you first touched my father."

Malila raised a hand, and a thin sheen of *void* danced along the outer edge. It called to Aran, and he felt something answer in his chest. A similar answer came from Nara's chest, inaudible but unmistakable to those who bore the mark.

Aran blinked, then cocked his head as he realized something. "The kind of military precision we saw below is unparalleled, except maybe by Ternus elite units. There's no reason anyone should ever reach that Catalyst. You let some through, don't you? People like Yorrak make runs at the Catalyst, because you want spies out in the galaxy."

Malila tilted her head back and gave a deep, throaty laugh. It went on for some time before she beamed a smile at Aran, then at Nara. "You aren't wrong, but the two of you are so much more than spies. You are more than the tools of Neith. Nor do you belong to Marid, or even to Virkonna, though she touched you before I did. You belong to me, Aran. And so do you, Nara. Even your names are of my creation. A reflection of each other. Fellow pack mates, destined to be hounds, as I am."

Nara's helmet hissed as she removed it. She took three steps closer to Malila, then glared up at the much taller demon. "So we're just a game to you? Everything we've endured...you find it amusing?"

Malila threw a leg over the arm of her throne. Her tail curled around her legs, almost of its own accord. "I sometimes forget how...urgent things are as a mortal. And how limited your perspectives are. I do not see you as playthings. Rather, you are my attempt to end a cycle that has been going on for over a hundred millennia. Krox and Nefarius have risen again and again, each trying to rule the sector. And each time the sector is torn apart, and we are lesser than we were. All while the true threat lurks in the darkness, growing stronger. Feasting on our apathy and ignorance."

Nara moved to stand next to Aran. "Then it sounds like we want the same thing. Are you strong enough to protect me from Talifax?"

Malila's posture changed, though subtly. Her eyes widened a hair, and a breath caught in her chest. It was minor, and gone quickly, but Aran knew those physical responses. She'd experienced fight or flight. She was afraid of Talifax, as it seemed everyone they'd met was.

"I cannot," Malila admitted. She straightened on her throne and fixed Nara with an intense gaze. "But I have given you the tools to do it yourself. Time will tell if that will be enough. The possibility you will fail, or give in to temptation, is as great...perhaps greater. Just remember—when you reach that fateful decision, that there may be a way to do as you are bidden without capitulation."

"We're straying into cryptic god-speak," Aran broke in.

He'd been down this route with too many gods now. "I'm just going to lay this out tactically, so we can get out of your hair. Krox is coming for Shaya. Voria is going to attempt to resurrect a goddess to fight him, but even if she succeeds we all know it won't be enough. We need an army, and we have to work with what we have. You said we needed to explain why we're here, but if you can see through my eyes you already know why. We need those ships powered up, so they can help us take down Krox."

Malila heaved a sigh of parental disappointment. She rose languidly from the throne, and walked to the edge of their perch to stare down at the mind of a dead god. "You've stumbled into the godswar, Aran. It isn't like any other war you've endured. Each decision we make must account for the distant future. This is why Neith empowered both Nara and Voria, so that they would be able to see the long ranging consequences of their actions."

"I get it." Aran moved to stand next to Malila's throne, and found her altogether too...normal somehow. Far below, Xal's magic called out to him, and he longed to fly down into that light, to claim more of it. "Those ships are tainted by Nefarius. Using them could potentially give a powerful weapon to our enemies. If we somehow finish Krox, then we're left weakened and unable to deal with Nefarius. Here's my problem. If we don't stop Krox we're all dead. Isn't it better to beat the enemy, and hope we can tackle the next one? If Krox wins, it's game over. Maybe he stops Nefarius, but will it matter to us?"

"No one benefits from Krox destroying Shaya," Nara interjected, lending weight to Aran's argument. "At least allow us to make mages. You don't want to power up the ships, and for good reason. But the ships are powered by mages. If you give Ternus *void* mages, they can power these ships, but they still have free will. They won't willingly serve Nefarius."

"Not at first." Malila sighed, then stalked back to her throne. She glared at Nara, as if the suggestion made it her fault. "But over time they will be corrupted and then consumed. Giving you this strength might help you prevail in this battle, but it will ultimately empower Nefarius, and that may prove to be all of our undoing."

"I'm so tired of hearing about hypotheticals," Aran said. He tightened his grip on his rifle. "I'm working with certainties. We take down Krox, or we lose. It's a simple equation. We might not like the consequences, but we need this cost if we want any hope of victory."

"Very well." Malila's tail flicked in clear agitation. "One hundred mages may approach the light. No more, and none of those blasted ships. I have but one stipulation."

"Name it," Aran said.

She leaned closer, giving a slow, predatory smile. "You and Nara must be among those chosen."

31

BOOTES VOID

Nara hovered in her spellarmor a few meters above the bleached stone, not far from where Aran waited. It was the first time they'd been alone since...well since it didn't matter. If being surrounded by demons counted as being alone.

Rank upon rank of horned monstrosities stretched into the distance, toward the sloping walls of the ocular cavity. Her enhanced senses made counting them easy, but she'd stopped when she reached ten thousand.

Today had still been the best day she'd had in a while. It was the first time any of her old friends had treated her like a human being since she'd been confined to that cell. It was the first time she felt like she was a part of something again.

How ironic then, that she badly longed to be back inside that cell, or in any cell really. She'd run events through her head over and over, and the conclusions were terrifying. She was meant to kill Voria, and Talifax was supremely confident that she'd do it. Assuming they survived what was about to happen, then the next place Aran was likely to head would be Shaya.

That put her alarmingly close to Voria, and within arm's reach of fulfilling Talifax's plans for her. She couldn't let that happen. It might even be better if she died here, removing herself from Talifax's twisted toolbox.

"You've got that look on your face," said Aran, interrupting her thoughts. His helmet hissed and he removed it, shaking sweat from his dark hair. His beard had thickened, but he'd been keeping it trimmed. It looked good on him. Aged him, in a positive way.

"I was just thinking about what comes next," Nara admitted. She faced the light—the Catalyst she'd dragged Aran into against his will. She remembered that now, and it shamed her. "I should be focused on Xal, but I can't help but worry about...after."

Aran tucked his helmet under his arm and turned to face the membrane covering the ocular cavity in the distance behind them. She followed his gaze and saw the *Talon* drifting through. It glided rapidly in their direction, expertly guided by Crewes. It stung that the sergeant so clearly disdained her now, though it was hard to blame him since it had been her actions that had caused all this.

"We'll have time to get it sorted. The flight back to Shaya's going to be long." Aran's deep brown eyes reflected the *Talon*'s approach. "I can't help but remember the last time we were here. A lot of the people going in aren't going to make it out. I hope the volunteers were told that."

"I'm starting to wonder." Nara replaced her helmet as the *Talon*'s sleek, golden form glided to a near silent landing a few dozen meters away.

Nara's armor sealed shut with a click, and her HUD came to life. The warm, rubbery feel against her skin was comforting, and no matter how much Voria and then Eros had tried to beat the tech mage out of her, it was here to stay.

She loved spellarmor and the protection it afforded, even if it did limit the use of true magic.

A ramp of azure magical energy extended from the *Talon*, and well-armed Marines began trotting out in four even columns. They carried spellrifles, which was a smart investment. Those who survived would emerge with a *void*-empowered weapon, making them all the more valuable.

Crewes exited the *Talon* directly behind them, like a sheepdog guiding his flock. Kezia emerged a moment later, her massive silver armor so at odds with the diminutive pilot. The drifter carried her hammer easily in one hand, the surface of the metal glinting violet against the backdrop of the Catalyst.

Bord huddled behind her in his smaller scout armor, peaking over her shoulder at the swirling ball of magic they were all here to enter. None of them addressed Nara as they began marching toward the light. The Marines' commander, someone named Kerr, paused near Aran and the two began chatting. Nara tuned them out, and focused on Kez.

Before she'd met and befriended Frit, she'd have called Kez her best friend. She and the drifter hadn't known each other well, but they'd fought together, and saved each other's lives. It hurt to see the indifference, and Nara wished there were some way to bridge the gap she'd inadvertently created. Of course, doing that would only make Kez more vulnerable to whatever Talifax ultimately had planned.

"Nara," Aran called in his confident voice, "can you bring up the rear with Kez and Bord? I'll take point."

Aran rose above the ranks, the purple light painting his armor violet. He moved at a steady clip toward the light, and the ranks of Marines crunched their way across the bone in a rhythmic march.

Nara trailed after, near Kezia and Bord. They weren't

really talking to her, but she still liked being near them.

"I don't think I can do this," Kez panted over the internal comms. "That light is...wrong. I don't want that kind of magic living in me."

"Don't go, then," Nara ventured. She drifted down to hover next to Kezia, no more than a few dozen meters from the hellish light. "Aran and I learned something from the Guardian. She can see through us, because we've been touched by...that. *Void* magic is powerful, but there are other ways to get power."

"You're on dangerous ground, Nara," Crewes snapped, his voice taught over the comms. "Don't be giving my people orders. You're still a prisoner."

"I was just—"

"Enough." Aran cut off everyone. "No one has to go in the light who doesn't want to. I know better than anyone the risks entailed. I'm going to walk in first, so I won't even see if you go, and I can promise you it will never be spoken of again. Make your own choice."

Aran's armor drifted into the light, and then disappeared. As soon as he entered, Marines began following him into the light.

"Yeah, I'm not going in there," Bord said as he poked out from behind Kez. "Kezia, my love, you do what you need to do, and I'll support you. Stay here, or go in the light—I got your back...side. I know you can't see it inside my helmet, but I winked when I said that."

Kez snorted at him. "How you can be such a bad mix of chivalrous and lecherous I will never know." She hesitated, and her armor turned to face Nara. She wished she could see the drifter's face. "It means a lot that I've got your support too, Nara. That light is joost wrong, and I'm not letting it touch me."

Crewes stomped his way over to stand next to Kez, then turned away from the light. "After that *dream* shit there's no way you could get me in there. I don't care how much you paid. These things get in your head, and they don't ever leave."

They stood silently after that as rank after rank of Marines trotted into the light.

Nara took a deep breath. She couldn't put this off any longer. She'd promised that both her and Aran would enter. "I'm already touched by it, and entering a second time probably won't make it worse. I'll see you on the other side."

"Be careful, Nara." Kezia's tone was...well, if not friendly, it was better than it had been.

Nara turned and guided her armor toward the light. She waited for the last few Marines to enter, and then plunged into the light just as she'd done with Yorrak's crew not so very long ago.

She felt a sense of the entire universe shifting one hundred and eighty degrees, and then something icy, like a pool of water, washed over her. When it passed, her perspective was different. She was elsewhere, and else*when*, she sensed.

She existed in countless places at once and her perceptions expanded to encompass galaxies. She saw in spectrums and possibilities that her mortal self could not comprehend or even perceive. She was a god, and not just any god, but an elder god who'd observed the passing of millions of years.

She was the infinity known as Xal.

Xal's demonic claws could pry apart a continent and his wings could cast shade that would deprive an entire planet of light. Whatever species he'd arisen from bore little resemblance to humans beyond having four limbs and two eyes.

But, at the very least, she knew that he had begun as a mortal, an eternity ago.

The god's voice rumbled through space, echoing through the mind of its intended target. "What have you summoned me to see, sorcerer? Speak, Talifax."

Panic flooded Nara's mind at the mention of Talifax, but there was nowhere to run.

Xal's colossal head turned, and his gaze fell on Talifax's dark armor, a tiny fly speck next to the planet-sized god. She mastered her terror. "Nothing here can hurt me. They can't even see me. This is just a memory."

"They cannot," agreed Malila's cultured voice. The demonic Guardian shimmered into existence next to Nara, her ghostly form translucent against the backdrop of the void. "We are witnessing a moment in the distant past, over a hundred millennia ago. I find it interesting that Xal chooses this memory to show you. The memory is always connected to the viewer, somehow. To your past, or your future."

Darkness surrounded them in all directions, broken by an endless sea of multicolored stars. It was one of the most beautiful tapestries Nara had ever seen, doubly so because she could perceive and understand each bandwidth of that light. Her sight, if it could be called that, extended to the edge of the known universe. She could see nearly everywhere, all at once, and she loved it.

Right now she—or Xal, she reminded herself—was focused on an area of the night sky that was nearly devoid of light. It was curiously different than every other area she'd seen. Instead of endless interwoven lights there were a few weak flickers here and there, broken up by vast stretches of darkness.

"Thank you for blessing me with your presence, Great

Xal." Talifax delivered a standing bow with both hands clasped before him. "My mistress will arrive in a moment. I beg your indulgence. Please, only a moment."

"Do not grovel, mortal." Xal did not bother to mask his disgust for Talifax, and Nara wished she could somehow warn the god not to underestimate him.

Space began to shift and fold, and a second colossal god appeared. This one was unfamiliar. A midnight-scaled dragon swam through the void, bits of light glinting off her scales. Her eyes were pools of deep *void* magic, so dark they, too, were nearly black. She blended perfectly against the stars, especially the strange area that was so curiously devoid of them.

Nara felt Xal's entire body tense as the god prepared for a combat he hoped would not come. He readied magics she couldn't begin to comprehend, but did not loose them. His horned head turned toward the Wyrm-goddess. "Why has your puppet summoned me, Nefarius? My time is not yours to command, and only my curiosity prevents me from leaving this place."

The Wyrm swam closer, and her leathered wings flared out behind her even as the light in her eyes intensified. "I have called you here because both of us are in danger, and I will begin by answering the question you did not ask. Why did I not summon the rest of the pantheon? Why only you?"

The dragon extended a clawed hand toward the empty region of space. "That is why I have called you here. For many millennia this region has quietly grown, and none of us have intervened."

Xal spun out billions of possibilities as he studied the strangely empty region. Nothing concerning appeared in any of them, though the void would grow over time. He turned back to Nefarius. Was this a trick? To what end? He'd never trusted Nefarius, despite the rest of the pantheon blindly doing so. Only Krox shared his fears about the Wyrm.

"Why would we intervene?" Xal was genuinely mystified by her motives. Nefarius was known to be the craftiest goddess in the pantheon, but she enjoyed neither jokes nor pranks. "This appears to be a natural phenomenon. Galaxies spin through space, and what's happened here is a haphazard pattern. Nothing more."

"Respectfully, Great Xal," Talifax interjected. "I do not believe that to be the case. This phenomenon is meant to look natural, but it is anything but."

Sudden realization dawned in Nara. She recognized that void. It had been categorized, and it was labeled on the galactic map that had always hung on Eros's wall back at the library. It was called 'Bootes Void'. She had no idea who Bootes was, probably some ancient Terran scholar.

The region had always fascinated her, because it was many millions of light years across, and contained almost no stars. The few galaxies that survived there were isolated, so much so that their night skies were probably filled with nothing but black. To them it would be the same as living in the Umbral Depths.

Xal's perceptions extended once more, and Nara was dragged along.

The god focused on Bootes Void, scanning it until he reached the very center. There he encountered something that she sensed the god had never dealt with. An area he was unable to perceive. A dark speck near the center of that galaxy drank in any light or magic that touched it.

"A tear in our plane?" Xal rumbled, turning back to the tiny mortal sorcerer.

Talifax's bulky form gave another bow. "Precisely, Great

Xal. Cleverly hidden, and so slow that it will take billions of years to swallow this plane. A takeover so insidious that even the pantheon might have been blind to it if not for my discovery."

Xal sensed the pride in the sorcerer, a failing that was not limited to their kind. He eyed Nefarius. "Why tell only me? Why not the entire pantheon?"

Nefarius folded her wings against her body, and pulled her clawed feet to her chest. It was the most vulnerable Xal ever seen her, but Nara was skeptical. The Wyrm's voice trembled when she spoke. "Of all the pantheon, you and I are the only gods whose magic is primarily *void*. Our magic is, in a way, linked to the Umbral Depths and they all know it. The ancient prohibitions prevent the denizens from working such magics. They are trapped. That means that this phenomenon must have been created by a god, or goddess, on our plane. Someone has betrayed us, Xal, and we will be blamed."

Xal spun out possibilities, and Nara watched as those possibilities led to his own distant death. An entire pantheon of gods—a few familiar but most completely new to her—swarmed over and killed the mighty titan. It happened so quickly she couldn't even perceive details.

"Yes," Xal said suddenly, returning to the present. "I begin to see. They *will* blame us for this. They already mistrust us enough as it is, simply because our magic is darker than theirs. I will keep this secret for now, and you and I will study it. When we know enough we will bring our findings to the pantheon, but only when we have a way to repair the tear."

"Of course." Nefarius bowed her draconic head. "Whatever you think is best, Great Xal."

32

HUSK OF XAL

Aran experienced a sudden weightlessness. He'd appeared in a familiar system, the same one where he'd witnessed Xal's death during his Catalyzation all the way back at beginning of this whole crazy adventure.

Xal's titanic corpse floated in the void, immense and somehow terrifying even in death. A host of other gods hovered around what must be the largest demon in the sector, feeding like piranha. He recognized the horrible, blazing star that must be Krox, though its surface swirled with far more colors than had been used at Ternus, and unless Aran was mistaken, Krox was far larger here than he'd been when they'd faced him.

Tendrils extended from Krox, ripping into Xal's body directly over the heart. The now familiar pulses of magic flowed up those tendrils, draining into Krox. Nor was he the only one feeding.

Countless Wyrms gnawed at the corpse, and Aran realized he recognized one of them. Drakkon, one of the smallest dragons present, was eagerly feasting on *void*-infused entrails.

"It's horrible, isn't it?" Malila's translucent form appeared a meter away, her arms folded and her wings limp as she watched Xal's memory play out.

Aran studied her out of the corner of his eye, still uncertain how to react or talk to a being of this age. He was left with the impression that she could snuff him out like a candle, and might if he said the wrong thing.

"Terrifying," Aran admitted, turning his attention back to the awful feast. Much of Xal's body had been eaten away, exposing large sections of bone and sinew. His head was still attached, for the moment anyway. "It definitely paints the godswar in a new light. We talk a lot about Shaya being holy, and the last dragonflight thinks that Virkonna is some sort of beacon of righteousness."

Aran shuddered. A sky-blue Wyrm, and a snowy-white Wyrm were feasting on Xal's heart, right beside Krox. He guessed he was looking at Virkonna and Inura. "She doesn't look very noble to me."

"Why do you suppose Xal chose this memory to show you?" Malila drifted a little closer, her dark gaze searching.

Why indeed? What was Xal trying to show him? Aran didn't answer immediately. He watched the memory play out. Time accelerated, and each god and Wyrm moved with comedic quickness. They swarmed over the corpse, and as years passed it shrank in size. The head vanished, presumably stolen by Malila, though time spun by so quickly that he couldn't be sure.

Time finally slowed, and all that was left of Xal was a desiccated husk. A few bones connected by lingering sinew —headless and lacking one arm. Aran glanced at Malila. "Are we observing the present now?"

"Approximately." Malila gave a very human shrug, completely at odds with the rest of her appearance. "The Husk of Xal still floats at the site of his death, and still possesses enough magic to sate those who seek it out. I was only able to save the Skull."

What would Xal gain out of showing him this? The memory seemed to have completed, or at least it was no longer advancing.

"You said you can see through my eyes, right?" The thought of it made him queasy. He was already being manipulated by too many divine beings, and he didn't like the idea that this chick was watching him on the toilet.

"I can." She nodded.

"Can you see through the eyes of everyone who's taken some of Xal's magic?" Aran turned his attention back to the body.

Malila was silent for a long while. Finally she raised a hand to brush dark hair from her face. "Theoretically, yes."

"Every god in the sector looks like they took a piece of Xal," Aran pointed out. "If that's the case, then you should be able to see what all of them are doing, including Krox. Maybe that's what Xal is trying to show us."

"It doesn't work that way." Malila shot him an irritated glance. "Xal doesn't know or understand that I am here. This is crafted for you, specifically."

The memory finally changed. Space dissolved into darkness, and he was suddenly elsewhere. This new system was much, much more familiar. He was at the Skull of Xal's present location, the barren system on the far side of the sector.

His perspective moved until he was staring into the glowing eye sockets of a dead god. There was no sentience there. No awareness, or at least nothing he could detect.

Both purple orbs flared, and twin beams of pure *void* magic lanced outward. They crossed the gulf of space incredibly swiftly, and yet it somehow also took an eternity to reach him.

Aran's senses exploded, and he could suddenly perceive entirely new spectrums and dimensions. He could smell starlight, and hear the passage of quanta and the lingering echo of the background radiation that had birthed the universe.

Part of him had expected something like this, and he relaxed into it. Perceiving as a god perceived had been heady the last time he'd been here, and if not for Narlifex he'd have drawn too much magic and died. He wrapped his hand around the sword's hilt, and was reassured when he felt Narlifex's presence.

Our Maker. Narlifex's voice was tinged with awe.

"Yeah, I guess he is," Aran replied with the same awe.

The magic should have been overwhelming, and yet it wasn't. He had no trouble adjusting to the dizzying array of new senses, and this time there was no desire to plunge into those orbs and attempt to gain more power. He was in complete control.

He turned to Malila, who studied him with those unreadable violet eyes. "Why isn't it affecting me like last time? And what is he doing to me? It doesn't feel at all the same."

"He is remaking you." Malila's voice sounded both impressed and a little frightened. She drifted closer, and did a complete circuit around him as she studied the magical transformation. "You're being imbued with *void* magic, but not like before. Before you were given raw essence, to shape as you will. This is a direct transference. He is crafting a specific magic ability, and imparting it to you. Something this complex could only have been formulated while Xal still lived. This is a part of his contingency. It must be. This is the realization of my vision, all those millennia ago."

Anxiety flitted across the corners of his mind. Neith had revealed that his entire existence had been shaped specifically to prepare him for some grand role in their endless war. Xal apparently had a similar plan, and there was nothing to say those plans intersected. What if they both wanted him to do different things? Which god could he trust?

Aran's back arched, and electric pain flooded every neuron. More and more *void* magic poured from the Skull into his chest, then rippled down into Narlifex. It played across its armor, darkening the metal, and making it both sleeker and a little larger.

Narlifex, stronger. The blade pulsed. *Mind... clearer. Smarter.*

The process stopped as suddenly as it began. Aran's breaths came in great heaving gasps, and cold sweat coated his entire body. He was still floating in space not far from the Skull of Xal, though, so it couldn't all be over yet.

He turned to ask Malila, but the words died unspoken. A dark shining mote of *void* danced in Malila's chest, and Aran could see it. He could feel it. He could, if he wanted to, even take it. All he had to do was extend a hand and claim the magic.

Vessel. The Skull's jaw opened as if speaking, and Xal's eyes flared. *You are my hound, born to harry my treacherous enemies. Track them to the edges of the void itself, or even into the darkness underlying all realities. Flay them, and devour their strength. Consume their magic, thus growing in strength.*

Aran realized that if he looked in any given direction he could feel faint pulses of violet light, in every corner of the cosmos. They pulled like the mote in Malila's chest, and Aran could only guess that each must belong to someone who'd eaten a piece of Xal's magic. There were thousands. More, maybe.

"He has elevated you, hasn't he?" Malila demanded. The quaver had grown stronger.

"I don't know," Aran admitted. "But I suspect it's something similar to what he gave you. I can feel you, and I can feel them. All of them." Aran gestured expansively at the night sky around him. "And he called me a hound."

"He's raised another." Malila licked very human lips, then flared very inhuman wings. Her hair floated around her like a sea of tiny snakes. "I have long wondered what my role in this epoch of the godswar is to be. I think you may have just answered that question. Leave here knowing you have made an ally. I cannot aid you against Krox, but it seems you no longer need my aid. Xal has given you something far greater than I could offer."

Malila bowed at the waist, and then her spectral form vanished.

Aran suddenly found himself falling, his body being drawn into Xal's titanic mouth. He plunged toward the overwhelming violet glow, passing between teeth that could have snapped apart the *Spellship*, and fell headlong into the magic.

33

VOID MAGES

Aran stumbled from the light, back into reality, and collapsed to his knees. His limbs refused to respond, and if not for the spellarmor he'd have toppled to the pallid bone. He drifted there, unable to control himself, magic crackling through his body, the aftershocks of whatever Xal had done to him.

After several moments the disorientation faded, and as it did he became aware of his surroundings. His armor insulated him from the cold, but frost crystals glistened all over the bony ridges leading back to the ocular cavity. He'd come out right where he'd entered, apparently.

An army of demons stood in neat, even ranks, observing his progress. They covered the plateau, every meter of it, and every last one carried a weapon and wore dark armor. The demons raised both arms, then brought them down as they chanted a single word. "XAL!"

It echoed through the Skull, washing over Aran in a wave of sound, and he realized that the gesture—cheering, maybe—was directed at him. He wasn't certain having demons be pro team Aran was really the way he wanted to go, but beggars couldn't be choosers.

The demons completed the odd ritual twice more, chanting the name of their fallen deity. Aran could only stand there and watch. The ranks of demons turned as one, and began marching away into the shadowed recesses that led down into the nasal cavity.

Something clattered behind him, and Aran spun to see Crewes approaching. The sergeant crunched across the bone, stopping next to Aran. His faceplate was closed, giving no hint as to his mood. He aimed the cannon roughly in the direction of the departing host. "Those bastards make me nervous, sir. And I don't like how they all just kinda cheered when you came out, like you were their gods-damned Messiah or some such. Demons are evil, sir. You know that, right?"

"You aren't getting an argument from me." Aran willed his armor into the air, and began drifting toward the *Talon*.

Nefarius had, evidently, spawned the word 'nefarious'. It didn't get any more evil than having a word named after you. Xal seemed less evil and more alien, but how much did Aran really know about the deity? Enough to realize that he'd been given the ability to rip magic out of people, which wasn't altogether different from what the ships they'd condemned could do. Perhaps that should be a wake-up call. What was he letting himself become?

Aran squared his shoulders, and tried to focus on the task at hand. He could mentally unpack everything he'd seen during the trip back to Shaya. "Has anyone else emerged?"

"You're the first." Crewes's faceplate snapped up. "This whole business is bad, sir."

Aran snorted a laugh. "You've got that right. I'm more

than a little tired of being a scale on a Kem'Hedj board, but if this is what it takes to save Shaya, then I'll do it. We can't leave Voria hanging. You were at Ternus. You saw the same thing I did."

Crewes shook his head, and spat on the bleached rock. "Don't mean I have to like it. This is why I wanted you in charge. You have to listen to me grouse." Crewes gave a grim smile. "I know you ain't got much choice in what happens here, but it makes me feel better knowing you don't like it any better than I do."

A shadow passed over the light, and a figure tumbled out. Then another, and another. Marines, men and women both, began to emerge from the light. It all happened in the space of a few seconds, and bodies piled up as more mages emerged.

"Let's get these people organized. Kez and Bord already back on the *Talon*?" Aran asked as he moved to assist the closest Marine.

"Yeah, I've got them prepping the medbay. Figured that could be useful." Crewes also moved to help a man to his feet.

Aran patted the man he'd helped on the back. "Head toward the ship. The disorientation will pass, and we'll brief you on what comes next."

He moved among them, gradually herding the dazed mages toward the ship. It took a while, but after maybe a quarter hour he paused and realized that the flow had stopped coming. "Sergeant, what's your count? I've only got 73."

"I've got the same, sir." Crewes shot him a sober look. "Rest didn't make it. We can wait as long as you want, but nothing else is coming out of that light."

As if on cue a final figure appeared. She didn't stumble

out of the light, but glided under her own power. Nara's borrowed spellarmor had been transformed in much the same way Aran's had. Her Mark XI was now darker, and slightly bulkier.

Her face was hidden behind her faceplate, but Aran sensed that something was off. Her arms hung limply at her sides, and she seemed barely aware of her surroundings. He cleared his throat into the comm, "Nara, you okay?"

"Hmm?" Nara's head came up. "Yeah. Just...kind of had a big bomb dropped on me. Godswar stuff. We can talk about it later. Where do you need me?" She glided a bit higher in the air, and surveyed the Marines Crewes was leading to the *Talon*.

"Get to the bridge, and get prepped for flight. I'm going to address the mages before we turn them over to Ternus." Aran started toward the ship, and considered what he was going to say.

He drifted up the ramp, and into the cargo hold. The newly minted mages clustered around the far side of the bay, and many wore the same haunted look Nara had. Aran waited for the last few to enter, then removed his helmet. *Void* pulsed from every Marine, and Aran could feel it in a way he never had before. There seemed to be a relative strength to each person, with some being nearly twice as strong as the weakest.

Most were already paying attention, but he strode to the middle of the room, then raised his voice, "I know better than anyone what you've just gone through. It turns your world upside down. You've peered into the mind of a god, and have been changed by it. We have that in common, all of us. Like it or not, we are all a part of Xal."

He let his words sink in, and glanced around the room to make sure he had everyone's attention before continuing. A sea of hard faces stared back at him. The governor wasn't going to like what he was about to say, and he was almost positive someone here would go running back to tattle. Oh well.

"You've signed contracts with Ternus, as I understand it." Aran walked over the ramp, and slammed the button next to it. The energy winked out, and the ramp began retracting into the ship. He faced them again, and noted that he now had all of them paying attention. "They're going to feed you to those new ships of theirs, and while they may have told you that all you're going to lose is some magic, it's important you know the truth. The magic you just absorbed? That's merged with you. It's a part of you. They can't take it without taking away some of what now makes you, you."

"What are you saying?" called a tall, blonde woman from the back ranks.

"I'm saying that what little I know of your history says you're fighters," Aran called back in a clear, confident voice. This was the right thing to do. "Don't let yourselves be used. Don't be taken advantage of. If you see yourself in a bad situation, and want out, get word to me, or to Major Davidson, and I'll do what I can." Maybe the words were empty. There was no guarantee he'd be able to do anything to help them, but he couldn't send them to the belly of those ships without some sort of lifeline.

"I can't speak for the others," the woman said, "but I need the money. My family needs the money. Doesn't much matter what happens to me." She shrugged, then moved to sit against the far wall of the hold.

Murmurs of agreement rippled through the crowd, and Aran realized that these men and women had been selected for a reason. Of course they had. Ternus would have picked people they could control, however that control needed to be maintained.

"Fair enough." Aran nodded his assent, suppressing his irritation at once again having been outplayed. "Get comfortable. We'll get you to your ships as soon as possible."

They had eight days before they'd reach Shaya. He had that long to figure out how to save these men and women, and to somehow help Voria stop Krox.

34

MY PEOPLE WILL LIVE

Nebiat flexed her magical muscles, and willed her newly created body elsewhere. She translocated to a spot deep in the Erkadi rift, over the world Krox had led her to not so long ago. The Earthmother's headless corpse lay below, surrounded by a nearly endless army of drakes, all of various ages, and covered by ancient trees.

I do not understand why you have returned here. Krox's apparent confusion satisfied a deep need in Nebiat. *These drakes are unsuited to form an army. A sufficient quantity will not be ready for several decades.*

"I do not agree." Nebiat hovered in the sky over the world below, and with her enhanced senses saw every last creature. Most looked up at her in primitive concern. Some hid. Others were blissfully unaware of her arrival.

It was the drakes she was concerned with, and even the most primal, down to the smallest, freshest arrival, stared up at her. They all recognized the presence of a god, and felt her immense strength, but they were too primitive to articulate it, which made them worthless to her, at least in their ability to fuel her with worship.

Nebiat studied the Earthmother's remains, and focused on the concentration of magic there. It was an immense amount of earth, dense and powerful, much greater than what she'd taken to crush Ternus.

Do not do this. Krox protested, finally seeing enough of her thoughts to understand what she intended. *If you destroy her, you give up a resource that will serve us for a thousand, thousand millennia. Nothing you could achieve with the magic is greater than the near countless armies we will raise.*

"Ah, Krox, you are so...obsolete." Nebiat's cosmic face split in a wide grin, the mouth growing only long enough for the gesture, and then disappearing from her face once more. It felt...right to have a body. "You do not understand our galaxy, or our role in it. What do I care for your endless war? That doesn't matter at all to me. What *does* matter is giving my people a future."

Your people? Krox's voice leaked anger, a rarity. *Your people are nothing more than the enslaved children of the Earthmother. Even were that not true, they are nearly extinct. Your father spent them as resources to ensure his own victory. He thought like a god. You think like a mortal. That route leads to our undoing, and if you seek this course I will resist you.*

"Will you?" Nebiat gave a soft laugh that echoed through the cosmos. "How?"

Krox raged against the confines her father had erected, but futilely. His rage was impotent. He could do nothing, and subsided. Nebiat ignored him and focused on her goal for coming here.

She took in every last drake, every nascent Wyrm, every hatchling, and even the clutches of eggs dotting the many forested valleys around the Earthmother's corpse. If this world were left alone for a thousand generations it would become a paradise that would spawn a draconic empire.

These Wyrms could rival, and eventually surpass, Virkon itself. Or they would if their creator didn't squander them in endless wars, and use them like cattle. That route explained why Krox had failed so many times. Because he didn't value mortals, or society, and didn't understand that in order to get mortals to believe in you, you first needed to offer them something of worth.

What does that entail? Krox asked suspiciously.

"Being a true deity," she explained, focusing more on the magic she was about to enact.

She plunged all four hands deep into the Earthmother's chest, and began drawing at the *earth* magic, just as she'd done before. This time she didn't stop. Wonderful pulse after wonderful pulse flowed up into her, and she grew correspondingly stronger with each one.

Wait! No, this is too much. Krox protested. She ignored him and drew still more power.

She drew until the pulses grew weaker, and then stopped entirely. Nebiat was suffused with an immensity of power that defied understanding, but she did not hold onto it for long. Instead she poured the magic into the planet, or rather the creatures on it.

Earth and *spirit* mingled, then flowed into every drake, every young Wyrm, and every egg. She touched them all at once, hundreds of thousands of dragons, and she evolved them. They grew larger and more intelligent. As one, they advanced. They matured.

Nebiat filled them all, every last vessel gaining some of the magic she'd taken from the Earthmother. She reserved but a small portion for herself. The rest, combined with *spirit* she drew from Krox, she gave to her people.

When the magic faded, countless faces stared up at her in wonder, and beheld their creator as sentient beings for the first time. She'd created a nation of dragons, a nation that knew no life but the one she was about to show them. In an instant her people were reborn, and the only cost was the loss of a headless goddess who meant nothing to Nebiat.

Will you bring your children with you to war on Shaya?

"A few of the most capable ones," Nebiat replied. Sudden weariness overtook her, and she experienced a similar need for torpor, as she had after absorbing the heart. She didn't fight it. "First, I will gather my strength. When I wake, I will bring my army to Shaya, and I will destroy it. I will pull Worldender from Shaya's corpse, and I will use it to kill any god who challenges me."

35

SAFETY OF A CELL

Nara was actually relieved to return to the *Talon's* brig. The cells were spartan, but comfortable, and Kezia had come down on the first day to bring her a scry-pad so she had something to do.

Frit and Kaho had mostly kept to themselves, and it didn't take Neith's enhancements for Nara to puzzle out why. Nara had been taken away with the squad, and when she'd returned they'd treated her like an ally. If she hadn't insisted on being put back in her cell she was fairly certain that she could have lobbied for, and gotten, Aran to release her.

That set her apart from her fellow prisoners, and it broke her heart.

She glanced over the waist-high cell wall into the next cell. Frit sat on her bunk, her back against the wall so she could face the cell door. Kaho lounged on his own bunk, which sagged under his draconic bulk. He had his tail clutched absently in one hand, while the other held up a scry-pad. His slitted eyes scanned down the screen, and he seemed oblivious to his surroundings.

Maybe now was a good time to talk to Frit. Nara rose and approached the bars. Frit stiffened, but didn't turn to face her.

Nara took a deep breath and opened her mouth with no idea what would come out. "I'm sorry. I know you're angry with me."

"That isn't it at all," Frit countered. She pulled her legs closer to her chest, and the heat of her skin sent a tendril of smoke from the bunk's surface. At least she faced Nara. "We're trying to decide if we can still trust you." Frit rose from her bunk, and stalked to the bars. She stopped and stared at Nara from just a meter away. "When they take us back to Shaya you're going to be punished, and then put right back to work. Kaho will be executed, and they'll probably do the same thing to me."

"I would never let that happen," Nara protested, but sudden desperation filled her. She didn't have the power to protect Frit, or even herself. "When we reach Shaya we'll share the same fate, whatever that fate is. I have a hard time imagining Voria coldly ordering our deaths. She's pragmatic, and needs allies against Krox, no matter where they come from."

"Is that what I am?" Frit hugged herself with her arms. "An ally against the very god that created my species? I don't even know where my sisters are, or if they're alive. I doubt they'd welcome me back. I betrayed them at Ternus when we stopped those bombs."

Nara's heart went out to her friend. Frit really had no home now. Not with Shaya, Ternus, or even with the Krox. She was truly alone, in a way that Nara could probably never understand. No wonder she'd gotten so close to Kaho.

"I promise I will never leave you," Nara said solemnly.

"And I mean that. We're in this together, and I'll even extend that to your...boyfriend."

Kaho finally seemed to realize they were talking about him, and rose from his bench to approach the glowing bars of his cell, his scry-pad still clutched in one scaly hand as his wings scraped sparks from the ceiling. "Earlier Frit said we were trying to decide if we trust you." He gave a toothy grin. "What she meant was *she* is trying to decide if she trusts you. I already do. I understand what it's like to be in your... unique position. No one will trust any of us, not ever again. We are each considered tainted, and all of us are likely to be put to death because of our actions. And besides, it feels good to have...companions? Friends? Whatever we are. I was never particularly close to my brother, and my mother... well, you've met her. She doesn't have friends."

Frit shifted so she could face both Nara and Kaho, and her smoldering lips gave way to a small smile. "I love your perspective, Kaho. You're always looking for the silver lining in any situation."

Kaho gave a draconic snort. "Yes, well, mother wasn't nearly as fond of that quality." He looked to Nara. "Do you think there's any chance Voria will meet with us before ordering our execution? Even if we are to be put to death, I'll happily tell her everything I know before we are slain."

Nara shifted her weight, then nodded. "I think so. She'll mistrust anything we say initially, but if you give her stuff she can verify, I think she'll listen. The question is, what can we give her? Krox has risen. A god is coming for Shaya. I'm not sure stopping Nebiat would even help. Do you know much about Krox? Anything we can use?"

Kaho's gaze grew introspective, and settled back against the bench. "I know a great deal about Krox, but little that's of use. I know that for him to have been resurrected it would have required a ritual of immense power called an investiture, one that my grandfather Teodros would have had to have been involved in. We know very little of the gods, particularly the elder gods, but in every story the only way to best a god was with another god. If every Wyrm in the sector attacked Krox at once, he would annihilate them all. Gods are on a different level."

Nara thought back to Xal's death, and remembered the sheer number of gods it had taken to bring the deity down. Krox was, theoretically at least, weaker than Xal had been. She tapped her chin, considering. "Kaho, what do you think Krox will do after Ternus? Presumably he could have reached Shaya immediately after he hit them. Why not do so?"

"That's a good question," Frit echoed. "If it were me I'd stomp out my big enemies as quickly as possible, so that they couldn't organize. Waiting is risky, unless you're waiting to increase your strength and resources."

"Maybe Krox is hitting other Catalysts," Nara realized aloud. "What's to stop him from going around the sector and, well, eating every dead god?"

Kaho shook his head, fixing Nara with an interested stare. "I don't think Krox will risk that. If the old legends are correct most gods would go into a sort of hibernation whenever they consumed a large amount of magic. Krox will be cognizant of that. I could see perhaps taking the Blazing Heart, since that was already a part of him. He might seek to reclaim others, though the locations of those Catalysts have been carefully hidden, or the magic has been taken by another god. I tend to think not, though. Particularly after your mention of Talifax. If Nefarius is a threat, then Krox will have to tread carefully, or risk being vulnerable when another powerful enemy rises."

Nara nodded thoughtfully. "Nefarius might serve as a check. At the very least it might force Krox to attack prematurely. Which brings me to another concern..." Nara retreated to her bench, and sat so she faced the others still. She felt so small. "Talifax is aware of everything that's going on. He knows that Krox will assault Shaya, and I'm sure he's positioned to take advantage of it. He considers me a tool, and I'm terrified that he's right. That somehow he'll get me to...to kill Voria. He says I'll do it, and he seems certain."

Frit shook her head fiercely. "There's no way you'd do that. I know you too well."

"Anyone can be broken," Kaho pointed out. He adopted a sheepish expression, which was altogether strange on his draconic features. "Binding can force anyone to do what you wish. Talifax is known for mastery of *void*, but he possesses many types of magic. It's not inconceivable that he could force Nara to kill Voria. He may have even planted a compulsion. It's possible she won't even feel the spell until it triggers."

Nara pulled her knees to her chest and clutched them tightly. "That's why I can't be let out of this cell. If I'm in here, then there's nothing I can do to hurt her. I'll tell her that when we meet. That's how I'll beat him."

"Can't bindings be detected?" Frit asked, shifting to face Kaho. "Voria is a powerful true mage. Let's ask her to inspect Nara. If you're really bound then she can probably remove it, and if not, then maybe you're right. Maybe she can keep you confined." She shuddered and her gaze went unfocused as if remembering something. "I-I don't want to live in a universe where Krox has sway. When we stopped by the Heart and I saw the way my people swirled around it...I won't be be a plaything for a god, and you shouldn't have to be either. There's got to be a way to remove Talifax's influence, and we'll find it."

Nara was still terrified, but it meant the world to her that she was no longer alone. A Krox and an Ifrit might be strange allies, but at least she'd have help when Talifax launched the last part of his plan.

36

MUH MAN

Voria gazed through the *Spellship*'s scry-screen, waiting, but the night sky over Shaya remained dark and empty. Aran's last missive put his arrival today, likely in the next few minutes. The possibilities she'd examined made that arrival a near certainty, but that still didn't banish the anxiety.

She had so many metaphorical plates spinning, and wasn't sure she could cast spells fast enough to keep them all aloft, metaphorically speaking of course. Ducius had been, to her immense shock, an absolute godsend. He'd been as good as his word, and had dutifully explained to their people that their aid was required to help Voria arise. It sounded so pompous. Eros would have loved it.

To her shock the people had responded, and responded in droves. They'd put aside their differences, drifter working alongside Shayan as they struggled to prepare for Krox's impending invasion. That possibility grew more implacable every day, and she could almost feel the dark god's approach. He'd be here any day, though most possibilities put his arrival two or more days away.

"Ma'am?" Pickus's voice came from the bridge's doorway. "You got a minute?"

"Certainly, Pickus." Voria clasped her hands behind her back, and pivoted to face the freckle-faced administrator. "If you think it warrants my attention, then it must be serious."

A tall man ducked onto the bridge behind Pickus, and Voria's hands snapped up, ready to cast a defensive spell when she felt the strength in him. Long, blue hair poured down his shoulders, quite literally. Every bit of hair, eyebrows included, was comprised of swirling blue-green water. His features were handsome, but not remarkably so.

"Holy shit, it's Drakkon. What up, muh man?" Ikadra pulsed. "I'd high five you, but like, hands and stuff."

Drakkon, evidently, gave a sardonic smile to the staff. "You have not changed, I see. I believe Shaya would be... amused to see the lasting effect she had on your demeanor."

"Welcome, Drakkon." Voria brought her hands down, and tried to recapture some of her composure by clasping them behind her back. It was difficult, especially with the reminder of just how ancient this being was. "The timing of your arrival is fortuitous. We're grateful for your assistance."

Drakkon raised a hand, which upon closer examination was covered in a myriad of tiny scales, so fine they resembled pores. "I am not here to battle Krox. I'd make an especially tempting target, as Krox would love to claim any portion of my mother's power that he can acquire."

Voria inhaled slowly, through her nostrils. Why would none of these divine beings actually stand and fight?

The breathing exercise failed to calm her, but she still managed to moderate her tone. "Respectfully, what plays out here may determine the fate of the sector for decades. Or longer. The Confederacy aided you when Nebiat invaded, and our need has never been more dire. If you seek to preserve our alliance, then your aid is required."

"Is that a threat?" Drakkon raised a watery eyebrow, and identical water slid down his arm, into his hand. It pooled into a slender spellblade.

"Are you even serious right now?" Ikadra pulsed. "You're going to pull a weapon on the woman who's going to save your ass? Man, you've gotten uptight in your old age, Drakkon. Your mom would be embarrassed."

Voria continued as if the staff hadn't spoken. "It isn't a threat. Our alliance will be at an end not because I intend you harm, but because *your allies will be dead*." She settled back on her heels, and waited for a response.

Drakkon gave a half chuckle, and the blade slid up his arm as quickly as it appeared. "Apologies, Major. Ikadra sees right to the heart of things, as usual. I admit that I possess the same arrogance most of my kind are burdened with. I do not enjoy being questioned, but I must remind myself who I am dealing with. Soon, you will stand above me."

"So, uh," Ikadra began, "why did you come, big guy?"

"I cannot intervene in the battle, but I have brought a gift." The Wyrm cupped his hands, and swirling blue energy filled it. It bathed his features with its soft light, making his eyes shine. "Millennia ago, on the eve of Shaya's death, my mother gifted her with a portion of her strength. I would honor Shaya, and honor you, Major. I would give you the same gift, a portion of my mother's strength."

Voria's rage dissolved. She slowly raised her hands and clutched at Ikadra. How did one respond to being offered the strength of a god?

"Be forewarned," Drakkon continued, as the glow brightened. "This magic is potent, and by itself will elevate you to a demigod. Absorbing it is dangerous, and costly. It will seep into your soul, and in so doing become a part of you. But you will need rest afterwards, perhaps as much as a day."

Voria hesitated. "It is a priceless gift. But I do not know that I can spare the time. What if Krox arrives while I slumber?"

"He will not," Drakkon replied confidently. He delivered a grim smile. "You will likely recover by tomorrow morning, or mid-afternoon. And my analysis of the timeline suggests Krox will not appear for several hours after your recovery. I understand that makes you anxious, but the power will be needed. You cannot win without it."

"Will it incapacitate me immediately?" Voria asked. There were many things left to do today, not least of which was welcoming Aran and the visiting Ternus dignitaries.

"No, quite the opposite." Drakkon raised his hand, and the swirling ball of magic spun up into the air. Its icy crystals spun off into spiraling arms, and it perfectly mimicked their galaxy. "You will experience sudden euphoria, and dizzying power. It will last for several hours, and then you will desperately crave sleep."

"Ikadra?" Voria glanced up at the lively staff's sapphire, which glowed with a flickering inner light.

"Hmm, I can't think of a downside, or a reason Drakkon would steer you wrong." Ikadra pulsed thoughtfully. "I'd say go for it. If you're going to have to brawl with a god you might as well have a fun evening first, right?"

Voria turned to Drakkon and smiled. "I'm ready."

"Very well." Drakkon gestured with a single delicate finger, and the swirling galaxy of magical energy spun closer and closer to Voria's chest. She shivered as it neared her, but nothing prepared her for the icy shock.

The magic crashed into her like a universe being born. It

rippled outwards from the impact point, and surged through every atom in her body. The *water* flowed everywhere, infused all of her. It was quite unlike previous Catalyzations, which had merely deposited magic into her chest. This magic was becoming a part of her, a vital part of her.

"I—". She had no words. Nothing she could say to express the wonder. "This is...amazing. It's so much."

The energy wasn't totally unfamiliar, as she'd already touched Marid when she'd clashed with Nebiat—what felt like a lifetime ago. This was so much...more. She could reach out to the stars around her. Could bring life-giving rain to the entire world of Shaya. She was...more than mortal, but still less than a god.

"It pleases me," Drakkon said suddenly, a smile creasing his fine scales, "Mother would have been pleased as well. May her strength aid you in your battle with Krox."

Ikadra pulsed in protest. "So, uh, Drakkon, what are you gonna be doing, man? 'Cause we could definitely use your help. I mean magic is great, but that kung fu stuff you do is pretty impressive. You could, like, karate chop Krox and Voria could, like, hit him over the head."

Drakkon gave an affectionate sigh. "I must return to mother, to safeguard her, and to nurture the drakes that have come to bask in her radiance. Already they grow larger and stronger. Soon the day will come when they are able to ride to war, but until then my place is with them."

Voria nodded. "I understand. You've done enough. With Marid, and with Shaya...I will find a way to defeat Krox."

"Ma'am," Pickus's nervous voice came from behind her, and she shifted to face the scry-screen. A Fissure had begun to vein across the umbral shadow. Aran had finally arrived.

37

REUNION

By the time Voria reached the conference hall there was a flurry of activity. Pickus stood at the edge of the room giving orders to an army of white-clad servants. A team of drifters began rolling in small casks of beer, which they set up on the far side of the room, away from the conference table. A few moments later, baskets of life apples arrived, and then pitchers of wine.

Voria picked a path through the organized chaos until she reached Pickus's side. The mousey tech no longer seemed quite so mousey. He waved off the last of the servants, then focused on her. "I think everything's taken care of, ma'am. I've got Ducius escorting Governor Austin, and he'll keep him entertained while you speak with Captain Aran. There's a small room through that door over there. The captain should be up any moment."

"You never cease to amaze me, Pickus." She gave him a warm smile, then turned to the room he'd indicated. "I'll keep the meeting brief, and then we'll come in to meet with the governor."

Pickus nodded, but he was already surrounded by a trio

of servants clamoring to have their specific needs addressed. More waited beyond them, not quite as bold, but equally persistent.

She hurried from the conference room, and into the adjoining office. Three hover couches lined the walls, but the room was otherwise empty. An antechamber, perhaps? Its original purpose didn't matter, and she knew she was just distracting herself. What was she even going to say to Aran? Him being here meant that her vision was that much closer to fulfillment.

Krox would arrive soon, and that was the part she was trying to avoid.

Footsteps sounded in the hallway outside the door opposite the one Voria had entered from. She squared her shoulders and wrapped a hand firmly around Ikadra as the door opened to admit a quartet of familiar faces.

Aran stood in the lead, wearing a quiet confidence she didn't remember. His serious face split into a smile, and he snapped a confederate salute. "Major, it is damned good to see you."

"It's okay," Bord said, muscling his way through the doorway and past Aran. "You can tell everyone how much you missed me, Major." He struck a pose, but lost it when Kezia elbowed him in the ribs. "Oww, I was just—"

"Being disrespectful." Kezia frowned up at him. "You owe her your life, literally. The least you could do is give her a salute."

"Aten-shun," Crewes barked. The company snapped to, just as they'd always done. All them faced her, their hands clutched before their hearts, just as they had been the first time she had gone into battle, and every time since.

"At ease." She smiled at Aran. "You're also a welcome

sight, Captain. We're sorely in need of any aid we can get, even those ships."

Voria noticed a fifth person lurking behind the others, and realized it must be Rhea. The girl seemed to want to keep her distance, so Voria pretended to ignore her.

Aran gave a visible shudder. "I get that we need allies, but being inside one of those ships was the worst experience I've ever endured. Worse than the mindwipe. Worse than anything Nebiat has put us through. Evil doesn't begin to cover it. As terrible as it is to say out loud, it might be best for everyone if there are heavy casualties in the Ternus fleet during the coming battle."

Voria gave a heavy sigh, and moved to sit on one of the couches. She placed Ikadra in the air, where he hovered under his own power. "We have precious little time before we need to go out there and put on a circus for the Ternus dignitaries. Can you catch me up? How did Yanthara go? And the Skull?"

She realized Nara wasn't present, and nearly simultaneously realized her mind was flitting about like a humming bird. This must be the euphoria Drakkon had warned her about. It was magnificent, even if part of her realized just how little she could afford it.

Aran's face grew more serious, and the expression paired with the thick, black beard made him look the new rank. Every bit of him was the consummate commander, and the way he walked promised swift death to any who challenged him. He'd well and truly become a master war mage, and goddess knew what powers he now possessed.

"I'll try to sum it all up quickly," he began, pausing to lick his lips. He gestured at the woman at the back of the room who'd yet to speak. "This is Rhea, the newest member of Aran's Outriders."

"So it did go well." Voria nodded respectfully at the young woman. Well, young Wyrm, she reminded herself. "Welcome. Your aid is timely."

Rhea nodded back, but said nothing. She looked a bit uncomfortable with the attention.

"The Skull went...less well," Aran continued. He heaved a sigh, then shook his head sadly. "We met the Guardian, a demon named Malila, and learned some troubling things. Anyone who's been touched by Xal is a conduit. Malila can see through their eyes, and distance doesn't seem to matter. Everything I've done, and everything Nara has done...she saw it all. The Guardian doesn't seem hostile, but I have no idea what her motives are in the long term."

"What does your gut say?" Voria asked. Sometimes it was the only reliable weathervane, when logic failed.

"I think she's on our side. She certainly has no love for Krox, or for Nefarius." Aran stroked his beard, and his eyes took on a far-away look, then refocused on her a moment later. "I debated telling anyone this, but it seems pertinent. Xal has given me the same ability to sense *void* and thus, those touched with his magic. Krox took a piece of him during the war, and I might even be able to use it to spot Krox's advance."

"Don't risk it," Voria replied. "Such magics can be traced, and if you peer into the mind of a god, you must expect them to peer back."

"Fair point." Aran looked toward the doorway leading into the conference room. "Austin comes across as a decent leader, but I'm already seeing that when he's pushed to the wall he'll screw people over without a second thought. He's been spending a lot of time with Skare, and with, ah, well, with your mother." He finally met her eyes when he said that last word.

Voria closed her eyes, and wished she could banish the euphoria. It was eroding her focus, and she needed that right now. She opened her eyes, and took in the company, who were all still watching her. "She's been compromised. Kazon warned me." It hurt to say, but she kept most of the emotion out of the words. "Right now I am more concerned for what it means regarding our new allies. If Ternus is also compromised, do we need to fear them stabbing us in the back in the middle of the battle? We cannot afford a second front, not right now."

Aran rubbed at the bridge of his nose, as if relieving stress. "I'd like to think they're going to support us today, at the very least. No one wants Krox to win here, and Ternus is even worse off than we are. But I think we should treat them as potential hostiles, starting right now. We need to be ready in case they turn on us. I hope it doesn't come to that, and I know that's the last thing you need to hear right now. But it's the truth."

"Shit," Crewes interjected with a proud smile. "Major can handle the truth."

"All we can focus on is tomorrow," Voria said, the euphoria stuffing her brain with cotton. She shook her head to clear it. "There's one other pressing issue."

"Nara," Aran said.

Voria nodded. "And her companions. Can they provide actionable intelligence?" She didn't dare get her hopes up.

"No." Aran shook his head. "Not because they aren't willing, though. You can perform whatever divination you like, but I suspect you'll find is that none of them are bound, and that all three are willing to help you against Krox. Kaho has no love for Nebiat, and is more than happy to tell us everything he knows. Trouble is, none of it seems relevant to a god assaulting our world."

"Ma'am?" Pickus's head poked through the doorway. "The governor is getting a little antsy, and doesn't seem to want to talk to anyone but you."

"I can do you one more favor, Aran." Voria decided suddenly. She glanced at the doorway he'd entered through. "I can spare you this farce. Take your Outriders and bring Nara to the *Spellship*'s brig. See that she and the others are safely ensconced, and then get some rest for tomorrow. I'll deal with my mother and our friends from Ternus."

Aran gave her a grateful nod, then twirled his hand in a circle. The company responded as one, and threaded through the door, back the way they'd come. Kezia gave Voria a little wave, and Bord gave her a big, stupid grin.

Voria could only smile back. She'd missed them so much.

She didn't know why, but somehow she knew to her bones that she'd never see them again. Not in this life anyway.

38

PRISONER TRANSFER

Aran was relieved to have avoided dinner with the governor. It wasn't as if the guy would have anything to offer strategically, and other than having his ego fluffed Aran couldn't think of what the dinner could accomplish. He deeply appreciated Voria diving on that grenade.

By the time they reached the *Talon*, Pickus was already there, his chest heaving as if he'd run the entire way. He stood next to the shimmering, blue ramp, his cheeks flushed and making him look a bit like a tomato under that red hair.

"Been a while, Captain." Pickus offered a hand, and Aran shook it.

He clapped Pickus on the shoulder, then released him. "Good to see you, man. I'll never forget how you saved our asses when the second burl blew up."

"Captain's right," Crewes agreed. "You did right by us, and now you're doing right by her." He gave Pickus an approving nod, which triggered a scandalized squawk from Bord.

"Well, today you've got a chance to pay me back." Pickus

gave a buck-toothed grin. "Voria said you needed to transfer some prisoners, but she didn't say who. I can help you get them to the brig, and then if you need anything else for the coming combat I can have it arranged. I'm kind of a big deal now."

"Administrator Pickus." Bord gave a snort and rolled his eyes, then turned to Kezia. "Yer not impressed by fancy titles, are you, luv?"

"The only title I want out of you is husband, and if you're lucky, maybe father." Kez gave him a coy smile. "Seeing as how a god's gonna be arriving and we have to play bouncer, why don't we spend the last of our free time relaxing?"

"Sir?" Crewes asked, raising an eyebrow and indicating Bord and Kez.

"I don't see why not. This is the last R&R anyone is going to see, and you and I can handle escorting Nara down to lockup." Aran walked up the ramp, crossed the cargo bay, then started down the ramp that led to the brig. Crewes fell into step beside him, but said nothing as they approached.

Pickus trailed after them, though he seemed more interested in inspecting the *Talon*'s internals than he did in following Aran to the brig.

They reached the base of the ramp, and Aran's skin tingled as he passed through the sound barrier. Nara, Frit, and Kaho all lounged on their respective benches, though they rose as soon as he entered. Only Nara approached the bars of her cell. Frit looked ready for a fight. Kaho had a half-curious expression, as if he couldn't quite summon the interest.

"Everyone up," Aran said. He moved to stand before Nara's cell. "We're moving you to the *Spellship*'s brig."

Nara's entire posture tightened, and he could feel her

tension even through the crackling bars. "Letting me out of here is dangerous, Aran."

Aran nodded in the sergeant's direction. "Crewes still has the control rod, and we're aboard the most heavily fortified ship in the sector. We're going to take a little stroll, then get you settled in, nice and quick. Voria's got other matters to attend to, but we talked a little, and I'm confident you're in good hands. She'll help you, Nara." He tapped the blue button next to the cell, and the bars winked out.

Kaho shuffled out, his wingtips brushing the ceiling. "I will offer no resistance. Frit, please grant them the same courtesy."

Frit's eyes narrowed, and wisps of smoke rose from the corners, but she gave a curt nod and strode from the cell, shoulders proudly squared as if she were choosing to be there, and not a prisoner. "Fine. I'm past hoping for fair treatment from Shayans, but maybe they'll surprise me."

Aran nodded at Crewes to take point, and the sergeant did so. Nara, Frit, and Kaho trailed after, and Aran brought up the rear. He kept his hand on Narlifex, just in case.

She will not betray you, Narlifex said, his tone confident. *Circumstances have put us at odds, but she cares for you. She seeks the same things.*

He nearly released the hilt of the blade. Narlifex had evolved more than he'd wanted to admit if the blade was capable of reading human social situations. He hoped it was right. Nara kept glancing over her shoulder, as if expecting to find something terrible there. She looked so distracted, and even stumbled once. Nara was one of the most graceful people he knew.

Pickus led them through a maze of corridors, and then took them into a lift. The doors slid shut behind them, and he moved to a panel with the Circle of Eight emblazoned on it. Pickus tapped the *void* sigil, then tapped three numbers on the neighboring panel.

A bright flash of light rippled through the lift, and there was a moment of vertigo that Aran had come to associate with teleportation. The doors slid open and Pickus stepped out.

"Come on," the fiery-haired tech mage said, "We're almost there."

The company followed him down a narrow corridor with smooth, grey walls. It emptied into a room of three-meter-by-three-meter cells that had clearly been designed by the same people who'd built the *Talon's* brig. The crackling blue bars were identical, as were the benches. The ceilings were higher though, which would likely help Kaho.

"Well at least they're just as luxurious as the last ones," Nara quipped.

Kaho made a noise that might have been laughter, while Frit delivered an annoyed stare.

"At least you haven't lost your sense of humor." Aran tapped the blue button next to the cell and the bars winked out. "See, safe and sound."

Nara, Kaho, and Frit each entered their respective cells. Aran was about to tap the button again, but hesitated. "Frit, would you prefer to share a cell with Kaho?"

Surprise flashed across her smoldering features. "That—I'd really like that." She walked from her cell and moved to stand in Kaho's. "Thank you, Captain. I'm not used to small kindnesses, but I should remember that you aren't Shayan. You're different than the rest of them."

Crewes barked a harsh laugh. "Lady, you know less about us than you think. It sucks that you had to live in that ivory tower with an ass-clown like Eros—no disrespect to the dead or nothin'—but that don't mean the rest of us are the enemy. The major is the best person I know, and she is most definitely Shayan."

Frit's expression grew somber, though she didn't reply. Maybe Crewes had scored a point.

He turned to Nara and lowered his voice a hair. "Listen. I know you're worried. Krox is going to be here soon. Even I can feel it, like a—I don't know, a pressure that's building. I have to believe we have a chance to win, and if we do...this Talifax isn't unstoppable, and we've got some powerful allies. Voria's about to get a whole lot stronger."

"I know," Nara whispered. She eyed him searchingly. "I just can't shake the feeling that I'm going to do something terrible. I know it isn't logical. There's no way out of this cell, and Talifax seems unable or unwilling to come here. It should all work out, but Aran, somehow I know it won't."

Aran gave a sympathetic nod. "I can't promise it will. But I can promise we'll do our best to help you."

"Count on that," Crewes echoed, giving Nara something resembling a sympathetic nod. "I may not like you, but I'm starting to understand that maybe you ain't the traitor I thought you were. We'll save your smug, elitist ass, and you can go back to hanging out with the major and drinking tea and doing rituals and shit. But first we've got a god to kill."

"Come on." Aran nodded toward the lift, where Pickus still stood. "I want one more good night's sleep."

Nara gave him a tentative smile as he departed, and Aran felt the tiniest bit better about everything.

39

UNLIKELY ALLIES

Voria remembered girding herself for the battle against Nebiat back on Marid. She'd feared her death, but had stalwartly ridden to war, with her battalion behind her. Stepping through the doorway into a dinner party felt a greater trial, and each step came heavier than the last. She forced a smile as she stepped through.

Most of the servants had disappeared, leaving four people seated around a table big enough for thirty. She instantly recognized her mother's laugh, even before she saw the severe white hair and the cruel eyes. Jolene sat facing the governor, the man she'd met briefly at Ternus. He was handsome, in an austere sort of way, but had the same cruel cast to his features that her mother demonstrated.

Skare sat two chairs away from the couple, sipping a goblet of lifewine. He raised it toward Voria, and delivered a smile as she approached. "Ah, Major, please, join us. We have so much to catch up on. I'm so pleased that you not only survived, but managed to acquire the *Spellship*. A true marvel, one that I hope our meager fleet can assist in the coming battle."

Voria pushed the euphoria away, and struggled to concentrate as she moved to sit in the chair next to Skare. She crossed her legs, and poured herself a goblet of lifewine, which she didn't drink. "Your aid is greatly appreciated, Skare. May I call you, Skare, or is that too familiar?"

Skare attempted to smooth an errant lock of hair, then gave up with a self-deprecating eye roll. "I'd like to think of us as friends, Voria. We've known each other a long time, and we share the same interests. Currently, at least." He sipped at his goblet, and gave her a mischievous wink.

"I suppose we do," she admitted. She took a small sip of the wine, then shifted to face the fourth person sitting at the table, Pickus. The fiery-haired engineer was wolfing down food as quickly as he could, and seemed to be desperately avoiding making eye contact with anyone. She freed Aran. Why not him as well? "Administrator Pickus, could I impose upon you to help Captain Aran transfer his prisoners to the brig?"

She watched Skare out of the corner of her eye, and was unsurprised to see his emotionless eyes fixed on her, as empty as the void. Perhaps he already knew who those prisoners were. But privately she hoped that he didn't, and now wondered. Petty, maybe, but one took what comforts one could.

"'Course, ma'am." Pickus set down his fork and rose swiftly, wiping his face with the back of his sleeve. "I'll get down there straight away." He shot her a grateful look as he all but sprinted from the room.

"Voria," Jolene's voice cut through the clink of plates and scraping of chairs. "I didn't see you come in." Her mother made no move to rise, but did raise her goblet in Voria's direction. "Your hospitality has certainly improved since you were stationed on that gods-awful ship, what was it called?"

"The *Wyrm Hunter*," Voria replied dryly. It brought her a small measure of comfort that Davidson had been given command. At least the ship was in capable hands.

"Major," Austin said, a touch stiffly. He swirled the contents of his goblet, then raised it to drink. The taste seemed to annoy him, and he frowned at the goblet, then set it down.

"Welcome, Governor." Voria kept her tone amicable as she rose and took the chair closest to Austin. Whatever else was happening here, he was the leader of her closest ally, and had come to assist her against a god. That took a certain measure of bravery or foolishness. Either amounted to a debt she owed. "You have my deepest sympathies for the state of your capital. Shaya thanks you for your aid. I know what we are asking of you. Opposing a god is no easy feat. You have my assurance that should we survive we will offer every magical remedy to help your people."

Austin's frown lessened, and he gave her a grateful nod. "Thank you, Major. Krox has made our colony unlivable. He's doomed hundreds of millions of my citizens to a slow death, and there isn't a damned thing we can do about it. What we can do, though, is get some payback." Austin nodded toward Voria's mother. "Thanks to the Inurans, we've got the tools to fight. The raid on the Skull didn't go as well as we'd have liked, but we came away with enough mages to staff the ships, at least. Skare claims they can go toe to toe with a god."

"And I stand by that claim," Skare confirmed. He set down his own goblet, then straightened the collar of his jacket, the blue fabric shining under the soft lights. "Gods are particularly vulnerable to the vessels' primary ability. The ships drain magic, you see. Gods are comprised of pure magic. I believe Krox will be quite surprised by the level of...

resistance Ternus is able to offer during the battle. The time of gods has passed, Governor. And now we have provided you the tools with which to teach Krox that very lesson."

Jolene gave a smooth laugh as if it were the funniest joke anyone had ever told. Austin's frown relaxed a hair and he picked up his goblet, though he didn't drink. "It will have to be enough. We may not be able to save our world, but we can ensure that Krox never does it to another."

"We will endeavor to do exactly that, Governor," Voria promised. As she watched, she realized that whatever magic Drakkon had given her was having another side effect.

A riot of colors exploded around her. Everywhere there was magic it leapt into sharp focus, and that magic glowed with the color of the corresponding aspect. The lifewine glowed a white-gold. The illusionary lights above glowed pinkish-purple.

But the people around her glowed far more brightly. Her mother's aura was multilayered, mostly the sky blue of *air* magic, but streaked with the white of *life*. Here and there, though, a new color had appeared. A purple so dark it bordered midnight itself. She knew it for *void* instantly, and while she couldn't identify the god it came from, she strongly suspected she knew.

Voria turned her attention to Skare, whose aura was remarkably similar to Jolene's, but with the addition of the fierce scarlet of *fire* and the soft brown of *earth*. None of that was surprising. Looking at Governor Austin was.

The young man wasn't magically active, or shouldn't have been. But his aura was overlaid with the same streaks of *void* that both Jolene and Skare bore. The scholar in her protested that it was possible he'd acquired it at the Skull of Xal, and that both Jolene and Skare had gotten it from a legitimate source as well. But she knew better. They'd all been touched the same dark god, presumably this Nefarius. At least she knew who her enemies were.

"Voria, do you have a battle plan?" Skare asked as he swirled the contents of his goblet. Why did people enjoy doing that so much?

"A rough one," Voria admitted, coming to with a start. Her newfound vision faded a hair, and in its wake came a tide of exhaustion. She stifled a yawn before continuing. "The Shayan fleet, what remains, is gathered over the tree itself, backed by Major Davidson and the conventional fleet you've so graciously sent. That is where we will make our stand. In my visions Krox has come with a thousand motes of flaming light, which I take to be Ifrit. That's where your fleet will come in. I'd like Captain Aran to lead your ships into combat, and to take down as many of those Ifrit as possible before they reach Shaya. If he fails the consequences will be...catastrophic." She recalled her vision, and shuddered.

"We're all exhausted I'm sure," Jolene interjected. "Why don't we let Voria get some rest? We'll return to our fleet and get prepared for tomorrow's...battle."

Voria realized that her mother was staring at her, and that her eyes shone with...well, some sort of emotion, certainly. Was Jolene genuinely worried for her safety? She hadn't even realized the woman was capable of experiencing that kind of concern.

"I could use the rest as well." Austin rose to his feet, and gave Voria a casual nod. "I'm sure we'll all need it for what we're about to face."

Something in his attitude was...off. Voria couldn't place it. He knew something, and that something was about her. Between the exhaustion and the lingering euphoria it kept slipping just out of reach.

"Good night, Governor. Mother. Skare." She rose to her feet and retrieved Ikadra from near the door. Inexplicable fear gripped her as she left the room. What was she not seeing? What did they know?

She was simply too exhausted to worry about it, tonight at least.

40

INESCAPABLE

Nara leaned back against the cell wall with a stretch, then began another set of exercises. The routine had been one of the first memories that returned, something they'd apparently taught her during her basic Zephyr training.

At first, practicing it had been hard, and Nara had been forced to admit that her physical conditioning had badly lapsed. It was understandable, of course, since she'd been studying to be a true mage. But now that she could remember what her body was capable of, she was more interested than ever in making sure she was in excellent shape. Lives could depend on it.

"Nara?" Kaho called from across the brig. The hatchling stood upright near the bars, his wings no longer nearly brushing the ceiling in their new cells. "Are you able to converse while doing your...mating display?"

Nara chuckled as she completed her next stance, tree pose. Mating display indeed. She bent nearly double into downward dog, a name that made no sense. The names were apparently so ancient many of the meanings had been lost in translation. "What did you want to talk about?"

"My mother's binding ritual for Drakkon at Marid was complex, I am told. You puzzled it out, did you not? That suggests you have some skill as a mage." Kaho began to pace back and forth in the cell.

Nara flowed into a standing position, suddenly interested. "Enough that I was able to modify it, though I don't pretend that I understood the entire thing." Though, now that she looked back with the benefits of Neith's gift, she realized that she *could* understand the entire thing.

"I've been considering the ritual of investiture that Voria is about to undergo." Kaho continued his pacing, his tone passionate. "A god does not possess a body, in the traditional sense. They transcend the physical."

"So what happens to their body?" Frit asked. She'd been watching silently from the bench in the cell she shared with Kaho, but now seemed interested.

"It must be obliterated by the magical energy." Kaho waved the comment away with a clawed hand. "That isn't what interests me." He paused and faced them both. "If gods no longer possess a physical form then they are effectively pure magic, as we understand it. But at its core the god must still possess the original spirit. Does that seem to make sense, Nara?"

She nodded along, following his logic. "If what we know is correct, then yes. A person's spirit must merge directly with the magic when the investiture is performed. There'd have to be something to serve as an anchor for the magic, and I guess the soul must be that anchor."

Kaho's tail flicked behind him, almost of its own accord. Whether in excitement or agitation Nara couldn't say. "Do you think it's possible you could somehow remove the spirit? Sever the anchor's chain, to follow the analogy. Perhaps it could be stripped from the magic, denying the god the bulk of its power."

"It's an interesting theory," Nara mused, though she was distracted by something else Kaho had said.

A spirit was needed to merge with a god, *not a body*. She wasn't yet sure how, but that tidbit seemed vital. The idea kept rolling around in her mind, though she tried to pay attention to the hatchling.

"Nara," Frit growled, her tone low and feral.

Nara followed her gaze and realized she was staring at an armored man standing outside the *Spellship*'s brig. Her breath caught when she recognized him.

Kheross's scarlet armor thudded on the metallic floor as he approached her cell, and stared at with those *void*-tainted eyes. She knew instantly why he was there, before he so much as opened his mouth.

"No," she whispered. "Kheross, please. Don't."

"Frit?" Kaho asked, his tone expressing his confusion. "Who is this?"

Nara tuned him out. She tuned out everything except for Kheross himself. The Wyrm held a control rod clutched in his right hand, which would allow him to remove her collar. She had no idea how he planned to get the cell door open, but it seemed likely he had a plan.

"You do not wish to be freed?" Kheross blinked at her. When she didn't answer he shook his head and moved to the bars. "It doesn't matter. Stand back as far as you can."

Nara backed away from the bars, and it was a good thing. Inky tendrils of *void* swam from each of Kheross's fingers, and wherever they touched the bars, the crackling, blue energy simply ceased to exist. He swirled his hands in a counterclockwise motion, and a two-meter, circular gap appeared in the bars.

She was free.

"Goddess, no," she murmured, hanging her head, but no longer able to deny the truth.

Kheross raised the control rod, and the collar snapped open of its own accord, and clattered to the floor. "Shall I free your companions as well? What do you say, Krox? Do you want out of your cage?"

"Please." Kaho folded his arms, and eyed Kheross skeptically, as if not believing he'd follow through.

Frit didn't reply, though she did move to the back of the cell.

Kheross walked to the second cell, and repeated his *void* ability until a similar opening was created. He smiled then, a wistful expression that seemed at home on his harsh features. "I've fulfilled my part of the deal. You're free to work whatever mischief Talifax has put you up to. My part in all this is done."

The Wyrm turned and strode from the brig, disappearing up the ramp.

Nara could only stare in horror at the gap in her cell, her mind going back to Talifax's words. What would she do when the weight of her fate was inescapable? Every barrier had been removed, and now she could, if she wanted to, sneak to Voria's quarters and kill her.

Thanks to the dream Talifax had sent, she knew the route. She knew how to reach Voria without being detected, and knew beyond a shadow of a doubt that she could kill her. But why? There seemed to be no reason, and she'd yet to feel any sort of compulsion forcing her in that direction.

The pieces were all there, and she felt so close to putting them together.

"Are you coming?" Frit asked as she leapt through the hole in the cell.

Kaho gingerly crawled through the same hole, wincing when his tail was singed by one of the bars. "Oww. What do we do now, Nara? Is there a way for us to escape this ship?"

That was the real question. What now?

She stepped out of her cell, and furiously tried to think of a way to avoid the fate Talifax had planned for her. There had to be a way to foil his plans, and yet if there were, wouldn't he have predicted it? He expected her to kill Voria, and seemed so damned certain it was going to happen.

Why? Why was he so certain? For that to be the case, then killing her must make sense to Nara. There must be a reason why killing Voria was the only logical course.

And then she finally understood. There *was* a reason. Theoretically the ritual could be performed on a soul. There was no need for a body. She remembered what Malila had told her. She could comply, without capitulation.

"Frit, Kaho, I want the two of you to sneak into the coliseum where they're gathering to perform the investiture. Here's what we're going to do..."

41

THE END

Voria reached her quarters an eternity later, and only in that moment wondered why she'd not thought to simply teleport there. She wasn't thinking clearly, which Drakkon had warned her would be the cost of absorbing so much magic so quickly. Hopefully sleep would remedy that.

"Thank the goddess." The golden door to her quarters dissolved, and she entered her spacious chambers. They bordered on opulent, and she didn't mind admitting she enjoyed it much more than the *Hunter*'s spartan quarters.

She deposited Ikadra in the air next to her nightstand, then sat and removed the ivory hair pick binding her hair. She combed her fingers through to remove the worst of the knots, then reached for her brush. Voria had many, many pressures each day. But this ritual was something she treated with the same sanctity she'd once reserved for Shaya.

Brushing her hair calmed her, and prepared her for sleep. It was a guilty pleasure. Shayan nobility, particularly women, were known for excessive grooming, and so she'd always avoided it with a severe ponytail, or bun, and an austere military uniform.

But in her quarters she could relax. She could, quite literally, let her hair down and be a simple woman for a few moments before bed. Voria hummed quietly to herself as she ran the onyx-handled brush through her hair, counting down the strokes from a hundred.

Thoughts flitted across her consciousness, but she didn't hold onto them. This too was part of the ritual, a sort of simple mindful meditation. Her breathing deepened, and by the time she'd reached her fiftieth stroke she was already ready for bed. She paused for a moment, and considered whether or not she wanted to finish the ritual.

"Voria!" Ikadra's sapphire pulsed, and she twisted in her chair.

Time elongated as her gaze slowly rose. It took in the hoverbed, the scattered maps on the table, the heavy Shayan tapestries on the walls, and then finally reached the ceiling. A figure crouched there like a spider, and wore some sort of enhanced body suit that was too small to be spellarmor.

The assassin already had a spellrifle trained on Voria. The barrel filled with *void* magic, a level three, more than sufficient for the kill. Voria had all the time in the world to watch the spell build, but none of the magic Shaya had given her, and nothing she'd gained from Drakkon made her the slightest bit faster. They couldn't prevent her death.

Nothing could.

She accepted that, even as she spun out possibilities. In all of them the spell ended her life. Millions became billions, but there was simply no possibility of survival. No hope, no hope at all.

She let the possibilities play out. She died, and Nara

completed the ritual. A god rose that the people assumed was her, a goddess they believed in. That power let this new goddess, Nara, challenge Krox.

In some possibilities Krox won, and Shaya was extinguished. The planet scoured away. The great spear, Worldender, pulled from the dead world. A tide of Ifrit surged from the massive star, and swarmed over the planet, burning everything they touched. The *Talon* and the black ships fought back, and in some possibilities they won. In others, they were overwhelmed and destroyed.

The greatest number of possibilities showed Krox emerging victorious, but in a few Nara drove him from the system. From there Voria's vision was...blocked. Someone or something had carefully obscured vast swathes of the multiverse. Talifax perhaps, or his mistress, Nefarius.

As the void bolt took her in the breast Voria's last thought was that no matter who won, her people had lost. Curiously there was no pain as her body unraveled, only a sense of relief.

She'd done her duty, and now she could finally rest.

42

THE BEGINNING

Nara stared down at Voria's still cooling corpse, and wept.

The major had been, in many ways, a mentor. Nara had always been desperate for her approval, and though grudgingly, Voria had given it. And this was how Nara had repaid her. She prayed desperately that her theory was correct.

"You MONSTER!" Ikadra's sapphire pulsed a deep, angry blue. "You killed her. I wanted to believe in you, and I told her you could be redeemed. And you killed her! Why? What could you possibly gain? You doomed us all. Unless... you're going to try to steal her power, aren't you? This is all some sort of con job designed to elevate you to godhood. And to think I actually thought you were hot."

The tears continued to flow, and Nara didn't fight them, but she did get to work. "Shut up, Ikadra." She picked up the staff, which was warm to the touch. With Voria dead the staff no longer had a master, which disabled his magical defenses. That was a good thing as Nara was fairly certain Ikadra would happily kill her right now, given the choice.

"Listen very carefully," she began, bending to inspect the staff. "you're a critical component in the ritual of investiture, right?"

"Right," Ikadra replied cautiously. The anger was still there, but at least the staff was listening.

"You're designed to channel the soul, right? So if you're elevating someone you must somehow store that soul, and then focus all the magic into it?"

"I guess. I mean that's what happened with Shaya. Why?" Ikadra pulsed suspiciously.

"Because I want you to pick up Voria's soul, and I want you to hold it." Nara placed Ikadra's sapphire against Voria's forehead.

"Uh, I can do that." Ikadra's pulsing grew more rapid and a note of excitement entered his voice. "Wait, you're still going to perform the ritual, aren't you?"

"Yup. Now get to work." Nara glanced over her shoulder, but there was no one there, of course. If Talifax was aware of what she intended, she was almost positive he'd be here crushing her spine, or something equally grisly. Either he didn't know, or couldn't do anything about it. She'd killed Voria, as he expected, and theoretically he still believed she was going to follow through with his plan for her.

"So, wait. I don't get it. Why did you kill her? That seems like a really messed up prank." A golden glow built around Ikadra's tip, and something ethereal rose from Voria, a golden mist that began flowing into Ikadra's sapphire at an incredible rate. It went on for some time. "She's going to be pissed."

"Because if I hadn't, then Talifax would have destroyed me long before I got to the *Spellship*, and he would have found another way to kill Voria," Nara explained while she waited for the soul transference to complete. "He was so certain that I'd murder her, and he believed that I'd go through with his plan to become a goddess in her place. At first I thought he'd bound me and that's why he was so sure, but the more I thought about it the more I realized the truth. He didn't think he needed to bind me, because he saw me killing her of my own volition."

"Binding you wouldn't have worked anyway," Ikadra said. "If you were bound, the *Spellship*'s security would have gone nuts as soon as you came aboard."

"Then he definitely thought I'd do it on my own, and he was right." Nara rose from Voria's body, and tried not to look at her sightless eyes. She cradled Ikadra to her chest and made swiftly for the door. "I think Talifax is either afraid of, or unable to, board this ship. I don't think he can see what happens here, either. He needed a tool to kill Voria, one that he could convince to do it without needing to bind them. That's also why he needed Kheross to free me. Because he couldn't or wouldn't do it himself."

It all made sense now. Nara hurried from Voria's quarters, and began to sketch as she walked. She cast an invisibility spell, and made the radius as small as she could while still covering herself. Then she trotted as fast as she could through the ship, snaking her way closer to the coliseum where the ritual was going to take place.

"What are you going to do now?"

"Now I'm going to pray that I'm right about this ritual. If so, we're going to go through with it just like we planned, and we're going to get Voria up and ready to save this world."

43

THIS WILL NEVER WORK

Pickus was about as nervous as a freighter down to one bad O_2 scrubber, and he had every right to be. The coliseum was absolutely packed with people ready to help Voria ascend. Their enthusiasm was infectious, and smiles and laughter were everywhere. You'd hardly guess a god was coming to snuff them all out.

Thanks to Ducius and his Caretakers they'd managed to convince the people that Voria would save them, but only if they did their part. They were ready to do exactly that, but unfortunately, there was still one major piece missing. Voria herself.

Pickus paced across the stage, and watched the door to the little room he knew she'd appear through, the same one where she'd met with Captain Aran the evening before. She should have been here nearly an hour ago, and the only thing Pickus could think was that maybe she was recovering from the magic Drakkon had given her.

He was about to send a runner when he remembered there were other options. Pickus fished his scry-pad out of his pocket and fed it a bit of *fire*, then selected Voria from his contact lists. The device generated a missive, which was basically a magical version of a comm call, so far as he could tell.

Several moments went by, and then the missive died. "Odd. There's no reason it shouldn't connect, unless..." Unless the person on the other end was either magically shielded, or dead. Both had catastrophic implications.

Pickus hurried across the stage to where Ducius stood chatting quietly with a few of his more loyal supporters. He nodded his greetings. "Caretakers. Pardon me, Tender, but I'm going to see if I can go find Voria. Would you mind watching over things until I return?"

"Of course, Administrator." Ducius clasped his hands before him and performed a standing bow. Pickus was still getting used to not being treated like engine grime, but thus far he was kinda liking it. "I'll keep them occupied, but I'd agree that getting her here sooner rather than later would be a good thing. We do not want their mood to ebb."

Pickus pivoted and hurried through the door into the antechamber. No sign of Voria. He headed to the door on the room's far side, which dissolved at his approach. He stepped through and was about to turn right when a warm, reptilian hand clamped down over his mouth. Pickus was hoisted into the air, and found himself face to face with a gorgeous woman...made completely of fire and rock.

"Hi there," the flaming girl said, as sweet as pie, "Kaho is going to release your mouth, and you're not going to scream, right?"

He nodded, and the hand came away. "Oh, crap, you're that Ifrit girl, right? And the guy behind me, he's one of those enforcer things? Ya'll don't eat people, do you?"

"Hello, Pickus." Nara winked into existence next to the Ifrit. She wore form-fitting armor that looked like it might have been produced on Ternus. He was almost as interested in the armor as he was the curves underneath.

Then Pickus went cold. Nara was holding Ikadra. "Oh, Nara, tell me you didn't do what I think you did. Please, tell me I'm wrong. I didn't want to believe what they said, but... you've really gone over haven't you? Or were you evil the whole time and just suckering me in? Man, I can't believe I fell for it. Well I can, but it's still shitty of you."

"Listen very carefully, Pickus." Nara leaned in closer, and fixed him with those pretty eyes. "Voria is dead."

"Oh my—". The scaly hand settled over his mouth again.

"Just listen," Nara said, continuing. "Her soul resides in Ikadra, and is ready to ascend, just like you planned. You can still do this, and she can still fight Krox."

Pickus thrashed in the dragon-thing's grip, and eventually it uncovered his mouth. "How? This thing only works if the people believe. I can't show them Ikadra and say empower this stupid staff—no offense. For us to complete the ritual Voria needs to be standing there. She needs to tell these people why their faith is well placed, and then, if we're lucky, they'll give her enough juice to do her god thing. So unless you've got—"

Nara's hand rose and she began sketching sigils. The first was a purple squiggle, quickly followed by a blue symbol kind of like a harp, and then another squiggle. The sigils fused, and the spell completed. Magical energy rippled over Nara, obscuring her features for a moment. When they passed Nara was gone, and Voria stood in her place, right down to the mustard stain on the sleeve of her confederate jacket.

"Okay, well, I guess maybe that will work," Pickus allowed, more than a little surprised that she'd so easily addressed the problem. "I mean, you've still got to give them a rousing speech. Do you think you can manage that?"

Fake-Voria gave a somber nod, and her eyes shone with unshed tears. "I can manage it." The words were given in a near perfect imitation of Voria's voice. The people who knew her best might notice something off, but everyone else should buy it.

"Nara." Pickus's voice cracked, but he didn't even care. "You didn't answer my question. I just don't get it. Why did you leave? And why all this? Just tell me there's a reason, and that you ain't...what they say you are. Tell me this Krox ain't what he looks like, neither."

Pickus didn't know what she could say that would make this okay, but looking at her, especially wearing the major's face...it was just too much to bear. He looked away, staring instead at the fire-girl.

"I don't have all the answers, Pickus, any more than we've got the time," Fake-Voria finally replied. She straightened, adopting Voria's imperious posture, almost perfectly. "For now we have a mission, and we're going to carry it out. Carry on, Pickus." She waved Ikadra at the doorway.

Pickus still had serious reservations, but at least the Krox set him down. He stared up at the lizard, who looked down at him with slitted, reptilian eyes. Somehow, though, the heat coming from Frit was more menacing. He glanced at her and she was smiling at him, but something in her eyes said that if he screwed this up she would space him.

He hurried through the doorway, and paused just on the other side to assess the situation. Ducius was just finishing a hymn, which the entire crowd, fifty-thousand strong, had sung in time. He didn't recognize the song, probably a

Shayan anthem or some such. Even the drifters seemed to like it. Seemed to mention trees and sacrifice a lot.

"Ma would have some choice words for me right about now." Pickus forced himself forward, and was quite proud that he didn't wet himself. Voria had called this the greatest con of all time, and now, it really was. He hurried over to Ducius, "Uh, we're about ready. I'm going to bring her out. Can you get them ready?"

"They are prepared. I will introduce her." Ducius gave Pickus a warm smile. "You've done much to engineer this moment, Administrator. I see now that she was right about you."

Pickus gave him a sickly smile, then waved a little as he backed awkwardly away. Ole Tex, let this work. He hurried back to the door and looked at Nara, "Okay, we're on. Ducius is going to introduce you. When he does, well, you gotta say some stuff to get them fired up, and then Ducius and his Caretakers will kick off the ritual."

Nara nodded, and stepped through the doorway.

There was no way this was going to work, Pickus was certain of it. Not like they had a lot of choice, though.

Ducius roared to the crowd, "I give you...Lady Voria, the savior of our world, and heir to Shaya herself." The Tender stepped gracefully out of her way, and moved to a large ritual circle, where his Caretakers were already arrayed.

Pickus could only watch, and hope, that Nara could pull this off.

'Voria' walked to the edge of the stage, Ikadra punctuating each step as his heavy end thudded against the bronze. She paused, then spoke in a high, clear voice, "I am humbled by the gathering I see before me. Drifters. Shayans. Ternus Marines. We've come together to accomplish something that none of us would be able to do alone. We seek to create a deity, so that we can oppose Krox."

She paused for dramatic effect, and did it masterfully. The crowd held their collective breath.

"I will ride forth on your behalf, and I will meet Krox in battle. I will triumph, and do you know why?" She held up a hand to her ear, and Pickus noted the sharp glance from Ducius. This kind of grandstanding was out of character for her.

The crowd called out a loose chorus of why's, and only then did Voria answer. "Because Krox is alone. Even his own children are deserting him. Even the Wyrms we have battled for so long will not stand with their creator. They recognize his evil. He is alone, and we are many. We will triumph."

Explosive applause echoed through the room, wave after wave crashing over Pickus. It went on for many moments until Ducius finally raised his hands, and spoke. "The ritual begins. Believe, my brethren. Believe in the power of your goddess, and she will be strong enough to save us all."

He returned to the ritual circle, where the Caretakers had already begun sketching sigils. Ducius took his place among them, and added a steady flow of white and blue squiggles to the spell. The crowd was utterly silent as they worked, and a few minutes later the spell reached a crescendo.

The sigils fused together, and a beam of pure white shot into Ikadra's sapphire. A soft, white glow rose from the audience, a tiny wisp arising from each person. They drifted toward the light in a growing wave of power.

Then, just as suddenly as the spell had begun, it sputtered and died. The light above the crowd winked out, and the glow around Ikadra faded.

The ritual had failed.

A few screams began in the audience, and Pickus glanced out to see what had caused the disturbance. People were pointing up at the dome overhead.

A second star had appeared in the sky over Shaya. Krox had arrived.

44

KROX RISES

Nebiat awakened once again, the last strands of torpor falling away to be replaced by awareness of infinite possibilities stretching into the distance. She spent long minutes analyzing billions of outcomes, and was relieved to see that nothing significant had changed.

Nothing that you can detect, Krox rumbled. *You must remember that many gods are adept at hiding possibilities until the moment of their fruition. If you are unaware of the parameters surrounding their desired outcome, then it can lead to the same hubris I've exhibited each time I've lost a confrontation.*

Either the deity's anger had faded or he'd suppressed it. Nebiat didn't care which. She twisted in the void over her new capital world, a world Krox had never bothered to name, and looked down at her children. While she'd slept they'd begun to organize. Groups had formed. A few had even begun practicing spells.

She considered the world, and its new inhabitants. The war against Shaya was important, but what came after? What came in a year, or a decade, or a century? She wanted this world to flourish, no matter the cost. That meant that while she could bring a tremendous army with her, it would also put her children at risk.

I approve of your sudden prudence. I still believe you have squandered the Earthmother, but since the deed is done, this world should be carefully husbanded. Your goal of creating a religion seems promising.

"My children," Nebiat said, her magic carrying the words to the ear of every Wyrm, hatchling and adult, all over the planet. "It troubles me to call upon you so soon after your awakening, but we have great need. We are at war, and even now our enemies seek to resurrect their goddess. If they succeed, every egg is at risk. They must be stopped. I call upon the strong to join me. We will take the war to them, and see that they trouble us no longer."

Draconic shrieks sounded all over the planet, every Wyrm crying out their defiance. The largest leapt into the air, and she smiled as they rose by the hundred. They sailed into the void, swirling around her like a swarm of bats.

Why not bring a thousand? Or five thousand? Your world could still flourish.

"Because if this war comes down to attrition we've already lost," Nebiat explained, rather graciously in her estimation. "I bring enough to subdue the remains of the Shayan's fleet, and whatever else she's cobbled together. Add to that our Ifrit, and Shaya has no chance of survival. There are many possibilities where Voria rises, but if she manages to, it will come down to a contest between us, and having a larger force of Wyrms will not change the outcome. Win or lose I wish to return to a prosperous world. Unlike you I plan to take the stewardship of my race seriously."

You are so young. You still think in centuries. Most species do not exist longer than a few hundred millennia. This world you so treasure will fall someday, and you will see the folly of favoring any single species.

"Perhaps, but until then I will protect my people." Nebiat held out her hand, and the Wyrms flew obediently into her palm. They settled there, all of them, so small compared to her.

She held her other hand aloft and Ifrit by the thousand felt her need. They flew toward the second palm, and pooled there. Nebiat willed *fire* into her hand, then used it to fuse several thousand Ifrit into a titanic star elemental. She repeated this process several more times, until she had a cluster of elementals.

It was certainly possible to create more, but Nebiat decided that this would suffice. She would use these Wyrms, and these elementals. If she lost today—a slim possibility, but one that still existed—then only these few followers would be taken, and she could return here to foster the rest. To encourage their worship, and thus grow in power.

"My children!" She thundered, her voice echoing across the cosmos in defiance of simple physics. "We ride for Shaya. In a moment we will arrive. Slay your enemies, and turn their world to cinders so that they may never challenge our rule again."

Nebiat concentrated, and then she and her children crossed the sector in the space of a heartbeat. They appeared in the sky over Shaya, on the opposite side of the umbral shadow, where their defenses would be concentrated.

As expected, Voria had anticipated that action, and re-deployed about half her forces to this side of the planet. A small fleet of traditional Shayan warships was supported by the Ternus fleet, the hated *Wyrm Hunter* among them.

Behind them lurked a new type of ship, one she'd not

encountered before. The wedge-shaped vessels were forged from a disquieting metal, one that resisted her senses.

I sense the taint of our enemy, Krox rumbled.

"Voria?" Nebiat asked, not understanding what he meant.

A far greater threat, in the long term. Nefarius, Krox corrected. *These vessels bear his touch. Take care in fighting them.*

"That's why I've brought minions." Nebiat opened her hands, and a cloud of dragons leapt from one, while a school of star elementals flowed from the other. They moved unerringly toward the enemy fleet, but their enemies fell back, avoiding engagement as they fled toward the other half of their forces near the planet's nadir.

At the head of that fleet flew the *Spellship*, gleaming brightly, an elder sibling watching over the smaller ships. It was the first time she'd seen the vessel, though Kaho had brought back footage of it from Virkon. It was smaller than she'd expected, colossal for a starship, but nothing when compared to a goddess. That didn't mean she shouldn't be wary, though. She didn't need Krox's 'prudence' to understand that, outside of Voria, that ship was the most powerful opponent in the system.

She considered engaging the defenders, but time was of the essence. Voria had not arisen, and that meant that there was no one to stop Nebiat from scouring life from the world below.

She extended all four of her cosmic arms and plunged them down at the shield surrounding the blasted tree. Each blow sent ripples along the shield, and she could feel it weakening. The shield might last for several seconds, but the moment it was gone she could rip that tree from the earth and claim Worldender.

Shaya was also down there, and after Nebiat devoured her body she would retreat to her world, and learn to master all her new power. For now, though, there was glorious killing to be done.

She was going to enjoy dismembering this world, and ending Voria forever.

45

INTO THE FRAY

Aran awoke in his quarters with a sense that something was desperately wrong. He rose from the hoverbed and picked up his uniform from the foot of the bed where he'd left it the night before. The *Talon*'s magic seemed to think of everything, and the gravy stain from dinner had vanished.

The unease persisted, and he knew he couldn't write it off as a simple dream. Something was wrong. He moved to his nightstand and picked up Narlifex, then buckled the scabbard around his waist.

The blade seemed to sense his agitation. *Krox comes.*

"Yeah, I can feel him, but it's more than that. Something's wrong with Voria," Aran murmured. Whatever the feeling was it seemed magical in nature, and as he examined his feelings he realized it had something to do with the ability Malila had given him back at the Skull.

Aran moved to the scry-screen in the corner, and fed it a mote of *fire*. He knew Voria was probably busy since this was the morning of the investiture, but hopefully she'd have a minute or two to put his mind at ease before he flew into battle. Seeing her face would go a long way to banishing his concerns.

The screen flashed, and then went dark. Odd. He blinked down at it and, for a moment at least, wondered if he'd miscast the spell somehow.

No. Narlifex countered. *You were right. Something is wrong.*

Aran cast another missive, but this time he targeted Pickus. It took several moments to resolve, and showed Pickus standing in the *Spellship*'s coliseum. Scattered screams came from behind him. Panicked screams. They hadn't broken yet, but the audience were all staring up at the dome above.

"Pickus, what the depths is going on? Where's Voria?"

"I—there isn't time to explain. Krox is here. I was just about to contact you. Aran, you need to slow him down." Pickus glanced over his shoulder, and when he looked back the blood had drained from his freckled face. "We're having problems with the ritual, and I don't know how long it's going to take. Or if it will even work."

"You want me to stall an elder god? Well this should be fun." Aran grabbed his jacket, and began pulling it on. "I'll get the *Talon* in the air, and the fleet into motion. Keep me posted."

"Got it. Good luck, Captain." The screen went dark and Aran headed for the door.

"Crewes, Rhea," Aran bellowed as he started up the ramp toward the bridge. "Bord, Kez...we've got company. Let's get moving."

The squad piled out of their quarters, with Rhea being the first to reach the bridge, closely followed by Crewes. Bord and Kezia were the last to arrive, but both were dressed and ready for battle.

Aran moved to the central matrix, and slipped past the

rings, into the floating command chair. He tapped *fire* on all three rings to deepen his link to the ship. "Crewes, Bord, you're up. Kez, you're standing second for the sergeant. Rhea, you're second for Bord."

"Respectfully," Rhea began in a tone that was anything but respectful, "if we are going into combat with a god, I'd suggest leading with your strongest Outriders."

Aran's senses doubled. He was seeing outside the *Talon*, which was still docked inside the *Spellship*, but it was overlaid across his vision of the bridge. Fortunately, he'd done it enough times that it was second nature now. "You're an unknown quantity, Rhea. I know Bord can keep us alive, and I know Crewes can make things dead, as well as run comms."

"I possess both *water* and *spirit* magic." Rhea moved to stand outside Bord's matrix. "That means that in addition to standard *life* wards I can also erect more nuanced defenses. Let me do my job."

"Your job?" Bord snapped. He rounded on Aran. "Is she seriously trying to replace me on her first frigging day? Tell the new girl to go sit down, Captain. This is bullshit. You know I can do my job good as anyone."

"Do I need to come over there, kids?" Crewes growled. His attention was mostly fixed on Bord.

"Uh, no, sir. Just trying to work is all." Bord hopped into his matrix and buckled into the chair.

That left Rhea for him to deal with. He chose the direct route. "Follow orders, Outrider."

Rhea gave a curt nod, then sunk into a lotus position a precise two meters from Bord's matrix. The move had a ritual look to it, and he'd bet this was some sort of tradition.

Aran guided the ship into the air, and considered the matter dropped. The *Talon* rippled through the *Spellship*'s protective field, and out into the Shayan system. Aran took several moments to study the situation tactically, and quickly realized that no matter how bad he'd thought things might be, his estimates hadn't been catastrophic enough.

Krox no longer resembled the blazing star he'd been when attacking Ternus. His form was now a towering multi-limbed giant comprised of cosmic dust and motes of magic that reminded Aran uncomfortably of Shivan, one of the gods he'd seen in multiple visions. Krox dwarfed the surrounding fleets, and was roughly twice the size of the planet he'd apparently come to destroy.

The god was surrounded by a cloud of white-hot stars in various sizes. Primal Ifrit, thousands upon thousands in a variety of sizes. The largest could engulf a starship, while even the smallest were large enough to threaten, if enough swarmed a vessel.

Sprinkled through the host were what he'd expected to see. Wyrms. What he hadn't expected was the quantity. There were at least a hundred, and quite probably double that number. Every last one wore the heavy scales of a centuries-old dragon, making them the equal of any starship in his ranks.

Aran was mystified by the size of the enemy host. It didn't seem possible. They'd been warring with the Krox for decades off and on, especially in the last few years; they'd killed dozens of Wyrms. Their corpses had been used by Teodros when he'd assaulted Shaya, which suggested he was scraping the minion barrel.

If they'd had an army this size, why not use it previously? Why not overwhelm Shaya during the first attack rather than make it a simple raid on the Chamber of the First?

"Crewes, get a missive off to Kerr, please." Aran guided

the *Talon* toward the haphazard Shayan fleet. The dozen or so warships sat a little ways away from the twenty Ternus vessels, which were arrayed in neat, clean ranks.

Aran surveyed the system and began formulating a battle plan. Krox had moved directly for Shaya, and it wasn't difficult to puzzle out the dark god's goal. He was heading for the shield, presumably to destroy it, and then the tree it protected.

His Wyrms and star elementals broke off in a massive cloud, and began making for the Shayan fleet. They had perhaps three minutes before the enemy closed to breath range.

"Got Kerr's attention. Putting him on now, Captain," Crewes said. He tapped a final *fire* sigil on the gold ring.

Fleet Admiral Kerr's grizzled face filled the screen, and he wore his concern openly. "All right, son, moment of truth. We're gonna put the engagement plan squarely on your shoulders, since we don't know squat about killing gods. What's the play?"

Aran took a moment to utilize the *Talon*'s senses. He studied the incoming enemy fleet. "It looks like the Wyrms are moving more cautiously than the elementals, which suggests that they're using the elementals as shock troops. Deploy your forces as a screen. Fire a few salvos at their forward ranks, then fall back. When the Wyrms respond we'll have the Shayans advance and counter their Wyrms. If you get into trouble dip down under the shield, then re-engage once they shift attention to another target."

Kerr nodded grimly, removing his cap, and smoothing the brim. "Austin ain't gonna like you putting us in the vanguard, and I can't say I like it either. But you've got the command, son. I hope you're right."

"You and me both, Admiral. Good luck." Aran nodded at Crewes and the sergeant terminated the missive. "Guess we're about to find out what a god can do."

46

UNINTENDED CONSEQUENCES

Nara had been through a lot of 'oh crap' moments in recent months, but the fury in Ducius's expression made the bottom drop out in her stomach in the way nothing ever had. She thought furiously, desperately struggling to compose herself as the Tender stalked in her direction.

He paused before her and his eyebrows knit together in disapproval as he stared down at her. "I thought so. Who are you, imposter? And what have you done with Voria?"

"Uh." Nara reached for a response, and the only thing she could find was the truth. "You're right, I'm not Voria, and I realize you have no reason to trust me, but we're out of time so I'm just going to lay this out and let you decide. Voria's dead. I think that's why the ritual failed. But her spirit is stored in Ikadra, which is a necessary step in the ritual. If you add me to the circle, I think I can modify the spell to make this work without her body."

Ducius's eyes narrowed suspiciously, and he glanced back at the Caretakers, then at her. "Who are you?"

"Does it matter?" Nara shot back. She raised Ikadra. "Look at the gem, Ducius. See for yourself."

Ducius did as she asked, and after a moment his eyes widened. Whatever wonder he experienced vanished almost immediately. "I can see a spirit in the gem, but I have no way of proving that's Voria. You'd have me trust someone I don't know, to elevate a goddess?" His face was split by indecision. "We have no other candidate. The people will not follow me, or anyone but her. Blast it, how did it come to this?"

"Douchie-ous," Ikadra snapped, his sapphire pulsing. "Get it together, man. There's a god up there, kicking the crap out of our fleet. I know you don't trust Nara. I don't trust her either, and I trust everyone, but we're out of options."

"Nara?" Ducius gave a snort, eyeing her like a piece of refuse on the deck. "There is no way I'll trust the word of a traitor. Your vile name is well known here. You killed her, didn't you? And this is a twisted scheme to take her place."

Nara considered a counterargument. She considered attacking him. Neither would work.

"Here." Nara offered Ducius the staff. "You deal with it."

He hesitated as if seeking the trap, then accepted Ikadra.

Nara squared her shoulders. She was done being kicked around. Done being used, and manipulated. But most of all she was done being judged. She folded her arms, and glared at Ducius. "Okay, you've got the staff, and you've got Voria's soul. Go ahead and do whatever you want. You're a true mage, right? So you should have no problem verifying who's in that staff, or modifying the spell to raise her? And you can do all that quickly, right? Because Krox doesn't look too patient."

She pointed skyward, at the dome over the coliseum.

The battle had spread, and now engulfed the entire visible sky. Bright red mini-stars flitted between the dark wedge-shaped starships, while Wyrms breathed acid, melting hulls on Shayan vessels. The *Talon* screamed by and loosed a flurry of void bolts that bisected a massive star elemental, the creature's body flaring briefly, and then going cold. Nara winced, knowing that Frit would be watching.

Ducius seized Nara by the shoulder, and started dragging her toward the ritual circle. "Come with me, child." He shoved her forward, and Nara allowed it.

She noted the crowd's reaction though. Ugly murmurs rippled through the ranks. They still believed her to be Voria, and no one assaulted their lady.

"What's happening, Ducius?" one of the Caretakers called, an ageless woman with waist-length blonde hair and exquisite blue eyes.

"Voria," Ducius began, then glanced pointedly at Nara, "is going to participate in the ritual. The energies apparently need to be focused on the staff, not on her. This will require some modifications to the spell, which Voria will perform." He glared expectantly at her.

Nara stepped forward with a confident nod, and tried to walk like she imagined Voria would. Nothing scared Voria. Nothing made her back down. Ever. Not even ancient Wyrms, or the gods themselves. She channeled just a bit of that resolve, even as guilt tainted the moment.

"We begin again," Ducius demanded. He stepped forward and began sketching *life* and *water* sigils. The other Caretakers followed suit.

Nara watched their work carefully. She'd already seen the spell cast once, and had a pretty good idea of what they were doing. *Life* and *water* combined to form the greater path of nature, known by some cultures as creation. Almost all transformational magic required it, and as Nara understood it, the process really was as simple as funneling the desired magic into the target.

Two of the Caretakers began adding *spirit* sigils, which caught her attention. She studied the intricate latticework, and quickly realized why they were being added. At the moment of transference they would usher the target's spirit from their body into the staff.

"That part," Nara pointed. "Remove the link to that entire section, but keep the rest of the sections around it the same."

Both mages looked about to protest, but Nara delivered her best imitation of Voria's 'don't presume to speak to me' face, the one that had always terrified her. Both mages fell silent, and removed the links to the areas she'd indicated.

She glanced up and tensed. The battle was not going well. Most of the Shayan fleet had been eradicated, and there were fewer of the wedge-shaped ships. At least the *Talon* was still flying, the golden ship twisting around a Wyrm, then flipping midair and reversing course so suddenly the Wyrm was caught off guard, and unable to dodge the disintegrate.

Nara returned her focus to the ritual, tuning out the battle. Aran could take care of himself.

Most of her work was done. The spell's energies would be directed by Ducius, and channeled by Ikadra, which the Tender still held in one hand.

If this was to work, though, she did still have one magical part left to play. There couldn't be an illusionary Voria standing next to the goddess they'd just raised, or people would always have questions. She needed to disappear from sight when the spell reached a crescendo.

A river of white flowed into the staff, and once more the

golden energy gathered over the crowd. Wave after wave of power, of hope, and devotion, and pure life, all poured into Ikadra. The *Spellship* itself began to shake, and light poured from the walls of the amphitheater, channeled not only from the ship, but from the world below.

Nara could feel the immense pool of magic on the planet gathering, and watched with awe as a beam of pure snowy white shot from the tip of the tree, into the *Spellship*, carrying with it not just the magic of Shaya, but that of all the people who believed that Voria would save them.

The sum of those energies was focused through the Caretakers, and directly into Ikadra. The gem began to glow, a brilliant sapphire star that was at once painful to look upon and impossible to look away from.

A peal like thunder crashed through the room, and a small crack spiderwebbed down one side of Ikadra's gem. As wave after wave of power slammed into the staff the crack widened, millimeter by millimeter. Nara clutched her hands to her mouth, and didn't stop the tear that trickled down her cheek. "Goddess no, please don't let this happen. It's my fault."

Killing Voria had seemed like the perfect solution to the problem created by Talifax, but now the cost was clear. The spell hadn't been designed to be used this way, and as powerful as Ikadra was even he couldn't handle the amount of magic required to become a god.

The crack spread another millimeter.

47

INNERSPACE

Aran's plan started to unravel the very moment the combat began. The Ternus ranks held their place, but not in the manner he expected. The newer Inuran ships were placed in the rear, behind the *Wyrm Hunter*, and the mismatched warships that had survived Krox's attack on their capital.

When the first rank of star elementals reached firing range the Ternus vessels opened up. The front ranks unleashed gauss cannons firing hunks of depleted uranium, backed by a smattering of nuclear missiles. They peppered the Ifrit, detonating spectacularly...to no effect. The Ifrit and the larger star elementals continued forward, seemingly unaffected by the conventional weaponry.

The black ships added nothing, lingering silently behind their technologically equipped brethren.

The star elementals didn't fire any sort of spell. They didn't need to. In essence, they were the spell. The living flame swarmed the closest Ternus battleship, the *Resolute*, each smaller Ifrit slamming into the hull in an explosion of incandescent debris.

In seconds the entire aft side of the ship was leaking atmosphere, and Aran winced as he saw tiny figures jettisoned into the unforgiving vacuum. A moment later the battleship detonated, bringing mercy to those unfortunate souls.

Only then did the wedge-shaped ships respond. They glided silently closer, and unleashed the unnatural black tendrils they'd used back at Xal. The instant each beam touch an Ifrit, its color changed. The Ifrit grew smaller, while the beam's color brightened to match the creature it was consuming. It happened swiftly, but each Ifrit disappeared in a puff, and the bolts reversed course and flew unerringly back to the black ships. They delivered their payload, and the hulls of those ships lightened to a deep, angry orange.

Three of the ships converged on the largest star elemental, itself larger than any vessel in system. Within seconds it shrank to a fraction of its original size, then disappeared in a similar puff.

"My gods," Rhea whispered, "They're...eating them."

Three more conventional Ternus ships exploded in quick succession. The only ship in the vanguard to survive the initial volley was the *Wyrm Hunter*, but smoke poured from a tremendous hole in the stern as she limped away from the line, toward the distant safety of the Shayan shield.

The wedge-shaped ships fired another volley of tendrils, and another. They devoured clouds of the smaller Ifrit but it was clear that no matter how many they killed their lines were going to buckle.

"Crewes, fleet wide. Fall back to the shield. Order Kerr to bring up the rear with the new Inuran ships." Aran tapped a *void* sigil on the silver ring, then the gold. Power rippled from his chest, rolling into the spelldrive and accelerating the ship.

They zipped toward the rear lines, and Aran took a few moments to study Krox with the ship's senses. The god seemed completely preoccupied by its assault on the shield. It raised a titanic arm, then brought it down with the force of a falling star. The shield rippled around it, the magic dimming considerably, then springing back, though thinner than before.

He didn't know much about the magic powering the shield, but he couldn't imagine it holding out for very much longer.

"Sir, I know we aren't turning tail and running," Crewes said, catching his attention. "What's your plan?"

"Doesn't matter how many Ifrit we kill. It won't change the tide of the battle," Aran explained as he continued to fly. "We've got to stop Krox. Someone has to attack the god directly, and keep it from beating on that shield until we can get Voria up."

Aran guided the ship low, and circled wide so as to stay out of Krox's field of view. He didn't know if the god needed eyes, but figured it couldn't hurt.

"This is foolhardy," Rhea protested. "If we attack that thing we're debris. Much as I hate to say it, live to fight another day. This world is lost."

"Nah, it ain't going down like that." Crewes gave Rhea a frown. "We don't leave our own. Our people are down there. My ma is down there. We stand and fight."

"And die, if we have to. But we do it smart." Aran seized control of the conversation once more. "Crewes, you picked up *dream*. Can you make the ship invisible like Nara did?"

"I don't think so." Crewes studied the slowly rotating

rings. "I mean I see how to give the ship the magic, but have no idea how to get it to do what we want."

"Illusion cannot be cast with *dream* alone," Rhea said. She folded her arms and gave Crewes a long suffering look. "You'd need access to *air* as well."

"I can supply that," Aran pointed out. He tapped the *air* sigil on all three rings, then waited for Crewes to do the same with *dream*. "Let's just hope this ship is advanced enough to figure out what to do with the magic."

The magic poured out of him in an azure torrent, into the ship, and once he reached critical mass he ordered the vessel to make them invisible. He was gambling that the ship, like Ikadra, could repeat previous spells that had been cast through it.

A moment later they flickered out of view, disappearing against the void. It had actually worked. He wasn't used to things going their way, not so easily. "Okay, Rhea, I want you to relieve Crewes."

"Sir?" Crewes said, raising a dark eyebrow.

"Trust me, Sergeant. Rhea?"

Crewes ducked out of the matrix, and Rhea slid gracefully into the seat he'd vacated. She deftly tapped all three *air* sigils, then repeated all three *spirit*. "I'm prepped and ready."

"Good. We're going to need everything you have put into spell wards." Aran focused on flying the ship, and he guided her in a low, tight arc that took them up and around the god's outstretched arms. He corkscrewed closer to the face, then brought them up around around to gain room to pick up speed.

It wasn't until that instant that it finally occurred to him what he was doing. He stared down at an elder god, a being so powerful it defied understanding. A being that was making short work of their planet's defenses.

A being that was too powerful to even bother with the small ships in the system. A being that was, quite simply, too big to notice them. A slow grin grew as he stared down at the titanic god, his star-studded body twisting as more blows rained down on the failing shield.

"Uh, sir?" Crewes's voice had gone up a half octave. "What the depths are you doing?"

"We lack the magic to fight back, right?" Aran poured *void* into the drive, and began his dive toward the elder god's face. "Well, Krox has got plenty, so we're going to go take a couple pieces. Rhea, Bord, now's the time. I want your best wards in place. We need to be able to survive the inside of a god."

Bord went up on tiptoe and tapped the *life* sigil on the bronze ring, then the silver, then gold. "Yes, sir. You're a crazy fooker, but if we pull this off everyone will know who we are."

Rhea's hands also flew across her matrix, and her magical strength quickly joined Bord's. The entire hull began to glow a brilliant white, the light increasing as they gained momentum. They rocketed past the fringes of the battle, gradually descending toward the god's throat at an angle that kept them in a blind spot.

"If this doesn't work," Aran said, glancing around the bridge, "you have my sincere apologies. Better luck in the next life."

He poured a fresh wave of power into the ship, and they streaked toward Krox's throat, the hazy skin comprised of multilayered cosmic dust, kilometers thick. The *Talon* plunged into the god like a divine bullet fired from a god-sized rifle. Aran braced himself, but forced himself to watch as they impacted.

They slammed into the wall of dust, which rolled around them in a furious storm as they pierced the outer layer of the god. The wards surrounding the ship began to unravel, layer after layer stripped away as they punctured the hide of a god.

"Can't keep this up...forever," Bord managed through gritted teeth. Waves of brilliant white poured from him into the deck, but each one was weaker than the previous.

Rhea fought a similar battle opposite him, immense amounts of *spirit* and *water* pouring from her in twin torrents. She gripped the arms of the matrix's command couch, and loosed a wordless yell as still more magic rolled into the *Talon*.

Those pulls grew weaker and weaker. Finally, she slumped against her chair and the flows slowed to a trickle, then stopped.

Bord roared a cry of defiance that mimicked Rhea's, and a final wave of brilliance spilled into the deck. The *Talon* shook, and the hull gave an ominous groan.

Then, as suddenly as the turbulence had begun, it was over. The *Talon* burst through Krox's skin and into...eternity.

An entire universe of galaxies spun out in all directions, impossibly vast. They stretched into the distance, their seemingly haphazard layout a perfect mirror of whatever movements Krox made outside. His body formed the bounds of this universe, which seemed to function much like their own, but in miniature.

Back on the ship Aran was aware of Crewes hurrying to Rhea, then bending to place two fingers against her throat. "She's breathing, at least. What the depths do we do now, sir?"

"It's all part of the plan, Sergeant. Maybe not a good plan, but it's what I got. Kez, get Rhea strapped into the couch against the wall. Crewes, you're replacing her. We're effectively trapped in the middle of a massive maze, but when we were at the Skull, Xal changed me. Now I think I know why. He's made me into a sort of a hound, with exactly the kind of senses I need to find concentrations of magic."

Aran reached out with the senses Xal had provided. He could feel bits of *void* scattered throughout Krox, and had no trouble locating the largest piece. A vast reservoir of *void* magic pooled somewhere in the god's waist, obscured by a dense green nebula. It was easily powerful enough to represent the magic Krox had siphoned from Xal's heart.

But it wasn't the only thing he sensed. There were massive concentrations of *fire* and *spirit*, and lesser concentrations of every aspect. Aran could, theoretically at least, take whatever he wanted.

He accelerated toward the pulsing *void* energy in the distance. "Let's see what happens if we start ripping out internal organs."

48

REST IN PIECES

The *Wyrm Hunter*'s hull gave a tortured screech directly over Davidson's head. A rip appeared and atmosphere rushed out, even as the temperature dropped sharply. A thick steel beam sheered loose from the ceiling, and crashed into the far side of the bridge.

Davidson seized the stabilizing ring, but his temple still slammed into the matrix's bronze ring. He saw stars, but gritted his teeth and regained his balance. He sucked in a deep breath and yelled over the rushing wind, "Status report!"

There was no answer. Davidson looked around the *Wyrm Hunter*'s bridge and his heart went cold. Rickard's body lay slumped over the stabilizing ring in her matrix, and the third matrix had been crushed, along with its occupant. Davidson couldn't even remember the kid's name—one of the spies the governor had sent along.

"How the depths am I going to get out of this?" Davidson forced several deep breaths, and considered his options.

He couldn't control the scry-screen as he lacked *fire*, but it still showed Shaya and the safety of the shield. That safety lay something like four thousand kilometers away, which normally wouldn't be an issue. Unfortunately, with Rickard down they had no engines.

Davidson's *water* magic wasn't of much use, though he did take a moment to conjure a ball of ice to cover the rent in the hull. The rushing of air slowed, enough that Davidson felt comfortable sprinting off the bridge.

His teeth chattered as he ran down the corridor, passing frightened techs as he approached the main hangar. Thankfully, the hit they'd taken was on the aft side of the ship, or they'd have been in real trouble.

"Sir?" a Marine called as Davidson entered the hangar.

"Get the men into crash stations," Davidson roared without slowing. They didn't have near enough escape pods for everyone, and none of the Marines wanted to leave when their brothers would be staying behind.

Davidson sprinted toward the tanks at the far side of the hangar, but knew in his heart he would never make it.

The starboard wall began to radiate heat, pleasant warmth at first, but that warmth quickly became lethal heat. The wall glowed white hot, and the Marines nearest it began to scream. They ran from it, their skin erupting into flame. Those closest were consumed when the wall buckled, and living flame poured into the hangar.

Davidson forced himself to focus on his tank. He leaned into a sprint, arms pumping furiously as he crossed the hangar. Heat washed over him in waves, scalding his arms, even through the uniform. Fifty meters. Forty.

The screams behind Davidson stopped, and he gritted his teeth as his uniform was cooked away. He reached desperately for magic he barely understood, much less wanted, and begged it to save him.

Water bubbled up around him, a cool balm that insulated him from the immense heat. It poured from his chest, pulse after pulse, and it kept the heat at bay. Or it made the pain tolerable at least. He'd still suffered second-degree burns, or worse. He thanked any god listening for the adrenaline masking the pain.

Davidson leapt over an ammo crate that tumbled past him, and the hull began to cant at a sharp angle as the hangar started to come apart. The oxygen around him burned away, and he saw spots as he fought to breathe.

He stumbled the last few feet, then in a fit of life-saving fury he vaulted atop the tank and rolled into the access port atop the turret. Davidson darted down the ladder, and tugged the hatch closed behind him. It sealed automatically, and he inhaled a thick, wonderful breath.

The tank hummed to life without any input from him, as if sensing his need. Davidson darted over to the command chair, and sat gingerly. Agony flared in both legs where the skin had cooked away, and he ended up in a half crouch over the seat, too damaged to risk sitting again.

Davidson flipped on the external camera, and instinctively seized the command sticks so hard his knuckles went white. The tank tumbled end over end, sprayed into the sky over Shaya through the flaming remains of the *Hunter's* starboard side.

The battleship left flaming contrails in its wake as it plummeted toward the shield, leaking debris. He couldn't hear the keel's tortured shriek as the vessel came apart, but Davidson's brain supplied it.

The *Hunter* detonated spectacularly a moment later, and the star elemental that had killed her flitted away to seek another victim. The ship that had survived a hundred battles and saved entire worlds finally succumbed to battle, and it broke his heart.

Davidson tumbled end over end, away from the shield. He hurriedly buckled himself in, and forced himself to sit, despite the pain. The agony was bad enough that he wrestled the medical pack from the wall. He fought the spin, eventually pulling loose the syringe.

He jammed it into his leg, and squeezed a rush of warmth into his thigh as the morphine spread. Davidson screamed, and his vision went blurry from tears. The tank continued to tumble, and he reminded himself that if he didn't get past this...he was dead.

Davidson grabbed another syringe, and jammed it into the other leg. He blacked out, but only for a moment. He pushed away the vertigo and tightened the straps around him. The tank had been built to survive re-entry. Unfortunately, he'd been hurled away from the shield, into the portion of the moon that had no atmosphere.

There was nothing to slow his descent as the tank spun toward the unforgiving ground. Davidson closed his eyes and prayed for the best. He kept time with his heartbeat, and had nearly reached two hundred when he was slammed into his restraints so hard his shoulder broke.

Davidson screamed, the pain keeping him from going unconscious. All motion ceased, but his body still thought it was spinning, and he fought the vertigo. The tank had crashed, but he was still alive. He struggled to focus, but kept drifting in and out of consciousness.

In the distance he heard hissing. He closed his eyes, and rested his head against the seat rest. "We're leaking O_2. How's that for a bullshit ending? I survived the crash, and skipped going down with the ship, and I'm going to die anyway." He thought of the *Hunter*, and didn't bother to fight the tears. "I'm sorry, girl. I should have stayed with you."

He folded his arms across his chest and gave into unconsciousness. At least there wouldn't be any pain.

49

WAKE UP

Voria returned to consciousness by degrees. She floated beneath a warm ocean of light, which cradled and protected her. It surrounded her, yes, but it also pervaded her. There was nowhere that she began, and the light ended. She *was* the light, she realized.

"Ikadra?" Her voice echoed into the distance, as if she were in a vast cavern. Where did it originate if she had no throat to issue it?

"Magic, obviously," came an amused feminine voice. "In the purest sense of a word. Your body's gone, kid. And I can say kid, because I was a goddess before it was cool."

Voria didn't have a head to turn, but she could apparently shift where her attention was focused. She was in a vast cavern, dozens of kilometers across. The ceiling was comprised almost entirely of roots, and below her, she realized, lay an ocean of magical energy. *Life* and *water* pooled together, swirling into one intermingled mass.

A ghostly woman shimmered into existence next to the pool of light, the pool that was Voria. She had long, dark hair, and a wide, friendly smile.

"Shaya?" Voria guessed.

"Of course," the shade laughed. "This is the moment I was created for. I knew the day would come when an investiture was needed, and well, here we are. Krox is here. I can see her up there."

"Her?" Voria asked, confused by the gender switch.

"Let's just say Krox is no longer himself." Shaya drifted closer to the pool. To her, Voria realized. How did one live as an ocean of light? "Someone else has seized control of the matrix, so to speak. I don't know who she is, but I can feel her inside of him. Controlling him. You can too, if you try. Anything I can do, you can do a thousand times more. Everything I am is just a shade of who you are. You can think of me as a sort of a snarky guide your annoyingly beloved predecessor left behind."

Voria frowned at that. "Krox is here, and our people are in danger. I need to get out there and fight. Just tell me how to do that."

"All in good time, kid." Shaya interlocked her fingers behind her head and relaxed into an imaginary couch. "What's going on right now? It's all in your head. Milliseconds are passing around you, so you've got, well, a few hours to get ready at least. Take your time. Understand who and what you are, and then defend your world."

Voria found the cavern claustrophobic, particularly because she couldn't see through it to ascertain how the battle was progressing. Aran was a fine commander, but he was as yet inexperienced and might benefit from her aid.

"You're going to have to let go of that micromanaging stuff," Shaya said, rolling her eyes. "Either this Aran can do what you need him to, or he can't. You can't get caught up in doing everyone's job for them. You've got to focus on building a team of people who can accomplish the things you're not around to do, and that starts here."

"Okay," Voria allowed. She couldn't fault the logic. Delegation was practiced by every skilled commander. "You say we've got time, yes?"

The shade nodded, then leaned forward in her imaginary seat. "You've got questions. Let's do this."

"I can feel a great deal of *life*, and a fair amount of *water*, both inside of me." Voria reached out experimentally, and could feel lesser quantities of other magics. They were minuscule in comparison to the *life* and *water*. "Theoretically that empowers me with nature, yes? I understand the greater paths conceptually, but not how to employ them. How do I cast spells?"

"You're still thinking like a mage." Shaya raised both hands, and began to glow with *life* magic. "See how I manifested that? I willed it, and it happened. It's more like being a war mage than a true mage. A true mage basically talks to magic and tells it what to do. A god IS magic. You're deciding what YOU want to do, and then expending a portion of your power to accomplish it. In short, think about it, give it some juice, and pow...spell achieved."

"And how do I counterspell?" Voria figured that would be of immense use in a brawl with another god, particularly one as strong as Krox.

"The same way you cast. As soon as you become aware of Krox doing something you don't like, then you think about something happening that will prevent it. If she summons a flight of dragons, you suck them into the Umbral Depths. If she throws a fireball—and she might—you throw an equal or greater amount of water at it."

"Okay, let's test this." Voria reached out with a dizzying array of new senses. She couldn't see through the roots above, but she could sense a vivid tapestry of powerful magic above.

Parsing friend from foe was trivially easy, as was inspecting Krox's magical signature. Though, before she did so, she spent a moment studying the shield protecting Shaya. Another blow or two and it would be destroyed, and the death of her planet would come in its wake.

She shifted her attention to Krox, and surprise flitted across her mind like quicksilver. She recognized the presence within Krox. How could she not? "Nebiat. I don't know how, but I'd know her anywhere. She must have been involved in Teodros's scheme."

"Sounds like you've got a bit of a grudge." Shaya gave a melodious laugh that reminded her a little of Aurelia. "My turn to ask questions. What are you going to do now?"

"My first priority is protecting my world," she reasoned. "I'll need to reinforce that shield, which it seems I can accomplish by fueling it with *life*."

"That will stabilize the ward, for a short time at least." Shaya folded her arms, and stared upwards. "But what then? Eventually Krox is going to break through."

Voria was silent for a long time. She spun out countless possibilities in a turbulent sea of understanding. In some, she stood strong. In most, she died. Krox was stronger than her. There was no doubt about that.

But she had allies, and at the end of the day she'd rather ride into battle with her battalion than receive any amount of divine power.

She realized something was missing. "Wait, why can't I see the *Talon*? It should be present in the battle, but about midway through simply ceased to exist. I don't see it destroyed, but...it's gone."

"I may not like the scaly bastard, but Inura is a crafty

Wyrm." Shaya shimmered into the air above Voria, and stared up at the battle. "It's possible that he may have hidden the vessel somehow. Or it could also be that the *Talon* is hiding inside of a larger entity, which would obscure it from all scrying. Either way, you aren't the only one who won't be able to see it."

50

THE SPELLSHIP'S TRUE PURPOSE

Voria appeared in the sky over the world where she'd been born. Nebiat—she refused to think of it as Krox any longer—pounded away at the shimmering shield protecting Shaya. Voria instinctively extended a hand, or tried to anyway. Then realized she had no hand. She was a floating ball of light, not at all like Shaya had been.

Shaya's amused laughter echoed through the void somehow. "You can change that. Envision what you want to be, and then...be it. You are an archon of creation. Handle it."

"Okay, let's see if this works." Voria envisioned a titanic reflection of herself. She pictured herself, complete with the confederate uniform, only far, far larger. Large enough to oppose Nebiat.

There was no slow process, no gradual change. She simply became what she wished to be, a goddess comprised entirely of light. Voria stood tall over Shaya, ready to defend her world. "I never imagined it would come to this, Nebiat. But as I've told you countless times, I will always oppose you."

Nebiat paused mid-swing, and drifted slowly away from the discolored shield, which now had ragged gaps eroded in several places. Not large enough for one of those fists to fit through, but close enough that a few more blows would allow Nebiat to crush everything Voria struggled to protect.

Yet her rival made no move to continue. She hovered there, folding all four arms as she peered at Voria. "I should have realized you'd recognize me. How many gods have a hand in this moment, I wonder? Despite all their meddling, I promise nothing will keep me from achieving my goal here."

"Is that so?" Voria asked mildly. She extended her newly created hand, and willed the shield to reappear. The gaps filled, and the shield's dim illumination built into a steady, vibrant glow. That glow was even stronger than it had been when the shield was created.

She turned back to Nebiat. "Let's settle this like warriors, Wyrm. Leave my world out of it."

Nebiat's hands extended, all four of them, and rivers of green flame rushed out, the tendrils snaking around every side of the shield, probing and searching for entry. Everywhere they touched, the *life* magic weakened, and within moments the vast majority of the shield had eroded.

"I am well prepared for this game, little goddess," Nebiat taunted. Her fists fell upon the battered shield, and fresh cracks occurred. "I will eventually break through, and when I do my forces will burn your world. You cannot keep me out forever, and you lack the magic needed to stop me."

Voria refreshed the shield again, though she felt the cost of it. How many more times could she shield her world? A dozen? Two? Eventually Nebiat would get through, unless she could find another solution.

"Is she right about us lacking offense?" Voria whispered

in her head. "I need a weapon. You can't tell me Inura didn't prepare something."

"We don't have anything flashy like *fire* magic, but that's why Inura and Virkonna made us tools like Ikadra and the *Spellship*. And the *Talon*. All three are designed to kill a god, or in Ikadra's case, to forge one."

"Speechless, then?" Nebiat called. The dark god continued to beat on the newly erected shield, and it was already cracking. It wouldn't be long before Voria had to refresh it a third time.

"We should do something flashy." Shaya snapped her fingers and her smile returned. "I've got just the thing. Want to see what the *Spellship* was really designed for?"

"Show me." Voria turned her attention to the ship where, theoretically at least, her mortal body still lay. It was long and slender, so unlike the sleek *Talon*. Given her current size it would probably fit in the palm of her hand.

"Go ahead, then," Shaya prompted. "Take it in your hand and see what happens. Trust me, you're going to love this."

Voria stretched out an arm, and willed the *Spellship* to come to her. The vessel obediently appeared across the palm of her hand, roughly the size and shape of a sword hilt. It vibrated suddenly, in greeting she realized. It was...alive. No less so than Ikadra, and like Ikadra it had been crafted to be wielded by a goddess.

Vast, brilliant light appeared at either end of the *Spellship* as her hand closed around it. The magic lanced outwards into long, thin blades of pure *life* magic, the antithesis of *spirit*, and *void*, and *dream*. It was a double-bladed staff, she realized. "My goddess."

"Me, you mean?" Shaya gave an amused snort. "Pretty

cool, right? You can melee gods with that thing. You've had training, right?"

"Not much," Voria admitted. She gave the staff an experimental twirl that ended with her opposite fist thrust outward. Her eyes darted down to the *Spellship* in sudden alarm. "There are tens of thousands of people in that ship. Are they...okay?"

"They're fine." Shaya waved dismissively at the ship. "It was designed for this. Your followers provide the power, and trust me, not even a god likes getting hit by that thing."

Nebiat had finally noticed the new weapon, and broke off her attacks on the beleaguered shield. She rose into the sky over Shaya, and flexed all four of her arms. "There's some fight in you, then. Good. I'm going to enjoy this, Voria. I've foreseen your death, many times, at my hands. I've tasted it so many times. Now I will make it real."

A cosmic fist sailed toward Voria, and she clumsily raised her staff to block. She narrowly deflected the blow, then backpedaled toward the sun to gain room. Nebiat followed up with another blow, and another. Voria desperately fell back, narrowly deflecting attack after attack.

Shaya's frowning face drifted into her field of view. "You're thinking two dimensionally. This isn't a school yard brawl. You. Are. A. God."

"Think like a goddess," she murmured to herself.

Voria teleported behind Nebiat, and rammed her staff into the elder god's midsection. The tip blazed where it touched her cosmic skin, and easily pierced her back. She brought the weapon up, and pulled Nebiat away from Shaya, flinging her toward the sun. A river of white *spirit* energy flowed from the wound, clustering in the air like droplets of divine blood, which maybe they were.

Nebiat gave a cry of wordless rage, twisting in the sky over the shield. She brought all four limbs to bear, each hand balled into a fist. Tremendous power built around each, then expanded toward her in four waves of green flame. She brought up the *Spellship*, and desperately parried one of the beams.

The other three slammed into her body, one in the leg, another in her chest, and the third her shoulder directly above. She couldn't precisely call what happened pain. Something more like utter mind-breakingly powerful terror, the knowledge that a part of her existence had just unraveled, and that if it happened again she would cease to be.

Her right arm, the one holding the *Spellship*, hung limply, unable to make use of the weapon. Voria desperately willed magic into it, forcing her body to return to its previous state. It came quickly, and easily, but not quickly enough.

To her shock Nebiat hadn't followed up on her attack. Instead, she'd turned her attention on the undefended world where Voria's previous followers desperately huddled.

51

ATMA

Nebiat had witnessed countless variations of this moment. It was a moment that Kem'Hedj players called 'atma', which meant death, or endless darkness, depending on your favorite translation. You left your opponent no viable choices, and they either gracefully conceded, or were systematically dismembered.

There was not a single possibility where Voria conceded, gracefully or otherwise, but Nebiat wouldn't have it any other way. She wanted to savor this, her rival's futile struggle. No matter what path Voria chose, she was about to die. Not a single possibility in the trillions Nebiat had perused offered her any chance of survival.

Nebiat thrust a hand toward the world below. A final rush of acidic, green fire rippled through the last vestiges of the shield, and her followers, Wyrms and Ifrit both, flooded through the gaps and began to assault the world below.

Her other three arms shot down, and seized the great tree itself in different locations. She willed her mass to increase, and slowly tore the wretched tree from the world that had birthed it. Tens of thousands died as branches snapped away and fell upon the settlements around the roots, along with mountains of soil and the remains of their structures.

As the tree tore free from the world, her nails dug into the wood, shattering it everywhere she held. Under the wood she felt something cold and alien. A life form, but one that lacked anything recognizable as a consciousness.

You have done it. Krox's voice held awe. *What you feel is Worldender, the oldest object in existence, so far as we know.*

Nebiat yanked the spear free from the remnants of the tree, laughing as countless fragments of wood rained down into the atmosphere, dooming the farming villages in the fields around the gaping hole where the tree had stood.

Behind her Voria had begun to rise, and had summoned her magic to heal herself, as she had in every possibility. And, as she had in every possibility, Voria went to the aid of her world. She summoned *life*, and *water*, and somehow undid nearly all the damage that Nebiat had inflicted.

Countless tendrils burst from Voria's hand like strands of blue hair, and the *water* magic twisted down around the city below. Cool water fell upon the Ifrit, burning them as surely as acid might a human. Spikes of ice pieced the Wyrms, jabbing through hearts, and skulls, and lungs. Hundreds of her minions died, just as she'd seen in countless possibilities.

Voria's crowning moment, the one that truly earned Nebiat's respect and admiration, came when she gathered the thousands of fragments of the wood raining down into the atmosphere. *Life* touched every last one, the tendrils as numerous as the *water* had been. They carried the fragments back toward the position where the tree had stood, and began welding them back together.

The gaps were filled in with magic, and it all happened

in the space of seconds. Many citizens hadn't even had time to fall to their deaths, and Voria managed to save them, depositing those who'd survived the initial impact back onto safe perches on her newly created tree. It lessened the catastrophic loss of life, but only slightly.

Finally, a new shield began to ripple outward from the tip of the tree, once more shielding the survivors from Nebiat's surviving forces.

It was all so very impressive, a fitting last act for her rival. Many citizens had died, but Voria had somehow saved a few. Only a god with the computational power she possessed could truly understand how great a miracle that was.

Her power is rooted in creation. This is where she excels. Slay her, and take that strength for our own. It will prove useful in many situations.

Nebiat could have countered Voria's magic. She could have prevented her rival from restoring the blasted tree, and even from restoring the shield. Instead, she chose a far, far more terrible fate for the people of Shaya.

She raised Worldender in two of her hands, steadying the weapon as she aimed at Voria's chest. In every possibility the ancient weapon ended Voria. There was no hope for her enemy's survival. Voria was exposed, a conscious choice on her part that had been necessary to save her world.

After her death Nebiat would take that world for her own.

She would make these people love her and worship her. She would teach them to revile Voria, and turn this into the first colony in her new empire. She would mold them into rabid warriors, and then unleash them to destroy everything the Shayans once loved.

Her revenge would be glorious.

Nebiat cocked the great spear back to throw it, and

Krox's elation surged with him. He too craved the death she was about to inflict.

Sudden agony roiled through her, a multi-layered wrongness as vital parts of her body ceased to function. Were she a mortal, she would have wagered that someone had just slid a dagger into her kidney. The pain, if it could be called pain, was acute.

"What—is happening?" She gasped as she sought a way to peer inside herself and find the cause of the disturbance.

In forging the body you have, you have rendered yourself vulnerable. You cannot perceive inside the confines of your own vessel. Not as we could using my previous form. I do not know what is causing the damage, but the weapon was either created by Inura or Nefarius. Either way, I can feel it pillaging our magic, growing stronger as it tears us apart.

"Can it kill us?" Nebiat felt the first stab of real fear since she'd learned that Krox intended to absorb her.

Another wave of pain washed through her, this time closer to the chest.

Not if we flee.

Nebiat considered that. No, not yet. She would not abandon this battle, not while Voria lived. She would never have a better chance.

52

HOUND OF XAL

Aran had never experienced the level of power, and of control, he felt while flying *Talon*. He guided the ancient ship through a forest of miniature galaxies, winding through Krox's body as he sought the pulsing *void* magic that had been stolen from Xal.

They flew in relative silence, with an exhausted Bord lounging against the wall, Rhea sleeping next to him. Neither was in any condition to fight, which meant they were screwed if they needed to defend themselves.

Kezia had stepped into Bord's matrix, as asked. She might lack his defensive capabilities, but her *water* magic could still prove useful, even if she was inexperienced at piloting. It beat having an empty matrix.

"I wish Nara was here," Kezia murmured under her breath. It was loud enough for Crewes, evidently.

"You know what?" The sergeant said quietly. "I do too. We're in the shit, and no offense, sir, but you ain't a true mage."

"None taken. I miss her too." Aran guided them around

a nebula, and smiled when he saw what lay beyond. "There it is, Sergeant."

A pulsing ball of liquid purple, darker than a heart wound and larger than any star, hovered in the black. Veins of dark energy flowed off the orb, and power pulsed away in a rhythmic heartbeat, snaking off into the vast distance that was the rest of Krox.

"That thing looks important." Crewes gave a slow smile. "Would be a real shame if something bad were to happen to it. I bet Krox would just love having his appendix burst."

"Yup, a real shame." Aran answered the sergeant's smile with one of his own. "Watch this."

He tapped the *void* sigil on all three rings, then poured as much strength as he could into the matrix. Dark waves of magic disappeared into the deck, one after another, until the entire vessel began to shake.

Aran seized the arms of his command chair, and gritted his teeth as he channeled the spell. A tendril of negative energy shot from the *Talon's* spellcannon, lancing into the pulsing ball. After a moment the pulsing stopped. The veins were suddenly sucked inward, as if subjected to tremendous gravity.

The entire orb shrank to a fraction of its size, all that *void* energy compressed into a tiny ball. Then it shot back towards the *Talon* at alarming speed.

"Uh, sir, is this part of the plan?" Crewes's voice was tinged with panic as the orb slammed into the ship.

"Trust me, Sergeant." Aran braced himself against the matrix's command chair, grateful he no longer had to deal with a standard stabilizing ring.

The massive ball of *void* magic slammed into the *Talon*, and rippled through every part of the ship. Darkness shrouded everything as the entire vessel filled with liquid magic, the blood of Xal, the most potent concentration of *void* still in existence, so far as Aran knew.

Icy pain shot through every neuron as magic flooded into him, drawn by the strange ability he'd received from Xal. Aran found he could manage the flow, and even distribute it, but he had to do so quickly.

He couldn't take it all. There was too much remaining, and he didn't dare give any of his friends more of the magic. Even if they were okay with it, and Rhea at the very least wouldn't be, it might kill them.

And then it occurred to him.

He sent a flow to Narlifex, which barely touched the reservoir still remaining. The rest, he gave to the *Talon*, fusing the vast *void* energy into the ship itself, empowering it just as he had his other weapons. The ship eagerly drank the energy, and he felt the *Talon* growing larger, and changing in shape and hue, as it absorbed the vast majority of the magic that had been stolen from Xal.

The ringing in his ears finally faded, and Crewes's gravelly voice broke the silence. "Let's never do that again, okay? I feel like someone just crammed their arm up my tailpipe, and left behind a bowling ball."

Aran took several deep breaths, and overlaid the *Talon*'s senses over his own once more. The awareness he sensed was deeper now, but still seemed to lack the ability to speak directly to him.

The area around him hadn't changed, other than the removal of Xal's heart blood. No dragons came roaring after them. No flood of Ifrit came sailing in.

"I've got bad news, Sergeant." Aran poured a little *void* into the ship, and spun it around as he scanned Krox's interior, searching.

"What's that, sir?" Crewes leaned over the edge of his command chair to look at Aran.

"We're going to do it again, right now. I mean, since we're here, might as well take some *fire* magic, right?"

Aran flew the *Talon* in a straight line, accelerating as he crossed the distance toward the largest star inside of Krox. It was a pulsing, red ball, fiery tendrils flowing out around it in long, slender neurons that snaked through much of Krox's interior.

"All right, sir," Crewes growled. "Let's give this asshole a heart attack then. I'm all about getting more *fire* magic."

Aran sucked in a deep breath and gritted his teeth. He tapped all three *void* sigils, and then duplicated the spell he'd used on Xal's blood. A tendril of negative energy shot into the heart.

That area of the sun darkened perceptively, for a moment at least, then the heart returned to full strength, and a flaming orb shot from where the bolt had struck. The *fire* magic streaked into the *Talon*, a massive amount, and yet still a tiny sliver of what the heart could offer.

The flame crashed through the vessel, and it took everything Aran had to channel it so that it didn't cook the interior of the ship. He struggled desperately to dump an equal slice into everyone, and then sent the rest into the *Talon*, which drank the *fire* as eagerly as it had the *void*.

Again the ship grew larger, inside and out. Aran didn't know everything the magic had done, but their destroyer was looking a whole lot more like a full cruiser, almost a third the size of the *Wyrm Hunter*.

When the moment passed Aran was left panting, sweat dripping down his face. He looked around the bridge. "Everyone okay?"

"Peachy, sir," Bord croaked from the couch along the side

of the wall. "But if you could let me off before you do that again, that would be great."

"Heads up, sir." The sergeant's urgency brought Aran back to the moment, and he observed the area using the *Talon*'s senses.

"Oh, crap." Now a tide of Ifrit were surging toward them. The divine equivalent of white blood cells, maybe. "Looks like the locals finally found us."

Thousands upon thousands of miniature stars rose from the heart, and began streaking in their direction. These ones were smaller than those attacking the shield outside, but that didn't make them any less lethal.

"Let's get the depths out of here," Aran roared. "Hang on!"

He poured *void* into the ship, and they streaked through a nebula, then down between the spiral arms of another galaxy. Behind him came an endless line of Ifrit, all bent on their destruction. Thankfully, the newly enhanced *Talon* was quickly outdistancing their pursuers. Not quickly enough for his comfort, though.

Aran poured more *void* into the ship, "Come on, girl. Find us a way out of here."

They wound further and further down into the body, but the number of stellar phenomena made it impossible to guess their location. Somewhere below the waist, maybe, but above the legs.

"Sir, why don't we just make a hole?" Crewes suggested.

"Looks like we may have to. Everyone add a share of *fire*, please." Aran tapped the *fire* sigil on each ring, and watched as Kezia and Crewes did the same. The *Talon*'s hull burst into nuclear flame, as hot as a star's deepest internals. "Okay, time to make a new orifice."

Aran poured still more *void* into the drive, increasing

their mass and velocity as they rocketed toward Krox's rear side. The *Talon* slammed into the membrane, Krox's skin, but the enormous heat melted through it, and they burst through, back into open space.

Spirit magic sprayed into space from the wound they'd created, a tiny cut when considered against the whole of Krox. That was just fine. They'd gotten out.

Now it was time to finish this.

The *Talon* twisted through the battle with impossible speed, easily avoiding the few Ifrit who attempted to attack them. Aran brought the vessel around high, and took a good look at the Krox fleet. Judging from the damage around the tree, some of them must have made it inside, but there was no sign of them now. The shield was in place, and the world seemed safe.

The surviving Ternus fleet, twelve of the black ships, had gathered into a tight ball directly above the shield. A few Shayan vessels dotted their ranks. Were those really the only survivors? There wasn't a single conventional warship, and Aran's anxiety rose like bile when he realized there was no sign of the *Hunter*. Maybe she'd made it to safety under the shield.

The few survivors were surrounded by Ifrit and Wyrms, each taking pot shots with their acidic breath or fire bolts. The Krox were working hard to form a blockade, and every Ternus or Shayan ship that approached the shield was quickly overwhelmed.

"Let's give them a hand. Sergeant, Kezia, bring that new *fire* magic online please. Pour as much as you can into the ship." Aran tapped all three *fire* sigils, then poured a healthy dose of magic into the *Talon*.

Kezia did the same, orange-white flame rolling out of her into the deck. "This is amazing. I've always missed it when you fookers got *fire*. Finally! I can burn things, just like you, Sarge."

"Yep." Crewes grinned at her like a proud father. He'd also tapped the sigils, but the torrent of flame coming from him dwarfed what was coming from Aran or Kez. Of course, Crewes had been to three *fire* Catalysts now, and was likely one of the strongest wielders in the sector.

Aran gathered the boundless flame into the spellcannon, and was pleasantly surprised to see that the *Talon* had automatically augmented the spell with the internal reserves it had gathered from inside Krox. He unleashed the spell, and could only gawk when a three-kilometer-wide fire bolt swept through the Krox ranks.

Every Wyrm it touched was incinerated, their smoking forms tumbling to the ground like broken kindling. The spell destroyed over a dozen in total, opening a gap for the Ternus defenders.

The Ifrit were unharmed by the beam, and quickly swarmed in to fill that gap. That wouldn't do.

This part was, unfortunately, all on him. Aran tapped each *void* sigil, and poured enormous strength into the ship. This was his aspect now, like it or not. He was of the *void*, but being so made him enormously strong. More than any mortal had a right to be.

The *void* magic pooled in the cannon, until Aran couldn't give any more. He gave an inarticulate cry of rage as he released the spell, channeling all of his hatred for the Krox, and everything they'd done. The cannon vomited a beam of pure *void*, easily a kilometer wide, which disintegrated everything in its path. Ifrit and Wyrm alike simply ceased to exist, widening the gap they'd created beneath the Ternus fleet.

Now it was enough for them to get safely beneath the shield.

"Crewes, get a message out to the Ternus fleet. I want every one of those black ships to attack Krox directly. Shayan vessels, get to safety beneath the shield."

Even a god must have felt the amount of magic they'd stolen. If the Inuran ships started taking more, then maybe, just maybe, the god would retreat.

53

AFTERMATH

Voria had watched every possibility play out a trillion times. She knew that she was going to die if she saved her world, and yet there seemed to be no better alternative. She simply could not live with allowing Nebiat to destroy her people.

Her heart shattered alongside the great tree itself, and fragments rained down over the endless fields she had whiled away her afternoons watching from her quarters in the Temple of Enlightenment.

She would not let this stand, and if this was to be her final act she would let it be a memorable one.

Voria raised the *Spellship* and aimed its blazing tip like a staff. She funneled her magic through the weapon, mildly surprised when the staff answered by supplying an equal quantity, thronging out of her followers in a vast divine song.

The magic felt endless, maybe even endless enough to subdue this tragedy. Time seemed to slow as the fragments of the tree rained toward the few desperate survivors below.

Voria arrested their momentum, and drew them together in a swirling mass of *life* and *water*.

She remembered the vision of Shaya creating the tree in the first place, her attempt to imprison the great spear Worldender. The very spear that Nebiat had stolen, and now raised in a killing throw. Shaya had made something good with her death, and Voria would too.

The magic coalesced into the exact form of the tree Voria had grown up knowing, the symbol of her people emblazoned on every flag, and every ship. Its roots grew deep into the world, filling the cavern where Shaya's body had lain.

Voria gave it more magic.

The energies rippled outward from the tree, washing across the endless fields, in an ever-expanding ring that raced across mountains, craters, and valleys. In its wake it brought life. Trees, and flowers, and lakes, and even oceans swept across the planet, as the atmosphere spread above them.

It covered not only the sanctuary Voria had created for her people, but the entire world. Life bloomed so strong, and vibrant, and diverse, that it no longer depended upon the tree. Clouds gathered, swirling and dancing, and bringing rain to parts that had never felt its touch. The magic seeped into the world itself, transforming Shaya into a lush, forested moon.

Finally, Voria replaced the shield, sheltering as much of the area as she could.

A fitting end for her short divinity.

Voria twisted to face Nebiat, to witness the fate she'd seen countless times, the fate that she'd embraced. Nebiat cocked her arm back to throw, but before she could complete the motion her cosmic body spasmed. A grimace passed across her face, and then her hand dropped to her midsection.

A moment later a tiny flaming ball shot out of Nebiat's rear, as if she were...

"You can say it," Shaya prompted.

"I'm not dignifying that with a response." Voria studied the flaming projectile. Was that...the *Talon*? It was larger now, and darker in color.

"Oh, come on." Shaya rolled her eyes. "A flaming ship just shot out of a god's ass. Are we really pretending that didn't just happen?"

A smile bloomed and something lightened within Voria. "I'm more eager to see where the 'flaming projectile' is going."

The *Talon* began belching immensely powerful spells, easily fifth level if she were to classify them. Perhaps sixth. Everything they touched simply died, and the *Talon* didn't lack for more spells. It kept casting, and tore through the enemy ranks in a storm of blazing death.

The vessel single-handedly created a gap around their Ternus allies, allowing the wedge-shaped ships to fan out and begin their counterattack on Nebiat herself.

The angry goddess had finally recovered, perhaps because the *Talon* was no longer lodged inside her. Nebiat brought down two of her arms, and fired twin flaming beams of acidic flame at the approaching ships. The magic swam as if alive, hungrily approaching the doomed vessels.

Voria spun out possibilities, and tried to decide whether preserving the present was worth mortgaging the future. If she saved those ships, they would be a problem. But without victory here, there was no future.

Voria swung her blazing staff down, and deflected both pillars of flame, shunting them off into space toward the sun. The unholy ships unleashed hungry, seeking tendrils, latching onto Nebiat's body, and greedily draining pulses of *spirit*.

A large vessel, black, but tinged with scarlet, streaked toward Nebiat, and she realized she was seeing the *Talon*. It had grown far larger, which was clear seeing it pass by the Ternus fleet. And it had grown far more deadly.

The familiar glow of a disintegrate built in the *Talon's* spellcannon, then lanced into Nebiat's chest. That part of her body swirled into a billion particles, and then dissolved, just as parts of Voria had done when she'd been hit by the acid flame.

The dark god's body rippled, and the horrible wound healed, but Voria felt the cost of it. And the sickly pulses of *spirit* magic were still flowing into the black ships, weakening Nebiat further.

Nebiat's hateful gaze settled on Voria, twin suns focusing all their attention on her. She held Worldender aloft, not to throw, but merely to brandish. "I have what I came for. I will see you again, old friend. It pleases me that you have followed me into godhood. If it takes centuries I will be the death of everything you love."

And then she was gone. The system was suddenly bereft of her immense power and the chaos Nebiat had wrought. Only a few Ifrit remained, and the remaining Wyrms were scuttling for the planet's umbral shadow as quickly as they could.

The *Talon* streaked by, ending three in the first pass, and another two on its reverse run. The Inuran fleet followed in its wake, eagerly devouring those Wyrms too slow to flee.

The Krox had been broken. They'd won.

Voria stood tall over the world that had given her birth. She tapped into the magic Shaya had given her, and used a simple spell to make her voice heard by every follower who'd just given of themselves to help save their world.

"For my entire life," she began, her blazing light illuminating the world she'd rebirthed, "I have lived upon Shaya. I have sheltered under her branches, or what I thought was her. I was taught that she would save us, and today she has. Shaya has bequeathed to me her legacy, and I now take up the same mantle she bore. I will protect not only this world, but all the worlds of this sector. Today we have proved that Krox can be beaten. Though the cost has been great we have driven him from our world. We have crushed his minions. And we have persevered. Now, for the first time, we will ride to war. We will sail into the Erkadi Rift, and we will put down Krox once and for all."

Voria could feel her followers, every last one. She felt them rejoice. She felt their hope, their adoration, and their affection. These people were ready to stand as one, and she had little doubt that they would overcome Krox.

"I'm coming for you, Nebiat," she whispered, peering across the stars at the vast expanse of purple on the far side of the sector. "It's time to end this feud."

54

SPARK OF LIFE

Nara sank wearily to her knees atop the stage where a goddess had been born, and stared up through the dome at the vacant space that Krox had occupied a moment ago. The terrified screams had stopped, and the people hadn't fled. Most began returning to their seats, or stared up in awe at the newly reborn planet of Shaya.

Ducius moved to the edge of the stage, where he began attempting to reassure people who didn't need it. Their goddess filled the sky above them—what did his reassurances matter? Always campaigning, that one. It wasn't her problem, at least. She'd done what she came to do, and had somehow managed to outwit Talifax. For now, at least.

Nara gave a contented sigh, and settled back on her haunches. Her part in all this was finally done.

Frit rushed to her side, close enough that she could feel the heat. "Are you all right? You're so pale."

"I could sleep for about a year." Nara stifled a yawn so large it made her jaw crack. "Raising a goddess really takes it out of you. Would not recommend."

She turned her attention to Voria's shining form hung in the sky above them, powerful, and clean, and, well...inspiring. She made the perfect goddess, and Nara was terribly grateful she'd avoided the small voice inside her that wanted the power for herself. She'd be an absolutely awful goddess, and she knew it.

Frit watched her for a moment, the heat close enough to warm, but not harm. She brushed a lock of flaming hair from her forehead, and glanced over at the Caretakers, who were all staring at Frit, and of course at Kaho. "Uh, looks like they noticed us. I was going to ask about running, but I guess the chance to do that has passed."

"I'm done running." Nara rose shakily to her feet, and her gaze fell on Ikadra, still bobbing up and down in the center of the ritual circle. How could she have forgotten? She rushed over to the staff, and her heart sank.

The sapphire, for the first time she'd ever seen, was completely dark. Cracks spiderwebbed across most of the surface, and the metal base was no longer warm to the touch. "Oh, Ikadra."

The cost had been high. Too high.

"Maybe he can be saved," Kaho offered lamely. "Some artificers are quite skilled, especially among the Inurans."

"He was built by a god," Nara explained softly, "and he was my friend."

A hot tear migrated down her cheek. She stared down at the weapon, the hardest casualty she'd had to endure in this war thus far. His loss was more real than the thousands of Shayans that had died in the battle. Even when he'd thought she'd killed Voria he'd still given her the benefit of the doubt. No one had trusted her like that. Not even Frit.

It took several moments for her to realize something had changed. Ducius's droning had faded. The crowd had gone silent, no longer panicked or awed. Just silent. She glanced up at the dome to see what had drawn their attention, but didn't see anything worthy of cause. Voria's magnificent shining form was...gone.

A sudden glow came from behind her, and Nara whirled to find Voria no more than three meters away. Soft, white light emanated from her skin, but she looked otherwise as she always had, not a hair out of place in her bun.

Nara plucked Ikadra and offered the staff to Voria. "Can you save him somehow? It's all my fault...I'm so sorry."

"Well, I should hope so." Voria raised an eyebrow, and stalked closer, though a smile threatened to appear, "You did murder me after all." Then she gingerly accepted Ikadra. "Still, I suppose there really was no better option. I certainly can't think of another way for you to accomplish what you did without Talifax's intervention."

"You...knew?" Nara blinked up at Voria, and scrubbed tears absently away.

"No, not at the time," Voria explained. She laid a hand over Ikadra's sapphire, and a pulse of multicolored magic flowed into the staff. "But a great many things are now clear to me thanks to the...snarky advisor left by my predecessor."

Voria smiled at the air, as if sharing a joke with a person Nara couldn't see.

A faint glow, almost imagined, came from Ikadra. Nara had never seen anything so beautiful. "Is he going to be okay?"

"I don't know," Voria admitted. "I'll need Inura to repair him, I think. But he's alive, if a little quiet for the time being." Voria offered the staff to Nara, who blinked up at her in surprise.

"Voria, you can't possibly entrust an artifact of that level of importance to a traitor," Ducius snapped as he stalked over. He'd kept his distance, but had apparently found the act offensive enough to speak up.

"Ah, Ducius, you're probably one of very few people still willing to speak to me in that manner." Voria, in all her power and glory, walked calmly to him, and stopped so close as to be almost intimate. Nara was desperately grateful that Voria's attention wasn't focused on her, though she was still mystified as to why the goddess seemed willing to forgive her.

Ducius's eyes widened, and his beautiful skin paled as he seemed to realize who he was addressing. "My goddess... well, I suppose that's you. Please, forgive me, Mother. It's just all so new. I apologize for my temerity, but to be candid, I will never like you, Voria. Goddess or no."

Voria barked a short laugh. "Never change, Ducius. I don't want your blind obedience, though it is probably more convenient if you save your...disputes for a more private environment."

Nara glanced out over the audience, who were all staring at Voria in silent awe. There was adoration there. They would die for her, every drifter, and every Shayan.

"What will become of us now?" Ducius asked.

"You're going to run this world," Voria explained as she gestured up at the dome showing the glorious world she'd given life to, a feat that left Nara numb with awe. "It will always need a Tender, and I can think of no one better to guide our people. I have made the world self-sustaining. What I have given cannot be taken away. Never again will our people be forced to sustain the tree. Instead, the tree will sustain them."

"And what about you?" Ducius asked, looking crestfallen, despite having his station confirmed by a goddess. "You're not staying, are you?"

"I can't," Voria admitted. "Krox isn't gone. Our ally's capital is in dire need of help. Help I might be able to provide now. And there are...other threats that need to be addressed." She met Nara's eyes, just for an instant, and Nara knew she was talking about Talifax.

"And her?" Ducius indicated Nara, and she straightened self consciously. She held Ikadra as if she had every right to. She'd be damned if she'd grovel before a Shayan noble.

"It's time to found a new religion, Ducius. Pompous as I still find it, I am a goddess, and I need a temple. That temple will reside in the *Spellship*, and the person I want running that temple is Nara." Voria took a step closer, and rested a hand on Nara's shoulder. "She's going to turn this ship back into what it once was. A center of learning. A place where magic can flourish. And together, we're going to reclaim this sector."

"I...see. As you wish, Mother." Ducius bowed stiffly from the waist, and when the audience saw the gesture fifty thousand people rushed to duplicate it as quickly as possible.

"Wait, you want me to do what?" Nara blinked up at Voria. "I don't know the first thing about running a religion, and even if I did, I find them useless. You know that."

"And this is precisely why you are in charge of mine." She faced Frit and Kaho. "I can see your minds clearly. There is anger, but there is no malice. Neither of you has anything but ill will for Nebiat. As far as I'm concerned that makes you allies. If you'd like, Nara will make a place for you here, until you decide you want a better one. Yes, Kaho, even you."

Nara could scarcely believe it. Not only had they survived, but they'd won, despite the heavy cost to the world below. She was surrounded by friends again, and it seemed all had been forgiven.

"Aran will be docking soon," Voria said. She smiled magnanimously at Nara, and the expression seemed completely out of place on her prim and proper face. "Why don't you go and welcome him home, officially, on behalf of the Temple of Voria?"

Nara didn't have to be told twice.

55

BROMANCE

The first thing Davidson became conscious of was his raspy breathing. He raised his head off his chest, and swung it drunkenly around as he tried to understand where he was. In his tank, the command chair.

He was alive. There was air. And it was considerably warmer than it should have been. Wait, was that thunder in the distance? That would require atmosphere. Had someone moved his tank while he was unconscious?

"Davidson?" called Aran's familiar voice from outside the tank. Metallic boots thunked down on the turret. "You alive in there?"

"Aran?" Davidson's throat ached something awful, and his voice sounded it. He licked his lips and tried again. "I'm down here! One sec. I can manage on my own."

Davidson rose shakily to his feet, and moved to the tank's ladder. He tested his broken shoulder and winced. Using only his good shoulder, he scaled the ladder slowly, judging each rung carefully as he climbed from the tank.

Every muscle ached, and exhaustion added a toll to each step.

He pulled himself up the final rung, and out into afternoon sunlight. Fat, white clouds dotted a blue sky, which wasn't protected by any sort of shield. Davidson looked around him in wonder. "What the depths am I looking at, man? What happened?"

Aran removed his helmet with a hiss, "Voria is a goddess now. Literally. She brought life to this world, and made it permanent. The whole thing."

"So she saved my ass," Davidson realized aloud.

"How so?" Aran asked. "You looked fine to me."

Davidson jerked a thumb at the tank below him. "I had a leak. There's no way my O_2 would have lasted. The only thing that could have saved me was...a goddess creating an atmosphere, I guess." Davidson's mood shifted suddenly, and he gave Aran an uncomfortable glance. "Did anyone tell you about the *Hunter*?"

Aran's face fell to match Davidson's, and his tone was just as somber. "I've watched the battle footage. She went down swinging."

"She was a good ship." Davidson sat on the edge of the tank, then reached over and popped open the aft compartment. He fished out a beer and tossed it to Aran, who caught it. Davidson removed a second one and opened it with a hiss. "To the *Wyrm Hunter*. She'll be remembered by every last soldier she ever saved."

"To the *Hunter*," Aran agreed, and raised his beer.

Davidson raised his beer and drank. The cool liquid slid down his throat, and set to warming his middle. If ever he'd earned a beer, this was it.

"I know it's a bit soon," Aran ventured, "but have you considered what comes next?"

"What do you mean?" Davidson savored a second mouthful of beer.

"Ternus doesn't have a conventional fleet anymore." Aran paused to sip his own beer. He seemed to enjoy it, though not like Davidson did. He just needed to spend more time around the guy, and that could be remedied.

"And?" Davidson prompted when Aran didn't continue.

"And you don't have a ship." Aran nodded behind him, at the *Talon*'s silhouette against the setting sun.

Davidson hadn't paid the vessel much mind, but now that he looked at her he saw the changes. He didn't know how, but she was more impressive than ever. "I think I see where you're going with this. Looks like you just grew some extra quarters."

"And I need officers." Aran gave him a grim stare. "Listen. We lost a lot, man. All of us. The *Hunter*. Ternus. Your own damned government. We've got the tools to get some payback, but not if we let them keep jerking us about like puppets. Do it on our terms. Join the Outriders. We'd be proud to have you."

Aran offered a gauntleted hand, and after a moment Davidson accepted it. He took another swallow of beer, and let it roll down his throat before replying. "You know what? I'm in. I love Ternus, but I'm not going to serve under someone like Austin. Not after what he ordered our fleet to do today. He sacrificed us as cannon fodder to screen his precious black ships. If he ain't loyal to us, then we sure as depths aren't loyal to him."

Davidson spit over the side of his tank.

"I couldn't have said it better." Aran took another swig of beer, then rose into the air. "Why don't we head back and get you some quarters?"

"Sounds good." Davidson rose to his feet, and looked

back at his tank. They'd been through a lot together. "I'm going to drive her back in myself. One last question, though. What rank are you sticking me with?"

Aran cocked his head, considering. "What rank do you want?"

"I'm not really interested in responsibility. I was happiest as a lieutenant. I just want to drive my tank and blow shit up."

Aran laughed, and then replaced his helmet. "Welcome to the Outriders, Lieutenant."

EPILOGUE

The universe shifted, and Nebiat appeared in the skies above her capital. Her wounds had been healed, but the memory was fresh. The pain of imminent non-existence wasn't something she was eager to experience again. Ever.

Yet the battle had been worth it. She extended an arm large enough to smash a continent, and marveled at the weapon held in her grasp. Worldender, the titanic spear, was clutched in her hand, pulsing with dark power.

This was your plan, then. Krox mused. *You never intended the death of your rival?*

"I'd have preferred to slay Voria, and that possibility existed," Nebiat replied, deep satisfaction welling up in her. "But unlike you I've lived my life as a mortal. I understand that sometimes people defy the odds. Voria has always triumphed, every time we've met. Even if that triumph was merely her survival. Part of me didn't really believe I would win, simply because I've never seen that woman be beaten. I was prepared for a loss today, and yet it was anything but."

She smiled down at her own world, understanding

Voria's need to protect her people. In that single way they were the same. Unlike Voria, though, her people were safe. An entire civilization waited on the world below, with the strongest of the Wyrms already building followings among the others. She took a moment to extend her senses, and to watch thousands at once. They competed, grew, and learned.

Somehow, she'd managed to preserve her people, the people that her father had very nearly squandered in his mad quest to raise a god. What's more, she now possessed a weapon that, theoretically at least, could slay a god.

"Tell me of this spear," she said, holding the weapon up for her own inspection. "Where did it come from? Who made it? And why is it so deadly?"

Worldender might be the oldest object in the cosmos, Krox theorized. *Rumors of its use stem from every epoch of the godswar, and Shivan's use to slay Marid was but the latest instance in a long line of gods felled. Even I do not know the weapon's origin, or the name of the god who forged it. Perhaps it already existed when our universe was created, a legacy of the denizens themselves. Whatever its origin, the spell can pierce any magic. It will nullify magic that comes into contact with the tip, and that includes you.*

The bit about the spear was important, but not the part that aroused the greater part of Nebiat's curiosity.

"Denizens? You mean the beings in the Umbral Depths?" Nebiat knew little of these creatures. She could seek the knowledge directly, if she wished, but Krox's memories were sheathed under countless strata, and the volume daunted her. She could spend a century simply witnessing, and still not see a fraction of what Krox had endured during his immeasurable lifespan.

Indeed. Perhaps they forged it originally, or perhaps whatever birthed them also created the weapon. Regardless, we have it now, and that is good. Worldender ensures that even Nefarius will be wary of us.

Nebiat considered that. She'd dealt a series of crippling blows to the Confederacy. Ternus was doomed. Shaya was depopulated. New Texas had been crippled. Only Yanthara and Colony 3 remained intact, of the greater worlds at least.

Virkon could be an enemy as well. Krox cautioned. *And you have not accounted for Nefarius, or the treacherous spawn of Inura.*

"Haven't I?" Nebiat gave a deep, throaty laugh. She made the sound perfectly mirror the laugh she'd borne before her ascension, and all over the world below Wyrms shot disquieted glances at the sky. She extended her perceptions, and took in the entire galaxy at once, seeing all her enemies. "I've retreated from the galactic stage, driven away by the mighty Voria. She stands in the open, over a ruined world. Now our enemies will look around. They will begin plotting, and scheming, and fighting. They will target each other, while they seek to pillage our world. They may invade the Rift, but they will underestimate us. They will assume we lurk here in the shadows, weak, and frail. And while they ignore us we will grow strong. We will let them spend their strength fighting each other, and I will spend the time studying my enemies. You will teach me of Nefarius, and of this Talifax. When they come for us, we will be ready."

Nebiat surveyed it all, and she smiled. No histories but her own would record today as a victory, but she knew that it marked the real turning point in the war. Soon, her enemies would feel her wrath, but not until she could deal a blow so total that none would survive it.

NOTE TO THE READER

Hey guys, thanks for sticking with me this far in the series! We're five books in and things are really starting to heat up.

If you're interested enough to want to know when the next book comes out, pop over to magitechchronicles.com and sign up to the mailing list on the right-hand side of the page.

I'll give you a chance to beta read the next book, work on the roleplaying game, and you'll hear about a small Magitech Chronicles Facebook group with like-minded readers where we talk about everything from the roleplaying game to what's coming in the next book.

We'd love to have you!

-Chris

Made in the USA
Monee, IL
26 January 2020